RIGHTEOUS FURY

AARON MITCHELL

Chaplapreneur Resources

Rockwall, TX

Chaplapreneur.com

"helping the entire world to see Jesus more clearly"

ISBN: 978-1-7354340-0-1 (Paperback)

ISBN: 978-1-7354340-1-8 (Electronic)

LCCN 2020915098

Any references to historical events, real people, or real places are used fictitiously. Names, characters, and places are products of the author's imagination.

Front Cover and Layout Design by Damonza.com

Printed in the United States of America

A Mitchell Holdings LLC DBA Chaplapreneur Resources

Contact Chaplapreneur Resources for permission to reproduce at

Chaplapreneur.com

Contact Us Page

Special Thanks to:

Laurie Magers,
Your edits made my words sharper and this story better. It was an honor to have your help with this project.

To my daughter Anna,
Watching you grow everyday is an inspiration and keeps me pressing forward through hard projects like this one. You truly are a special little girl.

Especially to my wife Heidi,
You inspire me to be better every single day. Thank you for being on this journey with me and believing in me to write this book, the last book and the next one. We have always been and always will be in this fight together. This victory is not mine but ours. We make a great team!

*This book is dedicated to Jesus Christ,
a fighter if there ever was one!*

*"In your struggle against sin you have not yet resisted to
the point of shedding your blood (Hebrews 12:4 ESV)."*

CHAPTER 1

GORILLA IN THE RING

WAITING IN THE wings of the arena, Thaddeus Class had been there several times before. At age 32 it was all too familiar. It was where he felt at home. He may have been living in New York City, but Las Vegas, Nevada, was his home crowd, too. He stood six foot one and was a solid 220 lbs., with the body of a Greek god — you know, the impressive ones like Hercules or Zeus. He made weight at 213 the previous day and was comfortable, fully hydrated, and ate a good meal yesterday, which made him strong. He ate light and natural today, which made him energetic and slightly hangry. He had studied the film of his opponent for the past year or more. Thad was confident that he knew Greg Wilson better than Greg knew himself. Thad had his fight preparation down to a science. He was ready! He knew it and The Baltimore Bomber was about to know it, too. Many were saying Thad was the greatest fighter the Octagon had ever seen!

He got his start as an average boxer and an elite collegiate level wrestler who was a two-time All-American, respectively placing 4th and 3rd in the nation. Those who knew him locally, and followed NCAA wrestling closely, knew that Thaddeus's Achilles heel was Lee Gardner, who wrestled at Iowa State. For some reason, Thaddeus couldn't beat him. He couldn't figure him out. Those last two seasons Thaddeus's only losses came to Lee at the nationals. His junior year he placed 4th, losing to him twice, and his senior year Thaddeus lost a close match in the semi-final to Gardner. After Thaddeus won big for third, he watched Gardner win by fall in the finals. Soon after, Lee was married and went on to be a successful coach on the college wrestling scene. He wasn't ever going to wrestle competitively again, much less jump in the Octagon with Thaddeus Class. But Thad's career was largely fueled by this setback and not reaching the ultimate goal he set out to do. During conditioning times in his training, he often went back in his mind and visualized winning those matches against Lee.

Even though Thad was a disciplined college athlete who also went on to be a great Harvard law student, he didn't always put his energy to good use. In his spare time during those collegiate years he channeled that energy into fights at parties or bars. He was generally well-liked by all, personable and fun to be around, but sometimes something would make him snap. Sometimes he would just go off. Sometimes it would seem to be over nothing. Other times it seemed to have great purpose. Because of the accident, he hated drunk drivers. On more than one occasion he grabbed someone from behind the wheel and forcefully let them know they were not going to be driving home. One man was beaten very badly; Thad's college coach somehow convinced the man not to press charges.

He knew that his anger had always lain just beneath the surface. It never truly went away. He was always ready to pop.

Since the accident he had dreams where he was beating complete strangers to death. He had one dream that was a recurring one about punching an enemy that just couldn't be knocked out. The person didn't hit back; Thaddeus only felt worse every time he hit this opponent. He would always wake up after his opponent started laughing at him and, to his surprise, the man would be unphased by Thaddeus's efforts.

This is what had always made him so exciting as a fighter. He was a true fighter, always looking to prove his value. If you doubted him, he wanted to destroy you. To watch him was pure adrenaline and you knew at some point in the fight the gorilla was coming out. Like the Incredible Hulk, his opponents would not like him when he was angry. He had a way under pressure and duress to become highly focused. His trainer, Rex, was always trying to poke the bear. I shouldn't say always. He poked the bear when he thought he needed to. Rex was like a father figure to him. When he first met Thaddeus, they hit it off. Rex had trained some of the greatest mixed martial artists in the world. He knew Thaddeus had the right attitude, work ethic, and talent to be an all-time great. Rex knew what Thad was right away.

When he came to GITR (Gorilla in the Ring) and expressed an interest in learning from Rex, Thaddeus was known as a very successful college wrestler but kind of a local punk who still seemed to need to prove something. Most trainers even in the fight world didn't want to deal with the type of baggage Thaddeus Class brought to the table. I am not saying they wouldn't have given him a shot, but they didn't chase him like you would think they might chase after an already accomplished athlete. Rex seemed to have a way of talking with Thaddeus which gave him the name "the Gorilla Whisperer."

Thaddeus was nicknamed The Gorilla because of his sheer size and strength, and he embodied everything GITR was about in the Octagon. He was a physical fighter, always in superior shape, and tough as nails. If you met him you wouldn't call him The Gorilla. He was a smiling, baby-faced white guy. Thaddeus was a physical specimen because he trained and had the genes to fight as a light heavyweight. He was fast, very fast. His hands moved like lightning. He had a long reach. He was very light on his feet and could move around the Octagon very well. He was tall for a fighter and usually couldn't be lifted off the ground.

He seemed to have been honed with the perfect combination of speed, strength, flexibility, mental toughness, and what was called mat intelligence. *Worldwide Sports Weekly* interviewed him and determined that he was the most intelligent fighter that had ever fought at that level.

In his spare time, he got his juris doctorate and passed the New York State Bar Exam. He was a licensed attorney. But an anger always crept just beneath the surface. He could snap at any moment. One time, in a media conference, a future opponent told Thaddeus that he was no match for his sheer strength and speed, due to his age. He claimed he would wear him down by mid-point in the fight, before he knocked him out. Those words provoked Thaddeus to throw a microphone past the opposing fighter's face that went through the wall behind him. Had he connected on that throw, he would have severely hurt the man with a deadly weapon. When your hands are already lethal weapons, the law is not kind to someone who makes a mistake like that, with press footage and literally a million eyewitnesses. When the fight came, Thaddeus embarrassed the man — knocking him out mid-way through the fight. Thaddeus told the press, "Well, he got the knockout right, but wrong fighter."

Thaddeus Class has always been a mystery. At age 32 he was 34 and 0. No one had ever even come close to winning the fight. He had 25 knockouts and nine technical knockouts. There were some great fighters in there who couldn't stand in the ring with him. Some of them wouldn't go down. The TKOs were called mostly so those opponents didn't get killed.

But this time was different. Rex knew it was different and was trying to treat this fight the same, but there was something wrong. Thaddeus had the same confidence. He had the same stamina, and there were glimpses of the same anger coming out, but something was wrong. Rex knew when a fighter was losing his edge. He feared his champion was losing it, or had already lost it. He hadn't slipped in strength or ability — well, maybe a little with age, but his experience far made up for it. He simply noticed that the same methods of frustrating and provoking his fighter were no longer working. In Rex's mind it was only a matter of time.

What was different for Rex was the close bond he had formed with Thaddeus. He feared the worst thing had happened. Yes, it had resulted in Thaddeus becoming more focused and more fearless. He had become a better human being. Rex no longer worried about seeing him on the eleven o'clock news. He knew now that Thaddeus not only knew the law, but actually obeyed it. In the past, he feared his vast legal knowledge only served him in seeing how far he could push the law, and possibly even represent himself in court if he had to (Rex's worst nightmare).

In many ways he was living up to what it meant to be a role model. He now had time for young athletes. He had spent some time volunteering and raising money for the community and some worthy causes. He even helped build a house for a family of four who lost their home in a tornado that year. He had helped some older fighters get back on their feet locally. He did many things for people and actually asked that they not tell anyone. He had been a very positive presence for GITR and the entire MMA fight world.

He traded in his cherry red Ferrari and picked up a white BMZ, which was still nice, but much less noticeable. He also got it for free, for being in their advertisements. He simply claimed it was time to grow up. He was a pleasure to be around. He was reading ancient writings and modern fiction. He stopped obsessing about what the sportscasters were saying about him and became more relaxed. He was starting to show signs of being a functional adult after this fighting gig was all over. Many people were waiting for him to mess up, but Rex knew Thad. He had been like a son. He was so proud of his fighter.

When Thad got something in his mind, he would follow it through to the end. Rex's greatest fear was the vice grip Thad had on the Bible in his hand. Even then it would be hard work to peel it out of his cold, dead hands. What an awful thing for Rex to realize, but it had truly happened. The unthinkable, Thaddeus "The Gorilla" Class had become a Christian. He read a lot and talked often about what he read. Thad knew how Rex felt about faith. Rex claimed himself to be an agnostic and hid behind knowledge. The truth was, it went much deeper than that. Rex believed in God and may have even believed in Jesus. But Jesus wasn't there for him at his darkest hour. His life was also marked by anger. Where was Jesus when he needed Him the most? Now Jesus was stealing his fighter's edge and the closest thing to a son that he had ever had.

Rex watched as Thaddeus masterfully warmed up in an empty hall leading to the arena. They were at the stage of the warmup where Thaddeus liked to be alone. He prayed, talked to himself, and bounced around in this empty corner of the arena. He had been there before. Now was the time, and as he had that thought the lights dimmed as his song began to play. It was loud and fierce like the man he knew how to be. Rex feared that he no longer was that guy; it seemed that he was a new creation. *Something created just for God to thumb His nose at me*, Rex thought.

Rex feared that the old man was gone and a new one was reborn in his place. This one was not afraid to live or die. He was not afraid to take chances, but the anger, fear, and a touch of insecurity were what made him great, and Rex knew that part of Thaddeus was dead. Rex silently thought to himself as he looked up and to the right, *Jesus, you screwed me again. I still hate you.*

Rex didn't have a good feeling about this. He grabbed Thad like nothing was wrong and let him punch his hands quickly. Rex slapped Thad's bare chest and yelled, "Here comes the greatest fighter ever, let's show 'em what's up!" Thad couldn't tell, but Rex felt his greatest fear was about to be realized. Rex and Thaddeus were about to be defeated, not because of the Baltimore Bomber, but because of Jesus. Again he thought, *Why again, Jesus?* Rex would get nervous for these fights; this was an exceptionally bad day, but he never showed it.

Rex had seen it before. Maybe not with Jesus, but something else eventually took the place of the passion, tenacity, and downright animal qualities a fighter needed to be great. With some they developed a business sense about the fight world, and that led them on into another career. With many it was women, lots and lots of women. Once that snowball started rolling down the hill there was no stopping it. The worst cases were drugs, or the sheer laziness that set in when money became no object at all.

What had made Thaddeus great to this point was he was disciplined and free from distractions. He didn't need women to get in the way. He was attracted to women, but groupies who never challenged him intellectually were not his equal. They cared about his body, success, status, but nothing deeper than that. Thaddeus was just a much deeper person than that. Thaddeus was pure class! It wasn't just a name; it was now an identity. At least it was becoming one, now that the anger was gone. Many still knew him as the same old guy he once was. But Rex, he knew differently.

Rex even thought to himself, *I wish it wasn't Jesus. I almost wish he did have a slight alcohol problem, or it was the girls. Why did it have to be the Son of God? Couldn't he just leave my fighter and my life alone?* Deep down Rex had a hatred that brewed towards Jesus. Then he comforted himself with the thought, *I hate someone who isn't even real.* He laughed it off and he was back.

Rex knew the dangers. He thought Thaddeus was different. He thought Thad could be focused to put the greatest fighting career together ever. He had talent, strength, speed, but most of all discipline. Make no mistake about it. Those things didn't come easily. God gifted him with discipline, not the others. Religion truly was the only thing that could stop Thaddeus, at least in the mind of Rex Metzger. Rex loved Thaddeus and wanted what was best for him. But in his mind, Jesus was a threat to his world. Jesus was not what they needed. It was not what either of them needed.

The Baltimore Bomber waited in the Octagon. Thaddeus made his way to ringside. He had on a warm robe with the right kind of fur on the inside. He had broken a cold sweat and needed to keep it going. His dark blue robe shone like a cape with the red glistening under the light and the bright yellow letters that said "Pure Class." He looked like a superhero and felt angelic. He knew his body was ready for war. He was as confident as he had ever been.

The arena smelled of beer, popcorn, and other concessions, which was some kind of mixture between hotdogs and nachos. His own sweat smell was mixed into that aroma, too. The crowd roared when they saw him. He breathed in and felt at home. This was his place. He was the Gorilla in the Ring and that night the Baltimore Bomber had fallen into his cage.

When Thaddeus got to the cage he smelled something else. He always did. Even though there was a preliminary fight, it still caught his nostrils. For many years he didn't understand why this happened. On his faith journey he became more awake. He began to study some of what made him the way he was. When he smelled the ammonia that was used to clean the mats he was always struck with fear. This reminded him of every wrestling match, every fight he ever fought. From second grade on, every time he smelled the smell he was struck with some fear and anxiety. Mostly because of how severely he was beaten on the mats at an early age. He was a tough and angry kid, but was embarrassed several times by well-trained talented kids. It wasn't until later that he became good at his craft. The smell reminded him of being lonely, fatherless, angry, and defeated.

It always slowed him a little and he would take a couple of deep breaths. Rex had a good sense of what was going on inside the head of his fighter, especially Thad. "Look, Thaddeus, a little kitten has fallen into The Gorilla's cage." Thaddeus looked up and saw him. He smiled and he was back. The Baltimore Bomber stood across the cage with his entourage. Their eyes met. This was the moment the ammonia fear went away completely. As Thaddeus looked him in the eye and grinned, he seemed to be able to turn the killer inside on at will. Thaddeus looked at the fighter. Funny how just yesterday he had a lot to say. But today was judgment day. The Baltimore Bomber looked back at him and smirked. The Bomber looked away slightly and in that moment they both knew who the alpha dog was. Greg Wilson, The Baltimore Bomber, still believed he would win, but he was reminded that this guy had been here before. *This is his cage and I need to rattle him early.* One thing Greg had on his side was he was a puncher. The Baltimore Bomber was getting his chance after being 19-0 with 17 knockouts. He was ready. He was a puncher, and just like the Rocky movies taught us, "A puncher always has a chance." Greg stood 6'2" and a solid 225 after the day before weigh-ins. He had a much bigger frame than Thaddeus. He had more trouble getting to 213, but he considered it the perfect weight for him. His high protein diet kept him strong as he worked with expert dieticians and strength trainers for maximum strength.

When it came to fighting, Greg wasn't just a puncher. Like Thaddeus, he was a college wrestler. He also had experience in Jiu Jitsu. But the most dangerous part of his background was his boxing expertise. He almost stuck with boxing, but he felt he was too well-rounded for that and could be a great cage fighter. So far, it appeared he was right.

Greg was no slouch and could fight with Thaddeus. Some

of the talking heads actually were giving Greg a chance. The thought was he could fight with him. He was in great shape. He was much younger at age 27. He might be at the peak of his career. If he stayed in there, he might get the champion on one to three of those bombs. It wasn't unreasonable to believe he could knock him out.

As the fighters went to the center, Thaddeus looked into Greg's eyes with a look that was somewhere between a kid's smile on Christmas morning and the watery drool a snake must get as it closes in on a rat just before breakfast. The referee said some words, Rex looked on. Everything seemed normal on the outside. Maybe there was nothing to fear. The fighters returned to their corners. It was time. Thaddeus was confident. Rex was a little disturbed that Thad looked even more confident than he had seen him before. He missed some of the fear and insecurity. That is what he missed, even though Rex wouldn't have those words for it. He was so worried that the rage appeared to be gone. The training this time was different. Everything was different.

Typically, this was where Thaddeus was great! The anger that lay beneath the surface was what made him memorable. It was what made him dangerous. It made him a Gorilla in the Ring. Rex thought, *Only God can help us now! But I won't ask. Thad will ask enough for both of us.*

Also in the corner with them was Billy Smith, also known as Billy "The Kid," and his main trainer, Larry "Quick Draw" Rossi. The next fight for GITR would be Billy the Kid, fighting for the world title in the heavyweight class. Rex and Larry had a unique relationship that went back 15 years. So when Larry started training Billy, Rex tried to get him to fight for GITR.

Thad was in need of a training partner, and it was the perfect marriage that a young fighter like Billy needed. GITR had the resources, connections, and the training time with the best fighter in the world just one weight class lower than him. Billy worked out a deal that he could keep Larry as his trainer but be a fighter for GITR, while Rex would assist Larry in Billy's corner. It was quite shocking that Rex would even consider this, but he knew it would be great for Thaddeus. Billy was already a good fighter, but he was on his way to becoming a great fighter and was a part of their fight club. He was actually the number one contender at the heavyweight class. Thad really poured his life into Billy. After this fight, Billy's title shot was the next project. He mentored Billy as a fighter and in life. They had become great friends, and this partnership truly helped to take maybe the greatest fighter ever to a level even higher.

That is what this fight world, or any individual sport, is really about though, isn't it? It is about the partnerships, the friendships, the brotherhoods that you have. It is funny — most of these guys get into this because of the individual gladiatorial atmosphere, but what it really becomes is this place where they bleed with and for each other. Billy would be there for support today and would be quieter than Rex or Larry during the fight, but make no mistake — he was every bit as invested in Thaddeus as Thaddeus was in him. He wanted his partner to win.

Larry had also helped Thaddeus with some of the finer points of his technique. He would be more vocal than Billy, but Billy knew three was a crowd. Billy would tell mainly Rex, but also Larry, things he noticed and they would relay the message to Thaddeus. Rex was the one who was in the fighter's head, while he had benefited from Larry's and Billy's knowledge of the sport. Even at this stage he had a large respect for what they brought to the club. But even Larry, during the fight, would mostly simply play an encouraging and supporting role. Most of his role was over already. He studied film and taught Thad what he saw and helped with the fight plan and the technique to execute. Billy and Larry also had some business to take care of tomorrow afternoon back in Manhattan, and would be leaving early in the morning.

Larry slapped hands with Thaddeus and reminded him he was the champ and no one could take that away from him. Billy barehand slapped his back, leaving a little red mark. Most people would think it stung a little, but to Thad it felt good. He was a cat ready to pounce on his prey. Larry and Billy stepped back and got into position. If they saw something Rex needed to see during the fight, they would point it out to him. Larry would help shout instruction, but it was understood that Rex ran Thad's corner. They helped greatly on the finer points of strategy. Billy didn't get a lot of the spotlight here. But make no mistake about it: everybody knew that Billy was what Thaddeus needed and vice versa to get to where they wanted to go. Thad, a great fighter, at this stage needed a young guy to push him more than ever, and Billy "The Kid" needed a mentor. It worked out because Billy was no kid anymore.

Larry and Billy were announced before Thaddeus and Rex. Larry, among his peers, was revered as someone with a lot of wisdom and coaching experience with the sport. But that wasn't enough yet. He wanted people to know his name. Billy was enjoying some new-found fame. With his baby face smile and cool wavy blonde hair, he waved to the crowd as he heard a new, more amplified version of the applause he was used to. Billy felt really good about the amount of fans he now shared with Thaddeus.

Rex saw Debra in the corner of his eye. She was nervous as ever, and sitting in her usual spot on the front row along the same side of the Octagon as Thad's corner. Thad would always wave to her one time before the fight. Most people called her Mama Class. She was the proud owner of Mama Class's Kitchen, a local diner back home. When the accident happened Debra wasn't working. Thad's father, Wayne, made enough for the whole family. Wayne was a small business owner. He owned a local dry cleaning business at three different locations and did quite well owning his own business. She loved Thad's father and when he died a large part of her died. This is when the anger started for Thaddeus, and Mama had to figure out what to do. That is when she opened Mama Class's Kitchen.

Her downhome cooking was what made her place the best little eatery in town. Her story and her recipes made the place an instant success. Debra was the kind of woman Rex would have been attracted to before she lost her husband and had to work. Debra, until the accident, was an excellent housekeeper. She did everything she could to hold the home together.

She would help Wayne with his business. She would be there for moral support or to bounce ideas off of. She made sure all of Thad's homework was done. She spent hours with Thad every day, telling him of the amazing plan God had for his life. She would do that back then and Thad never forgot it. She was filled with faith, love, and joy. She was a real homemaker. She wasn't jaded by the world at that point.

Wayne and Debra also helped out teaching children at church and were great examples of their faith. Everything seemed different back then. Debra still went to her little church. She loved the people and the church was so good to her after the accident, but Debra and God were not the same. She built her business up from the ground, and she wasn't going to ask Him for anything ever again. After all, how could He let this happen? Especially to Thad. After Wayne was gone Thad's anger began. She endured through many years of his anger. She knew of the pain in his life and in hers. Many people would look at them and say "they have everything." Debra was proud of her son, she was proud of what she was able to do, but she missed Wayne. She really missed him. She used to think she was mad at him for dying, but the truth is she was mad at God!

Rex looked at Debra after Thad nodded to her. They smiled at each other, but Rex knew she disliked him and, frankly, she was too much woman for him to be around. She was 5"6', 130 lbs., but a pistol. She was a fighter. He laughed to himself and thought, *Twice the fighter of her son.* There was no doubt in his mind who always kept Thad angry. She was one of those church-going people, which topped it all off for him.

Rex, being somewhat of a father figure, and Debra being his mother, often found themselves in social and family-type situations together. If you didn't know better, you would think they were some kind of past relationship that was still trying to be amicable for the adult child. They viewed the world quite differently. But their disdain for each other was mutual and more aggressive than passive, yet passive-aggressive.

The fighters were announced. When they announced Rex's name he simply put his hand up. Rex received a lot of praise for his club GITR, and especially for Thaddeus. Many people who followed the sport closely knew that he was not the primary trainer for Billy, but many people forgot to give credit to Larry for Billy as the primary trainer. Rex, even though he was kind of difficult and rough around the edges, was very sensitive to this with Larry. On one hand, he knew that Larry had helped Thad and his whole club go to the next level and he didn't want that to end. On the other hand, they were friends, too, and he wanted the guy to get credit for his work. Rex was very good in that way.

They announced Thaddeus "Pure" Class as the reigning champion and the crowd went crazy. New York was his home but Las Vegas, Nevada, was his home crowd. There was nothing like it. The man had become an icon. In that moment, Rex grabbed Billy by the back of the neck. He grabbed him in a way that would be hard for normal everyday life. But everyone's adrenaline was up. He whispered, "Soon it will be that loud for you, too." The exchange was a little awkward as Billy and Larry smiled back, but no one could hear very well over the crowd. It was time to fight!

The fighters met in the center and touched gloves. The referee said something but it was usually the same stuff as before. Thaddeus didn't take it in. Neither did "The Bomber." An interesting thing happened, though. For the second time in what started out as sharp eye contact, Greg looked away first. One of the things that made Thaddeus dangerous was his knowledge of this kind of thing. He had a brilliant mind, but throw the switch and he was an animal. He could psychologically look you over and break you down, but in an instant, he would expose your heart and your mind and eat your face. The champ felt good. Rex was a little nervous, but it was all about to go away, because once the fight started, there wasn't much you could do.

The training, the head games, the prayers and the preparation were what got them there. So much of the fight had already been fought. It was fought in the weight room, the earlier morning runs, the extra sprints, and the extra time sparring with Billy. It was spent with Larry and Rex breaking down film. It was spent in rest time and in icing down joints the proper amount. It was spent with Keith Mixon, the head athletic trainer, and having the right rehab exercises for injuries. It was spent in the pool when running was going to be counterproductive. As Thad stared at him from the corner, he knew this fight was already won, and he was convincing himself that Greg Wilson knew it too.

The bell rang and it was a bit of a chess match for several minutes. Thaddeus tried to grapple a little but often chose to stay out of the puncher's way. He was trying not to get set up for that vicious right hook. He worked tirelessly on that right arm, just as expected, tying up that wrist at every turn. Most of the first five-minute round was spent feeling each other out. Each fighter got a few good punches in, but neither was a clear winner of the first round. No doubt the first round scored for the champion, because that is how it is done.

Thaddeus, a great technical fighter, tied him up in the second round and had him on the ground getting great shots in on two occasions. But toward the end of the second round on their feet, as Thaddeus tried to box with the puncher, he was hit with that vicious right hook, followed by several uppercuts.

The champion looked like he was going down, but knowing he had another five seconds to survive before the bell (because he heard Rex yell that to him), he backed out and protected himself at the boos of the arena. Thaddeus couldn't remember being booed in that way before. The tide in the fight had shifted. The world appeared to be in shock. There was something about being booed that drove him crazy. He wasn't a people pleaser, but he was a champion, and he had a deep-seated need for people to see him win. Thaddeus got that look in his eye. It came later in this fight than Rex had ever seen in his entire professional career.

Rex knew the anger was there, the adrenaline was there, but he needed to speak words of sense into Thad in that moment. He had him in the corner for a minute before he must go back out for the next round. "Thad, hear me. He came here to knock out the champ. You have studied him. He is an emotional fighter. You need to be patient and then unload on him. He is the puncher, but you know this is when he makes mistakes. He has been able to knock everyone out after shocking them like that, but he will get sloppy. You know he will. Show him what 'Pure Class' is!" Those words pierced through the veins of the champion. He was class. In fact it was his name. His first name sounded like an ancient gladiator, but his last name proved he would do it with class, PURE CLASS!

For the minute in the corner Thaddeus sat and recovered. It had been years since he was hit like that. Greg was already on his feet. He never sat down the entire minute break. He was so pumped up and excited he ran back to the center of the Octagon.

Greg let his guard down as he chased the champion around in circles. Part of the mystique of Thaddeus Class for his opponents had been that he always seemed to get better as the fight went on. How did he do it? No one could quite figure it out. This was a special trait, even people who had studied him very intensely didn't get it. Yes, he was in excellent physical condition, but what else did he do that made him so much better late in the fight? He was even an older fighter now. It just didn't make much sense to the casual observer.

For an opponent to get him, they would have to spend time with him and talk to him. Without that, you couldn't possibly understand just how deeply he thought and the type of student of the sport he had become. Thaddeus was a thinker, and no matter how old he might get, this would always be a game changer, at least in his mind. In that moment his thoughts were what mattered most.

Thaddeus began to get some big shots in. Wilson was starting to open up. He noticed Greg leaving his left hand down a little after his right jabs. An anxious fighter would use that against the challenger right away. That just isn't how Thaddeus rolled. Thaddeus Class was always going to maximize his opportunities. He knew Greg wouldn't correct this error unless he exposed it. He also knew this was the one. Greg was disciplined and wasn't going to make many other mistakes. But as the fight went on, this one mistake would probably get worse, so long as he put the pressure on and he let him get away with this mistake. Thaddeus began throwing more punches and appearing to take more chances, although his positioning remained flawless. He really didn't overextend himself much, but he wanted Greg to feel more uneasy. Thaddeus also needed Wilson to feel as though he was getting to the champion and had a chance at a big knockout.

As The Bomber got a few shots in on Thad's head, he finished with that right jab. Thad made a habit of ducking out of the flurry, circling towards the right arm. As the round moved on, Greg landed larger punches while Thad only broke through on half as many as when he started to press, and his punches were only about half as hard as from earlier in the round. From where Greg stood, it was easy to believe that he was winning. Things were going his way!

Rex was a little nervous but he saw what was happening. Finally, after four minutes of mostly punching, The Baltimore Bomber connected on a few punches in a flurry. Greg left his left side completely open and extended himself twice as far as normal on that last punch, looking for the knockout. If you saw an instructor teaching boxing to second graders while explaining what not to do in slow motion, it would look something like that. Greg Wilson may not have been this out of position more than a few times since he was in second grade or so, in any type of boxing contest. But that is what happens when someone has been baited. The Bomber, who almost put the champion away earlier, was baited into believing he had him. He was tempted with opportunity.

Everything slowed down. Thaddeus knew it was go time! This time Thaddeus ducked the last punch and circled towards the lazy left arm. He timed three perfect uppercuts to the chin followed by one final hook across the face, knocking the puncher out cold. Thaddeus was expected to win, but not by boxing! He out-punched the puncher! He successfully out-smarted him. Thaddeus stood over him, proud as a cat who caught the rat and brought it back to the door for the owner to see. He had knocked him out, and he did it with pure class!

As Thaddeus ducked and connected on these four punches, he was facing his corner. Rex was relieved to see the giant of the Octagon appeared to have the anger back. He saw the look in his eye again and welcomed it like an old friend. He thought, *Not today Jesus! You didn't take him yet!*

Debra rose to her feet and screamed out for her son, "That's it, Thaddeus! That is my Thaddeus!" She also saw the look and, unfortunately, knew it well. She saw the same look on his face almost every day from the day he lost his father until recently.

She saw it when he bloodied the faces of two boys who were two years older than he on the church playground shortly after Wayne died. She saw it when he talked back to her as a child. *It will never go away as long as Rex is around,* she thought. She was so glad he won the fight, but sad to see that look in his eye again. She looked at Rex with an irritated spirit.

Rex was proud of his fighter, but felt he was exposed. It didn't go quite as planned, not like the other fights. Thaddeus wasn't the same. Some would criticize the end of round two, but most would look past it knowing the champion continued to prove he was unbeatable. However, Rex knew the difference and so did the other trainers out there, training their fighters. A puncher could very well be the demise of Thaddeus Class. As far as that night was concerned, though, he was proud of his fighter who may very well have been the best MMA fighter to that point in history. He was also concerned for his new interest that might ruin him. His disdain for the Son of God was back and oh, how he hated Him and His people.

CHAPTER 2

POST-FIGHT FALLOUT

REX WAS MORE nervous for the press conference than normal. Rex knew there was more opportunity for the story to come out about the newfound faith of his fighter. He typically was slightly uncomfortable in the past because of the trash-talking that went on, and when it came down to it he wanted the respect he deserved. Rex was uncomfortable during the questioning when Thad said something to the effect of, "letting the mouth of another praise him instead of doing it himself," which is a reference to Proverbs 27:2. He then quoted another Proverb explaining that, "Anyone who is great at something will do it before kings," which is a reference to Proverbs 27:29. Both are verses that are not typically referenced, and further evidenced that his faith was serious and that he was actually reading the Bible. On another hand it was ok, because the reporters didn't pick up on these verses that are not a common part of cultural Christianity.

The problem was Thaddeus never lacked boldness. He didn't lack the ability to be bold or say bold things. He was bold by nature. Rex legitimately feared for Thad, because Thaddeus had gotten into his share of troubles. He had said things that were mean, insensitive, and downright antagonistic. He had built a reputation of sorts that was about to come undone. You see, his public persona had yet to catch up with his private one. Thaddeus had not only become a believer, but he was growing rapidly in the faith. That could make for an interesting press conference and a very nervous Rex Metzger.

There was a press conference with the champion about one hour after the fight. The media was there and it was suspected that they would poke the bear until it ran at them through the cage, so to speak. It didn't take much to infuriate Thaddeus in the past. After a round of typical questions, Class was asked by Joe Johnson of *Attack Sports Weekly*, "Champ, at the end of the second round, that was the closest you have ever come to being knocked out as a pro. Do you think the fight would have gone his way had he had another minute left in the round?"

Thaddeus laughed a little, and simply said, "No. Next question please." Everyone laughed along with him. A shout came from a reporter in the back, "Good one, Thad! Great job." By trying to avoid the question it became a mutated disease that wouldn't go away. After everyone got the laughing down to a low chuckle, Joe started again. "The question should be answered. From where I sat it looked as though you were out on your feet."

Thaddeus then explained, "I never was out. I was conscious the entire time. I was a little slowed down by it."

Another reporter chimed in, "This photo here looks like you are out on your feet."

"I wasn't out on my feet. I got to the end of the round like I needed to and knocked him out in the next round." Thad was starting to get noticeably upset.

He went to his next reporter. Thad was flustered and had a little trouble remembering the reporter's name, then he remembered, "Tom, go ahead."

Tom was always nice to him and he could really use someone to be nice during this exchange. But Tom went in for the kill. "Some of us want to know, since we have never seen you in this position before, is age a factor?"

Now he was mad. But something was different this time. A few things were different this time, actually. For an undefeated alpha male fighter who knocked someone out and had never lost, he couldn't believe they were talking about his age. It also touched on an insecurity. It was like he didn't even consider that he was past his prime and that he was in danger of being knocked out until it came back to him in the press conference. It was all kind of new. In the past this would have been an easy lightning rod for the press. Thad was one of those fighters with whom you could usually have a newsworthy interview.

To try to get away from the questions that snowballed about retirement and everything else, he made the statement: "I guess I will do it as long as God wants me to." There it is was on the table. It was Rex's biggest fear about the press conference. The room was about to snowball in a different direction and Charles Pigeon, the world-famous fight promoter, was at the table with him promoting Thad. He cut the questioning off right then, when they started asking about which god Thaddeus believed in. Or what God had to do with it. Thad didn't say anything as Charles Pigeon ended the questioning.

Charles Pigeon, a sharply dressed, smooth-talking black man, grabbed him backstage and asked, "What the $*(@#)_*_@# do you think you are doing? They are questioning your age! They've got you on the ropes about the possibility of you being knocked out at the end of a round, and you come back with G-O-D. You have an image and you ain't Manny Pacquiao."

He came back with, "I am a Christian!"

Charles looked him up and down and said, "Since when?"

"About eight months ago I trusted Jesus!"

Charles explained to him, "You've got to tell me these things. You know you can't be going off script like that."

Rex looked at him and just couldn't believe it. What was happening to Thad? Where was his fighter going? And as such a strong influencer in his life, where did he go wrong to let him latch onto a crutch like Jesus? This would be the end of him as a fighter, and it wasn't helping their relationship any either. He thought, *Jesus, I guess you are setting me up again, and you seem to be taking your time before this knockout punch. But when you do it, I know you will hit me hard with it. I will be ready.*

Thad grabbed some food with his mother and headed for the hotel. He was about to go through the normal regimen of ice and Advil. Over dinner they talked about how proud she was of him and how proud Wayne must be of him now. The emptiness after all these years still showed up for both of them in big moments. It had never failed to not show its face in every single professional fight. They both hurt and the grief and the hurt never went away. It had gotten better, but had never gone away.

Back at the hotel, Thaddeus went his separate way from his mother and Debra was left all alone. She went back to her room which had a balcony that overlooked the pool. Thaddeus always booked her a room that was high and had a great view. She looked out over the water. It was peaceful. Vegas seemed peaceful from where she sat — and for Vegas. In the distance there were lights and excitement. Music was coming from somewhere, but that wasn't a concern for Debra.

She poured herself the first of three glasses of wine. She should be happy. Her son, whom she raised by herself from age eight, may be the greatest fighter ever. He had really found himself. He had a faith that was larger than even him. Maybe only noticeable to her, but he had a faith that was much larger than hers. She encouraged his faith and had raised him to be faithful to God, and it finally stuck as an adult. His entire demeanor had changed.

It was well known back in Curlsville she was a Christian. She attended church. The truth, however, was she had never forgiven God for her husband's death. At first, she seemed mad at the drunk driver, maybe sometimes Wayne. Then it was whoever was in front of her. After a few years she decided it was God's fault. *The Son of God has tricked me into thinking He has my back. We were faithful, my husband was faithful. He ran a business that was reputable. It was a pillar to the community.* Wayne owned three local dry cleaners. Upon his death she sold the dry cleaners to Tyreek Johnson, who was his manager and right-hand man for years. It was too hard for her to fully learn Wayne's role and deal with her own grief over the loss. She took the money and opened Mama Class's Kitchen and advertised capitalizing on her last name with ads saying, "Time to Class this Town Up!" When people saw her face on a billboard or heard her voice on the radio, this made for instant success.

The town grieved with her over Wayne. It is also important to know that she really kept everyone at arm's length after the accident. She couldn't share her true feelings with her son; she didn't want to publicly struggle with her faith. So she went into herself. Wayne was heavily involved in the community and a passionate lover of God. She thought about how faithful he was. She thought about the times he taught Sunday school, or even would tell people about Jesus on a park bench or wherever he was that day. He loved God. They loved God together! *Even though life isn't promised, you allowed him to just die. That drunk got away and just left the scene. He is gone forever. And no one even knows who did it. He just laid there and bled to death.* She chugged the last half of the first glass and screamed, "WHERE WERE YOU?" She missed him so badly. She hurt and she was angry at God, maybe Wayne for dying, and that jerk of a trainer Rex for keeping her son angry. She was mad all the time, but she didn't show it much.

No answer would satisfy her. Now what would she do? Thaddeus seemed to be moving on. She was glad that his anger seemed to be dissipating. A part of her was more sad because she feared he had forgotten his daddy, his faithful father who would be so proud of him now. But was he supposed to be angry forever?

Then she thought about Rex. She blamed that piece of work for keeping him angry all these years. He had a way of playing off his insecurities and pride to produce a product. He would tell Thad that the other guy didn't respect him, or would say things like, "Look at what they wrote about you, look what they are saying about you."

I thought maybe the anger, the killer, the animal was gone in Thad. But I got the perfect view before that knockout, she thought. *I got the perfect view of the anger that lies just beneath the surface, and that devil Rex brings it out. This will probably go on a lot longer than even his fighting career.*

Everyone thinks this killer in the Octagon is great now, but where were they when he had the night terrors? It happened every night for a year straight before there was a break. Then, out of the blue, in the eyes of her little boy that look of terror would go to that other look. The switch would come on. The anger that was always there in her sweet little boy. It was an anger that always lain just beneath the surface. The look would come out and he was ready to fight. Only who was he fighting? Was it his dad? Was it her? Rex didn't understand, or maybe he did — but she preferred to believe that he didn't understand. How could he? He wasn't there those times on the church playground when Thad would start beating another child and they couldn't get him to stop. He actually bloodied several older kids. The younger ones stayed away from him, but the older ones wouldn't back down. There were a few times that, had no one been watching, someone may have died. This anger was real.

She took her eyes from the balcony and looked to heaven. She exhaled and thought, *It was you he fought! Jesus where were you?* This whole story was different. *You tricked me.* She sat there and drank until she felt better, she drank a little more and passed out in the chair on the patio. Deep down she knew she had no right to be angry at the King of Kings, but she was. She never saw it coming and never recovered from the loss and sorrow of so many years ago. Her family was wrecked, her life changed, and she had to stumble through the upbringing of her son. She felt deceived by the whole story, the whole thing, and she wanted it back. *All that I put into it,* she thought. *I want it all back. Now my son even believes, but I am still watching a volcano erupt when he is in that Octagon.*

On another floor in the same hotel, Rex sat quietly, looking at a picture of a little girl in a Sunday dress. He took this picture everywhere he went. He had never seen a girl that looked so beautiful. She looked like her mother in the face, but had jet black hair like his — well, like he used to have. It was thinner and a little lighter now. Maggie was beautiful. She had a magnetic personality. She always believed the best about everyone and no one could ever tell her otherwise.

This picture was taken when she was just six years old. By the time she would have been seven she was gone. The sickness happened so fast and it was ugly. Rex and Mary began to have problems and they split up. He remembers how Maggie began having dreams about Jesus holding her. She had dreams about God very often. She prayed and believed God would heal her. They all did. Everything was different then. They tried marriage counseling every week for about six months. Mary always wanted to talk about it, but Rex couldn't get past it. Before it all happened they were involved in The Archway Community Church. Maggie was anointed with oil several times. Mary and Rex were both new Christians.

One Sunday morning, as they prayed over her, Pastor Rick asked her, "Maggie, do you believe God can heal you?" She exclaimed, "My God can do anything, Pastor Rick!" While she was really sick she would pray for the other kids in the hospital. She would try to understand how to be there for them, and she would say things about being blessed with two parents, where little Jo Beth didn't have a mother or a father, and was being taken care of by grandparents. She knew that some kids came from bad home lives or that some didn't have much money. How could she see herself as blessed? Rex could no longer see past his own hurt, and thought about how his daughter had been scammed too, and it was all his fault.

They prayed and believed that their little girl could be saved. They prayed and believed she would be spared and the story they needed would come true. He remembered how much faith little Maggie had. She had more faith than he had ever seen. She never doubted God. She never doubted that He had an amazing plan for her life. They even told her; they told her often.

While she was sick, Rex and Mary prayed for her and everything centered around her. They neglected each other to the extreme. But when Maggie was gone they didn't know what to do. People in the church didn't have room in their theology for God to not heal someone. There were no good answers. Mary dug deeper into her faith, while Rex refused to go any further. Mary began to understand that God heals, but it is up to God. We can have faith but sometimes it isn't His will. This answer helped her to have some peace sometimes. Rex hated that answer. He would think, *Why wouldn't he save my Maggie?*

Mary wrestled with whether she prayed enough or believed enough, but the clincher was little Maggie. No one believed more than she. What she saw that Rex couldn't see was that God was there for Maggie. He did comfort her, and the faith that resided in her could get her through anything, even an early death. Mary saw Jesus through the eyes of her little girl, and it was a Jesus who truly could do anything, just like Maggie said.

Mary moved out eight months after Maggie's death. They got divorced, and she was taken out by a heart attack two-and-a-half years to the day of Maggie's death. The medical diagnosis was a heart attack, but the spiritual diagnosis was a broken heart. Mary and Rex had reconciled and were working on getting back together the six months prior to her death. They forgave each other. They forgave Christians for the dumb things they said. Mary forgave God, and had gone to be with her heavenly Father and was praising Him with little Maggie by her side as this is written. Rex was working on it, but then when He took Mary too, he declared out loud privately in his car, "Jesus, I am done!" They both knew what that meant.

Now as he gazed at that beautiful picture, he was high on his own anger. He thought, *I am done, I told you, and now you are taking the only family I have left! You have to have Thad, too? You are taking away family! Not just a fighter!* His hate for Jesus used to startle him, but now his honesty about this anger and hatred owned the greater part of him in these moments. That is what anger, jealousy, and rage do. They blind us.

For several years the belief that a real Jesus walked the earth, lived a perfect life, died for our sins, and rose from the grave had been subdued. It is funny how disobedience to God Almighty feeds and fuels our distrust of Him. Our neglect and abuse of the sacred makes way for the thoughts of the secular to prevail. It is our turning away from Him that moves us further away. We actually get what we want, when we want to get away from Him.

Everyone has to give up something to have true faith. Your faith isn't real unless you have to sacrifice something. Rex had that moment of clarity before he found some programming that would take his mind off this. He was about to allow himself to be consumed by lust. He thought about all those things, and about the Jesus who couldn't heal his daughter, or maybe He wouldn't heal her. *Which is worse — a God who can't heal or one who won't?* He laughed as he thought about how ridiculous it was. *He either doesn't care, or is impotent and can't do anything anyway. Sign me up, Jack!* Rex turned up the TV and fell asleep to the hurt and the pain that consumed him. He felt most comfortable after he gave in to the idea, *Jesus doesn't exist.* That was better than deciding between *can't help* or *will not help.* When he could be convinced that it was all a scam, like buying land on the Gulf Coast, he found a measure of peace. Deep down the peace didn't last long. It wouldn't even last until morning. He would wake up two times before then, but rest for now; the champ got through another day. *I can at least be happy about that,* he thought.

In Thad's room, his body hurt, but he was very emotional. He was mostly joyous as he sipped on a hotel glass of champagne. He enjoyed the glass in private because it was weird to drink with Rex; he was always watching him and trying to help him, and he needed to turn that off for at least one night. He also didn't want to be talking about the next opponent or the next fight. He also didn't want to drink with his mom because he was pretty sure she would have a little too much, and he feared being a part of a problem. He wasn't sure if it was a problem or not. Who knew? He didn't want to ask her because that was awkward too. So he pondered by himself. He pondered his conversation with his mother and thought about his dad. Something was different this time, though. He didn't look at his dad the same anymore. He wasn't worried if his dad was pleased with him, he knew that he was. He had a new-found assurance that he would see him again. He felt truly blessed. He still hurt that his dad had been gone those last 26 years. He basically missed most of his life. But, no doubt he was blessed.

Thad's mind went back to the press conference, and then it raced back to the fight. He knew he was lucky at the end of the second round. He knew he won, but was his record tarnished? Was he losing the edge he had? He wondered, *Am I getting closer to retirement?*

He also noticed that he wasn't angry anymore. Personally, this was good, but professionally not so much. Thaddeus hadn't had a serious girlfriend in years. He had such a high respect for women because of his mother's influence, but for years was afraid of his own temper and anger. He had chosen to stay single, which wasn't too difficult. His training took up a lot of time and energy, and the girls who would try to get around fighters were really not women who challenged him. They were interested in Thaddeus the fighter. Even in his anger, he always knew there was more to him than that.

Thad also had a legitimate vocational fear to be concerned about. He didn't quite understand, but he was now fighting on ability and training, but that anger that gave him the edge was gone. He was still hungry and would train with passion. It kicked in at the right moment in that fight, but he also noticed that he didn't hate those opponents anymore. He wasn't motivated by the same things as before. In fact, that thought caused him a somber pain in his chest. Pastor Paul Adkins told him that hatred can grieve the Holy Spirit. He had even started to care about those people a little. Worse yet, with assurance there is a danger of becoming more relaxed. *I didn't get to this place by being relaxed,* Thaddeus thought to himself. Something was happening and it was extremely uncomfortable. If his edge was gone, he didn't want to continue to fight. He had an unbeaten legacy. He had a quick thought, *I need to get out before I start to slip.*

But I have to fight! he thought. *If I am not a fighter, who am I?* Thad had always been a loner. He had some people who would call him a friend, but Thad didn't really trust that many people. There was always a risk that people wanted something from him. Thad professionally had only known the fighting world. That was who he was. He was a fighter. Now what would he do if he couldn't fight anymore? Was God doing something different in his life? That's what he wanted to know. He was highly skilled and knew how to be an attorney. But, would he love that? He didn't know. He then sipped on his champagne some more and reviewed knocking out The Baltimore Bomber. He knew he still had it. He worried about how badly the press conference went, and what would happen with the media tomorrow, but he was greatly comforted knowing he got another knockout on an unbeaten opponent. He thought to himself, *This is magnificent!* He took the ice packs off, brushed his teeth, and went to bed.

He knew he was going to eat breakfast with Rex and his mother tomorrow morning. He was exhausted. Time to go to bed. He fell asleep, happy, content, and full of faith, but also knowing God was doing something wonderful in his life. Many nights he fell asleep sad and lonely, even after a big win, but not tonight. Tonight was another notch in his belt and special, because he now realized God had blessed his life. He put those fears behind after the thoughts of God Almighty consumed them like a wildfire. As Pastor Paul liked to tell Thad, "God must be seen as larger than life, and our problems must be seen as smaller than the Divine. That is what worship does for the believer and, in turn, that is the job of the believer to the world."

The next morning Rex arranged for them to have a private room in the hotel restaurant. They paid for it as a meeting space, but money was never the issue. Privacy was the issue. Thaddeus needed space and so did they. Rex and Debra also found it taxing in relation to their celebrity. If people couldn't find him (especially after a fight), they would try to find one of them to talk to.

Thad was different from other fighters. He had learned to hide a little, especially as of late, and he knew the media may be getting bored with him in the not-so-distant future. He used to have a poke-the-bear-type of switch that could be thrown when being interviewed, and he would go off. He may have thrown something like I mentioned about the microphone in an earlier press conference. Now he really wanted to avoid them. He hadn't gotten used to the new him. He had become a new creation in Christ, and as He found out last night, that could be more complicated than he foresaw. Pastor Paul gave him fair warning and coaching, but he didn't understand. Paul told him that he wouldn't get it until it actually happened, and Paul was right.

Rex was there early, drinking his coffee. He sat in the corner of the room that faced the door. There was hotel staff who had been paid to guard the door. This was to be a private brunch meeting. The hotel was not incredibly busy at 10 a.m.

Rex loved his morning coffee and having some alone time in a private room before the other two arrived. Debra showed up a few minutes early. She made her way through the dining area back to the private room where she nodded at the two-hotel staff. They smiled at her as she walked by and she slowly walked towards Rex.

Debra greeted him warmly to try not to show her disdain for Rex, "Our boy did it again, huh, Rex?" He stood to greet her and shook Debra's hand and grinned proudly, "Sure did! Sure did!" They made some small talk, but similar to homes that are broken they only made small talk to kill the time before the kid arrived.

Then Thaddeus made his way into the restaurant. He signed a T-shirt with his face on it as he made his way inside.

Thaddeus looked like he'd been hit by a truck. When they saw him they giggled a little as he hobbled, favoring his left leg and having trouble seeing out of the left eye. His nose was swollen with three large cuts on his cheeks, two on the right and one on the left.

Debra laughed and joked, "Not getting old are you, Thad?"

"No," as he labored to breathe a little.

"You are meeting with Dr. Jenkins when you get back home tomorrow still, aren't you?"

"Yes," he replied to Rex. Rex set up a doctor's appointment for what he called a Gladiator Physical after every fight. Rex cared for his fighters, especially Thad. After a moment of uncomfortable silence, Thad said, "Yeah, I am really looking forward to the rib portion this time. I might have cracked one again." They laughed it off. As brunch was very light conversation, Thaddeus ate until he had his fill. He was going to hang out in the hotel the rest of the day and fly back tomorrow, as was customary for him. He never wanted to rush home, because if it was a hard fight he would be sore.

He also sensed he was King of Vegas after a big fight. Even before his conversion he didn't really use it much to his advantage. He didn't go out and attract a lot of media attention. He didn't want to spend a lot of time in clubs because in the past his anger would have done him in; you know, when one of those wannabees would show up and want to fight. Other fighters could normally get away from that or they had some people who would keep them out of trouble. It wasn't his thing. He traveled light and was kind of a loner, like these two who were the closest to him as they shared some brunch.

As they sat there and ate, they got along like one big happy family. Both Debra and Rex felt as though they were doing it for the kid, so to speak. Even though Rex was okay with Debra, he knew that the Jesus stuff was largely her influence and fault. She was also this self-made mommapreneur who made him nervous. She was way too much woman for him.

The momma bear in her had a hard time with a man who felt he needed to keep her son frustrated and angry. She knew it was part of the fight world, but she wanted him to leave it all behind. He had proven himself to be among the best ever. He was getting older and enough is enough. Money was no object. After all, what did he have to prove? Was it for his father, for him, for Rex, for her, God? Who knows? *I don't even know if they could tell you at this point,* she thought. *Besides, his chances of major injury have to be increasing with age,* she continued in her head.

They all enjoyed breakfast and it was time to go their separate ways. Breakfast was almost over and as Thad was feeling better, Rex pulled out the newspaper. The headline read, "God's Fighter?" The article highlighted his past, the fighting, the anger, the pride, every negative interaction they could find. They even tracked down a high school football teammate through the middle of the night to get a statement. They must have called him minutes after the press conference.

Rex said, "I want you to hold onto this article and please keep a low profile." Debra didn't know what to make of the article. They both were positive in words to him, but were concerned because the press is brutal. Neither one of them wanted a discussion about church, theology, or Jesus. They were proud of their Thaddeus and didn't see this moment as the moment for a complicated conversation. They all went their separate ways.

Thaddeus checked his phone. Pastor Paul congratulated

him on another great win. He thought, *How cool is my life?* He texted him back and told him he would call him later. Paul was about to lead the Sunday morning church service.

CHAPTER 3

BACK HOME

BACK IN THE city, Thaddeus took the normal five days off after the fight. To his surprise, he checked out fine at the doctor. He would stop by the gym and check in with Rex. He also had extensive conversations with Billy and how to prepare for his up-and-coming title fight. Thaddeus did a little reading and some light working out. It was nothing too strenuous. He mostly just wanted to stretch and keep his metabolism going. If he had the opportunity to play some racquetball or play something recreationally competitive, he would.

He picked up his reading. He was reading some fiction and studying Scripture. He was really digging into the book of James. James' writing style reminded him of some of the professors he had in law school, well kind of. He was reminded of what they would be like if they were humble instead of what they actually were. He would think, *What if they would have allowed God to use them for His glory?*

Thad would eat many dinners with Billy. They wouldn't go to Thad's favorite place sometimes, but usually somewhere

Billy wanted to go. Billy would talk to Thad about what it means to be a champion, and Thad would layer those talks with what it means in light of his faith and witness. Billy wasn't extremely concerned about his witness, but he was interested in God being a part of what he was doing. Billy was a new believer on a honeymoon period with God.

One particular meal, Thad went into great detail talking about Abraham going out without knowing where he was going. He told Billy, "You know where you are going. You are going towards the HWT title, but that isn't even the best part. The best part is that God will use it for His glory." This type of stuff excited Billy, even though he had a look on his face like he didn't understand. Thad would take these conversations so seriously. He poured into Billy the difference between being motivated as a young fighter, to being motivated as an older, more experienced fighter. Thad also went into great detail about his mindset of fighting his best fight. It was kind of an obsession for Thad. Thad felt that if he fought his best fight, he wouldn't be able to be stopped. He would ask the question, "Can you be stopped if you truly hit your potential? What if your body hits its maximum muscular endurance, your technique is at its sharpest, and your oxygen never runs out? If someone has prepared and they are truly at their best, can they be stopped?

Billy's reply was always circular, "What if the younger fighter is just plain better, or someone comes along that your best technique doesn't match up with? What happens then?" The discussion always went circular like that, which is why Thaddeus liked to talk about it. You couldn't prove any of it.

Billy never understood why Thad poured into him like he did. He really didn't have anyone in his life that did anything like that. There was Larry, but Larry was actually pretty selfish. It was really about his money and him being seen at the end of the day. Of course he cared about Billy, but not at the same level as what Rex and Thad had built together. But in the mind of Billy, Larry was sort of a father figure that he tried to emulate, and Thad was a big brother to him. Maybe that made Rex like a distant uncle or something. Then there was his faith. He was a new believer and he had the faith of a mustard seed, and Thaddeus was confident it would grow. He didn't always understand how faith and fighting fit together. He couldn't always follow Thaddeus in those conversations. Billy couldn't quite get past how to fight and have faith and how they are not completely separate things. After all, fighting is violent and a dirty business. For Thaddeus it was a world that God would use His people in. Billy was also the first person that Thaddeus was truly discipling in a Christian way. He had always helped young athletes and was willing to help guys along, but now there was a faith component.

Thad began to pour into Billy about the fight. He began to remind him that, "Not only are you ready to challenge this guy, but you are a new believer now. That will help you through the training process. Jesus will help you to be ready for the title shot."

Billy chimed in, "Yeah, I guess."

Thad said, "What does that mean?"

Billy just kind of smiled, "I am happy and grateful for this new-found faith that we have, but I can't quite understand why God cares about if I am the champion or not."

"Ah, Billy, it is about platform, we talked about this."

"Yeah. I guess, I don't really understand where you are coming from with that."

"You will eventually," Thaddeus replied. They continued talking about the up-and-coming fight and preparation for the fight with Emmerick. Thaddeus was so excited to see Billy win the title. He truly cared deeply that his workout partner and someone he was helping along in the faith became the champion at the weight class above him. He cared almost as much about his partner winning the title as he did about his own title reign.

Rex would look on and think, *GITR will be the greatest club in the whole country by far. Soon we will be training lightweight contenders, too. Maybe in a few years, Thad will be ready to retire, and he can train people. Maybe we will have some lightweights or some middleweights to get ready for the big time.*

Thad loved to pour anything he could into Billy. Those conversations also happened after workouts. He was especially happy that he could focus on Billy, now that his fight was over. He wanted to focus on Billy's next fight and his spiritual development, and not focus on his own fight for a change.

Billy asked a lot of the normal questions to Thad about life after winning the title. He asked him about how people treat you differently from the day before you win, compared with the day after you win the title. He asked about a lot of the worldly things you don't think about, where to live, do I move, etc. How do you keep the people you want around you and stay away from the leeches that come after you for the opportunity? This includes everyone from businesspeople to women. Thad went a little too deep for Billy in regards to staying true and pure to God, etc. Billy had a small love for God, but fighting and being the champion was what he had worked for all these years. It was his main concern right now. There was nothing more important to him than the title and greatness as a fighter. He truly believed he had the ability to be where Thad was at that moment. Thad was helping him to get there, and even though Thad had changed, Billy could still see the young Thaddeus Class shining through. The young and selfish classless Class, who would take it by force. Billy had had the opportunity to learn from them both, for that he was truly grateful. Sometimes he missed the old Class. Sometimes the new one helped him just fine. But, underneath, Billy was hungry — and he was hungry for his first title. He believed he would be the world champion soon. So did everyone else.

After a fight Thad would also spend a lot of hours with Pastor Paul Adkins. He called him Paul. Everyone did, or at least he desired everyone to call him Paul. Paul had become a believer as a college wrestler himself. He referred to himself as an "almost" guy. The truth was, Paul was a pretty good college wrestler. Thaddeus found it sad. He always thought, *Man, someone could have made him into a killing machine* (in the Octagon). *Now he has to tell those stories in sermons and usually he has to look bad or it doesn't sound right coming from the pulpit.*

Paul didn't seem to need the sport anymore. He enjoyed coaching his kids and spending time with his family. Thaddeus envied this part of his life. It showed him there is life after fighting and more to life than fighting. The type of tenacity and discipline Paul trained with is what transferred over well for him in the ministry. He would preach messages that were prepared and convicting. He would work hard and pray hard. He studied the Bible and had a handle on the Word of God like no one that Thaddeus had ever met. Strangely, though, Paul spoke Thad's language. Paul understood Thad's world. Not like him, but he got it in a way most people don't. He knew about big victories and embarrassing defeats. He knew about what it was like being out there in front of hundreds of people and not having a team around you. He got it. He understood the training and the loneliness it takes to really go for it. He knew what the training and dieting were like.

What Thad really loved about Paul was that Paul didn't treat him differently than anyone else. He didn't treat him like he was better than anyone else. He didn't treat him like a celebrity, and most of all, Paul didn't chase after Thad. They had a genuine kinship and Paul knew that Thad had a lot of people following him who wanted to be some kind of fight groupie.

Paul wasn't there to be seen, get money from him, etc. In fact, Paul was the one who talked him out of tithing. Here was a guy who was trying to make his church float. He was trying to grow a group of people that stayed the same size for a number of years. Every penny counted. Everything that came in mattered. Paul was telling him how pastors rely heavily on the Old Testament to come to that conclusion, and to obey the laws of tithing in the Old Testament we need to consider this was also the tax plan for a nation. We need to consider it is pre-church. We need to consider how few times tithing comes up in the New Testament and how many of those times it is mentioned in a negative way. But Paul wasn't letting anyone off the hook. He preached that Jesus owns everything and we are stewards of His resources, to be spent in the best way for God's glory. Part of that is supporting the work of your local church.

Reasons like these are why Thaddeus was so intrigued by Paul. Thad was by far the richest person he knew personally. Because Paul didn't hit Thad with guilt, condemnation, or shame, it changed him. That is true discipleship. Without going into it, Paul's family and the church had different concerns about their financial situation because Thaddeus now gave a lot of money to the church. A typical pastor would maybe not hold Thaddeus accountable, or would go the other way and hold him to extreme accountability to make sure he was compelled to tithe or give. But not Paul.

It was hard to tell who had the biggest new-found interest in fighting — Bob Rickets, the building committee chair who was blessed with a lot of options, or Dolly Wright, an 89-year-old woman who headed up the city feeding program. I will go with Dolly. You should have seen her watch the fights. She was a feisty one!

With Paul, he kept getting better to Thad because, even after the change, many began to change a little towards Thad but Paul never did. Paul still held Thaddeus accountable. Thaddeus was absolutely certain that Paul cared for his soul. When he talked about money and explained how it is something God gives us for His glory and we shouldn't over-value it, worship it, or treat someone differently because of it, Thad believed him.

Thad had even tried to bring him along on fights, but most of them were on Saturdays. Paul couldn't get away from the church, family, and coaching responsibilities. Paul was a true friend; Thad wasn't sure how many friends he truly had anymore.

Paul had only met the champ one time before his conversion. It was one of those things where they happened to be in the same place. Paul had invited him to the church, but at the time Thaddeus thought he was just after his money, like he had been conditioned to think.

Not long after that, Thaddeus had become a Christian and didn't know what to do with his new-found faith. He heard Paul speaking on the radio and remembered meeting him when they announced the name of the church on-air. Thaddeus then sought him out.

Paul was only two years older than Thaddeus. It had been a long time since Thad saw the type of faith Paul had, and the consistency at which he lived his life. Thad was blown away by the consistency of his faith. He had seen that type of belief before, but not since he was eight. Then, on that fateful day, God took his dad away. His mother also carried a different presence about her faith before that day.

Thaddeus needed to stop by and check in with Rex before lunch. Thaddeus pulled up with Paul and started walking into the gym while Rex pulled up close to them in his normal spot in the parking garage. Rex drove a cherry red Ferrari, like the one Thaddeus used to drive. Rex's car had a vanity plate that read BEATDWN. You could tell by the paint job that it was something special. It was a unique shade of red.

Paul saw Rex getting out of his car and shouted, "Hey, Rex!" Rex rolled his eyes slightly as he got out of the car.

Paul said, "There it is! You got that new car, huh? Wow! Rex, this car looks real nice. I love the paint job!" Rex didn't mind Paul as much as he minded what Paul represented. Paul represented the Christ who was powerless to change his life. He was powerless to save his little girl. But as far as an ex-wrestler who understood the fight world, he was ok. But he didn't trust him. There were only two kinds of people in church, as far as Rex was concerned: those who are taking and those who are being taken.

Paul, having been a college-aged convert to Christianity, understood how hard it was. But Paul was going to keep loving him. They talked about the car for a few minutes. Rex expressed that he was going inside to get some paperwork done. Paul, a little overly-anxious, looked at Rex and said, "Hey, we are going over to Carm's Pizza for a bite. How about you come with us?"

Rex said, "Paul, I get what you are doing."

Paul said, in a slightly sarcastic way, "Getting pizza?"

Then Rex let him have it. "You seem like a sincere guy, but I don't want to talk faith with you. I don't want to be sold your hippie Jesus. My experience is pastors and churches will take you for what they can get!"

Paul looked a little shocked at his straightforwardness and then said jokingly, "Would you consider it if I paid, then?"

Rex, having a clear and angry agenda, couldn't help but be broken up by the humor of the entire situation. This pastor clearly made a lot less than any of them standing there and his comeback to pastors being criminals is, "Let me pay!" Rex gently shook his hand, laughed it off, and went inside. "Maybe another time," he said as he walked inside.

Thaddeus spoke after Rex went inside. He said, "He really is a nice guy."

Paul jokingly said, "Who?"

Thad continued, "He has been through a lot. He and I have always been close since I met him."

Paul said, "The great thing about being us is people need what we have. They need Jesus and the Gospel. Eventually, over time, people are willing to let me pastor them, because they encounter something where they need answers. They need a pastor, a church family, advice, etc. They need it and they need it now!"

Thaddeus spoke up to interject, "Paul, he already had that moment. He had two and the church wasn't there. You might have missed that train, man!"

"You can fill me in a little over lunch, if you don't mind. But, whatever it was, Jesus is still the answer." Paul waited in the car while Thaddeus went inside to speak with Rex and some of the guys.

Thaddeus convinced Paul to go to Cornerstone Café. Paul knew they would end up there, he was just messing with him about the pizza, he knew there was someone he wanted to see. Paul was one of the only people in Thad's life that Thad really wanted to be around for long periods of time. Thaddeus insisted on paying every time. Paul tried to pay a few times, Thad was too quick. Finally, Thad explained to him that he wanted to bless his pastor, and if he didn't stop trying to pay he wouldn't eat with him anymore. This was one of those moments where Paul realized they had the potential to have a two-way friendship. Much of their time was Paul downloading what it means to be a Christian into Thad's mind. Paul understood the competitive world. He understood the fighting world because of his background. He knew about lifting hard and making weight. That wasn't a problem. He did, however, struggle to understand Thad's world right then. For example, Thad paying for everything. He didn't understand the money, fame, and some of the daily challenges. Thaddeus liked to frequent some local places where he could slip in and out the back; sometimes they called ahead and would slip through the kitchen into an empty dining room.

They ate in the banquet room. Other times, like today, they would walk in the front door and speak to a few people and explain that he had a meeting with Paul and would be seated away from people. The waitresses were always tipped well, along with the hostess and anyone who would help them to be shielded from the public. Thad was an extrovert, but not so much of one that he needed the attention all the time. In fact, he found it really hard to be him at times. Some wanted to gawk at him, some groupies and gold-diggers played their hands for him at times. There was an occasional late bloomer wanting to prove something and even pick a fight, if you can imagine that, as well as sometimes people wanting to get some money or something from him. Being Thaddeus Class in public was a full-time job.

Paul had gotten to where he could use all of these things happening around him for good. They also found if they frequented some of the same places, the same people got used to protecting his time, the same people knew they would be tipped. The same people would see him in the restaurant, etc. This created an atmosphere where it wasn't such a surprise.

His favorite place to frequent for lunch was Cornerstone Café. He had gotten to know the owners and found out from the owners that even though they didn't highlight it much, their establishment was named because of Jesus being the Cornerstone of their lives. You can't remove that stone or it all falls apart. Jesus Christ and Him crucified is central to owners Tommy and Rita Hightower, the middle-aged couple from South Florida.

Paul wanted Thaddeus to understand his world through the eyes of Jesus. Thad was really taking to this concept. During lunch, Thad engaged the hostess, Lisa, and told her he would pray for her about her daughter who was struggling in school. Now Sally the waitress — that was a different story. The truth Thaddeus couldn't hide very well was that Thad went to Cornerstone Café almost exclusively these days because of Sally. She liked to make fun of him because of his black eye, and would make jokes about how the pastor gave it to him.

There was something about Sally that drew Thad in. He was interested in her and her story. It had been about five years since Sally's husband left her. He ran off with another woman. There were no kids involved; Sally didn't have any children. They had only been married about two years and it happened out of the blue.

Sally picked up the pieces and moved on. She worked very hard as a waitress at Cornerstone Café. She loved it there. The people wanted to sit in her section. She was very loving and accepting of people. Sally was a Christian, but didn't talk much about it. She tried just to live her life. She enjoyed the attention Thad gave her, but fought internally with it because she *"ain't no groupie"* and she *"wasn't trying to land no fighter, neither."* At least, that was what she told herself.

As they sat down it started. She snuck up on the table while the two men were talking with each other about something deep. While Thad was in-mid sentence, she said, "Wow! I heard you proved to be the alpha in another one of those cage beatings at the pound this week."

Thaddeus fired back, "Yeah, you watched it this time, didn't you?"

"Yeah, I was going to but only if there was nothing better to do. I went with giving my dog a bath and chewing my toenails."

"What's wrong, Sally? Is two men fighting too scary for you?"

"No, I find it comforting that if he hits you too hard I won't get bullied by you anymore. The truth is, I did watch it. They had me on these tables in here. You know, they always turn you on in this room and you can choose to sit in the Thaddeus Room (she made air quotes with her fingers), or out in the other room if you don't want to watch the fight, or have your kids watching the fight."

"So, you saw the fight then?"

Sally quickly fired back, "Well, yeah, people in this room always tip better. Why do you think I put up with this (she motioned with her two pointer fingers around the table) all the time?" She turned to Paul and said, "Sorry for ignoring you, Pastor. How are you today?"

"Entertained, as always, Sally, how about you?"

"Always good." Sally took their orders by saying, "The usual?"

Thad smiled and said, "How about make sure they make mine with a little more love and attention this time? I find the atmosphere a little cold out here."

She fired back with a "Wow! Kind of a dad joke without any kids? There is no end to your immaturity. It must have been those shots you took at the end of the second round." Somehow, when she said it, it didn't hurt. Paul got a little uncomfortable with that comment, thinking she struck a nerve.

Thaddeus simply looked at her with bright eyes, smiled and said, "You did watch it!"

She said, "I told you, I have to be able to relate to my audience in here. It is about the tips! The pastor understands. He works on tips. Isn't that right, Pastor Paul?" She brought Paul in to soften the conversation. Paul just laughed along and nodded. "I will be back with your drinks."

While she was off working, Paul asked him, "So why don't you ask her out?"

Thad was able to talk because there was enough of a buffer zone, but he chose not to. He put it out there, "She is too young for me." Sally was only 27, so there was a five-year age difference. But that was not the real reason, and anyone with a brain listening to their conversations knew it.

"You obviously like her," Paul challenged.

"Ok, the truth is, I have no self-control."

Paul, thinking he was talking about lust or sexual sin, tried to talk to him about how to prayerfully date someone, "and when someone is a Christian it might be easier to not sin together, and it is why a lot of devoted Christians get married faster."

Thad got a little red because he was this big, tough, giant who was now feeling like a fifth-grader talking to his father about the birds and the bees. Thad interjected, "Stop, stop, stop! That is not what we are talking about. The anger, the violence, the man I was once was. I have never trusted myself. Anger and pain are part of my past. I keep most people out of my inner circle. You, my mom, Rex, maybe Billy are really the only people who I feel really know me. Another person is a crowd."

Paul looked at Thad and said, "Champ, you got to take a chance."

He looked at Paul and said, "I thought you were going to be teaching me some faith lessons today."

"I am. The risk is worth it. But the greatest cage fighter on the planet already knows that, huh?"

Thad looked up at Paul and said, "Ok, I will think about it."

"Hey, so how is 'The Kid?'" Paul was referring to Billy "The Kid" Smith. Paul had played a part in helping get Billy back into church and even saw a type of recommitment to Christ moment. Paul had baptized Billy. But he was gently trying to help Thad along as a primary discipler of him. In

Paul's words, "It works better this way, you are in each other's world."

Thad said, "He is good. I am still not sure that I am the one who should be teaching him the Scriptures or anything. He needs a lot of attention."

Paul chimed in, "You have helped him to become a great fighter, haven't you?"

"Well, yeah."

"Then what is the problem?" Paul goes in for the kill. "It is all the same. You are discipling him to be a fighter like you. Help him to live a life like you."

Thaddeus made a quick, awkward joke about ketchup — he was obviously looking to escape the subject. Thad never found Paul that annoying because not many people held him accountable, but oddly enough the people who were closest to him did just that.

They ate, had lighter conversation and paid the check. Thad gave Sally an even bigger tip than usual. Thad and Sally smiled at each other and he and Paul left. Thad needed to get back in the gym tomorrow so Paul and he were going to spend some time together today. It was important for Thaddeus to be around Paul to do his post-fight soul searching. It was nothing official, it was just something Thaddeus knew he needed to do and Paul had come to expect it. Maybe things were changing or about to change. He didn't know, but he needed to know before training for the next fight.

The next day, Rex had his second cup of coffee and his paper. He was about to finish up his morning routine and get to the gym. In front of him on the cover of *Americana Today,* there it was. There was a picture of Thaddeus with a swollen eye in the press interview after the fight. It seemed they caught him at just the right moment, and maybe even photoshopped the picture to make him look a little more battered. The headline read in full color, "As Long as God Wants Me To…" Rex just shook his head as he read the article.

It was very predictable. The paper built a case against Thad, seeking to prove how maybe he isn't the fighter he once was. He wasn't the killer he used to be. He didn't have the anger anymore. Something was different. The paper, having a touch of an anti-organized-religion bent to it, sought to build a case against a fighter that was being made soft by Jesus. What made Rex really angry was that he agreed with the sentiment that Jesus wasn't going to help his fighter, and may be his downfall. It made him sick to his stomach.

Rex was concerned for his Thaddeus. He'd had enough of Jesus. He was going to defeat Jesus. Jesus took his Mary and his Maggie and he wasn't going to let him take Thaddeus and his ability away. Rex was ready for the fight of his life. Thaddeus was going to have his faith. But, his faith wasn't going to interfere with the fighter he still could be. Rex felt he needed to fight Jesus so Thad could continue to fight everyone else. He felt extra motivated and got ready to get to the gym.

Later on, Thaddeus arrived after Rex was already at GITR. The fight calendar atmosphere after a fight is relaxed a little and gradually gets more intense with some reset times along the way. This is true especially when you know you will have an opponent, but there isn't one yet, or even a fight date. But strength and explosive power training are a large part of what happens right after a fight. Diet becomes a little more relaxed, although Thad had to make a few changes because of age. In other words, a 25-year-old champion can eat and rest much differently than a 32-year-old fighter.

There was never a shortage of workout partners in GITR who wanted to strength train with Thad. He had lots of encouragement from Rex, Larry, Pete, Joe, Billy, and several others who took part, making themselves available for the purpose of one day getting to where Class had arrived to.

Early on in the workout, while doing some cleans in the weight area, Rex pulled out the newspaper clipping. He held it in front of Thad's face and screamed, "THEY ARE SAYING YOU ARE DONE! WHAT DO YOU SAY? ARE YOU STILL THE *$%#* CHAMP?" This wasn't abnormal behavior for this gym. It wasn't abnormal for Rex to motivate in this way. The others joined in with words of encouragement and reminding him of his knockout. "IS THE CHAMP STILL HERE? IS THIS STILL HIS HOUSE?"

The fire was back and the workout was awesome. He got an extra rep or two on about every exercise. There was screaming and yelling. The champ was getting that between-fight power back. He could feel it. Rex knew how to touch the nerve. He also rode that nerve the rest of the workout. He went after that nerve like he was picking leftover raw steak from between his teeth. Like an animal provoked, the look in Thaddeus's eye was back. It was pure adrenaline at GITR. If you have never been around fighters training, it is quite a thing. There is ego, adrenaline, rude comments, etc. They don't usually train where there are smooth-moving, controlled workout machines. They normally are in the PIT, the weights are dirty, the room is smelly. There are loud bangs and yelling while men throw hundreds of pounds on their backs for sport. When they go down for that last rep of squats with four- or 500 pounds on their backs and don't bring it up, they scream and throw it off their backs. The atmosphere smells like the zoo, tastes like adrenaline and the dreams of what might be. With every intense rep, there is a growing belief that the fighter training will be the one left standing once again. It borders on it being a doctrine or an idol, or a religious law to follow. "Outwork the other guy. Give it your all and you will be the one left standing." Those who sparred with him were aspiring fighters themselves, oftentimes with their own fights coming up.

Soon the focus would be shifting to Billy. Billy was going to be fighting for the HWT title very soon. It would be a great day for GITR to have both titles. They would be the Light HWT and the HWT champions of the world. The reason this workout wasn't as focused on Billy was there was kind of a ritual about this sort of thing. There was something about getting that first intense workout in that said to the fighter and his psyche that he was back. He wasn't going to be at the top of his game or the peak of his training, but he was working hard again. He was going to spend some extra time in the weight room and was going to gradually spend more time on the mat.

He would also spend a lot of time with Billy and Larry: Larry being the primary trainer for Billy, while Rex was the primary trainer for Thaddeus. Sometimes it got a little confusing or territorial around there, but it worked. Thaddeus cared deeply about the success of Billy. Under Paul's direction he had even begun to disciple him as a new believer in Christ. He mentored him as a fighter. There was also a great deal of competitiveness between them. Sometimes Billy would refer to Thad as "Old Man." There had also been times when the two had been grappling and Thad would say something like, "Not yet, kid," before a big takedown. It was a healthy, competitive atmosphere. Healthy for some cage fighters included a lot of ego. There were fist fights even on days when there was no striking, but there was a great deal of respect they had for each other. Imagine if Billy won against Emmerick. GITR would have the two champions at the last two weight classes. It was an incredible feat. It was a dream come true for Rex, and as far as anyone could tell, it was pure joy for Larry "Quick Draw" Rossi as well.

But behind closed doors you should know that sometimes Billy had his day. Sometimes Billy hit some moves on the champ that usually didn't happen out in front of the crowd. Billy had benefited from two great trainers and working out with maybe one of the greatest fighters ever. Thaddeus truly had a heart to make him into a better person and disciple him in Christ. He wanted to see fruitfulness that would last beyond when he was too old to fight.

As he got closer to the fight it would be interesting. There would be days when Billy, being the fighter who was getting ready for his big break, would be outfighting Thad. It was kind of expected when someone was training for a fight on a certain day. There is a real art to what is called peaking. How a fighter eats, trains, and rests all centers around performing on that one night. As it gets close to that night, we might see something new in this gym.

Thad had been beaten by the larger Billy "The Kid" Smith, but not on a daily, consistent basis. The champ had always been able to put him back in his place. But there was something exciting happening here and it had been good for business as well. It had been good for building a program and endorsements because at the two heaviest weight classes was where winning had been done. When others started working out there, they wanted to see them compete against each other. Rex and Larry knew what this did for the environment.

But what happened two hours later after the workout was done was what startled Rex. As Rex tried to poke the bear, it seemed Thaddeus was able to leave it there. He was able to leave the anger, animosity, and insecurity all behind. He did everything he could in the weight room that day, and he was going to leave it there. One of the things Rex said, "Wow! You really convinced a lot of people you were all washed up at the end of the second round there!" These were easy comments Rex had made in the past that touched the insecurity of Thaddeus and would maybe even trick him into going out for a two-mile run at the end of the workout.

Thaddeus, still short of breath, just looked at Rex and said, "Ah, Rex you told me not to trust what those lined papers say. We showed the world already."

"Someone is always coming for you, Champ."

"I know, Rex." With that, Thaddeus grabbed his stuff, told him he would see him tomorrow morning, and off he went.

Rex knew things had changed in the mind of Thaddeus, but whoa! This used to really get him going. Not today. Not this time. It seemed that Jesus was outsmarting him again. It was fascinating how every time Rex allowed himself to get close to someone, or have something for himself, Jesus seemed to get in the way. Now he was really afraid that this change of perspective was going to hurt both their careers and ultimately the bond they had. Rex had gotten to the place where when he thought of it, he cursed at the Son of God in private. He wasn't so noticeably in favor of Him in public either, but it was even worse in his own head.

Rex went into Larry's office. He gave Larry a little office just off the weight room area. It had a desk, an old comfortable leather chair, a TV that was only used for watching film.

Larry was an expert at scouting. He had taught everyone at GITR a lot about how to read an opponent. He was very good at pinpointing tells. Tells are things that a fighter does before throwing a punch or making a move. Sometimes they are nervous or superstitious habits. Other times they are bad habits, or a matter of getting into the right position. Everyone has them; a great fighter will get away from them. Part of what made this partnership great was since coming to GITR, not only had Billy and Thad become better fighters, they had become great at reading each other.

Billy had especially become great at scouting Thaddeus. Many times Thad would beat Billy on the wrestling mat or in the boxing ring, or sparring in the Octagon, and Larry would help Billy to fine-tune for the next time. That is what made this partnership so beautiful. Truly, the best fights ever may have happened in that room, with only a few people there to see it.

Rex walked into Larry's office visibly upset. Rex and Larry had a no fluff policy. He just blurted out, "What do you think, Larry? Is Thad on his way back down? Has he hit the top of the mountain?"

"Why do you think that Rex? He hasn't lost a fight. He is focused and trains hard."

"Larry, he is a special fighter and I care that he doesn't ruin his legacy. Was he out in that fight?"

Larry chimed in, "Yeah, you know he was. Everyone says it and even Thad knows it. But, it happens. Some of it is technical. He gets lazy on his left side late in a fight. He leads with his face on his shots without clearing the guy's arms late in a fight. But, it happens."

Rex fired back, "No, not to Thad it doesn't. I am worried that this faith thing is getting the best of him."

Larry agreed, "I don't know that it is ultimately what is best for Thad or Billy. Billy spends a lot of time with Thad. They talk about the Bible and some Christian leadership stuff. I mostly tune them out when I hear it."

Rex chimed back in, "The great thing is, Thad has always been focused. He used to get in trouble, but for the most part there was anger and something to prove. Now God has everything. There isn't an urgency anymore. The fire is about to go out. I see it, but he doesn't. Things are not the same. To him he has always been winning."

Larry stood up from his chair and grabbed Rex by the shoulders. "Rex, he was already great when I got here. He continues to improve. He has at least two more wins in him. He still watches film. He is great at helping Billy along. He is competitive enough that if he loses to Billy too much in practice that will keep him going. I think your goal is to get through two more fights unbeaten and see where you are."

"Maybe you are right, Larry. Good thing you are here. Thanks." Rex smiled and left the room to go home.

CHAPTER 4

COMMUNITY

FORTY-FIVE MINUTES AWAY in Curlsville, Debra rushed around with her normal duties at the restaurant. There was a Bible study that met at Mama Class's Kitchen. She would make sure they had everything they needed. She was once very close to all the women who attended this study. They were there for her when Wayne died but she stopped getting around them, except for Barbara. Her and Debra still talked. Barbara, Ruth, and Vicki took her at her word when she told them life was hard being a single mom and starting a business, and she just couldn't come to the Bible study. She retreated into her shell not too long after the accident.

She went to church for Thaddeus, and it didn't hurt her business but Jesus was no longer her friend. She missed her husband, but in a way she felt at times like she had found some kind of realist awakening. She found out that if she worked a lot she made more money. She found out God didn't kill her if she worked on Sunday. She felt her eyes were open, but then at times feared her disdain for God.

Wayne always told her, "You can be mad at God. He can take it!" When she found herself still talking to God she would quickly stop. After all, *The life we had, what did it get us? Where was Jesus in all of this?* Wayne never missed church. He knew more Bible than most of the pastors she had ever met. *My son was going to have a near-perfect Christian upbringing. Where was Jesus in that?*

Thaddeus was so angry. The truth is, so was she. There were many nights when they held each other and cried. Wayne held this family together and now like a cruel joke he was gone, and for all intents and purposes, Jesus was gone from their house too. *For many years Thaddeus fought, and now he is a professional fighter under the thumb of an angry, insecure trainer who needs him to win another fight for him, do it better — for his glory!* She stopped in her mind and took a breath.

These thoughts all happened as she watched the women from the church coming into the restaurant. Barbara walked in with a smile on her face. "He did it again! Nice fight the other night!" She knew Barbara and Vicki probably didn't watch it, but Ruth told her how it went. That was the pattern — they cared, but fighting wasn't their thing. Debbie didn't have any grudge about that; if it weren't for Thaddeus, she would never have gotten around it either. But she was a tiger for that child. She would love her boy Thaddeus until she no longer could. She would be there for him, no matter what. Barbara knew Debra hadn't been the same since the accident. She knew her faith wasn't the same. She knew things about Debra because they were friends and she would let her in. She knew the hurt and pain she suffered. Barbara, like every other time, invited her: "Come in. We are talking about Jonah. This book we are studying is quite fantastic. It talks of Jonah's racist and religious bigotry. It is deep stuff."

Debra simply said, "Yeah, sounds good, but we are short on some wait staff today and have some real breaks in the dam. You know I always appreciate when you ask, though."

"I won't ever stop. You know that!" Debra gave her a busy woman's nod, and as Ruth and Vicki entered, Debra opened the door. They had some casual conversation for a minute; they also congratulated Debra on another win for Thaddeus. They were off to their study while Debra disappeared into the kitchen and her office in the back.

She loved seeing her friends, but kind of liked when they left too. Pain was her reality, even after all these years. Guilt said, "I could have done something different or been better!" Grief said, "I will never get over it. I will always hurt like this!" and Bitterness shouted from deep within and with utter despair, "Jesus where were you?" She would sometimes think about Martha meeting Jesus on His way to come see her brother after he had died, "Lord if only you had been here, this wouldn't have happened." But the fact was, it did happen and there was nothing that could be done now. She came out to send them on their way when they closed down at 2:30 after lunch was over. She hurt but she hid it well, or so she thought.

Thaddeus went to eat with Paul's family. Paul's wife, Ella, was not what you think of as a pastor's wife. Many pastors seemed to be married to women who liked to stay home and have a lot of children. Ella was a career woman. She liked to keep you on your toes, meaning she never wanted you to feel as though you had her figured out. Ella would tell kids in the youth group she used to be a firefighter or a ninja. She preferred this to even her current position of CFO at a local but thriving accounting firm.

She did her job well and was herself. She didn't desire to fit into the stereotypical role of what others felt a pastor's wife should be. Early on in Paul's ministry he gave her the freedom to be herself and stuck up for her at every turn. Sometimes within a church, leaders and their spouses have to break molds and trains of thought for the good of the people there. He explained to her how being herself was the best method of discipleship to use.

Simeon and Elizabeth were their two children. Simeon was ten and Elizabeth seven. Paul lived in an average house in a very nice neighborhood. They chose the location for the schools and Ella loved the house. She had a knack for making the house into a home.

When Thaddeus pulled up into the driveway of the home, the house was lit up. Simeon and Elizabeth were outside playing basketball in the driveway. Thaddeus brought with him an expensive bottle of wine. He walked to the door with a fresh black eye. Simeon, a young wrestler, and Elizabeth, who liked playing soccer, were used to his look from seeing him in church. They both greeted him. Simeon liked Thaddeus's fighting stories. Ella would get a little uncomfortable with some and Thaddeus would try not to offend her. She was a former athlete herself, but the violence of his sport made her a little cautious as the little ones listened on. Thaddeus respected her, and actually feared her a little, in that around her kids things were going to be done her way.

Finally, it was mealtime. Thaddeus loved to talk about food and grilling. Being single, and somewhat of a celebrity and an aging athlete who enjoyed being alone sometimes, meant he had a need to cook for himself.

Ella brought out some ribeye steaks that were one-and-a-half inches thick and very large. There were some baked potatoes that were grilled to perfection alongside those steaks. Thaddeus liked his steak somewhere between medium and rare. Ella used the perfect amount of spices for the task. Thaddeus's steak was heaped with mushrooms and onions on top, while the smell of gently cooked animal carcass soothed his heart and made him feel tough at the same time, like a real man.

They laughed and talked about the current events in their lives. For Thaddeus, Paul was the celebrity. He was larger than life. Thaddeus looked at what Paul had, and he desired it for himself. Not in a way that is weird or sinful. He didn't want to take Ella from him, or his kids, but in a healthy way he knew that even though he had the entire world at his disposal, something was still missing. Something was incomplete in his life.

Thaddeus and Paul helped clean up the kitchen. They left some of the plates in the sink. Paul pulled Thaddeus outside on his humble little porch he jokingly called "the lanai." Thaddeus told Paul, "Man, I love hanging out with your family. Your wife's cooking and the way you guys all joke around with each other is priceless. I really am thankful that you let me into your world."

Paul replied, "Yeah, they are great. We all have our struggles. Ella and I have our trials too, but working hard on our marriage for all these years does a great deal to help with that as well. It doesn't just happen. It takes work, just like training for a fight. It takes prayer. We pray together. We are there for each other. She is my equal. I help her with her career. She helps me with mine. I listen to her, she listens to me. We don't always see things the same way. Sometimes we may even argue, but at the end of the day, Jesus wins for both of us and in our marriage."

Thaddeus responded, "So, it isn't just about finding the right woman then?"

"Not completely, you both need to be found in and by Jesus," Paul responded. "Look, what I mean is: Jesus is central. Our plans have to revolve around and lead to His plan for us. The same is true for your marriage and what God is doing in the lives of my kids."

Thaddeus thought deeply for a minute. "Wow, it is a lot to think about, huh?"

Paul came back with, "Not really; it is like a Sunday school teacher asking little kids questions in Sunday school. The answer is always Jesus."

Paul went on, "Discipleship is always the answer. Once you know what you are shooting for… (he paused). You know, Thad, I have had several people approach me about you."

Thaddeus was a little alarmed by that statement and asked, "What does that mean?"

Paul continued, "Well, people with an evangelical mindset look at you and think, 'Look at the platform he has. He has such a testimony and he can reach a billion people with a book or something.' Someone else will look at you and say, 'Wow! I want to use someone like Thaddeus to reach my community for Jesus.' Those are not bad things, but I tell them not now."

Thad was confused and maybe slightly hurt because he was a doer, and responded, "Why?"

Paul went on, "Many reasons. You are just growing into this. You are putting anger behind you like we have talked about. You are struggling with newborn struggles and have to do it publicly, that is difficult enough. You are finally just learning Who you belong to, where your worth comes from, etc. You are also more than a fighter, you even have a law degree. God is doing something awesome. He is writing a story that is beyond words, yet I still don't know what it is. That is one of the things that makes Him God, right?"

Thaddeus sighed, "I guess." Paul had a way of speaking to Thad's heart that was unexplainable and unique. Even though he was similar in age to Thaddeus, he had walked this walk ahead of him and was sort of an older, much more experienced brother to Thaddeus.

Paul went in for the direct hit, "Why don't you date, man?"

Thaddeus smiled a little and humbly said, "I don't trust myself, I guess. I had a girlfriend in high school I treated really badly and I didn't like the person it made me. I went to law school and stayed away from serious relationships. I have been around groupies who like me because I am a fighter. I didn't feel like I fit in at law school, probably because I was getting my fighting career started then and didn't hang out with many classmates. But when it comes down to it, I like that from a distance I look good and I don't want to mess it up."

Paul said, "Is that why you don't ask her out?"

Thad smiled again, "Who?" They both knew they were talking about Sally.

"Look man, she would give you a run for your money. She would push you. She would disagree with you. She wouldn't dote after you because you are a famous fighter. She would push you to be better, and she would stick up for you, even though that might be hard for you to imagine. Look, it might not work out, but it is worth a try."

It got a little uncomfortable. "Thaddeus, back to what others want from you within the church and why I don't entertain these ideas."

Thaddeus says, "I know, I am not ready."

"Okay, but that is not the complete answer. I want to pastor you and you are my friend. I am committed to you in those ways. I don't go looking to get anything from you," Paul tenderly responded. "Sally isn't perfect, she knows you are not either, but are you perfect for each other? Maybe you are, maybe you are not."

Thad asked, "But what if she doesn't talk to me anymore?"

Paul jokingly said, "I guess you will not have very good conversations while you are ordering food. Is that really the end game? The risk is worth it, right?"

Thaddeus cut in, "Something else has me down."

"What?"

"I think I might be losing the desire to fight. I still enjoy it, but my edge may not be there anymore. I know Rex sees it. The media sees it. The Baltimore Bomber exposed it."

"What do you mean?"

"Anger!"

Paul jumped in, "You need to be angry to fight?"

"No, but I don't know what I have to prove."

"You still looked good to me," Paul cut in. Paul started to ask a few questions. "Do you love training?"

"Yes."

"Do you still desire to fight and develop that legacy, and will you train in a way that will not damage it?"

"Yes, I think. I just am a little confused. Jesus is reshaping me, but taking my anger away affects me."

"Is Jesus asking you to quit fighting?"

Thaddeus thought for a second, "No, well I don't think so. I just get very confused. You have competed at a high level. Is fighting sinful?"

Paul was a little taken aback by the question, not because

it hadn't been asked before, but he happened to be looking at someone who was possibly the greatest to ever step into the Octagon. He thought about how much of a heart for Jesus this man really had. It seemed for someone who let it go in the Octagon, he had developed this survival skill of playing it safe. His mind raced as he put the pieces together thinking about why he didn't ask Sally out. Why he kept such a small circle of people who really knew him. Paul's response was quick, "I don't believe your sport is sinful unless Jesus asks you to do something else. Many people are not going to understand your world, but what a great story you have to tell already and will be telling. Many pastors will not tell you this because they play it safe and, quite frankly, they don't understand how two men can beat each other to near death and still go have dinner together and laugh about it later. I had a guy tell me in college that he was puzzled by how I can love Jesus but get into more fights in the wrestling room than anyone else."

Thad cut in, "It truly is a different world."

Paul went on with, "That is exactly the point. You can't fall into the mold they want you to fall into. You are cut from a different cloth. As for this new creation you have become, it is important that you understand the methods for your success in the past may have been built on insecurity, pride, anger, and a host of things that are not godly. This is the time to redefine your training and understand who you are in Christ. He will give you a better method, if continuing to fight is what you need to do. You already started to train, but only you know if you want to or not. Most importantly, don't let that girl get away. The hero has to get the girl." They laughed about it and hung out a little longer.

The next day after his morning workout, Thaddeus went

to Cornerstone Café to see Sally. If he got there about 8:30, she would not be working as hard and would have time to talk with him. Sally was happy to see him walk in. She walked over to the table and said, "Wow! Just wake up?"

He said, "No."

She continued to rip on him about his black eye by saying, "If someone beat me up like that I would stay in bed, too."

"You keep picking on a defenseless little fighter like me, I might have to call the police."

They smiled. She said, "Cup of coffee and the Western Omelette."

"With love, yes." He nodded.

He looked at her and thought *this is the moment.* "Can I ask you something?"

"Yes," she said.

His voice got a little squeaky as he continued, "I am a very boring person when it comes down to it. I kind of avoid people a lot of the time because people know me and expect something much more exciting. But, I would like to spend more time with you and know you better."

Sally seemed a little shocked. It was like this thing they had going was good enough for her. She got a little nervous. She said, "I – I – I do like you a lot. I don't want to hurt your feelings, but I don't think it would work between us. I am going to get your order in." Then she quickly walked off.

This was possibly the most awkward moment Thaddeus had experienced in many years. No one told the man no, aside from his trainer. This was a very hard thing for him to handle. Immediately, he processed all the things in his mind that he must have misread. Was there something about him that was going to keep him from ever having a real relationship? What was wrong with him? He thought about how fascinating it was that he felt like he needed someone all these years, and when he stepped out like this it caused him so much pain. He got mad at Paul for convincing him to pursue Sally. He took out a book and started to read to pretend he wasn't injured from the exchange. The truth was, he would choose being beat on by a great fighter any day of the week to the feeling of rejection. Good thing he always sat where he was hard to find and others wouldn't know. He also processed how he didn't think Sally was all that close to the people she worked with either. Even after she brought him his food and they had more awkward engagements the rest of the meal, he didn't let up thinking that she probably liked him too. It was hard to understand. Most importantly of all, Sally became even more attractive to him.

Later that night, Sally processed her own life. She processed how perfect her life seemed just a few years earlier. She processed how Jase convinced her he was a really good man. He loved Jesus. He loved her. It seemed like a fairy tale. It turned out none of it was real. He found something and someone better and it was over. It even turned out it was over before she thought so, as he was out with her long before the end of it. She churned with turmoil and thought to herself, "It seems that the world is a much better place when I keep to myself and don't get too close to anyone. People's lives on social media and in pictures are not real."

She learned from her father growing up that if she pushed him too far she would get back-handed. She got pretty tough, like the time he tried to take a swing at her when she was 17 and she knocked him out cold. He was drunk and surprised. Secretly, Sally had taken self-defense classes. She knew that it was time for her to live with her grandmother as she finished school in the city her senior year. Things hadn't been easy for her and that was why she was jaded by life.

Which brought her to Thaddeus. Wow! He seemed great, but he couldn't be like that all the time — and in his earlier fights and interviews she saw the look. She knew the crazed look and the anger that consumed. But this guy was a professional fighter, not her fat old man. What would a woman her size — or any size — ever do if a man like that hit her? She would surely die. Deep down she feared Thad. She sensed she was wrong, but she learned that this is how you live. She learned it from her father. She also learned from her fat old man you could be an awesome deacon in their little Baptist church in their little community, and could make her mother look really bad, while he smelled like roses.

Thaddeus Class was not the same at home as he was in public; no one is. That was how she ended up with her ex-husband. He was skinny and not overly attractive. He had a great sense of humor and she thought they had something real. The truth was, they both tried to play it safe. She was scared and he liked scared. It turned out he was controlling and jealous too, probably because he was looking for the door.

One thing was for sure, she would never end up with a public legend known for fighting. No one ever gets rid of the anger. She loved Jesus but she also knew anger and the permanent resident known as fear that she lived with resides with us as a result. Thaddeus Class, as perfect as he seemed, would never be who she was supposed to end up with — that is, if she was supposed to be with anyone at all.

A couple of days later Thaddeus and Paul met up for lunch. On this day they got some pizza delivered to the church office. This was Thaddeus's idea. Although only shortly into his training, Paul, having been a competitive wrestler, knew this was weird. At this stage in Thad's career he was very disciplined and wasn't going to violate his diet like that. There wasn't any good reason for this violation of his diet, but maybe he just wanted pizza. Paul was confident Thad was probably just stalling on asking Sally out.

Thad came in and said hello to Paul's secretary, Bernice. Bernice was sitting in the outer area to the main office. Bernice was everything you would want in a church secretary. She had a calm voice. She was well trained for when someone called the church with bad news, or in case of an emergency. This was essential in having a church in the New York City area. She also had been at Trinity Bible Church for about the same amount of time Paul had been alive. She knew the church inside and out, and probably the clincher for her hire was she had more than 30 years in age on Pastor Paul. This woman loved being a church secretary; she loved Jesus. She loved His church and was essential to the body. Bernice Hopkins turned down serving on the board several times, and had always gravitated towards greeting people on Sunday mornings or teaching her elementary school age Sunday school classes.

Bernice gave a warm greeting to Thaddeus, "Hey Thaddeus, looks like you got some more bruises. You might need to borrow some of my cover-up for that eye."

Thad fired back, "Come on now, it ain't that bad. How are you, Bernice?"

"Good, just loving this weather."

Thad found her joy over the current erratic temperature drop to be a little weird. But, that was who Bernice was. She enjoyed a very simple, peaceful Christian life and shined light on people wherever she went.

Just then Paul came out of his office. As Paul approached, Thaddeus poked at him, "I was wondering when you were coming out to see me."

Paul said, "Well, you can wait, but here comes the pizza guy." Paul had a credit card in hand. This was typical of Paul. Most of the time he let Thad pay because they had this type of understanding. But Paul would try to sneak it in once in a while.

"Pastor, you are going to get jacked." Thad put his hand out and had the money ready to hand to Rick the pizza boy who came walking in the door.

Rick saw Thad and told him, "Hey, good afternoon to you, Champ! Nice fight last week, but man, that black eye!"

Bernice piped in and said, "Yeah, I told him he needed my cover-up."

Rick laughed. He was very comfortable around Thad and Paul. Rick McCloud was a young college student who everyone liked, but was a struggling new Christian who seemed to get himself in compromising positions. Thad gave him double what the pizza cost. He joked and said, "I like it better when you pay, Champ." He gave a friendly punch in the arm to Paul and said, "See you Sunday, Pastor."

Paul responded to Rick with, "Someone else might get a black eye around here." Rick laughed and left. Paul and Rick had a great relationship. Paul had been there as Rick had tried to be serious about his faith with one foot in each world. There was nothing malicious about any of this exchange.

Paul told Bernice that he would be back in one of the adult classrooms for lunch away from the phones. "Tell anyone who calls that I am in a meeting. Tell them I will be back by two."

Thad looked at Bernice and laughed, "He is afraid I will

get pizza sauce on his collection of Luther sermons or his John Wesley commentaries."

"Aw, Thad, those are fighting words," she laughed.

Paul said, "If you must know, I have a hard time preparing a message about sacrifice when I smell my favorite combination of pepperoni, cheese, and mushrooms."

Thad said, "So eccentric anymore! You are right, you can pay next time. I can't have my pastor getting spoiled." Bernice shook her head and laughed.

They started toward the short hallway through the narthex area of the church, the back hallway that held the classrooms. No one would be in the church today. If someone did show up, they would hear them coming, so there was an element of privacy. Paul said, "I love Nick's Pizza. This is good."

"Yeah, me too, I thought this was a great idea."

Paul replied with, "Because of the pizza?"

"Yeah, that pizza is awesome."

Paul, with the nosy, aggressive method that always seemed to gain information, continued to pry, "Yeah, but we had a good thing going at the coffee shop. We were set up in the back room. People had limited access to you. And the best waitress in the city. The food is great."

Thad sarcastically replied, "Do they teach you that crap in seminary?"

"What?"

"This thing where you keep prying on me until I break."

"I either learned it as a competitor or it is a spiritual gift," Paul replied.

"Oh, I thought all this time people were talking about your *anointing*, but really it was *annoying*," Thad snickered.

They sat down, Thad nodded, and Paul prayed for their

food. It seemed there was a moment they took a break from their harsh language towards each other, so they took their first bite of the pizza and began to talk. "Well, you broke me," Thad said with a mouthful of pizza.

"What on earth are you talking about?"

Thad continued, "I asked Sally out the other day. I sat at the usual table. We were laughing and joking around and I thought, *this is the moment.* Everything seemed to point to this being the moment that I would ask her out. When I asked her out, everything changed. I can't figure out what it was. I told her I don't go out in public much, but I would like to find a way to be out with her. I talked to her about how I would like to know her better. I feel like I offended her in some way. I was shocked that she said no. I messed the entire thing up."

Paul asked a few clarifying questions. They talked further, turning over what he said exactly, and if she was offended by the way he asked her out, or talking about not being in public, did that bother her in some way. Paul just listened for a period of ten minutes or so, not saying much. It seemed much longer.

Finally, Thad looked to Paul and said, "Give me something to go on here. You were the one who told me to ask her. Now it is out there and there is no going back."

Paul laughed and said, "You are definitely right; I am surely at fault for your ability to ask a girl out. I told you to ask her out, not scare her." He laughed it off.

"Paul, this is serious. I put myself out there and she turned me down. I misread the entire thing."

Paul got serious for a minute, "I am sure you didn't, because I see how you talk to each other."

"Well, that is it. I failed," as Thad put his hands up in the air.

Paul, seeking to be more pastoral, tried a different route as he put his pizza down, "This isn't about you. It doesn't sound like she is attached to anyone else. It doesn't sound like she doesn't like you or anything like that. One thing I have learned as a pastor is it is very hard to predict someone's behavior. People do often make vows, like we have talked about before."

This was not new to Thad, as he and Paul had wrestled through some of this with his anger problems. Paul continued, "She might never want to depend on a man ever again, she might not be ready for a serious relationship, she might have made a personal promise to never get married again, she might not want to date a fighter for some reason. But, as you know, personal vows are not anything to overlook. Something made her say, 'I can't be with this guy,' and that is why she changed all of a sudden. It is like with the pizza. I have a need to not be perceived as the begging pastor. We have talked, I know, it is better for you to pay, you want to pay, you want to help me do what I do, and that is your contribution to the Kingdom, but my personal vows get in the way of you paying at times."

Thad laughed and said, "We can devote some time to that, if you want."

"On one hand, Thad, this is good for you."

Thad, a little offended, said, "What? You wanted it to work out like this?"

"Well, no, but be honest. Who in your life ever tells you no? Ever? Only me, your trainer, and your mother. That is it. You are not selfish. You don't take advantage of it like many people would, but you are a local hero and a face people recognize anywhere you go. Her telling you no is hard, because you haven't experienced that much personal rejection. It is hard for you to see the criticism that people bring up in the media, but personally this is going to be something that is hard because you don't go through it much. Unfortunately, your response to it is to run. You are not doing what you would do as an athlete, and possibly you made another promise to yourself about not going through that again. We should be eating down at that coffee shop. This isn't over yet, unless you don't think she is worth it."

Thad paused and took it all in. "Huh, that is why I buy the pizza."

Paul laughed, "Haven't you read in Acts about Bar Jesus, 'you can't buy the Spirit'?" They laughed it off and moved on to some other topics.

Thaddeus was inspired by Paul in a way no one else could duplicate. Paul was also inspired by his friendship with Thad. Not because he was a great fighter, but because this guy loved Jesus and Paul was helping to mold him like a piece of fresh clay. God was doing something that excited Paul, but he didn't know what that was. That is what makes God, God. Sometimes Paul was able to look back and understand why his dreams of greatness on the wrestling mat didn't come true. Only a few years prior to meeting Thaddeus he would have wrestled with feelings of jealousy and regret.

After lunch, Thaddeus took some time to himself. He needed to be back to the gym for a strength training workout. When he arrived at GITR, he walked in and talked to Rex. They sat there and visited for about ten minutes before going after it. Rex seemed slightly different this time. He seemed anxious and just a little odd, much like a parent who has to have a difficult conversation with an adult child.

They made small talk about TV shows and cars until Rex brought up that Charles Pigeon called him that day and was looking to set up the next fight. He told him about a young Jiu Jitsu specialist with a bit of a boxing background, that happened to be eleven and zero with eleven KOs. He was a physical specimen and quite a student of the sport. His name was Hunter Adams. Hunter was a Brazilian. He was quite a scrapper.

Thaddeus knew all of this and wasn't surprised. He had listened to some talking heads on the sports channels comparing him to the young fighter. Some had already projected this could be the guy to dethrone the champion. There were similarities to how Thaddeus had come up in the ranks and how Hunter "Gladiator" Adams was coming up through the ranks. Fight comparisons were drawn between his first eleven fights and Hunter's quite often. Hunter was just making a name for himself and wasn't the name Thaddeus was, but those within the sport were interested in the card.

Thaddeus looked at him and asked the normal question, "So when is the fight, Coach?"

Rex paused, "I told him not to schedule it yet."

"What? Why? You know that if you hold off on scheduling, Charlie will turn this into a media circus. I don't know much, but with Charlie it ain't about show friends, it is about show business."

"I know. I just want to make sure," Rex said slowly.

"What are you talking about? I know you and you wouldn't put this off unless you were not sure. What are you holding back from me?"

"Thaddeus, you are like a son to me. You are the only family I have left. I care about you far beyond you as a fighter. You are being talked about as the greatest fighter ever. At some point everyone starts to decline, and something else takes the place of fighting; 35 and zero with 26 knockouts and the rest being TKOs is very impressive. No one has gone the distance. But I am worried."

Thaddeus was now becoming very angry, "What on earth are you worried about?"

"You, Thaddeus! You! You don't look the same! I noticed the difference in that fight. He almost put you away!"

Thaddeus interjected, "Rex, you tell me all the time that a good fighter can always get caught."

"You didn't get caught. He beat you at the end of that round. You were out on your feet. That didn't used to happen to you. I am afraid that it might because you don't know when it is time to start thinking about retiring."

Thad was hurt, "Where is this coming from?"

"Something always distracts a fighter at the end. You have your faith and your pastor friend who is hanging around here. That is fine, but you aren't trying to prove anything anymore! I am trying to talk to you about this to protect you."

Thaddeus was a bit relieved now, and less offended than he was agitated. "So, that is what this is about? This is about my faith. Or is it about your lack of belief?"

"You're the fighter, not me!!! But I am tired of fighting the Son of God only to see Him take everything away from me that is mine! Did you know there was another little girl in our church whose sickness went away? Do you know their family stayed together? Do you know they lived happily ever after? It is all a scam. This time the scam is bringing down my house again."

Thaddeus replied with, "How could I know that? You will not talk about it! It bothers me that you think this way, because I feel like I am better than ever now. You have always believed in me and that is part of the success we have had. I have never been so sure of myself."

"Thad, that is just it. Can't you see it is a scam? You feel more confident, you weren't as careful, you're getting older and you almost got your head knocked off. GO WATCH THE FILM! You weren't the same. I am not saying now is the time, I am just saying that I am concerned. I would love to make more money. I would love to keep fighting another 15 times or so. But, I care about your legacy."

"Rex, I believe you do. This might also be about your problem with Jesus, too, huh? Maybe trusting in the Jesus you perceive as letting you down strikes a nerve and you prefer something to be different. I am sorry you lost little Maggie and your wife and everything else. I can't explain why it happened, but God does love you."

"I allowed myself to think that once and that is how He, or it, or they get you. Champ, Jesus is about to steal your crown. You think you are better than ever, I see you are not. That is the scam. This confidence you have. You used to just believe in yourself. Look, it has helped you to have Billy training here too! That might just be the boost you need at this stage. But it is hard to stay on top this long."

Thaddeus got calm and was noticeably calmer in this exchange than normal. "Rex, I am going to get changed, so we can work out now."

"Thanks!"

Thaddeus got changed and was able to put this whole thing behind him. Things were obviously different between Thad and Rex that day. No one else noticed, because Rex said things that were encouraging to Thad's ego about being the best fighter in the world, and Thad was extra motivated to show him he still was. The weights went up easier, there was some good wrestling mat time that happened, drilling the same five or six moves over and over again, and some live goes without the striking, which was wrestling with submission locks and chokes.

Thaddeus felt good about the work he put in that day. He learned some things. His conditioning was still there from coming off the recent fight, but he was trying to put his between-fight strength back on, it was right on schedule. He felt good physically. He still loved it most of the time. But no one really likes it all the time.

After the workout he got something to eat and called his mom for a few minutes. He talked about how after every fight he had some doubts, but this wasn't anything out of the ordinary. He told her, "Mom, maybe there is more to life than fighting."

She laughed, "You think?"

"I mean, maybe I need to be thinking about the rest of my life."

"Wow, who is this? What did you do with my son?"

"Ok," he paused.

Debra saw the opportunity to address her concern. "Maybe you need to be thinking about starting a family."

"Whoa, Mom! One step at a time."

"You're right, you might want to try to get a date first."

Thad honestly responded, "I tried that. She turned me down."

"Wow, she was strong enough to turn down my Thaddeus. She sounds like the one. I can't wait to meet her. That is exciting."

"Funny and productive as always, Mom. I will see you

Sunday afternoon." They said their goodbyes as Thad now seemed to have a new worry on his mind that added to the original one.

After Thad hung up the phone, he went for a long drive. He always felt at peace behind the wheel of the car. He loved to listen to music; he would listen to preachers and even pray. But he could drive for hours, just thinking. He liked to get out of the city and drive towards some hills and trees.

His mind was racing. Why did Sally not want to date him? Did Rex have a point about him being done? *Does my faith make me less of a fighter or much more?* Will he and Rex ever be the same, in light of his faith? *How many more fights do I have in me? I am not as angry. Maybe I don't have as much to prove.* His mind turned over and over. *I guess it is ok, if the war is done. Am I ready for it to be done? Huh?* He could go on and on like this for hours in his mind.

As he prayed and thought deeply, he considered that he got to where he was because he felt like he had so much to prove, coupled with the anger that always crept just beneath the surface that was mostly directed at God. God stopped him from knowing his father past a very young age. Part of accepting Jesus' forgiveness and payment for the sins in his life was having to deal with the pain and torment and anguish of being unforgiving towards God. He no longer blamed Him for this; now was this hurting him in the Octagon? The answer to this question was important for his future.

He came back to that question as he continued to think about it. *Does God still want me to fight? Man, there is so much to think about.* As would occasionally happen, Thaddeus would feel himself falling into a deep sadness. He drove, consumed with it most of the way. The sadness gripped him and would hold him down for a few hours, and he could usually shake it off. This time he hurt. He hurt beyond his capacity to define why he hurt.

He shook the sadness with some prayer, Bible reading, and some comedy on TV. He came back to knowing that right now he was the best fighter on earth. He didn't know what he was doing with his future, but it seemed as though he was training right. Maybe Sally would still go on a date with him. Rex had always been good to him and he could trust him. Paul was helping him to know Jesus and His purposes for his life better. This was the difference between Thaddeus, the new creation, and the old Thad. God was active and present in his life and he was victorious moment by moment and not just in the fight. With some more reading that night, Thad was able to fall into a peaceful sleep, but how long he had left in the Octagon was becoming a real question.

The next morning Thaddeus got up and enjoyed a three-mile run. He had some mat work that he was going to do later that day. It was an off day for his lifting program. By 8:30 he was ready to get a cup of coffee and some breakfast. He went to Cornerstone Cafe and sat at his usual table in the back. He was afraid Sally wouldn't wait on him.

She came over, "Hello, Thaddeus."

"What is happening, Sally?"

"Not much, just another day in paradise."

He joked and said, "Huh? I always wondered where that was. This is what Jesus was talking about, 'Today I will be with you in paradise.'"

"Wow, creative! Paul is rubbing off on you, even a Bible reference."

They both smiled and were extremely uncomfortable.

Sally was worried that she had hurt Thaddeus's feelings but still had no intention of going out with him. Sally started to say, "Hey, about the other day…" when Thad cut in, "No big deal; it is good for me."

"You like taking a beating, huh?"

Thad smiled with fascination and thought about how he was sure he had never met anyone like her. Kind, likeable, but tough as nails. Beautiful but sarcastic and treated him differently than other people did. He simply smiled and said, "I guess so."

"The usual breakfast meal?" she asked.

"Yes, that is me." Suddenly, the interaction gave him hope. He wasn't ready to ask her again. He wasn't ready to make any sudden movements. But he felt comfortable for whatever reason. He got out a book and started to read. It was a fiction book. Thaddeus used fiction to keep his mind off training. He sought to have balance, even though to perform at the level he did at this age he needed to be obsessive. As he got closer to the fights he was downright maniacal.

She came back with his coffee and made a quick joke, "Here is that coffee you need to keep up with those young guys in the ring."

"Funny," he said.

Thad just continued to read, while Sally walked away. She didn't understand why she felt embarrassed or cared so much what he thought. She tried to go off and do her own thing, but her eyes were always being drawn back in his direction, as he continued to read. She was fascinated that Thaddeus could take rejection so well. She didn't think she would see him in this restaurant anymore, because someone like Thaddeus Class wasn't used to losing or getting rejected, ever. She noticed he was sincerely into his book. The title was *Into the Storm*. She thought to herself, "What kind of storm does he know about?"

She came back to check on him. "Everything all right, Thaddeus?"

"Yes."

She said, "It is really good to see you in here today. I was a little afraid you wouldn't come back and see me anymore."

"I didn't come here to see you. I am here for the coffee. You — I have been beaten up by tougher people than you before."

She smiled, "You sure?"

"Maybe," he smiled and laughed. When it was time for him to leave he left her double the bill which was typical for Thaddeus with her.

Later on in Curlsville at Mama Class's Kitchen, Debra was balancing the books. The restaurant was doing well, but she sat there feeling lonely. She still missed Wayne after all these years. On the outside she looked fine. Everything appeared to be good at the restaurant. Her son was known as a great fighter all around the world. He was successful and seemed to have his life on track. But, it hurt. She sipped her wine and looked at her lonely office. She hurt. She felt empty. She remembered the days when she trusted Jesus so blindly. She remembered the days when things came easily. The business was thriving and marriage was good. Thaddeus was happy. This was all before reality happened. The reality she thought of was, *it can all be gone in a second and all you really have is yourself. You must make it happen. You must make sure the bills get paid, you have to recreate yourself.* In the moments when Jesus is supposed to be the most real, He wasn't — but the reality that came to the forefront was the reality of Debra and, sadly, the reality of death and decay all around her.

She sat back in her chair and suddenly chugged the remaining glass in her hand and started to pour another. *It seems that this is becoming a problem,* she thought as she chugged another half-glass. Then she thought, *Says who? Where has it gotten me?* She poured another glass and smiled. Just then, even though it was evening and Mama Class's Kitchen was closed, someone knocked at the door. It was Barbara. When she looked out they made eye contact through the glass in the front door of the establishment. Debra came out and looked out the door. Debra tried to hide her drunkenness but needed to walk towards the door. She thought, *Right – Left – Right – Left.* She opened the door and Barb looked at her with a very forgiving smile.

Debra said, "Hello, Barrbaarra," as she tried not to say much. She wasn't interested in talking right now, but the alcohol kept her from realizing how strange it was that Barbara was knocking on the door to her restaurant (that was only open for breakfast and lunch) after dark to talk to her.

"Hey, Debra. Are you all right?"

"What dur yur mean?"

"Well, I didn't get a chance to talk with you earlier, and I thought maybe you were having a hard time. I know this Sunday is the anniversary of Wayne's accident."

"Come on, Barbrraa, that was years ago. Come on in." They walked back into Debra's office. Barbara saw the almost empty bottle of wine and the empty glass beside it. She knew with Debra to never be judgmental and to always be loving. She acted like it wasn't even there.

Debra looked and said, "Is everything ok?"

"Yes, I am doing ok."

"Good, Barb, glad to hear it! Amen, right? By the way, why does He hate me?"

"Who hates you, Debbie?"

"God!"

"God doesn't hate you."

"Yes, He does. It is all a joke. He has taken my Wayne away. I had to start this restaurant and raise a kid."

"You did a great job, by the way. He is great at what he does and may just turn out to be a truly upright citizen."

"Barbara, you might be my only friend. I want you to understand something, though. I am sure God hates me, and I hate Him, too! The feeling is mutual. Why would He let this happen?"

Barbara knew to only listen. She knew not to challenge Debra's wit, even when she was toasted on Zinfandel. She listened as Debra went on for about another hour. At some point she started to sober up for a minute and she said, "Wait! How did you know that I was here, or that I needed someone?"

"Sometimes, God is there for us even when we don't want Him to be. I knew I needed to stop here!" At that Debra just cried some more and they talked lightly for another hour. Barbara agreed to take Debra home and drive her to work in the morning, leaving her car there.

CHAPTER 5

BILLY'S BIG SHOT!

IT WAS A Thursday and Thaddeus was going in to work out with Billy. For Billy to defeat Gus "The Knight Crawler" Emmerick, he was going to have to polish up his technique and scrapping ability. Thaddeus was trying to spend more time with Billy. Billy was a young Christian. He had been a Christian for even less time than Thaddeus. Billy didn't mature at the rate Thaddeus did. Rex and Larry were glad Thaddeus liked to spend a lot of time with Billy. They both saw him as having some coaching or training in his future. Mentoring and coaching sharpens a fighter as well, especially one who is disciplined and cares about integrity, like Thaddeus. They weren't keen on the faith lessons, but Thad would continue to pour everything into Billy that he could.

Billy asked, "Thad, what was it like to win the title?"

He responded, "Everything changed. It is like one day I woke up and it was all different. How people looked at me, how I was treated. I had to learn what it means to be a champion. I had to learn what it means to be in an opponent's head. Some people, you have them beat before you get to the Octagon, but the best fighters are going to give the best fighters their all. So I got most of the best efforts of the best contenders. My faith has also changed how I look at it, too. It isn't everything anymore. There is more to life than the fight."

Billy chimed in, "No, I don't want to hear that. I need to be the champ here. I need to focus on that."

Thad said, "No, you don't. You need to be thankful and obedient to the One who made you. He will protect, prepare you, and sustain you. When you focus on the opponent, you set a low ceiling. Do you think 'The Knight Crawler' is concerned about you?"

Billy said confidently, "YES!"

"I do, too. He will watch your film. He will know you. He will know me too, and our style. But he will know himself better."

"True, but really, does God even care about fighting?"

"Heck yeah, Kid. He cares about what we care about."

Knight Crawler was no joke, sort of a late bloomer, but no joke. He was the heavyweight champion standing only about 17 wins and three losses. He fought very comfortably at 240 lbs. Billy was comfortable weighing in at about 230 lbs., so he was an even smaller heavyweight. This is what made him a good workout partner for Thaddeus, which, oddly enough, could mean a very challenging matchup for Emmerick. This matchup would be the first time in years that Night Crawler would face an opponent that was small and agile and could keep up with him on the ground. The training Thaddeus did with Billy was essential. They did a lot of mat work without striking.

Billy worked out in the weight room for an hour and was waiting on Thaddeus. He was doing some drills by himself.

Larry walked into Rex's office, "Where is Thaddeus? He hasn't been here on time all this week."

"What do you mean? He has been here, getting Billy ready all week!"

He looked at him, "Rex, have you forgotten what it is like to get ready to challenge the champ?" He sternly looked at him, "We have 30 days! In 30 days he needs to be ready!" "This type of thing doesn't happen when Thad has a fight," Larry said under his breath.

Rex fired back with, "What does that mean?"

This was not an uncommon exchange. Rex also knew the stress of the up-and-coming fight. This wasn't a normal fight. Larry and Billy could voice their concerns; Rex was a little annoyed because of the friendship they had. He simply thought, "Whatever. They have to know that I am extremely interested in having two champions around here."

Just then Thad came walking in dressed and ready to go. He nodded at Billy and apologized for being late. Larry said, "Whatever." He quickly got warmed up and they began to work out. This workout was largely focused on technique and Thaddeus helping to sharpen the technique of GITR's next great champion.

Larry and Rex settled their difference as their fighters sparred together. "We have created a beautiful thing here, Larry."

"Yes, we have," he nodded back. Everything seemed to go back to normal.

The next day, many of Thad's same workout partners who got him ready for the last fight would be stopping by. There would be a fresh, capable body on Billy constantly. Thad and his partners would prepare him for fighting a smaller, quicker, and more agile fighter than the other heavyweights he fought.

That night Sally was fast asleep. She had a dream that she was talking to Thad in the restaurant. There were lots of people around wanting his autograph and talking with him. She was poking jokes at him, as always. "You want to order, or are you too famous?" She started thinking about how perfect it was and maybe they really could be together. The people started to leave. The restaurant was closed and it was night-time. There wasn't another person that could be seen for miles. She walked back into the room where she had left Thaddeus drinking coffee and he was no longer there.

Thaddeus was gone and her father was standing there. He stood up and ran at her. "Expecting something else?" He threw Thad's coffee cup against the wall and tossed his own beer bottle at her. He was dressed in sweatpants and a sweatshirt he would have relaxed in at home. He screamed, "You can't have him, I won't let you!!!!."

She woke up and stared at the clock; it was 6:33 a.m., time to wake up. She felt her face and ran and looked in the mirror. She thought he had beaten her up again. She thought, "Men, what do I need them for? I have never met one that brought me anything but trouble."

The next day Thaddeus stopped at the restaurant again. He stopped by and sat in the same seat he always sat in. It was in the back room; everyone knew where he wanted to sit and everyone knew who he wanted to wait on him. He sat there in the same seat that only a few hours before was in Sally's dream.

This time when Sally saw him he made a joke. He tried to joke around with her about her hair or something, and it didn't come out right. Thad could tell something was wrong. "You ok, Sally?"

"Yeah, just kind of an off morning. Is it ok if I don't talk about it? Do you want the usual?"

"Yes," he replied.

She said, "I will be right back."

He decided this was the weirdest thing he had ever seen. He couldn't understand what it was. *Do I smell? Am I that ugly? What is it?* He prayed, "God help me." Sally continued to avoid him most of the meal. He finished reading his book, *Into the Storm.*

She came over to him to drop off the check. He knew exactly what the bill was and handed her double the bill in cash. He grabbed her hand and said, "Thank you."

"For what?" Sally snapped back.

He looked surprised and slowly got out of his seat, "For being my friend."

She seemed to be back and looked at him with sarcasm, "Are we friends now?"

He said, "I am here for you."

She said, "I am sure you think you are, but I have heard that before."

"From me?"

"Does it matter if it was you or another guy?"

Thad smartly said in an on-air voice, "According to recent scientific studies, not all men act the same, so yes!"

She said, "My case study has proven differently. Case closed. Look, you come in here and try to impress me with who you are and your jokes. You're reading a book about storms, what do you know about storms? You don't live in the same place the rest of us live."

He snapped back, "I do know something about rejection now, thanks to you."

"Everybody wants something, don't they?"

He suddenly realized that some of what made her so attractive was her toughness and her independence. For the first time, Thad saw the anger and the resentment for what it was. It was almost as if she mistook him for someone else.

He simply paid her and handed her the check. This time, without touching her hand, he simply gave her the check and the money and said, "Thank you." Then he turned around and left. It was heart- wrenching. He ached in a way that he hadn't felt in many years.

When Thaddeus got to the gym that day, he was already hurting. He walked in and saw Larry and Billy sitting there. He said hi and they knew he wasn't excited about being there. Thad walked away to get changed for the workout. Larry looked at Billy and said, "I think he only gets excited about his fights. Doesn't he realize there are about to be two champs around here, now?"

Billy replied, "Maybe that is what it is."

Thaddeus and Billy started their workout. From Thad's perspective, everything seemed fine. He didn't notice Billy was especially feisty that day and was trying to make him feel every move that was practiced. Thad was already suffering from a broken heart. This pain was way worse than anything else. *She was so mean to me. What did I do to her?* he wondered.

There was something odd in the air that day. Have you ever walked into a room and realized something wasn't right? As they drilled and practiced moves and counters, it was like Billy wanted Thaddeus to feel every exchange. There was usually a different feel to a workout when you got close to a big fight, especially the biggest fight of someone's life. Billy was about to find out what he was made of. He had unanswered questions:

did he have staying power? Was he going to be a champion? He had to beat a great fighter to win the title. Because Thaddeus had some idea about what Billy was going through, he didn't even give it a second thought. To be the champ, you need to fight with a chip on your shoulder, especially when you are closing in on the final weeks before fight night.

They finished drilling. Thaddeus usually helped the younger Billy "The Kid," as they were working on technique. But not today. He could tell that Billy didn't want technical help that day. That was ok with Thad. Now it was time for the other workout partners to join in. They were drilling with each other and warming up, and the intention was to work out with Billy when they went live. When one fighter got tired, another one would come in fresh, keeping Billy in there the entire time.

When it was time for the live goes, Billy said to Larry, "No, I want the champ."

Rex jumped in and said, "What do you mean?"

Larry said, "He wants to fight just Thad first."

Rex said, "He is still coming off a fight. We've got his partners here that helped him before the fight."

Billy, now with mouthpiece in, said, "I helped get him there! I am about to fight the champ in my weight class. I need the champ!"

Thad said, "Ok, I will go."

Rex didn't like it, because he had come to understand with Larry and Billy both that there is always ego involved. Rex said to Thad, "Just give him the first ten minutes, one ten-minute go." This was one of those odd situations for Thad. As he aged as a fighter, he wasn't usually back in the room going live with one of the best fighters in the world so soon. But, jerk or not today, Thaddeus cared deeply for Billy. He had been discipling him as a believer in Christ. He had been teaching him everything he could about fighting. He had unselfishly poured into him, just as Paul Adkins told him to. "Don't be great just for yourself. To be great for God you need to show up and be there for others as well." Oddly enough, being there for someone of this caliber meant you needed to fight him.

Thad had every intention of winning this fight. Billy may just have been on his way to being the next heavyweight champion, but Thaddeus had always been his big brother in this room. Larry "Quick Draw" Rossi and Rex Metzger looked on as their two world-class fighters began to go at it. The clock was set for ten minutes. They had fight gloves and headgear on, and they were going to go for the entire ten minutes. It was going to be brutal. People would pay to come and watch this fight if it were open to the public. The other workout partners there looked on and watched intently. Some of them wanted to know how to beat either one of them. Some of them just wanted to improve. They looked on as people who helped get these two to where they were. From the young to the seasoned, they felt they were a part of something big. They were a part of GITR. A part of them also felt like fans. Fans who couldn't cheer or say much, but they knew this was going to be good. Some of the best fights ever had happened between these two and no one but their trainers were even there.

But something was different this time. Billy struck Thaddeus hard on the chin and let him know he wasn't playing today. Thaddeus, still being down to weight somewhat, was just starting to get the between-fight power back in the weight room. There was lots of hand fighting and striking. Many fighters and trainers would be uncomfortable with the amount of striking going on in the training session between these two great fighters. You don't want to get hurt, but the philosophy between these two was that no one was going to give them the fight they had the opportunity to have with each other. They needed to take advantage of it. Billy would fight "Smokin'" Joe and "Slippery" Pete and the young guys later, but his main focus for these ten minutes would be Thad. The first five minutes were filled with scrambling, but they caught each other with some good punches. They fought upper body, trying several times to lock and throw. They took shots at each other's legs. Thad especially absorbed some big punches to the face.

Both fighters were very competitive, but in the last three minutes Billy got in deep on his leg and took Thad down. He was able to punch downward. He was winning! Billy seemed to be beating the best fighter in the world. A few things were happening here. Billy was training for his up-and-coming fight; Thad had had his and wasn't in the same place. Rex and Thad didn't like losing, but they understood the nature of training and peaking. In other words, it was annoying, but it wasn't a surprise that Billy would start winning these practice exchanges while he was in the closing weeks of fight preparation.

At the end of the go, if you'd had to award a winner, you would have picked Billy. This wasn't the first time Billy had bested the champ, and they both knew it probably wasn't the last. But for Billy, something different was happening. He sensed that soon he could be champ.

Billy said something smart under his breath to Larry about the big picture on the wall. He said something to the effect that Rex would have to put his picture up there soon. Rex and Thad just shook it off. For Thad, these were the types of things he was trying to help Billy with. He saw this as a spiritual opportunity. For Rex, he began to slightly take note. The workout continued after a short break with the other two workout partners, "Slippery" Pete Durkin and "Smokin'" Joe Latimore, subbing in and out on Billy. Pete got his name from being slippery — he could roll, and hit submissions. He would strike sometimes but he liked to grapple. Latimore was a beast. He was a larger-than-life physical black specimen of a fighter. He was a brawler, and had been a top tier fighter for years, but had never broken through as a top contender yet. Latimore was very experienced and mean.

These fighters were fresh, and Billy had just bested the champ. He continued to fight strongly, with both of them switching in and out on him for another go, and he finished out with some conditioning at the end of the workout. Thad continued to work out as well. He spent some time running and jumping rope. At the very end, when Billy moved on to some conditioning and both the trainers were focused on him, Thad grabbed Slippery Pete and worked on some of the finer points of his technique.

Things happen in practice, but it seemed that something different was happening now. It was on the subconscious level. In most ways it was very exciting for GITR to have a new up-and-coming great. There was a great sense that GITR would now have two champions at the two heaviest weights. This would be the premier place to train for everyone over 170 lbs. This was going to be exciting.

If you looked closely, you could see that many of these workout partners had come a long way as well. Slippery Pete and Smokin' Joe Latimore were now fighters who could stand in front of anyone in the world. This was the dawn of a new era, but as for Rex and Thaddeus it was a little unnerving. For

Rex, he was wondering if Thad was nearing the end. It would be great if they had another champion, but the fighter who got them there wasn't going to be around much longer. For Thaddeus, the talk about his career ending was becoming more evident, and he didn't like the vibe he was getting back from Larry. Larry Rossi was a kind of "mad scientist" of the MMA world. Larry knew scouting, training, technique. He could add value to any fighter, any trainer, and any club.

At the end of the day, Thaddeus and Rex both thought in their minds that they were headed to greener pastures. Yes, all along it had been mostly about Thad, but this nervousness was just about something different coming about in the life of the club.

The fight was approaching. Leading up to the fight, Billy was getting nervous and excited. He correctly understood that one of the biggest moments of his life was approaching. He had trained with the best in the world and had come to a place where he had clearly beaten him in practice. Two giants sat at the table the day before the weigh-ins. Gus "Night Crawler" Emmerick to the left, and Billy "The Kid" Smith to the right, with their people on either side of them. Charlie Pigeon was in the middle. He was the mastermind behind the promotion of both of these fighters. How did this same promoter end up at the center of the money with these great fights?

Charlie promoted Gus "Knight Crawler" Emmerick the same as he promoted Thaddeus and Billy and all of the great competitors. Both Gus and Billy looked hangry. They looked as though they could bite each other's heads off. On Billy's side, Larry took the first seat followed by Billy, along with Rex, and finally Thaddeus Class taking his proper seat at the end of the table. On the other side of Charlie Pigeon was

Emmerick's trainer Dustin Fields, then Emmerick and assistant trainer, former contender Damarius Dunkin. They had noticeable chips on their shoulders as did Larry and Billy. Rex seemed a little relaxed for the occasion, and Thaddeus was just happy to be there.

The press were a few feet in front of the table with only a white line and the elevation of a small stage separating them, with some cameras behind them. The questions started. A female reporter in the first row stood to her feet and addressed the champion. "Mr. Emmerick, for the first time as champion, many are projecting your defeat in this fight. What would you like to say to the naysayers out there?"

He looked at her and said, "Look, what do you want me to say? My opponent is a great fighter. He is being trained by the best and works out with a great champion in Thaddeus Class. But this is still my time. I intend to prove that two days from today. *Betcha World Today* still gives me the edge. So place your bets on those fringe sites you are talking about, and get the odds."

The reporters laughed it off. That was so Emmerick. He had business sense and a sense of humor. It was part of what made him a high-quality fighter. He was a competitor. Don't bet him for money at anything, because suddenly he is really good. This was a big fight, but he was going to play it cool.

Billy could feel his head beginning to sweat. He was so irritated with the champion. He thought, *Larry was right. I don't seem to get any respect. This guy doesn't know what he is up against.*

The next reporter addressed Billy. A gray-haired man in the back stood to his feet and asked Billy, "So, Billy, tell me about the training staff you have with you and what it is like to train with Thaddeus Class and speak to the advantage that gives you."

Billy was so irritated right then, mostly due to his own insecurity. *This is supposed to be my day,* the voice in his head was shouting. He went on to think, *Larry and I are sitting in the seats of honor and we got this guy asking about Thaddeus and Rex.* Billy smiled, "I have been waiting for this opportunity for a long time. Larry has been my main trainer and has been here from the beginning. He has been a father figure for me in many ways. Now, obviously, us working through GITR and assisting with the other fighters has been great; the many workout partners the facility brings and, of course, working out with the great Thaddeus Class helps."

A dark-haired man Thaddeus knew through his many press conferences stood up in the middle and said, "Thaddeus, many have alluded to you being an older brother in the sport and life to young Billy. What does it look like for you to be in a mentoring role to someone who could potentially win a title and be around this sport much beyond what you have left?"

Thaddeus laughed uncomfortably. "The truth is, Richard, I figure I've got about another 30 years left doing this. I will probably outlast you." There was a roar of laughter from the crowd. This press conference was now off script, but what do you expect when Thaddeus is part of the equation? Charlie was beaming from ear to ear. Rex was chuckling. Even the opponents' side cracked a smile, but not Larry and Billy.

Thaddeus caught Billy in the corner of his eye so he tried to be diplomatic and careful with his words. "Look. I have the opportunity to work out with a great fighter. I am excited for our club that we will have another champion. We have trained hard, and Billy is helping me to successfully stay where I am as well. Larry has brought a lot to our club, especially in the way of studying the sport. Now, I hope to continue down this path for many years. I feel most of all truly blessed to be friends with Billy. Which, I think you guys should be asking him questions. This guy is about to fight for the HWT title! I am old news right now."

Billy didn't really even notice that Thaddeus tried to divert the attention back; if he did, there was some sense of entitlement with it that wasn't normal. The problem was jealousy is detrimental and hard to deal with when you are fighting and trying to collaborate together. Billy didn't possess the emotional intelligence that Thaddeus had, but in those moments it wasn't that Thad didn't notice, but he considered it part of what he was helping Billy with. The truth was, his commitment for Billy and the brotherly love he had for him outweighed how nasty the sinful nature was that spewed out of him. In the back of Thaddeus's mind he got past it, so Billy could grow out of it too. So even the jealous moments created a sense of purpose for him that gave him a heart for Billy. Thaddeus desired to truly mentor him, and be the big brother in the sport and in the faith that he knew he could be. He truly didn't get angry with Billy much; he would laugh to himself often and think, *Sounds like someone I used to know.*

It is funny how sin works. It is funny that we are comfortable with a sin nature that is similar to our own, but if someone sins differently we find that repulsive. Deep down, Thaddeus knew that Billy needed to repent of this attitude and condition of the heart that made him like this. Billy was a new believer but was still acting this way. Thaddeus understood because he was kind of the same way and he needed to grow out of it. He just set his heart on helping Billy, which made him a little blind.

Rex noticed that the conversation was getting away from them and decided to try to help. He noticed the awkwardness and insecure look on Billy's face, and the irritated look on the face of Larry who had also waited for this moment. Rex said, "If I can say something. What we have done here at GITR has been truly remarkable. Larry has remained the primary trainer for Billy as I have with Thaddeus, but we have worked well together, being longtime friends and all. I believe we could just prove in a few days that we have the two best fighters in the world at the two heaviest weights. There is no limit to what they can do. We look forward to a great contest with Mr. Emmerick, who is a heck of a fighter himself."

With typical people this would have been a good way to smooth this over, but Larry and Billy fed off of each other's jealousy. They wanted the spotlight so much, and under-standably so; they had worked hard to get there, but they also couldn't forget that training with Rex and Thaddeus Class had been a huge part of that story.

Larry and Billy didn't get to talk as much as they normally would have because Thaddeus and Rex took up much of the conversation, and after Rex's comment the reporters went back to Emmerick (as they should). Emmerick was asked, "What is your prediction for the fight?"

He said, "Look, we are excited to defend the title against GITR. Thad and Rex have been great. The Kid has been great so far. It will be a signature title defense for us and we look forward to the opportunity."

For Emmerick it was just business. "Let's get on with it." He was thinking, *I ain't playing these Mickey Mouse games any-more. I am going to get in the Octagon and show him what is up.* For Emmerick, he had been there before and the talking had just become routine to him. Yeah, he played the mind games with the press conference and the weigh-in, but the fight was truly in two days. All these games were great and all, but the first time someone took a crisp punch in the mouth, all the talk was for naught.

Emmerick loved being the champion and had worked hard. He was insulted that the betting odds were against him and was particularly motivated to get the win against maybe the best fighter he had fought. So much of what Billy did was similar to Thaddeus, only he was younger and bigger. Arguably similar in speed.

When the press conference was over everybody got to their feet. The two fighters took a photo op standing face-to-face. Stiff eye contact was made; Gus smirked, half-winked and broke eye contact first to reach down and look at his hand to shake with Billy. "Good luck, Kid. I look forward to it."

Billy looked at him with steam in his eye, fire in his veins, and what looked like foam coming out of the corner of his mouth, "You shouldn't," he said with a smile as he shook his hand. The gaze he gave him looked right through him.

Emmerick, an experienced champion, was taken aback and in his mind was on notice. Something about the exchange to him said, "I am about to jump in the cage with a real animal." For the first time in a long time, he was a little shaken. After all, this was a fight with GITR and the greatest fighter of their time was in his corner. Most of all it was a look he used to have. It was how he got there. It was a look he still had from time to time, but he no longer would grit his teeth until it hurt. He no longer foamed at the mouth or felt it in his veins the same. The hunger he recognized, but maybe it was a little lonely at the top and he couldn't help but wonder later if he wasn't much closer to the end than he first thought.

Thaddeus was so proud. He had had extensive conversations with Billy about this type of thing. They had had extensive dialogue about when a fighter is vulnerable, and the fight before the fight, and the psychology behind it. You must keep the eye contact. You must be really confident and not fake it. You must be ready to fight your fight, and have a deep-seated belief in yourself that comes from prayer, training, mental preparation, etc. At that, Emmerick and his team walked away and things got chaotic with the press.

Rex and Thaddeus had already forgotten about the other things in the press conference, while Billy and Larry continued to be haunted by it for a while. But much of this got lost in the excitement of the common goal. Charlie Pigeon met with the four of them after, just as he did with Emmerick's corner. Charlie Pigeon talked with them about business stuff. As they talked, it was about to get more detailed; Charlie would let everyone in on the marketing plan and the plan for the future if the fight was won, and then the downside — when the fighter wasn't around — about what happens if he loses.

While they had some basic conversation about the fight before he excused Thaddeus and Billy, Charlie looked at Billy and said, "This is a great opportunity. It might seem unfair, but it could be the only shot you have. I think it is your turn, but you have to decide — and if you are a champion we can make a lot of money together." Billy shook hands with Charlie and said, "I will be a great champion, Mr. Pigeon."

Charlie looked at Thad and said, "Hey, Thad, teach him how to be classy." Charlie, Larry, and Rex went off to have a drink. They needed to talk business so they went off to a private area in the hotel bar.

As they walked away, Thaddeus and Billy started walking by themselves in the other direction. Thaddeus grabbed Billy by the back of the neck. "Ah, Billy it is going to be great. You are going to be a great champion. I can't wait. Can I do anything to help?"

Billy stopped and, oddly enough, there wasn't anyone around. This wasn't typical, and they would surely be spotted shortly. Billy looked at him, "Look man, it is hard being in your shadow."

"What do you mean?"

"Well, look, we have a press conference and they want to talk to you and Rex. This was supposed to be about me winning the title."

"Sorry, man, I can't control that. Maybe I shouldn't be at the table anymore."

"Look, I don't know, but I need to get alone and process this stuff. I need to think about the fight and get by myself. I am going to grab something to eat and go back to my room, where it is quiet. Can I talk with you tomorrow?"

Thaddeus smiled, "Look, I am sorry. I am not trying to get in your way. I have a little bit of skin in the game here, too. I want to see you win."

"Yeah, so does everyone else, Thad. They want to give you credit."

Thad looked puzzled. "What do you mean, Billy? No they don't. People know that I helped you and you helped train me. What is the big deal? You can't do this all by yourself."

Billy looked at him. "Look, man, I do appreciate it. Maybe I am just on edge because of the fight. I am going to get by myself. Just forget it."

Thaddeus said, "No problem!" as he gave him a gentle closed fist to the shoulder. "If you need anything, Kid, I am here for you."

At that, Billy walked off and Thad was left to think about what was going on. He settled in to thinking about his own championship fight and how many people he apologized to afterwards. His mom, Rex, even a cab driver he needed to go and try to find. The pressure was intense. The stakes were high. Thad was comforted by this thought.

Billy went back to be by himself and was able to relax and stay away from the media. Larry and Rex were busy with business, and Billy ate some dinner and was able to watch a little TV. He tried to walk off his dinner a little, but found quiet spots on the hotel floor. He was able to look out the windows and see Las Vegas. He was still bothered by the press conference and nervous for the fight, but he was finding solace in devising a plan to take the title.

He went back to his room and sat on the floor, visualizing the win. He visualized the takedown, the direct hit, a kick to the face and the submission hold. He saw how it could happen. He watched a few of Emmerick's old fights, but then settled down with some mystery type stories on TV.

Billy fell into a peaceful sleep, at least for a while. At four a.m. the phone rang. It was Thaddeus. "Hey, Kid, I need you to walk outside your room and answer a few questions for me. It will help me greatly."

Billy jumped to his feet and walked to the door. As soon as he opened the door, there were fifty reporters all dressed in white asking him questions. They had phones to record, there was a TV camera, there were lights. They all wanted to know about Thaddeus. Some of what they said, "Billy, can you ever be the champ Thaddeus is?" "Is Thaddeus a great coach?" "Will your victory cement Thaddeus's legacy?" "What does Thaddeus eat for breakfast?" At the last question, Thad answered, "My opponents!" Everyone laughed; everyone laughed except Billy.

Just then he woke up and was wide awake. He looked at the hotel phone. It was hung up. He looked at the door. He opened it and looked outside. There was no one there. He turned the light on in his room and looked at the clock. It was only 1:12 a.m.

It was all just a dream, but clearly Thaddeus Class was on his mind, and more than he should be when within 48 hours of a title fight. Clearly, Emmerick was who he should have been more focused on. Thaddeus was becoming a distraction. He continued to turn and toss, and even though it was illogical, focused on being angry with Thaddeus.

The next day before the weigh-in, Billy and Thaddeus met in the hotel lobby and walked to the car where they would drive about five minutes over to a high school workout facility for a light workout. They got on the mats that were provided for them. Last night was a good night for Rex and Larry to be out talking with Charlie Pigeon, because the day before the fight Billy was always well-studied. The game plan was in place. Rex and Larry both decided with Billy and Thaddeus that they would let the other fighter work them out and get them ready for the big fight in the last 24 hours.

Trainers can't stop being trainers any more than a mother can stop being a mother. What that means is, the creative part needs to be over and you have to go with what you have. If Thaddeus found a few tweaks, that was one thing. But Larry and Rex could tweak things and make changes all the way up to the fight — and it could become very confusing, where

Thaddeus's changes would only be little variations in technique and little adjustments based on Billy's strength, versus the strengths and weaknesses of "Night Crawler."

Thaddeus, looking more like a coach than a fighter, was standing in the lobby when Billy came down. He was talking to a couple who wanted a picture with him. He was standing there in sweats but drinking his morning cup of coffee. Billy, looking agitated, rolled his eyes when he saw him, not in a fun, playful way but in a "not again" way.

Thaddeus saw him coming off the elevator and said, "Hey, you should get a picture with this guy. Get a picture this last time before he becomes the champion." Billy smiled; he greeted them and got a photo op with the guy, both holding closed fists at each other. They went and got into a very nice rental car and pulled out. Thaddeus already had the address in his phone and he was off to the facility that was only about five miles away. Thaddeus drove and Billy rode shotgun. "The Kid" seemed agitated and not quite awake yet maybe, but that was ok. This was normal for the day of a weigh-in except for heavyweights. Billy didn't need to lose any weight, but it was also normal that a fighter was noticeably agitated as the fight got closer.

Thad began to try to talk, "Hey man, you got this. I am excited for you. I am here for you if you need anything."

Billy smirked, "I got this, Thad. I am going to be World Champion."

"Yes, you are Billy, there is no feeling like it."

"I know, Thad, you have told me thousands of times."

They got to the facility and walked inside. They were able to go in and they warmed up with some jogging and stretching. They both got into themselves a little and didn't talk much. There was a lot of just drilling, no hard striking or kicks, but rolling around, common- type movements. They sparred at about 70% without any striking.

Billy was feeling quick. He was about to hit his peak. When a fighter or any highly-trained athlete peaks, they are at their very best for that season. You can really only hit a peak once every 3-6 months. It is a very intentional process. Training is breaking your body down. You break it down with weights and live matches in the practice room, and agility workouts and an endless amount of activity. There are times when you are training with heavy weights. As you get closer to the fight, the weights are lighter and the reps are up. When it comes to running and jumps, and all of the training that goes on, you want to break the fighter down, but when he or she recovers they feel strong. They feel better than ever. They are quicker. Their lungs can go longer. They are stronger, more athletic. It is exciting.

It was important that Billy felt really good and began to see what peak performance looked like for him. Billy was at the age where it was all coming together. In his mind, he was going to fight his very best fights over the next two or three years. Billy was hitting things with speed and timing. He was moving like he had never moved before. He set aside all of the negative things he was feeling and was moving faster than he had ever moved before. He felt strong. It was all coming together. Both of them got excited and were becoming excited about competing the next day. Billy was shocked at what he was able to do.

Billy began to hit counters at rapid speed. Thaddeus tried to emulate the movements that Billy would see from Emmerick, one of which was a lazy kick that Emmerick took a shot at late in a fight. He left himself wide open for a left hook on the other side if a fighter was quick enough. Emmerick had never fought anyone yet who was quick enough or skilled enough to expose this. As Billy looked towards the next day, he knew it was all going to change.

As Thaddeus saw the ability Billy was showing, he became so excited he started to yell. "Nice! You got this!" "Your day is here! His days are numbered!" "Who is the champ?"

Billy hit a crisp takedown and yelled out, "I am!" Their short, intense practice came to an end and it seemed that Billy remembered they were friends. He high-fived Thaddeus and said, "I am ready! I got this!"

Thaddeus said, "Yes, you do! I am glad I don't have to fight 'cha!"

They left, and Billy had now completed his last training before the fight. Weigh-ins were in a few hours, which meant nothing to a heavyweight as light as he. There would be some mind games later at the weigh-in and there would be press and excitement, but other than that, the fight was his for the taking! Billy was ready. He felt it. He knew he could beat Emmerick! On the way back, Thaddeus was relaxed and so was Billy. Thaddeus told him, "I am so proud to be a part of your journey. You have helped me to stay on top and have been there for me. I am excited for this fight. Thank you!"

Billy replied, "You, too, Champ! Tomorrow at this time we will be preparing to have our second champ at GITR."

"That is right, Billy, we will be champs together!"

Billy decided to spend the fight morning alone. He didn't want to talk with Rex, Thaddeus, or even Larry. He sat in his hotel room. As he just sat there while his mind raced, he was a conflicted soul. It was no secret Thad was always trying to help Billy with this aspect of his life. Yes, his childhood was bad. His dad wasn't there. Yes, he had to be the "man of the house." Yes, he had his doubters, but what makes a person not see how much people have helped him? He always felt like he needed to stay angry. He needed to prove all the doubters wrong. He had built an entire existence on that. Being self-made had always been important to Billy. Yes, he trusted Larry. Larry had played a fatherly role in his life, but he was never sure that Larry would stick around if it all went away, if he declined as a prospect. In fact, Billy was pretty sure that Larry wouldn't stick around for him. That might have been because of Larry. It might have also been because of what Billy experienced growing up. Most likely it had to do with both factors.

In his long talks with Thaddeus, Thad had often tried to teach him how the self-made narrative worked against his faith. For Billy, he had ears but he couldn't hear, he had eyes but he couldn't see. Billy was a baby to this type of deep conversation. He simply didn't understand. Part of it was that being self-made was a narrative about himself that he had always loved. His dad wasn't there. His childhood wasn't great. He had to grit his teeth and do it, and he overcame. Look at him now. The problem when you explain to a baby Christian that the self-made narrative goes against faith in Christ and the grace that He brings, is that it is strange to him. It doesn't sound right, because we mix our self-help, motivational talks together with some Bible verses and we end up with this try-hard type of thing called faith. The hard part about faith is it starts and ends with God. So our responsibility is to respond to Him, to be God-made and not self-made. Thaddeus knew that Billy just didn't understand this part and had to pray and wait to see what God would do. In this way, Thad wasn't naïve — he was just hopeful, as you should be as someone modeling these things for Billy.

As Billy sat there and tried to relax, he knew this was the day he had always longed for. He longed for the day that would put the doubters away. He would put the champion down and he would be the champion. The battle in his heart and mind continued on with many layers to it. The voice in his mind said, *But will this day really do that? People will always credit Thaddeus for making me. They don't know what it was like growing up like I did. They don't know where I came from!* Deep down his anger was real, which was why he didn't like to think too deeply. When it came to fighting, he wanted to be an animal. The animal inside was about to be unleashed, and it would be unleashed on Gus Emmerick!

Instead of getting mad about the fight, he would sometimes get mad about Thaddeus. *They don't know,* he would think. *They don't get it! They don't realize I am helping to make Thaddeus. They don't realize I am the one helping him to stay on the top! We help each other.* Thaddeus admitted it and even credited Billy a lot, but this jealousy was something that God needed to work out of him. It was downright blinding and a real handicap to Billy.

He went back to thoughts about Emmerick and forgot about Thaddeus. He was now onto the fight in his head. At that there was a knock at the door. Rex and Larry stopped by to let him know they were looking forward to the fight. They wanted to make sure he got the right amount of sleep and tested how he felt. They brought him some breakfast.

He drank a lot of water, some skim milk, and ate some chicken and eggs for breakfast. He desired to stay strong for the whole fight. He didn't want a huge breakfast, but it had the right amount of protein and carbs involved, with a little bit of strawberries on the side. He felt good, lean, muscular, fast. In fact, he didn't think he had ever felt this good before.

Larry looked at him, seeing he looked like he could spit nails, and told him, "We have waited for this day for so long. I can tell you are going to do it! This is the last day you will wake up not knowing how it feels to win the title. You will go through a tough fighter, but you got this. He hasn't fought someone like you."

Rex said, "I am looking forward to having another champion in my club. We believe in you."

Billy looked at them both and was excited. "I want to relax and not think much about it for the next few hours. I am going to eat and watch a little *Law and Order*, probably walk up and down the hall to work off my food in a little bit, and read. I know I am ready and focused."

Rex chimed in with, "Have you talked to Thaddeus today? That guy knows how to prepare. He has the last 24 hours of the fight down to a science."

Billy looked up from his eggs, "Yeah, I know, Rex. He has downloaded it all on to me. I told him to kind of hang back this morning. I just need to read, think, watch some TV. I am ready."

At that, Rex and Larry got up to leave. They decided they were going to get some breakfast themselves. At another corner in the hotel, Thaddeus sat in his hotel room by himself. He desired to talk to Sally. He wished he could go to breakfast and eat at Cornerstone Café. He wanted Sally to harass and joke with him. He just wanted to see her. So he decided to do something kind of weird. He looked up Cornerstone Café on his phone and clicked on it to call. Loretta, another waitress, answered the phone, "Is Sally there?"

Loretta said, "Yes, she is, can I ask who is calling?" Loretta knew who was calling, but didn't want to ask if it was Thaddeus. She recognized his voice and knew that he liked talking with Sally.

Thad said, "Ah, tell her it is her not-so-secret admirer."

"Got it, Thad. Good luck to you guys tonight."

"Thank you, Loretta."

She went and got Sally. Sally got on the phone and said, "Hello."

"Hey, Sally."

"Come on, Thad, what do you need? I am working here."

"Sorry to bother you. I just wanted to make sure you knew I would be on TV tonight. It is important because the camera makes me look younger."

She gave an awkward giggle, "So you will be younger with more muscle like Billy on TV."

"Ha, ha. Just thinking of you, that is all."

"Thanks, Thad. I needed that today. Let's continue this awkward conversation when you sit in my section and fumble around in a few days."

"Sounds like a date to me. No take-backs. Got to go."

Sally laughed and said, "Bye."

Thaddeus said, "Bye." He hung up the phone and had hope. So did she. He thought, *She is great.* He went off to get something to eat before needing to meet up with Billy and the team later.

He was glad he got that out of the way, because things would get a little busy before the fight. Latimore and Durkin would be flying in, along with some of the other practice hands. Keith Mixon was also already there and would become a little more available as the fight got closer. Billy truly didn't have many injury problems to deal with. He knew how to ice his joints and take care of himself. But Keith would be around more to make sure he attended to all the prefight needs that he had.

As the fight time approached, Thaddeus walked into the mat area designated for Billy. Billy was in the corner, sleeping. Some lightweights were beginning to warm up on the other side of the room. Thaddeus recognized them as the Hood brothers, Michael and Kevin. Michael had a fight later that may prove to be very important to him getting a title shot.

Thaddeus came in and sat down by Billy and looked on at the lightweights who both knew him and nodded. Billy continued to sleep for about five minutes.

Thaddeus didn't wake him up. Billy woke up and scratched his head like he was sleeping pretty deeply. Billy looked at Thaddeus, just sitting there watching the Hoods for a few minutes. Thaddeus was really into thinking about them and their situation. He knew that Michael was the one fighting, but even if you didn't know you could tell. He could tell by the nervous look, the glimmer in his eye. The excitement, the nervousness, and the way he was putting things together. He was moving at lightning speed. He looked as though he was going to win.

Billy knew that Thaddeus was thinking deeply about it, so out of curiosity he tried to get him going. "So, you think Michael wins tonight?"

"Yeah, Billy, I do. I see the look in his eye. I see the crispness in his movement. I see hunger. It is exciting. I think he might even knock him out."

"All that from watching some drills?"

"Yeah, you know me. Look, Billy, this is your time. I

can't wait to see it. In about three hours you will be crowned champ."

Billy still didn't understand why Thaddeus wanted this for him. For Billy, since he didn't really have the parental figures in his life and the ingredients of secure people around him, he couldn't help but think it was misguided of Thaddeus to want this title for Billy and, ultimately, it was something else he would get credit for.

Thaddeus remembered what it was like to be in Billy's shoes. In some ways he wanted to go back there. He knew he was closer to the end of his career than the beginning. He knew that it was time to quit soon. He thought, "What if I could go back and do it all again?" He thought about how maybe it would be nice to go back to when not many people knew him. This chapter with Billy had been a new lesson.

"Hey, I will come back in and warm you up in an hour. I will make sure you are awake in 40 minutes." Billy was truly relaxed. He was young and could fall asleep on a wrestling mat, even with people working out on the other end of it. He had done everything he could possibly do to get to this point. He had done it, but now was he going to do it? He had very little doubt, but it would not be easy, that was for sure.

Billy drifted off back into a nap and knew that when he woke up it would be the last time he woke up before becoming champion. As the first fight was about to start, Thaddeus went and stood in the hallway leading out to the arena. Michael Hood made his way to the ring. He was the picture of con-centration. He looked his opponent in the eye and gritted his teeth, while climbing into the Octagon. Michael was a heavy underdog, but he was going after the older, seasoned fighter right away. From the opening bell, Michael attacked and didn't let up. He was relentless. He fought as if he would never have the chance again. He fought like a champion. The older fighter, Ricky Hernandez, seemed to have no answer for his kicks, punches, or takedowns.

The crowd was watching the momentum build. Excitement was in the air. Round one ended, and to everyone's surprise, with Hernandez feeling like he had been beaten up severely. He walked with his head down back to his corner with a very bloody cut above his left eye. Ricky saw the excitement of the crowd and tried to rally in the second round. As the fight continued on into the fourth round, it became apparent that Michael was, in fact, going to pull the upset. Time approached to go back and work out with Billy. When Thaddeus went back to the matted area assigned for Billy, he walked into a room with only Larry talking to Billy and Rex sitting up against the wall. Rex tried not to step on Larry's toes; this was a big night for him and for Billy. It was also a big night in the life of GITR.

Billy smiled and appeared to be well rested and relaxed. He began to jog around the room a little and skip and break a sweat. He grabbed a jump rope and jumped for a few minutes and then went into a series of stretches. He and Thad began to practice some takedowns and some counters and some situations where he would be able to punch. He practiced exposing the weaknesses of Gus Emmerick. About 20 minutes after he started he was moving at full speed. Billy had never been this fast. He had never looked this good. The man was on fire.

About when things slowed down a little, someone who assisted with GITR walked into the room and said, "Michael Hood by knockout. The guy looked tough."

Just then Thaddeus turned to Billy. "Remember what I

said, Billy, he had the look. I knew he would win. You have that look. You are about to be the champ!"

Thaddeus was happy! Billy was really happy! *Just like the day before*, Thad thought, *Billy has hit his peak!* As they got closer to fight time, they knew it was time to slow down a little.

Billy slowed his pace way down for a little while and would gradually pick it back up again briefly before going out into the arena. But as he felt the excitement building, his mouth began to water as the HWT title was now in reach! It was time for Billy to settle down a little as they were about to make their way towards the hallway. The challenger would be called at any moment. Thaddeus looked at him and said, "You are ready. I know you are." He put his hands on him and prayed for him.

Billy looked at him and said, "Thanks."

"No problem, Kid. You got this."

When they saw Billy coming they announced his name. Billy was walking with intentionality. He had an appointment. It was an appointment with destiny. He was made for this. Fighting and making a way for himself was the only thing he truly understood. It was his time. His mind was set to attack mode. The crowd loved him and cheered for him. As he stood in the Octagon with his team, they announced Larry as his head trainer who got some cheers. They then announced Rex, who got a few more cheers, and the house came down again for Thaddeus "Pure Class." Even in this moment it seemed to Billy that he was in the shadow of Thaddeus Class.

Billy channeled that energy back to Emmerick as he saw him making his way to the Octagon. Billy bounced back and forth and kept his eyes right on him. There was no doubt who was ready. Emmerick may be ready, but Billy was definitely in a different state of mind. Everyone at GITR knew Billy was a competitor. They expected him to break this fight open right away. They knew there was about to be a new sheriff in town. They played Emmerick's song. It was a new song called "Danger." The lyrics were hard to understand, but the point was he was dangerous. This guy was fierce; he was an animal. He trained hard to be the champion, but he saw this as a signature fight. As "Night Crawler's" group made their way to the Octagon, he had fire in his eyes as he climbed the stairs and looked across at Billy, "The Kid." He grinned at him, but he looked away first after a few seconds. He knew Billy was no kid.

Thaddeus laughed and Billy knew why. Thaddeus simply said, "You see that, Billy?"

"Oh, yeah, I did. He is mine. He knows it deep down inside."

Rex smiled as he and Thaddeus left the Octagon first. Larry was a little nervous but was mostly excited, knowing that he would finally be the main trainer for a champion, and it was well deserved. He was ready for it! He looked Billy in the eye. "You are the champ in this Octagon. You are about to be! You have worked for it! It is your time! This guy can't hang with you and tonight is not his night. You got this!"

Billy grinned and pushed his teeth together as it was time to shake hands. Emmerick seemed to be looking through Billy as he was slightly taller and almost looking over his head. They bumped gloves as Billy smiled.

A bell rang and the fight started; Billy almost ran at the champion like an animal. He was on the attack. He landed a series of punches right off the bat. He got deep on Emmerick's leg and got the takedown. He found himself sitting on

Emmerick's chest early and pounding his face. He had him trapped on his back and knocked the heck out of him for what seemed like a long time. He landed some vicious blows to the face. Oftentimes this type of fight would have been stopped, but you can't stop the champion and give it to the challenger only seconds into the first round. Emmerick was usually the animal in the ring. No one had ever taken it to him like this.

Billy continued to land blows to the face. As Emmerick squirmed to get out of that position, Billy found himself on top of him with a knee on his chest and he was banging on his ribs. His knee slid up into his throat as he squirmed. This entire exchange lasted about two minutes, which left Billy tired, but the champion was really tired. He was already bleeding. His cheeks were heavily brush-burned and swollen. Emmerick knew that his rib may have been cracked from the landing of the knee. He had never fought anyone like this before.

Billy was fighting the fight of his life. The commentators on TV had declared that this was history in the making. They were starting to see that Billy may indeed win and this may not be close at all. They mentioned several times on-air, "The man is fierce!" "He is a specimen!" "He is just awesome!" "This is crazy!" The truth is, it was crazy. Billy was taking it to a seasoned champion! Many thought he would win, but to embarrass the champion — who would have thought that? That is exactly what would have happened if Emmerick hadn't fought back so hard.

Back at Cornerstone Café, Sally looked on as she saw the man was bloodied, and the owners, Tommy and Rita Hightower, looked on as if they couldn't believe what they were seeing. They were watching Billy destroy a great fighter. This was Thaddeus's workout partner. It was now his time, too! All of the people at Cornerstone were watching on TV. This was historic.

Thaddeus already had his picture in the place getting his hand raised after a title defense. The Hightowers planned on surprising Billy with a blown-up picture in the restaurant as well, to be kept in the back room. What they were witnessing was unbelievable!

Emmerick squirmed out and somehow got back to his feet up against the cage. He landed a few brutal jabs to the head that slowed Billy down. Emmerick knew he needed to strike and he did. He took some chances and landed some big punches. Emmerick began to get some punches in and even got in on Billy's leg a few times. There was a lot of countering and grappling. You could begin to see why this guy was the HWT champion. He may have been out-classed but there was no quit in him. He was going to fight until the end.

As the first five-minute round came to a close, both fighters were tired and looked like this fight had already gone the distance. All of the judges awarded Billy the first round victory of 10-9.

When Billy returned to the corner, he sat down. Larry was excited. "We got him where we want him. We knew it! I knew it! You knew it!"

Thaddeus said, "You got this! This is your night."

Rex chimed in, "Let's get it!"

Billy went back to the center of the Octagon as they called them both back in. Emmerick tried to get him to chase him to the edge. Billy changed up his style to kind of hang around the center and wait for him. He didn't want him on the edge. He wanted to put the champ away in the middle of the Octagon.

There was no doubt, it was all coming together. Billy was

fast. He was smart, intense, and relentless, and now was showing patience. He circled and waited. He bobbed and wove. Emmerick made a move and caught Billy by the leg. He had him down and landed a few punches. But a scramble happened and Billy found himself behind the champion. He caught him in a chokehold. He had him tight. He squeezed with all he had. He had both of his legs behind, pinching his sides. He had it locked in tight.

Emmerick knew this could be the end of his reign as champion. He began to get small. He tried to roll. He reached back and pinched Billy's calf. The hold loosened enough for him to scurry out the side. He got to his feet and kicked Billy on the back of the knee, making him bend down forward. Billy then took a knee to the face. The tables appeared to be turning. Rex yelled, "Get out of there!" Somehow, Billy in a scramble ended up with Emmerick's leg and landed on top of him again, punching down in his face.

For a moment he thought *I am going to win*, but he was tired. He saw Emmerick's tired and bloodied face. He slowed down for a second, but landed a vicious blow on Emmerick's upper lip on the right side. For a second, in a state of exhaustion, Emmerick looked like Thadddeus and he landed two of the hardest punches ever seen. The average man may have died. Many would have been knocked out.

But the tide changed very quickly back in Billy's favor. The champion was beaten and spent. Billy was a protégé of Thaddeus Class. He was a GITR fighter and he was going to win. He was the beast! He was the alpha today! The champion had no answer. If Emmerick didn't do something different, he may just get killed today.

Emmerick squirmed out again, getting to his feet, but

spent the rest of the round trying to slow Billy down and keep from getting hit. He wanted to slow him down and get out of the round. Billy got some more punches in and a swift kick to the back of Emmerick's knee as well. Billy continued to punch on him and think, *My time! Yes, it is!*

Round three began and Emmerick decided to match the pace of the young challenger. He bolted towards him, faked a weak punch, and caught him with a swift kick to the back of the knee. At that, the champion began to punch on him from above. He was now spinning behind him and he got two shots in the back of Smith's head before knocking him back down to the ground. Billy sprang up and somersaulted away. Emmerick, sensing the awkwardness of Billy, chased him, but Billy caught him with an uppercut. He caught him then with a hook. He kicked him and began to just brawl. He gained his composure and switched back to wrestling. He took the champion down and Emmerick, sensing he was losing momentum, began to fight back hard. They rolled and countered each other. Emmerick got some licks in. Billy got some in and the fight continued at a vigorous rate. Both fighters were exhausted when they hit the three-minute mark, and the rest of the round slowed down. Many punches were exchanged, but as far as the scorecard was concerned, Billy and Emmerick were pretty close, so the judges all gave it to the champion 10-9. It looked like going into round four it was going to be interesting.

The corner was a little different after round three. "Billy, listen," Larry said, as he was only inches from his face. "You've got to continue to fight. Look, you think you are tired, look at him. The third round was yours, but you need to push him. I need you to set the pace. I think he let it all go last round. Remember, he will get lazy on that one side, just like we talked about. As he slows down we can knock him out." He screamed, "This is your time!!!"

As they went back to the center, Billy got there first this time and he began to go to work. The champion tried to continue to keep up with him, but he couldn't as Billy got more shots in. He got shots in the stomach, in the face. Billy shot in on a double left and landed on top of him in front of the cage. They were back on their feet. It looked like for the minute the champion was beginning to get the upper hand as he got some shots in. Billy appeared tired; he kind of stepped in sideways and dropped his hands.

He seemed to fall into the signature hook of the champion. Emmerick saw it coming and he raised up, trying to sink that hook. Right as Emmerick stepped in, Billy dropped and countered, just like Thad had practiced with him. He came up with a vicious uppercut while the athletic champion was exposed. No one had ever exposed him before, but GITR did. Billy did it!

Billy knew when he hit him. There were two hits. Billy hitting Emmerick and Emmerick hitting the ground. He landed on his face and no one believed he was getting back up. Everything seemed to slow down for Billy. Everything had changed. He was now the champion. He was now worth something. He now proved everyone wrong — his mom, his dad, his fourth grade teacher who told him he wouldn't ever make it. He proved wrong every girlfriend who thought he wasn't going anywhere. He proved it to them all. He was one bad $#@)&*($Q&)* and now the Heavyweight Champion of the World!

A picture was snapped. Larry was holding him up. Billy was in the air. Thaddeus had Billy's arm and Rex was standing there by them with his hands up in the air, celebrating the championship of the world. GITR was now great, things were changing for this club. They were changing for Billy and Thaddeus.

Rex thought in that moment, *I can't believe I am here with Thaddeus and my longtime friend Larry. I can't believe this club is getting there.* For a second he wouldn't admit, he thought *God is blessing me.* It was a moment he wouldn't forget. Rex's club was now the greatest club in the world as it trained the two best fighters. Who knew what would happen? Maybe Thaddeus would retire and focus on coaching Billy and some others. The future looked very bright.

Billy grabbed hold of Thaddeus as he was covered in sweat, blood dripping from the top of his eye, and said in his ear, "I have never experienced anything like this before. Thank you for helping me get here."

The moment was pure and very satisfying for Thaddeus. Billy was young and tough and selfish. But Thaddeus always had grace on him, because that was who he used to be, too. That was his story and a moment like this was what really made it worth it. There was hope for Billy. It appeared to be a moment where he could think past himself and have gratitude. It was Christian fruit in a moment of success.

Larry grabbed hold of Billy and they looked at the crowd as Larry had Billy by the neck, hands in the air; they pointed, and the crowd went crazy. They looked at Rex as someone in the corner grabbed the hats and put them on. The hats said, "GITR WORLD CHAMPS! ONE-TWO PUNCH!!!"

Then a picture was snapped with the hands in the air and an exhausted Billy holding the belt. Afterwards, he put the belt around his waist and they were whisked away into the night. Larry grabbed Billy and said, "This is just the beginning!"

On the other side of the Octagon, Emmerick hadn't been knocked out before tonight. He was outsmarted, and just didn't look good. Billy fought like a champion. Emmerick was hurting. They attended to him as he was escorted to the locker room. He barely stood for the hand-raising of his opponent and there was no doubt that even though he couldn't think straight in that moment, Gus would never forget this moment. It would be a defining one for the rest of his life.

Billy couldn't believe it. He expected to win, but now that he had he was shocked! It was an unbelievable feeling. Rex knew that any fighter over 170 lbs. would now want to train at GITR. This was just the beginning. Rex and Larry felt like kings in Vegas. They hit the blackjack tables. They talked fighting with anyone who would listen until late into the night. Rex felt truly accomplished. Larry and Rex both felt like they were the champions and had done something special. Something amazing was happening at GITR. Rex wouldn't admit it to himself, but he felt truly blessed.

The next morning Thaddeus got up and went for a run. He was up early enough not to be seen by the fight fans. Since they were up late watching Billy, not many of them were out and about during his run time. Even though it might not be the smartest idea, he liked to run away from the streets and go out into the desert. Once in a while he was startled by a little lizard or some type of animal movement, but he could look back and see where Las Vegas was. Athletes who cross train with running, but are not true runners, know that if you run out two miles, you still have to get back. That is the reason he ran out two miles, so he wasn't tempted to stop early. No one wanted to walk slowly from out in the desert.

As he ran he listened to music. He was particularly motivated this morning. This was the first time that he had a practice partner who was a champion. Thaddeus Class had now been a great champion and mentored another champion who fought at the weight class above him. He successfully helped reproduce himself in Billy. He thought about if he quit now, how he could focus on coaching Billy and some others. He could help Rex build the brand even more. He thought about speaking and what that career could look like. Or, *Maybe I will write a book,* he thought. The future was wide open.

He thought about Sally and how he saw some hope now and that maybe there was a future there. He saw he wasn't angry at God anymore, and life was good. Thaddeus didn't ever remember feeling like this. This wasn't a feeling that he could ever remember having. He felt fulfilled. Maybe more than championships or anything else, this was what he had been longing for all of this time. He just wanted to give back in a way that mattered. He wanted to be at peace. He wanted to feel as though God was happy with him.

He thought about Billy and thought about how to pray for him and how to better mentor him. *I need to be able to move him towards being in control of his own peace like this. I know what it is to be where he is. It feels good for a while, but your circumstances can't be what gives you peace. There must be something more to it.*

As the next song ramped up, Thaddeus picked up the pace. He was working hard. He wanted to be able to stay with Billy. Thad understood that Billy was at his very best right then and he needed to be able to stay with him in practice.

He wanted to be able to still win. As Thaddeus continued to run, he began to think about what was next. *What is the next defense?* Maybe he was getting towards the end. Maybe there wasn't anyone else left to fight out there. Maybe it was over and he could do something else. He could help Rex at GITR. He could do something else. He then thought, *No way. I have just helped train a champion. I am a champion. I am at my best. It is time to secure my legacy in this sport.*

He sprinted in bursts on the way back, marked by cacti and rocks. Thad was motivated for the moment, but deep down he couldn't help but think that maybe he didn't have anything left. Maybe it was time to get out. He wasn't sure. He knew he wanted to continue to mentor Billy. He knew he could help him with his walk with Jesus, and teach him how to be a true champion with integrity. When he finished his run, he knew he had trained hard and planned on enjoying the rest of the day, knowing he helped someone else get to where he was.

Billy woke up with a strange blonde woman in his room. He seemed to have forgotten what happened after the fight. He felt dizzy and a little slow. She, oddly enough, felt odd too, and maybe wasn't sure that she should be there. When Billy woke up she was getting dressed; she now had all of her clothes back on. He looked at her and remembered. He immediately said, "What, no breakfast?"

She touched his face and said, "You were great last night, but I can't be here." She kissed him on the forehead and said, "Congrats again, Champ!"

In the corner of his eye he saw it as she was walking out of the room. They both knew that this was where it ended and they were both fine with that. But in the corner of his eye, there it was. He had chased it all of these years. It was the championship belt. Billy "The Kid" Smith was the Heavyweight Champion of the World. He then began to have some regrets about the woman who stayed with him last night. He hoped Thaddeus hadn't seen her leave. He felt sorry for it because he knew that it wasn't something he should do as a Christian. Then he began to remember the night and the regrets seemed to be minimized. He sat there and looked at the championship belt and he couldn't believe that it was his. He got there. He achieved it! He was the best fighter in the world at the HWT class. He thought, *Man, my life has changed. In one day almost everyone will know who I am. This is crazy.* He stared at it. He thought, *Thaddeus was right! There is no feeling like it!* He closed his eyes and fell back asleep.

In a moment he was asleep and into a dream. In his dream, Thaddeus knocked on the door. BANG! BANG! BANG! Billy knew it was Thaddeus as he stumbled to the door. He opened the door and said, "Hey, man, what is up?" He was feeling a little drunk.

Thaddeus said, "Come on, man, I just saw the girl leaving your room. She walked down the hall and left, she came from this room. Come on, man, is that what we represent? Is this what it looks like to be a Christian to you?"

Billy looked at Thaddeus with anger. "You had your time when you were younger. Now you are trying to be different. That isn't me."

Thaddeus continued to press with his arm in the doorway. "Is this what being a Christian is to you?"

Billy screamed, "NO! IT IS WHAT BEING THE CHAMP IS TO ME!" At that, Billy knocked out Thaddeus with one punch and slammed the door.

Billy woke up, now sobered up a little, shocked at his own dysfunction. He didn't know what to do with all of the feelings he had. But deep down he resented Thaddeus and there was no getting away from him. He couldn't escape him. There was no escape. Now he was ticked at Thaddeus again as he looked at the belt and thought, *Will I be in his shadow forever? I can't take this.* He huffed and rolled over and was back asleep in seconds because of how exhausted he felt, and annoyed that Thaddeus even bothered him in his dreams.

CHAPTER 6

LOST

Rex heard the phone ring about eight one morning at the gym. It was Charlie Pigeon. Rex said, "Hello."

Charlie jumped right to it. "Is the famous Rex Metzger there, the beautiful genius who trains those killer animals at GITR?"

Rex, in his very dry sense of humor said, "Charlie, what did I tell you about calling me beautiful? How is it going? Ha, ha, ha!"

"Not how, Rex, who?"

Rex, trying to keep up, said, "What do you mean?"

Charlie said, "How do you feel about a rematch of your boy Thad and Freaky Freddy Patterson?"

Freddy Patterson was someone Thaddeus had beaten a couple of times. He hadn't fought him for a few years. Freddy had worked hard. He had improved and had worked himself into being a top contender once again. He had a record of 24-4. He was a Brazilian Jiu-Jitsu-type of fighter, with a mean kick, but well rounded. He could punch with the punchers and grapple with the grapplers. He was kind of a fluky type of fighter. He would mix it up and roll around and end up in very dangerous striking or submission positions.

Rex responded with, "Come on, Charlie, Freaky Freddy? What happened to Hunter Adams?"

"Well, Rex, I like that card, but it will be really big if we let him win a few more. I am going to bet that Thaddeus will still be around — for a little while longer, anyway."

Rex found this really odd. He didn't understand the angle. There was no guarantee that Thad would be around that much longer, and if this fight could bring in a lot of money now, why wouldn't he want it? Thad could decline or retire and Hunter Adams could lose a fight to someone else. This could cost all parties involved millions. He knew Charlie didn't play that one straight. Something was a little off, but he couldn't figure it out. But Thad was the champ and, in Rex's mind, they were in the driver's seat, so he lost interest before asking the question, "Isn't there anyone else out there?"

Charlie sighed and actually said, "Not at the moment. We have a few that we want to give their moment to like Hunter, but it is too soon. Look, obviously we want Thad to keep winning. It isn't profitable enough for me if he loses to Freaky Freddy, but we need to have a fight in between this one and the next big one to keep building his legacy. I wouldn't offer it if I wasn't sure he would win. Besides, Thaddeus wins, but you know Freddy will put on a show!"

Rex laughed a little. "When would it be?"

"It would be five months from today," Charlie added. "Is that enough time for him to be ready?"

"Yeah, but I don't understand. Why Freddy again?"

"They have history. It is a good story and it will be entertaining. Freddy will get some good licks in. Like I said, it will be entertaining and good for your club. Other than Freddy, you are about twelve months away from giving anyone else a legitimate shot. Viewership and interest in Thad is up due to his undefeated legacy and entertainment value. I think we are looking at paying at the same margin as last time with an expected return of about ten percent increase in revenue coming in."

"Ok, I will talk it over with the team. If it all looks good, we will sign the paperwork this week."

Charlie finished off with "Sounds good, talk to you soon."

Rex said, "Bye."

After some short discussion, which involved meeting 15 minutes before their morning workout was supposed to begin, Thad, Rex, and Larry agreed to the fight. Thad was familiar with "Freaky Freddy," and was ready to start training.

The spirits were high at the gym. Thaddeus was training for his fight with Freaky Freddy. But now there was a second champion. After all, the press conference stuff had died down and Billy had been in the gym a few times for some quick workouts to loosen his muscles up; it was time to get serious again.

Typically, it was a day the fighter would be getting back in the weight room, but he wanted to celebrate by getting on the mat and sparring some. He wanted to drill and work out with Thaddeus, which Thad was ok with since he was getting ready for his fight. Thad started out joking around with Billy. They would roll around and drill takedowns. It wasn't very structured. They didn't need to hit the same move over and over again or anything; they would take whatever their opponent gave them and hit a move from there. There was no striking, just wrestling-type moves. Obviously, the takedowns were to set up submission holds, or strikes.

The first few minutes the two of them sparred and went back and forth. At times it looked artistic. A good drill partner lets the other guy do the move, and there is a skill to it. You don't give them everything, but you don't hold them up or tighten up on them. As the drilling continued, as was typical, it became more intense. There were celebratory type things being said by "Smokin'" Joe and "Slippery" Pete. "Look, we got two champs in here now! We can all be champs!" Others working out looked on as the workout became more intense.

Billy decided to practice some throws, which Thad was ok with. It was his day and he needed to get that first big workout back in. It was important. Billy hit a perfect throw, arching his back and planting Thad to the canvas. Larry chimed in by saying, "Rex, did you catch that? There is your picture, you can put it up there beside Thad."

Rex got louder and said, "Not yet! You see that picture? That was Thad's third title defense." Almost immediately, Billy hit a fireman's carry, tossing Thaddeus off his back, and smoothly coming back up to hit the next move. This time he stepped in and threw him over his head. "How about that one?" said Billy.

Thad began to encourage Billy, "Nice throw."

Billy came back with, "I know, right?"

Neither Rex nor Thaddeus was bothered by the giant chip on Billy's shoulder. He was the champion. He beat a great champion and he may have a great future ahead of him.

After about 30 minutes of intense drilling they got a drink. Billy said to Thad, "All right, get your gloves on. First go as champ versus champ."

Thaddeus looked at him, confused. He said, "I understand the mat drilling, but what is up with going live already?"

Billy looked at him and said, "I am young! What, you don't remember what it was like when you first won the title? They say you can't be beat. You're training to fight. I feel good. Let's go! Just ten minutes."

Typically, Larry would weigh in and want to work on technique at this point. But he didn't say anything. Rex looked at Larry and said, "Is he sure? He just fought."

Larry just shrugged his shoulders. The older mentor champion Thaddeus Class couldn't pass up the live go. After all, this is what made them great. Thaddeus had been coming up short in the live goes in practice lately. Granted, they didn't go full-on strike mode much, but when they did, Billy had been beating Thaddeus. However, these last few weeks while his workouts were no longer focused on Billy, Thad began to look more like a fighter in training. He had a big fight coming up now, with Freaky Freddy, so he was going to train hard.

Thad said, "Let's go, Champ!" and the time was set. Anything went for the next ten minutes. It was kind of understood that they were not going to injure each other, and Rex and Larry reserved the right to stop it at any time.

For the first few minutes there was a lot of feeling each other out. They took a few conservative swings, or some shots where they dove in on a leg but backed out quick. Both of them were trying not to get caught with each other's right hook.

Some of the greatest grappling went on in this fight. There was a lot of scrambling. In some ways it looked like when they were drilling, but they were trying to punch each other. Thad got in on the big guy's legs several times, but it only served to make him tired. He wasn't quite in fighting shape yet. About eight minutes in, Thad caught Billy on his back and unloaded some great shots to the face. The young champion rolled out.

Billy caught Thad with a vicious uppercut, just like he pictured it, just like he thought about knocking out his mentor many times. This punch was a perfect MMA-type of uppercut, almost pulling him over Billy's body. Billy locked up high around his back, putting his own head under Thaddeus's chin and tossing him belly to back, hitting his head off the cage, dragging his face down it.

Typically, in practice this would be time to stop. But he let go, coming up partially to his feet, and unloaded on Thad's face. Thad, at this point, was out cold, while Billy screamed in his face, "There is a new @#$%^&%^&*% sheriff in town @#$%#@%#&$!!!"

Rex jumped to shield Thad from Billy. Thad was still unconscious. Billy put his hand in the air mocking the picture on the wall. Larry chuckled a little and said, "I think it is time to quit."

Rex looked at them both in front of everyone watching and said, "What is wrong with you two? We have something great here."

Larry said, "Maybe we are sick of hearing how great you are, and your celebration of Thad's greatness. You have a new champion now."

Rex, looking at them both, asked, "What are you talking about? We are a team. We have helped each other." Pointing to Thad, "He helped you both."

Larry said, "And you both have been paid, haven't you?" He pointed to Thad lying there, bloodied and still waking up, "He can't stay on top without us. You said so yourself."

Rex screamed, "Get the $^#*&($^#@& out of MY GYM!!!"

"Yeah, that is what we both thought. Everyone knows that even though this is the house we helped build, it is your gym."

Rex looked at them and said, "What good is it if you destroy the house you build?"

Larry grabbed Slippery Pete and Smokin' Joe and said, "We've already got a place across town," Larry knew that both of these guys were not under contract and Rex would gladly let him and Billy out of their contract now. They grabbed their bags, their lockers were already cleaned out, and they left. The young workout partners cleared out — some of them to train with Billy and some of them just didn't know what to do, so they went home.

Wow! They sat there. Thad was just waking up. The well-paid head medical trainer of GITR, Keith Mixon, came out to attend to Thad. Rex and Keith went way back to when this all started. Keith was used to egos and the injuries fighters got. After a good look-over, Mixon said, "He is going to need to go into concussion protocol. He took some brutal shots. This is going to set back his training."

Rex was hurt on a heart level. He knew hurt, but this caught him so off guard. He walked out in the hallway, sat there, and teared up. He couldn't believe this. GITR had their second champ, he thought he was training with a close friend. It turned out he was no friend at all. Not only were one champ and several fighters leaving, but Thaddeus was hurt. He snarled up and to the right at heaven; he clenched his fist and yelled, "You think this is funny?"

Once he composed himself and cleaned up some blood, Rex was going to go in and talk to Thad and make sure he was OK. He blamed himself. He thought, *How could I let this happen? Was I just greedy? Did I let the wrong people in? What was wrong with me? I almost got Thaddeus killed. This is really bad.*

Then, as Rex thought about it and started to look at the blood left on the floor of the cage, he thought, *They go to church together. Thad has been mentoring him in everything. They have those annoying Bible conversations right here in front of me. It bleeds into every conversation. Wow! What a hypocrite.* The annoying part for him after thinking this was that Thad wasn't a hypocrite and this was the beginning of the end for him. Rex then entertained this new train of thought. *I knew Jesus was going to bring Thaddeus down! I just knew it. This is where it ends for him. He has lost his edge.*

Thaddeus was in with Trainer Mixon. There were a few practice hands in the training room hanging out a little long with their ice packs, shocked about what happened, but nosey more than anything. Rex quickly cleared them out and told them they needed to leave. When Rex entered the training room, it was Thaddeus who was lying there on the training table. The trainer was trying to loosen his back up. He was trying to release tension in his neck and calm him down. Thaddeus began to cry. He started choking up, and then it was a roar for a moment like an uncontained child. Only this was The Gorilla. He was in a full-bore roar for what seemed like a long time, but it was only about 15 seconds.

Keith grabbed Rex and pulled him into the corner, "When I get him calmed down, I am going to check him for a concussion. It is too difficult right now, though."

"Your timetable Keith, just make sure he is all right."

Rex put his hand on Thaddeus's shoulder and said, "Hey, Champ. You've got to calm down. Relax." Rex said, "You're hurt. Does your head hurt?"

Thad said, "I hurt everywhere." He then changed the subject, "What was wrong with him?"

Rex, at the risk of sounding stupid, asked "Who?"

"Billy! It was almost as if he was trying to kill me. But we are like brothers. I am as happy about his success as anyone else. We have been there for each other through all of this. What is wrong with him?" Thad started to push himself up from lying on his chest and said, "I have to go talk to him. He is young. He needs me to understand how to deal with the pressure of being a champion. I can help him be a great champion."

Rex was overwhelmed with thoughts running through his brain. He was thinking about how on earth Thad could not see this man had tried to kill him. It was an act of hatred, or jealousy, or something, but they couldn't have them working out together right now. And were they trying to leave GITR, and where would they go? Where were they going to run to, what was going on in their heads? *Where is my friend and business partner going?* Surely they weren't leaving. But he didn't show much concern for Thad.

Thad said, "Let me up, Keith. I need to go get them. I need to go see where they are. I need to talk some sense into Billy."

Rex finally had a moment of clear thought. He just blurted out, "It is over, Thad."

Thad said, "What?"

Rex: "This whole thing. Larry is jealous, and now Billy. They are champs now and they don't need us. I thought it was about us, too, and we were building something, but they are burning bridges with us."

"Why?"

"I don't know, Thaddeus. I just know that what just happened wasn't normal for celebrating a victory. You don't just try to kill the club's reigning champion and signature fighter. You don't just come in here and do that if you don't have a point to make."

Thad finished getting checked out. He considered it a miracle from God and thanked the Lord that there was no concussion or sustained injury. As Thaddeus thanked God in his heart, Rex looked at it as a very disciplined and finely-tuned athlete could walk away from much more than the average person. Many people would have died with that exchange, which had always been the concern with these live go's between the two of them, but they usually seemed to know where to draw the line with each other. In the past when things would get out of hand they would stop, but even then there was a mutual friendship and brotherhood that bound them together. There was respect and a sharing in the other's success.

Whether Thaddeus realized it or not, Rex knew that things would never be the same. Something was different about Billy lately. Something had been wrong for quite a while, it was just that Rex didn't want to see it. Rex knew that Thad couldn't see it, just like he couldn't see it with Larry. Rex thought to himself, *Thad didn't see it coming. He is so blinded.*

"That is what God does to you," a voice in his head told him.

"You don't get it, God. Stay out of my life. You always let me down and it seems like you don't let me alone." Rex then realized that he didn't know what to do, but now he was talking in his head to an imaginary something that he didn't really believe in. Rex then laughed with lightning in his eye and stopped. He was really angry. Still standing there in the training room, he blurted out, "I need some air."

Trainer Mixon said to Thad as he tended to him, "I have never seen a connection like you and Rex in this sport, and especially with him. You are his fighter, but he cares for you."

Thad said, "Yeah, we are like family."

Keith looked at him and said, "Sorry that your training partner turned on you."

"Aw, Keith, he will be fine. He and I get into some arguments and all, but I will talk to him. There is new stress that happens when you become the champion."

"Thad, I don't think he is coming back to GITR. You know that wasn't normal."

Thaddeus put his head down and began to sob again. That was what he was upset about before, but the denial had set in. "Thanks, Keith, you are a great guy." Thad left when it was over and went off to get a shower; he didn't truly yet understand what had happened. Keith was a solid Christian guy who happened to go to the same church and knew Paul very well.

As Thad was leaving, he walked by the Octagon where the blood had been cleaned up. He stood there and looked at the giant mural of when he was a young champion. He was a giant in his own mind then. As he breathed in, he didn't smell sweat, fight, or tears. He didn't smell any of it. It was a little old and a little musty, but the giant killer was the ammonia. He thought about how the mats had been cleaned and the cage was sprayed down to get rid of the blood. He thought about the thousands of times he had smelled this smell. He was struck with fear. He thought about being nervous and anxious; he thought about it all. As he stood in a lit area of the room, he looked up at his prideful face with a hand in the air, in awe of how he had gotten this far, and wondered if maybe Rex could be right — that "the new me" could get himself killed. Then he saw some blood on the cage. *They missed some.* He thought, *That is my blood.* He stood there in awe at what was happening. A deep sadness came over him. It was one that he knew well, but had been gone since his new life in Christ began. He felt sad and all alone.

Thaddeus sat down and thought, *I need to call Billy.* He called Billy's cell phone.

Billy said, "Hey, Champ." He sounded like nothing had happened.

Thaddeus thought he was going crazy for a second. In a mentoring, older brother type of voice, Thad went first, "Hey, man, what is going on?"

Billy said, "What do you mean?"

Thaddeus was shocked by this, in light of their friendship. To Thaddeus this was hurtful and odd, but they were fighters — that isn't how he would describe it. "Come on, man, can we go get some food or something? You're like my best friend here."

Billy's voice cracked a little. "Thanks, Thad, for being my training partner these years and helping me get to where I am going, but you are holding me back now. Things are already in motion. We are not going back now. Sorry."

Thad understood Billy wasn't really sorry but was just acknowledging that he hurt him. That was how Billy seemed to handle apologies, but as far as brokenness over hurting Thad or Rex, that wasn't what Billy was feeling.

Thad said, "What do you mean?"

"I mean I will not stay in your shadow. It is time for me to fly. Charlie Pigeon will be calling you guys. Maybe my new club will give me the credit I deserve."

Thad, sensing that he was about to be hung up on said, "Wait!"

Larry now had the phone. He said, "Thad, get ready. We

are coming for you. It has been a pleasure working with you, but now we are coming after you. You'd better get ready."

"Larry, come on man, I trusted you. I thought we were friends."

"Thad, Rex is right about you. You have lost something with this faith kick you are on. Stay away from my fighter. We are going to beat you."

At that point Thad yelled, "WHAT?"

"You heard me, Class, we are coming after you."

Thad chimed in, "I won't fight Billy."

"You will tarnish your name and Rex's name if you don't. You are a smart guy, Thad, too bad you think with your heart. You will fight or we will embarrass you."

Thad yelled, "What is wrong with you?"

"We are just after what we have always been looking for — the respect that we deserve, the respect you have. See you soon!" At that, Larry hung up.

Thad was at a loss for words. He realized he couldn't sit there and just think about this. He needed to do something about it. His mind was racing. He looked back up at the picture. He didn't want to fight anymore. He thought, *Maybe the champ in that picture is going away.* He began setting his heart to retire. He thought, *Maybe Rex is right. I don't have the same feelings about it anymore.* Thaddeus thought about all the reasons that he didn't want to fight Billy. He poured so much into him. He helped him with how to think about his place in the world (or so he thought). He encouraged him to be baptized. He thought they had a deep friendship and connection. They had something that mattered, or so he thought. Thaddeus thought, *Maybe he was just using me, but I still want him to figure it out. I don't hate him for it.*

The old Thaddeus would have kicked his head in. But the anger was gone. He still wanted good for Billy, even after this. When you are a fighter, you can't second-guess. You have to be committed to dominating your opponent, and he no longer was. If Billy was his opponent, then it would be too hard to fight him.

As he put his head down, he heard the door open from outside and someone walked in. Thad didn't move, he heard someone walking towards him. He thought, *What now?* It was Paul. "Paul? Why aren't you home with Ella?"

"Someone in the church was having an emergency; comes with the title."

Thad asked, "Who?"

"Keith called me. You want to grab some dinner with me?"

"Sure. But, I will not be very fun to be around right now. But let's do it."

As they drove off, Paul called his wife on the phone and told her that he couldn't be home, but that they needed to go out to eat. "Honey, I need to be the champ's wingman tonight. He can't seem to ask this waitress out right if I am not there."

Thad, in the background said, "Stop. We can't go to Cornerstone."

"I am driving. What are you going to do about it?"

Ella, knowing she is on speaker phone, sarcastically said, "Watch yourself, baby, I have seen that right hook. He hits a little harder than your board members do."

"Tell him, Ella! He is always picking on me."

They hung up after a minute of sappy love-yous and small talk about one of the kids' friends and the other one's homework. There was a part of Thaddeus that wanted that for his own life. He thought about it especially after the night he'd had. Thad thought, *Maybe this fighting thing really has run its course.* It scared him a little, because that was what he had always done. He asked the question in his mind, *What would it look like for Thaddeus Class to have a real job?*

So, they got out of Paul's Honda and went inside to Cornerstone. Usually Thad would have something smart to say about Paul taking him to try and get him a date. He would have some creative joke or something of wit to say. But this time Thad didn't know what to do. He was hurting so bad. He had nothing to say. So, when they entered the main area, the owner, Tommy Hightower, took them to the other room. Thaddeus started to walk towards the back but he went to the bathroom instead. Sally came over to Paul with their drinks. She knew something was a little off. She just kind of looked at Paul with a serious face. Paul looked at her, "Don't act like I told you, but take it easy on Thad today."

"What happened? He looks horrible. Did someone beat him up?"

"Um, sometimes things are confidential. If he tells you, that is one thing, but I will not tell you about it."

At that, they saw Thaddeus walking back from the restroom. She said, "Hey, Thad, nice black eye. Pastor said you got beat up."

"What? Why did you tell her? Aren't you supposed to keep things confidential?"

"Yes, and I didn't tell her, you just did." Sally simply smiled back at him.

Thaddeus laughed a little. Sally said, "I will be back with the usual stuff, sound good?"

"Yeah, that sounds good," Thad and Paul both said.

Thad got a little sarcastic. "She surely can have fun with

me as a friend, but we are not going to be anything more than that. She is having fun. And you, I told you that I didn't want to come here. I already feel low enough. You told me to disciple Billy. He got baptized, I thought I was helping him to live better and be better. He seemed to really be soaking it all in. Now my trainer thinks I am weak because of Jesus, and Larry and Billy are saying that I am not the same because of it, so they are cutting out. Now he wants to fight me."

Paul gasped, "What? But, he is a heavyweight."

Thad starts again, "He can get down if he wants to, and if he does it right, he will be incredible."

Paul jumped back in over top of Thaddeus, "Yeah, but you will beat him. You have mentored him and you are the best fighter at your weight."

"Paul, I don't know. I think I am done. I am hurt and broken. I took joy in seeing Billy succeed. He also made me better, and to tell you the truth, we fought in the gym, but most clubs won't have their two signature fighters strike each other much. We bent the rules because we wanted to fight against the best, but we didn't really try to permanently hurt each other. (Pause) Until today, that is."

Paul cut in, "But you have fought him, and could fight him, right?"

Thaddeus jumped back in, "I don't have the same drive to fight now. I lost my friend who made it easier. We were working together, I was making him better, and he was making me better. Even now I hurt, but I don't have the same anger. Maybe Larry and Rex are right, I am losing my edge. I don't want to hurt him, I feel bad for him."

Paul sat there puzzled for a second. Thaddeus looked at Paul and said, "What?"

"I was just thinking about how most of my pastoral conversations are similar to something I have heard before, but I have no reference for counseling a spoiled, rich, cage fighter." Thad laughed. Paul continued, "So let me put my ex-wrestler hat on. You are not the same fighter that I met at first. When you were young, you were exciting because you were always ready to snap. You were raw power and speed. You are still technically good, but you might not be as fast or as strong as you were a few years ago."

"Thanks, Pastor, I really need this pick-me-up today. Is this going somewhere?"

"No, Thad, listen. As far as your mat intelligence and your ability to know your opponent and adapt to your opponent, that is what makes you a better fighter than when you were younger."

Thad jumped back in, "But, I was a killer, a gorilla, when I was younger."

"Maybe, but your signature wins came as a result of your ability to think under that anger and duress and come out with wins, knockouts."

Thad jumped in, "But, what do I do if I don't want to fight Billy, or even fight anymore?"

Paul slowed down how he was talking, "Then, very simply, you must quit. You must retire if you don't have anything left, or you can't train to fight Billy, or if there is something keeping you away from fighting. But if you know deep down that you will not be able to take it, then you can't quit. You will know that you left something on the table. Then you know you have to fight. Most people quit and have regrets, they have something left. But you are not most people. If God wants you to quit, He will give you peace about that. He will give you peace."

Thad was finally starting to crack a smile. Thad said, "So, is this the pastor hat now?"

Paul joked, saying, "I don't know who I am."

Thad then says, "Me neither."

Paul got serious again, "Only a joke, Thaddeus. I am a child of God and so are you. Your identity is not a fighter or any of these things. This is what you do, but God loves you no matter what." Thaddeus still looked horrible on the outside, but here they were seeing something happen to him on the inside.

Sally came and sat down at the table. She seemed to have a knack for the awkward. Sally said, "I am not here to pick on you, but I just want you to know that this little part of town is really proud of you. Every time you come in here, people out there marvel at what you can do. But they respect you because of who you are as well. You are not mean to them. You hang out here and are willing to know them. I just wanted to tell you that."

"Thanks, Sally (he smiled); that means a lot. I sure don't come here for the service."

"Ha! Ha! I will be back with your food in a second." She left the table.

Paul looked at Thaddeus and laughed a little.

"What?"

Paul just shook his head, he added, "I knew she could cheer you up." They ate and had some relatively normal conversation after that.

The next morning Rex got a call at GITR from Charlie Pigeon. "Charlie."

"Hey, Rex. I want to talk with you."

"Ok."

"Bad news. Freaky Freddy is dealing with a shoulder injury. He may need some surgery. We are going to cancel the fight."

Rex said, "Ok. Well, Thaddeus still needs to have a title defense in that six-month period, we are down to four months. What do we do now? Do you have another plan?"

"I do, actually. I just spoke with your former associate and I am really sorry to hear about what happened between you and Larry and Billy." Rex was caught way off guard and got a nervous feeling in his stomach and a tingle in his throat; he paused. Charlie continued, "You know, though, for me this is about business, and at the end of the day I feel bad about this division you are having, but you do have a challenger. That challenger is Billy."

"What? He hasn't fought at Thaddeus's weight class. He has to get his weight down in this four-month period."

Charlie spoke up. "They said the weight will not be an issue. He is young, and fighting closer together is how he wants to do it. They feel you will need more time to prepare for them than vice versa."

"Wow, Charlie, this just came to me yesterday, we had a big blow-up here yesterday, we didn't know about any of this. When did they talk to you about this?"

"They met with me a day or two after Billy's title fight. I also met with them again last week in their new facility. They had the equipment set up and the offices moved into. It looks nice."

"Last week? What?"

Charlie, wanting to move on, commented, "I am excited about this fight. Sorry you're finding out this way. I am not good at feelings and stuff, though. Give me a yes or no after you talk to Thad. You might not want to, but this will be Thad's and your biggest payday by far. If he is destined to lose, this could be better going out against someone like this. If he wins, the discussion of his legacy as a fighter is completely solidified. Because The Kid is good."

"Charlie, I know he is good, I helped to train him."

"That's right! The marketing on this will be through the roof. Let me know today, if you can."

"Charlie, how come you didn't tell me? This is a real snake move."

"Rex, you know this is just business. Let me know today, Rex. Let's make beautiful music together. Got to go, bye."

Just as Rex hung up the phone, Thaddeus came into the gym. He started walking towards Rex's office. Rex was still startled by the conversation he'd had with that devil, Charlie Pigeon. Thaddeus walked in the door and sat down on the couch that was in front of the TV used to watch film on opponents. He walked in and looked at the floor and sat down. Rex turned his chair around. He wasn't sure where to begin. So he went with, "You sleep well?"

Thad's reply was weird for a fighter who went through what he had gone through yesterday. "Yes, actually. Oddly enough, I did."

"How? I barely slept at all. I think I am going to sleep on that couch today."

"I went to eat with Paul last night. I had a long talk with him; I think it's time for me to retire."

Rex was stunned. All he could blurt out was, "What? W-w-what?"

Thad said, "I think you are right. I have had a great career and it is important to know when it is over. Maybe it is time to do something else. I don't know that I can get ready for this next fight."

Rex was having a lot of emotions over this that he didn't understand. He knew that if Thad fought Billy they could win, show them, show the world, and get paid more money than he had ever dreamed of. He started with, "You don't have to get ready for Freaky Freddy. He called the fight off, he needs shoulder surgery."

Thad's response was, "That is too bad. I will call him this week and tell him I am retiring and wish him luck."

Rex jumped in, "What is that? Why are you concerned with him? You lost a friend yesterday! Our club lost a fighter. I lost a friend! This sucks!"

Thad jumped back in, "Yes, it does, but what am I supposed to say?"

Rex paused, "I have something."

"What?"

"Here it is. Charlie also told me that he wants you to be on the same title defense timeline. There is a fighter who could be ready in four months."

"Who?"

"Billy!"

Thad looked at him with eyes of pain, "No!"

"But Thaddeus, listen to me. I wouldn't accept this if I didn't know you could win. They are tearing our business apart, they hurt you."

"Revenge isn't a good reason."

"What are you talking about, Thaddeus? Where did you go? When I found you, you wanted to prove it to everyone. There is a guy and his trainer out there who beat up the best fighter on planet earth behind closed doors. They spit on everything we built together. They want to discredit us and kill GITR. They are going to try to embarrass us, and all you can say is it isn't a good reason to fight! What kind of reason do you need? You are Thaddeus Class! So Jesus has finally got you! Pastor Adkins has finally told you that fighting is evil!"

"Rex! Paul was a competitive college wrestler!"

"Thad. don't give me that. You got beat up and blindsided here, and your pastor friend convinced you not to fight, you even said so!"

The screaming was now getting louder. "No, Rex, that is not what happened! We talked about reasons and why to fight versus why not to fight. He never told me what to do. You don't want me to get in the Octagon if my heart isn't in it, do you? Look around. Where are my workout partners? Where is Slippery Pete and where is Latimore?"

"They called, they decided to go with Larry and Billy."

Thaddeus shook his head. "Look, Rex, I am going to work out, I am going to lift and run. Can I just work alone today?"

Rex got serious for a moment. "Three things. One, I just want you to know I believe in you and nothing is going to change that. Two, we are family and I know that I have a lot of things going on in my mind over this. I believe you need to fight this one. I believe it hurts your legacy if you don't, but that is your decision. Yes, it matters that you will make double the last fight and set you up to make more again the next time, but it can't be about that. Last thing, I want you to get the weight workout in but hit the speed bag after a good four-mile run. This is a good day for it since your lifting is light. Have a good workout, Thad. I've got to go anyway, I will see you tomorrow. Think about the fight, will you?"

Thad replied, "Ok," then went to get his workout in.

After leaving the gym, Rex had another idea. There was someone he needed to talk to. He was so mad that it had come to this. He was going to corner him and really tell him what he thought. He had lost all respect for him and couldn't take it anymore. He was sure he would explode. He was tired of people messing with his life. He might just walk in there and beat him half to death in front of everyone; he would see what happened. *That would be quite a story,* he thought. He walked in the church office doors and saw Bernice sitting at her desk. He stomped right by her. She said, "Can I help you?"

Rex yelled, "NO!"

He stomped back through the short hallway and saw Paul sitting at his desk. Rex yelled his thoughts out loud, "What are you doing today, preaching a sermon that will mess up some people's lives?"

Paul, acting cool and unintimidated, tried to calm the situation. "Rex, good to see you, what can I do for you?"

"Cut the garbage, Paul, I am tired of you messing with my fighter's life."

Bernice looked in and said, "Pastor, should I call the police?"

"No, Bernice, I don't think that is necessary, but you'd better ask Rex. Do you think you can bring it down a decibel? We've got a mom's day out thing going on back there."

Rex calmed down and Paul motioned to Bernice and said to shut the door, it was fine. She said, "I sure am glad you can speak their language."

Paul replied with both palms up and extended towards Rex, "My mission field. Rex, I've got a clean mug over here, have you tried this s'mores-flavored coffee from Local Roasters? You like it black, right?"

"Yeah, how did you know?"

"I pay attention."

Rex was noticeably calmed down now and he looked at the table beside a couch that was used for people to sit and meet in Paul's office. There was a picture of Paul after a wrestling match in college. Rex laughed, "You know, I would have trained you. I remember watching you when you were in college. You had potential to be a fighter."

"Why didn't you track me down?"

"Well, that isn't how it works. The way it works is you need to come to me, or show up at one of the events where we are looking for talent coming out of other sports."

"That is encouraging, but those days are over for me. So, Rex, let me know why you are here. You seem mad at me."

"Thaddeus is going to retire. He said he was going to retire because of a conversation you had with him last night."

"Rex, I didn't tell him to retire. Last night he was hurting pretty badly because of what happened. I told him about what it would look like to retire and that he had to be sure. I wanted him to understand that people could perceive his legacy differently, and that he should probably fight this one. But he did mentor Billy. I can understand him not wanting to fight him, but I do know what it is like, Rex, to be a competitive athlete in a hand-to-hand combat-type of situation. It took me years to be able to go watch a fight or a wrestling match. When it was over I didn't want it to be, but it was. Look, Rex, I know what regret looks like on a smaller scale, and I know what fulfillment looks like. I don't think he should quit unless the desire to compete isn't there. That is what I said, and if I told you what he said I would be breaking the rules." Rex was a little taken aback and embarrassed that he got the situation so wrong.

Paul continued, "You should know. I care deeply that Thaddeus is a success. The reason is, he is my friend. Yes, I am helping him, but I have gotten more disciplined in my workouts again. I have decided to take my health more seriously. I am running and lifting and doing those things. Thad motivated me in that direction. He pushes me and inspires me. I want whatever is best for him, and plan to be friends with Thad, whether I serve a church that benefits from his giving or his presence or not. I am not a bad guy. I have people here trying to get him to do certain things at the church and get more involved. It isn't the right time for that now. So, I chase them off. That is my two cents."

Rex sat there, shocked at how wrong he had been about Paul all this time. Maybe he did judge him through the lens of the pastors he knew or had met or seen, but there was something different about this guy. Rex suddenly became more respectful, "Pastor, my club is in disarray. He lost his practice bodies as well, they are going across town to workout with Billy. We have kind of an emergency brewing. Thad needs someone to run drills on. No striking at this point. Would you come in and work out with him in the morning?"

"Ah, Rex, I am not in mat shape."

"So, it is a yes, just come in for an hour at seven a.m. It looks like your office hours start at 9. You can be showered and up here by nine."

"Who would have thought you could come in here ready to kill me and get me to do something for you?"

Rex replied, "Who would have thought that I would be seeing you as the guy who could remotivate my Thaddeus?"

As Rex turned to leave, he looked at the picture again. "I really would have trained you, Pastor."

"Thanks, but I am old now, don't get any ideas."

"I won't."

Paul laughed out loud. "Hey, Rex, can you make up with Bernice on your way out? Try being nice to her next time, ok?"

Rex actually apologized to her on the way out. She immediately walked into Paul's office as they looked out the window while he drove away. She laughed, and Bernice said, "What a weird guy."

"Yeah, sorry about that. Pastoring takes you to some weird places sometimes."

The next day Rex was at the gym in the office, shuffling some papers, waiting for Thad to come in. Thaddeus came into Rex's office. He sat down and said, "Look, Rex, it has been a good run, but I don't think I can do this. I just don't want to fight Billy. I know I can beat him, but this has been a lot. A few days ago I had a good friend who was also a champion. We had another trainer that I thought had my best interest in mind. We lost Latimore and Durkin. I just don't see it."

"Stop, Thaddeus. What am I always telling you?"

"I know, respect the process. But look, Rex, maybe it is over. He nearly beat me to death the other day. You even think I am not as good as I once was. I don't want to hurt him; I feel bad for him. I feel bad that we were friends not long ago. I'm just not in a fighting mindset."

To Thaddeus's surprise, Rex remained calm in his response. "Look, I think we can both agree that this was a traumatic experience. Let's hang in there for a minute. You love to work out, don't you?" He smiled and continued, "Look, he ain't Billy, but I found you a workout partner for this morning. I might have convinced him to stick around here. You need to get in there and drill with him though, he has some office hours he needs to attend to." Rex was noticeably entertained, feeling like he really had something interesting going on, but couldn't stand it anymore.

When they walked out to the matted area, Paul was out there stretching out. "Your pastor decided that he didn't want to run today, but that he wanted to be on the mat with you. He isn't going to go live."

Paul walked up and said, "Let's go, man, I am going to drill with a world champion today."

Thaddeus was really confused, so he just said what was on his mind. "Ok, first of all, Rex, you have been very clear to both Paul and me that you don't like Paul, and you don't like what he represents. Second of all, Paul, you have been working out, but you told me you left this life behind."

"Oh, I did, and I am sure I might regret this, so no live goes right now, and you've got me as a wrestling partner; I am not going to punch and kick with you. By the way, Rex, Bernice asked me to tell you to make an appointment next time."

Rex looked at Thaddeus and scratched the back of his head, "Yeah I kind of barged into Paul's office and told him what I thought about him. It turns out he thinks you should fight this fight, too. Maybe he isn't as bad as I thought. You were right."

Thad smiled a little, "I was what? Wow! When do you ever say I was right?"

Paul jumped in, "Now, Rex, it has to be something he wants, but I do think it could be the fight of his career — and not fighting it could damage how people see what he built."

Thad looked at the ground, "Paul, I told you, I don't know."

Rex, sensing it was time to move on, said, "We are going

to do the mat drills for an hour, then you will go into your lifting and running workouts for the rest of the morning. But let's get going so Pastor Adkins can get up to the church. You don't have to make a decision today."

Paul was in excellent physical condition. He was a little awkward in his own moves, but they were slowly coming back to him. He never lost how to fall or apply the right amount of resistance in being a good drill partner. Thaddeus and Paul drilled hard for most of the hour. It was a little different for Paul, because the drilling he did as a college wrestler was to try to take someone down and put them on their back. MMA is different in that you are setting up a choke, a submission, or a strike. Somehow, Paul's presence relaxed Thad and he had an incredible workout. He still hadn't committed to fighting Billy. The truth is, he just wasn't feeling it. Rex was lining up workout partners, just in case, but wasn't sure what was going to happen yet, either. After some intense lifting and running he felt good about the body of work he put in for the morning. According to his schedule, he needed to come back and put some mat work in in the afternoon. He knew Rex was scrambling to find workout partners. There were some college wrestler types that he liked to bring in, but they were not the caliber of Thad. He also had some local boxers that he liked to bring in, to keep him sharp, who were better boxers than Thad. That is what would probably be helpful today.

Thad showered, changed, and grabbed his book. He was going to go eat breakfast by himself at Cornerstone. He kind of walked in and went to the back where he normally sat. Sally walked up to him and told him his order. He got his cup of coffee; he was now reading *Treasure Island*. "Interesting choice, Thad, you going looking for treasure?"

"No, Sally, I am just trying to read something that makes my problems go away." Thad's response was a little more serious than she was used to. "Sorry, Sally, I guess I am going through a little bit of stuff right now."

Sally looked at him and said, "It's all right. You don't need to impress me. Judging by those sweatpants, I don't think you are trying anymore anyway." He laughed. "Let me get your order." She turned and went to get him another cup of coffee.

Thad immersed himself in his book. He was utterly captivated with Black Beard and buried treasure. He enjoyed the story, even though he knew the mutiny was coming. It seemed a lot like his own story. He didn't know how to completely escape the sadness he felt, but he escaped it a little as he read. Sally didn't come back much; she was busy, and what Thad needed was very predictable. His diet would change a little if he fought, but for now she knew the drill. *The man is consistent. I will give him that,* she thought.

Just then on a sports talk show that was on that typically talked about the NFL or the NBA or some other mainstream sport, they went to a live feed. It was the new facility of the fight club, New Horizon. Thad looked up, and it was just across town. It was Larry, talking to the camera and Billy was there. So was that rat, Charlie Pigeon. There was an announcement being made with lots of press there. Larry stood at the podium. Larry shuffled some papers and began, "Ok, time for the announcement. For those of you who do not know me, I am Larry Rossi. I am the founder and head trainer of New Horizon and the head trainer of World HWT Champion Billy "The Kid" Smith. We were part of GITR and trained alongside club owner and trainer Rex Metzger, and the great world champion, Thaddeus Class. We are grateful for our years there, but through much pain and contemplation we have decided to cut ties with GITR.

"This decision wasn't easy, but was necessary for two reasons. Number one, much of what went on at GITR was centered around their legendary champion, Thaddeus Class. Since there were now two champions fighting out of GITR, Billy and I both needed something different. The second reason is they have something we want. We believe Billy is the future of this sport and he wants to challenge for the Light HWT Title. Currently, we sent an offer to GITR about the possibility of a fight. Because Billy doesn't have any fights in Thad's weight class, it is Thad's option to make him fight someone else in this weight class before him, pushing his defense to Billy back. This offer included a money pot double the size of his last fight, and an opportunity to be a double champion, being the HWT champion as well. I ask you, why would we not get a response? The answer is simple. Billy has surpassed the champion, he is now the superior athlete between the two, which was part of the tension we experienced. If the fans do not get to see this fight, it will be tragic. But just so everyone knows, if I were Thaddeus I wouldn't want to fight Billy either. Thank you all for coming today." He walked off and ducked back into an office.

Some people in the restaurant caught the story but they were not about to ask him about it. There was only one person who would dare ask him. And here she came. Sally sat down. "You and I both know that wasn't true. What is really going on?"

Thad was a little emotional, "I don't know. I guess I saw his and my friendship differently. I wanted the best for him. I was happy about him winning the title. I intended on helping him along for the rest of my career. I have a hard time seeing myself fighting him."

Sally was confused, "But I have seen you come in here, sometimes he had a black eye or you were limping around. This is what you do. You have probably fought him more than about anyone else, right?"

"I guess, but that desire to hurt him, or embarrass him, is not there."

"What does your pastor say?"

Thad laughed, "Rex has him working out with me some."

Sally covered her mouth so she wouldn't spit, "I'm sorry."

"I know it is weird, but he was a good wrestler in his time."

Sally came back to the point. "So he thinks you should?"

"Yes."

"Don't mistake grieving and hurt feelings with your desire to still do what you do. Fighting will end for you one day, but not yet. You still have it. You're grieving, I get it. Work past it."

"Perfect. Since we are working past things you will eat dinner with me tonight then, won't you, Sally?"

Sally paused, "It seems that you got me there. It isn't a date, though."

Thad snapped back, "That is fine, you can dress up; I will stick with the sweat pants. Where can I pick you up at 7?"

She gave him her number to text. He paid and was off to the gym for round two. But first he needed to see Paul.

He walked into Paul's office and said, "Hey, how do you feel?"

Paul looked up, "Good. I can't believe I worked out a world champion this morning. Me, an old pastor. Ha! ha!"

Thad got serious for a second, "Look, I just need you to help me with something. Larry and Billy just blasted me in a press conference. I am down about all this. You are not into revenge and you always say it isn't a good reason to do something. I don't want revenge. But I hurt over this. I think this is the challenge I need. I know I can beat him, but it will be tougher than any fight I have had. He also has been scouting me for years."

Paul looked at him and said, "I know you, and you aren't worried about your legacy as much as if you didn't fight him and see. Now that that is off the table, let's look at something else. Will you be able to deal with their smugness and the prideful way they are going about this? Maybe you still have a lesson to teach them. I know Billy, through you. I want what is best for him, but what is good for you is you taking down your greatest challenger. What is good for him is to lose to you. Maybe while they are calling you soft and considering you naïve for how you approach your life, maybe they need to see faith in action. Maybe Rex needs to see something different. Maybe little people like me need to be inspired."

Thad jumped in, "Will you assist in my corner? I need you to give me spiritual insight. I want to keep the main thing the main thing. I need you to keep working out with me. I will save my live go's for some others, but I want those partners to come in fresh. But my drilling partner will have to help me change my whole style. They have film on all my fights and even my practices fighting Billy. It was all conveniently kept on Larry's laptop. They know me inside and out. Larry and Billy have been scouting me for years. It was just annoying at first, now it is really messed up. This is going to be the hardest thing I have ever done in my career. I need you Paul."

Paul said, "Make sure Rex is good with it."

"He is."

Paul smiled, "I'm in. But you do know if I ever take you down I will tell everyone."

Thaddeus looked at him with a renewed look in his eye. He found the why, and was now working on the how and the what. He smacked Paul's chest beside his tie. Bernice came back and said, "Is this another one of those weird situations?"

Paul, "Um, yeah!"

As Thaddeus was leaving, Paul told Bernice, "Bernice, I told you I live a strange life."

Paul immediately called Ella to tell her.

CHAPTER 7

COUNTING THE COST

THADDEUS DROVE OVER to the gym. He walked in and caught Rex watching some younger fighters. He looked him in the eye and said, "Hey, we have a fight in about three and a half months, don't we?"

Rex said, "Yes, we do! Let's sign the paperwork so that jerk Charlie and Larry don't start more trouble with the media."

As they walked to the office, Thad began to tell Rex what he thought they needed to do. "I want to change how I fight. I want to spend an extra three hours a week on the mat this time, just drilling. I want to change and fight left-handed to start. I also want to develop some left-handed throws like Gomez (a fighter who gave him fits in their fight). The plan will be to be able to switch back to the old me at some point and throughout the fight, but not until he is tired. I want him to be surprised. He has been scouting me for years. I am going to out-condition him, but most of all outsmart him. This fight is going to be fought in my head."

Rex was excited and hopeful. "Let's get started!"

They walked into the office and pulled up the film on Billy. It was odd to scout Billy, but it was time to teach this kid a lesson. They watched as Billy would start out swinging and then back off. His aggression was in short bursts. He had also become very good at knowing his opponent, so they knew some of the film would not be helpful because he could adapt so well. They also knew they were preparing for a much quicker Billy. They knew Billy would be slim and lightning fast. They projected he would be both much quicker and still stronger than Thaddeus when they fought. Smith was young, naïve, and coming off winning the HWT title. He had momentum. At the same time, Thaddeus and Rex had battled with whether Thaddeus was on his way back down the mountain.

When you scout a fighter, you need to look for tells. That is what Thaddeus and Rex were doing with the film. Before they strike or shoot in on a leg, do they have any habits? Do they have a favorite setup? Do they leave themselves vulnerable in some way? Rex and Thad learned a lot more about scouting from Larry. Larry really knew how to scout, which was the scariest thing of all. Larry worked hard on helping Billy close the gap on Thad while he was there. Larry and Billy would watch practice film of Billy and Thaddeus off of Larry's laptop. As Thad and Rex watched one of Billy's fights, they remembered just how much footage Larry had to work with. He had hours of practices recorded on his laptop. It made them both sick.

Rex said, "To win we need to become a whole new fighter."

"No, Rex, we need to become a whole new fighter for half of the fight. We can show sparks of the old me, but the setups have to be new. We need to study film of me and scout me as much as we scout him. We need to anticipate what he will have up his sleeve. We know how Larry thinks. We can do this."

Across town, only a few miles away towards the southern tip of Manhattan, Larry and Billy were extremely motivated. They knew how Class and Metzger thought, and had no doubt they would say yes. They knew the fight would happen. Thad had never backed down, and Billy especially knew Thad cared about his legacy and integrity in fighting. He knew Thad would rather lose than have his integrity as a fighter and his legitimacy as a champion called into question. Larry and Billy watched a little practice footage on Thad. They couldn't wait to get at it. They felt free. Everyone was there — Smokin' Joe and Slippery Pete were ready and working hard in the weight room. Billy was now working for power as he was coming down in weight. He wanted to have strength and muscular endurance and try to burn fat. He wasn't lifting for raw power anymore, it was for match strength. A championship fight is five rounds of five minutes. There is one minute between each round. Your shoulders have to still be strong to punch. Your legs and back must be strong in the end to lift. A fighter's biceps must be strong if you get an opportunity for a choke-out or submission. You must be strong at the end, just like at the beginning of the fight.

With this in mind, with his workout partners in his face, they screamed. Everyone was there just like always, but no Thad or Rex. This bothered Billy a little, but when he thought about beating the best fighter ever, it was easy to forget. In his mind there was the idea of *Thaddeus, the one I must defeat,* and the Thad who was his friend and mentor. It was somehow separated out, which gave him some peace. He seemed to reason that Thaddeus would do the same in his position. Thad always spoke of how hard it was to stay on top and that there was always someone coming through the ranks, you always had to be ready for all challengers. Sadly for Thad, he really didn't see this one coming and he poured a lot into helping Billy. It turned out to be a very big risk.

Billy didn't see the world quite like Larry did, but he knew that life wasn't so black and white either. Larry didn't seem to care much about who he hurt or how he got there, he just knew he wanted to be there. Billy was getting there. For Smith, it was hard to be young and a new champion and know that you could beat the one who had never lost. Billy wasn't going to be in his shadow anymore. When he entertained a thought like this in a workout, he would have a surge of power or energy.

With all of this running through his mind, Billy trained like never before. In three and a half short months, the fight of his life was about to happen. He liked Thad and maybe even felt a strong sort of brotherly respect for him. After all, what he did for him was priceless, but it was his time now. Thad had had his time. He had gotten more than he deserved. After all, Billy helped him get there. Thaddeus Class even said so. As he had that thought, Larry screamed it, "IT IS YOUR TIME NOW! YOU'RE THE CHAMP! YOU'RE THE BEST IN THE WORLD!" He curled dumbbells to failure doing ten hard reps, not perfect kind, but match-situation kind. He arched his back and cheated his butt off to get the dumbbells up. Intensity was the key. Larry screamed, "FASTER!" The dumbbells dropped to the ground. "Who is the champ?"

"I AM %#*@()&%*#)&%#@*," the giant man screamed, as he picked up a set of dumbbells five pounds smaller apiece. He did the same type of set, screaming all the louder. He dropped those after ten and picked up an even smaller set. Larry said, "GET TEN AGAIN!" He hit 13 reps on each arm, and dropped the weights and roared in Latimore's face. The onlookers inside the gym thought they were glad they were not going to step into the Octagon with him next. He looked in the mirror with fury, looking more cut up and physically strong than he did as a heavyweight. The weight was coming off and he was getting stronger. People around there like "Slippery" Pete Durkin and "Smokin'" Joe Latimore were starting to think it would be a bad day for Thaddeus Class. The truth was, they were all a little jealous and were all looking for something of their own. Larry compensated them and promised them a lot. The truth of it all is the fight world is a dirty business.

In Billy's mind he was about to prove to everyone that he was the greatest. The intensity of those workouts was increasing. He noticed that without Rex and Thaddeus running the show, their workouts were even more passionate and unhindered. There was nothing that held them back. Without the faith talks during and after with Thaddeus, there was a much more animalistic, raw, or unhinged feel to the place. There was more cursing, more anger, more fights among workout partners. It was raw, semi-caged fury, and Larry Rossi liked it that way as he trained his animal. His animal was about to prove that he was the greatest beast of all time. Maybe Larry would finally get the credit he deserved, too. He comforted himself with the idea that *Thaddeus is getting too old and is way too nice to train like this!*

Across town, Thaddeus showed up at Sally's apartment. She answered the door wearing a beautiful casual dress that was never worn before. It was shiny; it screamed casual yet was simple and beautiful. She answered the door with a smile and said, "Hello, Thaddeus."

Thad smiled, "Hello, Sally. Wow, you look great!"

Sally replied with, "You like?"

Thaddeus found it funny how with Sally the sarcasm never ended. Thaddeus had made some reservations at Moedoe's, a really nice place that Sally had not dared to try.

He said, "Well, I thought we would go to Moedoe's for 7:30."

"Ooh, good call on the Moedoe's," She jumped in. "But not the movies. I like going to movies and you and I can go to the movies another night, let's just sit in the park or something and talk. I can't talk to you in the movie."

Thad saw the opportunity to seize a quick burn. "Wow, Sally, I think you just agreed to another date without me even asking you. You might be falling for Thaddeus, huh?"

"Yeah, it is important for you to know where you stand, buddy. Back off a little, haha."

Sally was a confident type of awkward, but was also guarded. She didn't want to get hurt again and she really wasn't very quick to say yes, even to Thaddeus's advances.

They went to dinner. Their reservations got them right in. They were seated in a more secluded spot in the restaurant. Thaddeus tipped the hostess and instructed her not to give his location to anyone. The hostess spoke about how she was a fight fan and that her ex-boyfriend got her into it. Thad took a quick selfie with her; she was elated.

Sally looked at him, "This is the type of thing I worry about. This type of attention is hard for me."

"Maybe a little for me, too. But my trainer always promises me it won't last forever. There will be another fighter that will come along and replace me in their minds and hearts locally."

She smiled, because she thought her next words would

be funny, "Yeah, aren't you going to fight him? Billy is my favorite fighter."

Thad actually teared up a little and just said, "Yeah, a lot of people like him."

Sally again felt awkward, "I am sorry; I was just joking around. That situation with you and him is not something to joke about, I realize that."

Thaddeus laughed, "Ah, it is ok. We were close once, but love 'em and leave 'em. That is what I always say."

Sally laughed, knowing he was joking. "I personally don't understand how Billy can't be happy just being the HWT Champ. He got a lot of attention and notoriety just from that."

"Yeah, he wants more. All of us fighters always want more. It is kind of like a sickness. I understand it. But I am not really like that anymore. That is why I have wrestled with giving it up at times."

"Gasp!" Sally said sarcastically. "But who is Thaddeus Class if he is not knocking someone out?"

Thaddeus fired back with, "Just one of God's loudmouthed children, I guess." Sally smiled.

They had a great evening. They walked in the park after their meal. Sally spoke about her first marriage but not her father. She was more relaxed than normal, but not as relaxed as Thaddeus. Thad walked her to her door. Sally felt a little nervous. This was usually the moment that changed things. Thaddeus looked at her and said, "Thank you, Sally, for coming out with me tonight. I hope we can do it again."

Sally smiled and said, "Me too."

"Can I kiss you?" She nodded. So he bent down and kissed her. It was a good kiss and he looked at her and said, "Good night, Sally."

She said, "You know, for a fighter you are not that bad."

"Haha," he walked away. Thad knew he wanted to kiss her again, but didn't want to end up on the other side of the door. God wants you to be committed and Sally deserved that.

Sally shut the door and thought *Wow! That is the first time a man took me out and didn't try to impose his will onto me — and with a fighter. Wow! Now I kind of wish he would have.* Then she caught herself and realized that wasn't right. She was a little surprised in herself that she let herself feel so much for this guy. But then she rambled in her head back and forth, *he isn't going to fight forever, and he is a lawyer, too.* She couldn't calm down. Then she started to think about all of the awkward things she said to him.

The next morning Thaddeus was extra-motivated. He got to the gym early. He was there earlier than Rex. Thad had a key. He went into Rex's office and began to formulate a plan. He watched all the film on Billy that he could. There were many instances where Thad was in the corner or when he shouted instructions, much of it Thaddeus remembered. It hurt to see it again. It seemed that they did have a genuine connection. How is it that they could have this genuine connection, but Larry took him away? He began to look at Larry and hate on him when he was on the screen, but the Holy Spirit spoke to him. "You can't hate them and help them at the same time."

Thad paused the video for a moment when all four of them were on the screen. He knew deep down inside that he had an opportunity to show all of these people, including Rex, something different, even himself. He closed his eyes and thought, "Lord, save these people. Help them to know you. Direct me to follow hard after you and do your will. Amen."

Then he unpaused it. He saw it. Thaddeus had always tried

to help Billy correct this thing. Thad thought, *Surely he will address this, because I tell him all the time, if I were fighting you I would go after your left side when you get really tired.* Billy was great technically, but as a young, quick and powerful fighter he did have some habits that he got away with that were not going to fly against Thaddeus Class.

Larry did a good job of minimizing this tendency to reach with the same arm and the same leg side and stand there flat-footed for a second. Larry addressed it by how he was to stand and work the ties with the fighter he was fighting. That is why Thaddeus Class had to become an entirely different fighter. He must completely change. If he did slip into his old style, he had to do it from the new style. First of all, he needed to be left-handed. He needed to punch with his left. He needed to change his lead foot. He needed his quick jabs to be left-handed. He needed his grappling shots to be left-handed. This would especially shock him, because he was a huge proponent of not needing to grapple both sides the same. In other words, shoot one type of shot on one leg and another on the other, but shoot with the same arm and leg, because it was too hard to learn to do it another way. Was he really going to try to do this in three short months? It seemed that the only way to win for Thaddeus was to focus on being the smartest and most technical fighter.

He also wanted to sharpen his Jiu Jitsu. He wanted to be able to roll and grapple into positions to set up submission opportunities from his left-handed grappling. He also looked at some kickboxing opportunities. The more different he became, it could slow Billy down. When Billy became tired and was gasping for air, he would reach and make this mistake.

Just then Rex and Paul came in, surprisingly getting along.

Paul walked into the office to say hello to Thaddeus. Thad had already been there for almost two hours. Paul quickly went and got changed. Thad showed Rex, "This is what I am thinking. We need to build our entire attack off the fact that he will make this mistake."

"Oh, Thad, let's be real. You know Larry will have him coached to feed off of your attack to keep him away from that."

"Exactly, Rex, that is why I am becoming a completely different fighter. I am not going to chance it. You see, he will resort to those bad habits if I surprise him."

Rex chimed in, "Ok, but you have three months. How much different are you going to be able to be?"

"But, Rex, that is the formula. I am smart enough and good enough to change."

"Ok, Thaddeus," Rex kind of spoke slowly like a father speaking to a child. "If anyone can do this, it is you. But I don't know that we can change everything. You are talking about going entirely left-handed. You want more mat work."

"Don't forget boxing and kickboxing, too."

"When do you go back to the stuff you are good at?"

"The last round,"

"But you have to have your old stuff sharp, too."

"He needs to be surprised every round."

"No one goes the distance with you. This is the problem with this plan. You are not the younger, stronger, faster or more athletic fighter anymore."

Thad jumped in, "No, I am the smarter one. Trust me, he will not know what hit him. I have actually told him how unnecessary it was to make changes like this and learn how to do things left-handed that you normally do right-handed. He will not know what to do with it."

"Ok, Thad, this is what will happen. Larry will adjust. You must go out and win the first two rounds. He may win the next two, and when he is tired, because you have to be in superior shape, you beat him in the last round. You are both champs so you can't rely on getting the decision based on that. Ah, Wow!" Rex shook his head and scratched the back of it.

Thaddeus looked at him, "Rex, do you believe I can do it?"

"Thad, you know I do, but this isn't going to be easy. We need to have some great people in here for some live goes. Billy is the second-best fighter I have ever helped to train. If anyone else was fighting him I would say no, but you can do it. But this will be hard. If we start down this road, there is no plan B."

"Rex, we have never had a plan B."

"We have never needed one, Thaddeus!"

Thad smiled at Rex and said, "Exactly!"

Thaddeus had a renewed sense of confidence. It was because Rex believed in him, Sally was willing to date him, Paul was there helping him. It was truly something to be seen. He was also very focused, but life wasn't all about fighting. It had future, hope, and joy. He had the right people around him and in his life. He had community.

Paul walked out to the matted area. He warmed up and stretched and started drilling. Thad was now at five takedowns practiced to Paul's two. Thaddeus was now doing everything from the opposite side. He seemed awkward, but he did the same single leg takedown over and over again. It was the only move he drilled for the entire time. Oddly enough, it was the very move he swore to Billy he would never learn to the other side, because he had another shot to that leg that only required the same step and the same arm to reach for it. This seemed like the perfect place to start.

Paul enjoyed being a part of this. He had never gotten to help train a fighter like this before. Paul hadn't been around a lot of guys like Thad that were so tedious about drilling one move over and over again. By the end of the hour, Thaddeus appeared to be able to do this move in one fluid motion when the opportunity came up. After the workout, Thaddeus focused on jumping rope and some agility type things.

The other thing that happened was Paul began to do for Thaddeus what Thad had been doing for Billy. After workouts or when they would eat lunch, Paul would continue to tell Thaddeus about God's glory, and that it was important to let go and realize this is not the most important thing in the world. Jesus is, and your witness is the most important thing. Your larger purpose carries you through.

In Thad's mind this was going to be a strange fight because he was becoming a different fighter. If it went badly in the first two rounds, there truly was no turning back. The reason was he couldn't give Billy confidence by trying something new and failing, then trying to go back to the old style. Because Billy would think, "Thaddeus knew he couldn't beat me with how he normally fights. He tried something else, now I will destroy him fighting like he always does." Those first two rounds needed to be filled with a lot of smoke and mirrors. Billy and Larry both knew Thad's tells, they knew his moves, his counters, his stances. He needed to come up with new setups, strikes, and kicks. He needed to become a better scrambler. The Jiu Jitsu guys coming that afternoon would help with that. He truly was going to war, but peace was coming over him. The scene had been set and they all knew that judgment day (Fight Night) was coming. He planned on being prepared beyond what anyone could realize. Thaddeus was starting to believe it was going to be the fight of his life.

One morning Rex overheard one of their faith conversations and decided to push back on the reverend. It was time for Thaddeus to move on to some lifting, and this allowed them to talk alone. Thad had learned over the years that talking religion with Rex was a very difficult thing to do. It was emotional, and it didn't seem to go anywhere. It was like getting into the Octagon with a really tough opponent, only Thaddeus never felt like he won.

When Thaddeus walked away, Rex said to Paul, "I like you. I am not a Jesus fan, but I like you. I like that you bring Thad's spirits up. He is more than a fighter to me. I have been kind of a father figure for him through some rough stuff, so his faith has made him better. But don't be telling him that Jesus is more important than this fight."

Why not?"

"Because great people minimize distractions. They minimize superstitious thoughts and behavior. This is a big stage. Listen to great athletes and they will tell you how focused on the goal they were and will not mention beliefs or faith or any of that."

Paul again, still asking questions, "Says who?"

"Says the guy he is fighting, the trainer I am competing against. They sat in here and learned how I train Thad. They learned him. They studied hours of film on him for practice. Then when they left they took all that with them. They are obsessed, and that is what we need to be. Look, Pastor, faith is something I tried once and I lost everything. It is ok that he believes it, and I have even come to like you, but Jesus wasn't there for me, I learned the hard way I was on my own."

Paul took a chance, as Rex was now close to Paul and looking at him straight in the eye. "Rex, I know about your daughter. I know about your wife. I know about your pain."

Rex chimed in, "That is just it, Paul. You don't know anything. You don't know me or what I have been through. My little Maggie looked at Pastor Rick as he prayed and said in front of the whole church, 'My Jesus can do anything.' My marriage fell apart. It killed the only woman I ever loved. God took my baby away. Did you know also that another child in our church got healed at the same time? The people in our church didn't know how to be there for us. God was silent. I used to think He might even talk to me or direct me. My faith died with Maggie, and it was buried with Mary."

Paul looked at him and said, "Rex, I am so sorry."

"You see, Paul, that is just it. You can't do anything or say anything that will make me want God, church, or any of it anymore."

Paul looked at him and said, "You are right."

Rex stood up straight and felt justified. "Not the response I was looking for, but ok. I can't believe that you just admitted you're powerless against my faithlessness."

Paul smirked, "I only agreed with your assessment that I can't make you want God or church as a part of your life. I can't make you believe. It is God's job, and it is your job to respond when He calls you. Rex, much of what comes out of your mouth on the subject isn't that God doesn't exist; it is that He isn't and wasn't there for you."

Rex added, "At my lowest moment!"

Paul came back quickly, "Yeah, that is what I am talking about. You are talking about someone who wasn't there but had the power to be there. That isn't faithlessness, that is distrust. After all, how can you be mad at someone who doesn't exist?"

"You're right, I don't not believe, I just hate Him. I hate the Son of God for killing my family, destroying me, and now He is taking my fighter. God hates me! So I hate Him! There isn't any faking it with someone who knows everything, is there?"

"Wow! I knew it was a good day. I found out the great Rex Metzger really does have faith!"

Paul had a way of knowing how to close a conversation out and rebuild any walls that were broken. Paul looked at Rex and said, "I've got to go to the office. I will see you tomorrow morning."

Rex laughed a little, "See you, Pastor."

As the day went on this interaction bothered Rex. He didn't understand how Paul could be so right and he didn't realize it all this time. Rex was angry at God. He believed in Him and he reflected back on a sermon years ago he heard before Maggie was sick. Everything was right. He sat there with Mary and Maggie in church, and Rick spoke about Ecclesiastes 3:11. Pastor Rick kept referring to eternity being placed in the heart of man. There is something in us longing for something more than what we have. God is here somewhere. We know life isn't over. He also referenced the Psalms when speaking about creation revealing the glory of God.

At the time he thought about how evolutionary scientists or weather experts who observe climates or seasons, who know we are exactly the distance from the sun we need to be, and how people can look at all these things so closely and not believe. He thought about how he had allowed himself to sit and believe the lies. He believed the lies he told himself. Now he must be honest, he believed in God. He even believed in God because of what he had seen and heard, but Jesus — Rex would not follow Jesus because he hated Jesus and Jesus hated him, too.

CHAPTER 8

CHANGE

BACK IN CURLSVILLE, Debra came up on a stop light and without even realizing it, drove right through it while it was red. She didn't even slow down. It was like she was somewhere else. The driver of the car she hit survived and walked away. Debra was out cold. They called the police right away and took Debra to the local ER. Debra suffered from some head trauma and wasn't making much sense to the other driver or the police when they showed up. The officer was Benny Jergan. Benny was an experienced officer who knew Debra well. He was a regular at the restaurant.

Rex answered the phone and heard that Debra had been in an accident, that she was in ICU and unconscious. Thad had just gotten showered and dressed. Rex saw Thaddeus walking out of the locker room area and past the weight machines down the hall. He could see he was about to leave.

He said, "Thad?" The way it was said gave away that something was wrong. Thaddeus looked up at Rex. Rex just blurted out, "Your mom was in an accident a block from the diner. She is in ICU at County Regional Hospital."

"ICU!? What?"

"Thad, she is unconscious. She was a awake a little after the accident, but now she is out. They are examining her head. She hit her head. Come on. I will drive you there."

It was a long drive. What was normally 45 minutes without traffic became one hour and 15 easily, with traffic. It felt like forever for Thad. Something about it brought everything back to that day when he was just eight years old, and the hate he had for that drunk driver. *He took our family away. How could he have done that?* They walked into the ICU and were directed to her room.

Thad saw Benny. They both briefly greeted Benny and went in to Debra, who was conscious now. She looked somewhat normal. It had been about two hours since the accident. Benny said, "Yeah, it is one of those things. She wasn't making sense at the scene but now she seems to have her wits about her. Good to see you, Champ. I am glad your mom's going to be ok."

Thaddeus looked at Debra who was now awake, "Was something wrong? What happened? Were you texting or something?"

"No, Thaddeus. It was just one of those things. I guess I am getting old, or I have a lot on my mind or something."

"Glad you are ok. It isn't good to lose the most important person in your life to an accident. We have been down this road before."

"Not going anywhere, Thaddeus," Debra perked up. She quickly changed the subject. "So how is that girl you have been telling me about?"

Rex jumped in, "What girl? You need to focus."

"Ah, Rex, you can't control love, man."

"So, it is love now? We've got a fight."

Debra jumped in, "If it makes you feel better, she is pretty tough — like me."

Rex said, "No, that doesn't make me feel any better."

Thaddeus jumped in, "Now that I know you are ok, I will be right back. I need to go to the bathroom. It was a long car ride."

"You can use this one, Thaddeus."

"No, I will use the one down the hall."

"Ok, not a problem."

Thad left Rex and Debra to another awkward moment. Debra said, "So, how is my Thaddeus, do you have him nice and angry towards his old friend? I am sure The Gorilla will be ready to knock his head off. By the way, don't discourage his new girlfriend. I need grandchildren."

"Funny, Debra, not my main concern."

"What do you mean? Don't you watch over those things?"

Rex interjected, "I watch over a lot of things." Rex was extremely irritated with her, even though he knew it was the pain meds making her say what was on her mind — but it didn't make it less offensive that it was on her mind. He had been in her state before, and he knew that she was just being honest. He wasn't sure why he cared what she thought, anyway. He paused, "You know I know, right? Thad doesn't suspect it, but I notice things."

"What things?"

Rex continued, "I notice an awkward family friend, who is the officer, who abruptly leaves without giving much information. I see a woman who has been driving for 50 years running a light she drives through without texting or really being distracted. You didn't make sense at the scene. They were worried about stroke or trauma. The truth is, you were drinking. Now you have had two hours without a drink and you are feeling better."

"What do you know, Rex?"

"I know about love and loss. I also know about addiction, because I need to see it in a fighter or the people around him. I also know it because I lived it. You need help."

"I need help! This coming from the guy who keeps my son so angry. He has more money than he will ever need. You work his insecurities until the last nerve."

"Debra, Thad's dad was killed in an accident by a drunk driver. He would be heartbroken to know this."

Debra said, "Rex, so you think I am not good enough for my son. Are you going to tell him not to come around me?"

"No, I am relieved, though. I thought you were perfect all this time. I am concerned that you think you are enough of the exception that you are willing to become the person who took your love away." At that she began to weep.

Suddenly, Rex felt bad. It is funny how when you see someone crumble whom you perceive to be tough as nails, what that does to you. For Rex, he suddenly had more of a heart for Debra. Maybe he even wanted to help.

At that awkward moment, Barbara came into the room and, at that, Debra got herself together. Thaddeus came walking back in and Rex said, "I think I am going to get some fresh air, take your time Thaddeus. Glad you are ok, Deb."

Debra was hurt by the exchange, but because of herself. In a weird way it was the first time that she thought, *Maybe this guy isn't such a bad guy.*

Barbara said to Debra, "Looking good, Debbie! I like the gown and this place you are staying in, wow!"

"Barb, come on now. You just wait until you need a hospital visit."

"Oh, Debra, we both know you aren't going to come and visit me." Thad kind of hung back.

Just then Dr. Maze came in. "We have a few concerns and we need you to stay overnight."

"I can't, doctor, I need to open the place in the morning. My manager just quit, I can't do it."

"If you have any brain bleeding or swelling, or if you did have a stroke, we need you here for the next 24 hours. So, we are talking about maybe two nights."

"Doc, my manager just quit, there is no one who can take care of the place."

Thad chimed in, "Mom, I know someone who can take care of the place for you, and she is tough as nails."

"Ok, if my Thaddeus trusts her, so do I. Call my head cook, Carlos. He will be there the next two days. Tell him, and make sure Sally can do it."

"Wow, Mom, you even remembered her name."

"Praying for grandchildren here, Thaddeus."

"Funny, Mother." Thad kissed his mom good-bye and would try to call Sally from Rex's car. "Love you, Mom. Try not to be too bossy and let these people take care of you here."

Barbara laughed a little, "Good call, Thaddeus!"

Deb looked at him and smiled, "I will be ok. Love you."

Thaddeus walked outside and got into the car with Rex. He dialed Sally's number and said, "Hey, Sally."

"Uh, Hello? Who is this?"

"Funny."

"Oh, you are that guy I went out with the other night."

Thad snapped back, "Yeah, the name is Pete."

"Whatever, Thad."

"So, I have something very serious to ask you."

"Thad, you are not going to propose to me over the phone are you? You see, this is why you stay single."

"Funny, like I would ever propose to you, but no, I need you to run my mom's restaurant in Curlsville for two days. She was in an accident. Her manager quit and no one is going to be there to run it. There is a cook named Carlos who knows the kitchen, but my mom needs someone to run the place. Are you up for it?"

"Where is your mom?"

"She is in ICU. It was a bad accident, but she is ok. She is awake and making decisions and might be in the hospital for two days. I didn't want her to get out of bed and hurt herself. I am sorry, I realize this is a lot to ask, but I don't have any friends."

"Yeah, why wouldn't I do it? My first chance to run a restaurant and the first impression I will make on my boyfriend's mom is me messing up her dreams and ruining her restaurant, while she is in ICU. Why would I not do this?"

"Ah, you said boyfriend."

Sally snapped back, "Mistake. You never asked me."

"So, you will do it?"

"Yeah, I will, and Thad I am glad your mom is ok. Are you sure she is ok? Is there anything else I can do?"

"Thanks, Sally, this is a big enough job, I will text you Carlos's number and you can work it out with him. I am sure you will need to be there about five a.m."

"Also, Thad, thank you for trusting me with this responsibility. It actually says a lot."

"I told you, Sally. I just don't have any friends. Talk to you later." They both said their goodbyes.

As they got off the phone, Rex chuckled a little. Thaddeus knew that he was going to say something about distractions or not having a girlfriend when it is time to train, or focusing or something along those lines. But he bit anyway.

"What's funny, Rex?"

"Nothing, Thaddeus. I was just thinking about my family days and thinking about how there are more important things in life than fighting."

Thad laughed, waved his hand in front of Rex's eyes as he drove and said, "Where is Rex, what did you do with him? Take me to your leader."

Rex looked at him and said, "You know, seeing your mom in the hospital and me not having great hospital memories, I was thinking. Let's come back in the morning and make sure everything is going ok there. I can meet your girlfriend. We can then come back and double up in the afternoon."

Rex added, "Oh, and bring Paul, too. He can call it a visitation, right?"

At that, Thaddeus had no idea what was going on. It wasn't normal for Rex to all of a sudden give Thad the morning workout off. At that, He just said, "Ok."

The next morning Thaddeus and Paul packed into Rex's red Ferrari. But before they did, Paul nicely broke the ice over Rex's license plate. It said, BEATDWN. "So, is the license plate what you do to someone else, or how you make them feel, or is it how you feel? What exactly do you want me to address today?"

Rex kindly said, "Get in the car. Thad, let Paul get up front."

Paul marveled at the car. It had every upgrade permitted. Some of the interior was specially made for him. This was not something that you see every day. The leather was silky smooth light gray with the GITR logo on the seat. The mirrors above the driver and passenger seats had the GITR logo in the corner. The sound system was incredible. Paul loved it!

Rex looked at him and said, "Kind of sinful to have a car like this, isn't it, Adkins?"

Paul said, "Not anymore, now that you let me ride in it."

"Yeah, Paul we are not there yet, so don't push it. I might let you out early."

As they drove the early morning drive they listened to some music and talked about life. Rex never watched what he said around Paul, or anyone, for that matter, but at least he wasn't trying to annoy him on purpose. He seemed to not be angry towards him anymore — or at least not today.

Paul marveled at the sound system and touched the side of the seat and loved the real leather feel of it. It was incredible just how comfortable this car was. There was a time early on when Paul really wanted to be a Thaddeus Class or someone like that. Money and what the world looks to as success drove him and inspired him a little too much. Now he was mostly past that. Sometimes he thought about what he could have done instead, especially being around Thaddeus. *What a beautiful car,* he thought.

When they got there they walked inside. It was still early, but even on Saturday this was a busy day. Thaddeus walked straight into the kitchen to see Sally. He hit many hands along the way. The long-time employees knew him and yelled things like, "Hey Champ!" Sally walked over to him and said, "Hey, trying to run a kitchen around here!"

"Sorry, Sally, I thought I should come by and let you know I am here and willing to help you. I know you want to make sure my mom thinks positively about you and all."

"Come on, Thad! If you tell her you were helping me, that doesn't make me look good."

"I figured you would say that. I am here with Rex and Paul."

She said, "Wow! You are amazing. How did you get the devil and Jesus to eat breakfast together?"

Thad laughed, "Hah, common project I guess. All right! I will get out of your way." He laughed as he walked out of the kitchen and a very focused Sally turned around and started talking to Carlos and Tina, the ones who knew how things were normally done.

Thad walked into a corner of the restaurant that was secluded because Rex picked it out. It was just a habit when in public with Thaddeus, like he could go unrecognized there, the regulars and the townies knew him so he would not get harassed here like he normally did. Thad sat facing the kitchen, so he could see Sally coming out of the kitchen and working. He tried to engage Rex across from him and Paul beside him, but he was focused on Sally. He thought about how natural it was for her to be in charge here.

These people didn't even know her. They were coming in and asking questions about Debra. Of course, everyone already knew about the accident and they wanted to know if she was ok. This also made the restaurant busier. It was amazing to Thad how she could multi-task and be an amazing PR person with the customers. The restaurant didn't miss a beat. To give credit where credit is due, Tina and Carlos knew how to run everything and she took a lot of cues from them. There were things Sally just didn't know about and they went ahead and did them. There wasn't much sense in trying to teach her anything, since Debra would be back, it was more about survival. But in case there was any doubt, Sally belonged at Mama Class's Kitchen.

One customer saw her talking to Thaddeus, Paul, and Rex, and yelled out, "Watch out, newbie, the champ will tell his mom if you mess up their order."

She yelled back, "This one, he's a puppy!" Something about it made everyone laugh. It really wasn't very funny. Some people call it anointing, or gifting; whatever it is, sometimes people are standing where they belong and you can see it. Sally didn't know the people there. She didn't know who they were, or what their story was. She actually had never run a restaurant before, but she came in that day and owned the room.

Thaddeus was no puppy, but he felt something — it might be love. Rex made a joke about it. "Thad, I tried to tell you not to get distracted, but this one might just keep you in line. She might be the only one tough enough for you."

Paul wanted in on it, too, "Hey, Rex, gotta give the preacher credit for pushing the timid little champ."

Thad jumped in with a smile, "Ok, let's talk about something else."

Longtime waitress Jana took their order. Jana had been a part of the Mama Class system since Debra started it all the way back when Thad was little. Jana, being about retirement age, but a hard-working woman who didn't want to retire, joked with Thad a little. "Hey, Champ, I was thinking. It seems like this Sally girl likes you a little too much. If you want I can slow things down and talk about how I used to change your diapers and what a bratty kid you were."

Paul reached his hand out to shake Jana's, "Hi, Jana, I am his pastor. I need some stories for the pulpit. Do you have more of the bratty, selfish ones?"

She knew Rex already. He chimed in with, "Do you have any stories of shame I can use during a workout? Unfinished business? Something like that."

Thad spoke up, "Ok, Jana, if you stand here long enough Rex will put you on the payroll; that is what happened to Paul."

She laughed it off. Jana said, as a caring elder to Thad who had been there for this family through it all, "Seriously, though, she is a great manager, but she is even better for you. I am sure she will really boss you around."

Rex added, "We can only hope!"

Sally walked over, "I think my ears are burning."

Paul piped up, "Ah, Sally, you know things aren't all about you. Everything is actually about Thad."

Now they were all laughing. Thad, a little red, said, "They are just fascinated that I finally found someone to boss me around."

Sally said, "As long as we are all on the same page."

Rex said to Sally, "Really, though. Great job."

"Thanks, Rex, good to see you in person. I have only seen you on TV and yelling in Thad's corner. If you can work with all this (as she motioned over his head), you are my hero."

He laughed and said, "Nice to meet you. I have only heard good things about you."

She talked with them for a minute and went back to work, but Thad was truly happy that Sally was there, and had come through in such a big way. She was even better at this than he thought she would be. The people loved her. After the meal,

Thaddeus paid for his clan in cash and gave Jana a tip matching the bill — which was all Jana ever allowed him to give her.

Sally approached, looked at Thad and kissed him on the cheek. The locals in the restaurant began joking around. "So that is how you slow down a tough guy."

Thad looked at her and said, "Sorry. They are hard on me around here."

Sally looked at him and, for a change, was serious, "No, thank you," she said softly. At that, Thad and the guys left and went to meet up with Debra at the hospital.

When they pulled up to the hospital they all got out and went in. Several people greeted Thad and Rex on their way into the hospital. One guy looked at Rex and said, "Keep our guy winning, brother. We love our Thaddeus First Class around here."

Paul responded, "First Class? Why didn't you guys ever go with that?"

Rex said, "Because look at him! He doesn't get dressed up for anyone."

They got to Deb's room. She was sitting there, looking a little annoyed. "Mom, what is wrong?"

"Nothing, I am just stuck here thinking. Why am I here when my future daughter-in-law is running my restaurant? She might even mother a grandchild of mine, I don't even know her yet. Jana called me and she can't believe how good she is doing there, and how she harassed you in front of your friends and all the locals."

Paul and Rex laughed a little. Rex tapped Paul on the arm and said, "Hey we love her. She beats him up all the time."

Rex felt comfortable with Paul now. He had finally gotten past some of those barriers, like believing Paul was going to pass a collection plate at some point or something. Thad jumped in, a little serious for the moment, "They are saying you need to stay through tomorrow. I am sure we can get her over here to meet you."

Debra said, "No! She isn't meeting me in the hospital!"

"Ok, ok! Got it! All right, I will bring her by when you are out at the beginning of the week."

So things settled down and Rex began to tell Debra, "I will tell you what: that place runs great with her running it and not you."

"Thanks, Rex. Classic Rex," Debbie said.

They had a quick visit and Paul said, "Debbie, can I pray for you?" She gladly accepted. Paul prayed a great prayer for healing and recovery. Thad kissed her good-bye and they walked out of the room.

They had almost gotten to the car when Rex said, "Oh, I left my jacket on that chair. Here are my keys. Pastor, drive my car. Thad, watch him. I am trying to have something to sue Jesus for," he joked.

Paul looked like a kid at Christmas. "Oh, Rex, you will regret this!" Everyone knew he was joking.

Rex went back up and walked directly into Debra's room. Debbie looked up from the TV and said, "What are you doing back here?"

"Just missed you. I left my coat."

"Oh, you forgot something."

"No, I left it and your son's Pastor is driving my car around the parking lot against my better judgment so that I can speak to you."

"Oh!"

He reached behind a hospital chair off to the side of the

room where he had hidden his coat on the floor. He put his jacket on and reached into the left pocket.

"Your son and Paul even don't realize what happened and I am still not going to tell them. But I am going to do something about it."

"What the $*#()& are you talking about, Rex?"

He handed her a pamphlet introducing her to a group for alcoholics. "I want you to go to this. It is after hours on Sunday. They will help you. It is 30 minutes from you towards the city. It is anonymous enough for you there. No one will know you there."

"People know my son everywhere. You know what it is like. It is like that for me, too."

"The people in this group are good. They have a special commitment to keeping it quiet."

"Rex, this isn't your concern. I will not be any more trouble to Thad. I know you have the big fight coming up. I know you think this is a distraction and how this works for you. Life happens, jerk! He has been the champ all this time, I am not hurting him."

Rex looked at her very seriously. "Thaddeus is not distracted by this. I am. I don't know what it is. Thad is my only family and you are the closest person to him, maybe second to his new girl."

She smiled and said, "I am ok with that," she laughed.

Rex continued, "I was an addict — or am one who recovered, or am recovering, I don't know. But I care about your son. He is my family now, which makes us some kind of step-relative or something, but you are not only going to go, I am going to be your sponsor."

She laughed. "You're joking, I will be accountable to you? You're the guy who kept my kid angry all these years!"

"Yes, and I will even look past how little you think of me to help you. You're not at your best right now. Sundays Thaddeus and I have minimal contact until we get close to the fight. I am going to drive up and meet you and take you to these meetings. You will go. I will sponsor you and you will do it, because you are better than this and the mother of the toughest kid I have ever met."

"Do you think you are going to walk in here and tell me what I am going to do?"

"Yes, I do. Your training starts a week from tomorrow, Mama Class. See you then, Debbie." He smiled and walked out, this time with his jacket. She sat there, gazing at that pamphlet, and then looked up at the doorway through which Rex had just left and wondered if it was possible that Rex actually cared about her enough to try to help her through it. She laughed to herself about how unlikely that was, and how rude he had been to her. He had pretty much told her what she was going to do. No one did that to her, but she kind of found it flattering, somehow. Then she thought, *Someone must have put some Merlot in this IV. I know I am not fascinated with that beast of a man.*

Rex went down the stairs, particularly impressed with himself. He walked out to his car where Paul willingly started to get out of the car. He looked at Paul and said, "Hey, you want to ride this back to the city?"

Thaddeus looked up, "Wow!" They all laughed about it and Paul got back in the driver's side of the car and began to get ready to drive the beast home.

Something was changing in Rex. Maybe he was becoming

more content in his older years. Whatever it was, something was different. Thaddeus didn't get it, but he knew something was different. They enjoyed the ride back to the city and didn't talk about fighting one time. When they got back, Rex and Thaddeus knew it was time to go to work, and Paul left to go to his office at the church.

Back in the city across town, Red Jackson came to visit. Red was a mentor to Larry. Along with him he brought some workout partners from the college. Some were boxers, some were wrestlers, some were Jiu Jitsu types. Red was a true academic ruffian. They spent some time watching Thaddeus' practice film. They knew his every move. They knew him in the first round, but most importantly they knew him in the later rounds. When he got tired, they knew his habits.

They began tailoring their set-ups to how they would strike against Thaddeus Class. They planned on taking away all of the things he did best. They knew his best punches and takedowns. Everything at this stage in the training was about beating Thaddeus Class.

For Billy there was no greater opportunity than this fight. This kid was going to be striking hard, he was going to be striking fast, and he was going to be in the very best shape of his life. He had beaten Thaddeus enough in the practice room to know that he could do it. He felt very strongly that if he fought his fight and made himself into the best fighter he could be, he would win the fight. He would defeat a guy that was being called the best ever, who had never lost, but was on his way down. Also, Thaddeus had never fought someone he had taught everything he knew. He had never fought someone who knew him so well. He never fought someone who was so much superior to him in athleticism, strength, and speed. Billy was also convinced that Thaddeus had never fought someone as great as he.

He knew Thaddeus so well that he even knew when he woke up in the morning. He knew that Wednesday mornings he liked to sleep in a half-hour longer. On those days Billy got up and ran, because he knew the great Thaddeus Class was still asleep. Billy took those runs outside, whether it was cold, snowy, icy, or rainy. For a fighter at this level, so much of it is in their head. So many head games are played. Thaddeus had even taught Billy the secrets of his head games. Ultimately, the head games were played with themselves, inside their own heads.

Sure, Billy had taught Thad a few things, but Thad literally taught Billy everything he knew about being a professional fighter. That included the mental part, the faith part, the physical part. Everything Thaddeus learned he poured into Billy. Billy felt he was clearly in the advantage. Several times Billy had the thought, *This fight is mine!* With this thought he would grit his teeth a little and the corner of his mouth would water. He had never felt better than he did training for this fight, and they all knew Thaddeus was going to be rudely awakened with Billy's own new set of skills. With Red Jackson on board, this was going to get crazy. It had its cost; anything worthwhile in life does, doesn't it? We all have our cross to bear, but after this fight Billy will have arrived at a place he and Larry had always aspired to be. The HWT title wasn't good enough, they wanted to be historic.

That is where Red Jackson came in. Red analyzed film and technique in practice alongside Larry. He literally stood over Billy in practice and tweaked technique over and over again. As he practiced the same takedowns, strikes, setups, and movements, they were focused on new things that would defeat Thad's style. The thinking was basically that Thaddeus Class had always been the same and he would not change much. They wanted to design Billy to be a fighter that was even harder for Thaddeus to fight.

Back at GITR, Rex and Thaddeus were intensely watching Billy's practice film. Since Larry took his laptop that had most of what they had stored, they didn't have the same resources on Billy that Billy had on Thad. They had some recent practice footage saved and could watch his recent fights. So they poured themselves into this task.

With Billy coming down to weight, his potential for improvement in athleticism didn't have a ceiling. He would be leaner and meaner. They correctly understood they were facing a Billy Smith that was already a champion, in the prime of his fighting career, and would have sawed off his own leg to be the first person to beat Thaddeus Class. He knew Thaddeus so well, and knew he probably couldn't change much. Billy knew that, as for himself, he would be faster and not much weaker at the new weight class. He took great comfort in this fact.

As they watched the film, Thaddeus was typically overly optimistic and confident (if you can say that about someone who has literally won everything). But this time he looked at Rex and said, "We really do have to change everything, don't we?"

"Well, he will be our toughest opponent so far. He will be faster at his new weight. He will have you in strength and speed. He is technically good, but most of all, Larry and Billy both know us both so well." Rex pointed at the screen where Billy and Thad were fighting and said, "They will have a plan against you that will win if you stay the same. If you can successfully learn how to fight differently and stick to the plan, we win, though. He isn't as smart as you. He isn't as experienced. You can do it, but it will require a lot of drilling. You're going to have to be in top physical condition, like you always are when it comes time for the fight. We need to have you hit your peak that weekend right on schedule, strong, fast, lean, lungs, technique — it all has to come together for that night."

They went out on the matted area and talked through a lot of situations. They decided one of the main things they needed to do was slow down the right hook that Billy has successfully ended many fights with. That punch was important, and it seemed that he could hit it from a scramble or a counter. It was Billy's best weapon, and the thing about a puncher is if they get you, there is no way to make your head harder. You have to know how to get hit. Every time there is an opportunity to hit that punch, Thaddeus needed to catch the arm at the elbow. From there, knock it out of the way and go, but either way it was going to be a major concern.

The risk was very obvious. If Rex and Thaddeus were wrong, Thad could get his hand broken by putting his arm in the way of Billy's fist, or he could still get hit, hurt, or knocked out. But they knew they had to take away Billy's best attack. Rex exclaimed, "I don't think this is something that has been done at this level of fighting, so it will be a first. But if you can do this, it will slow him down and help our whole attack. We need to take it away and go on the attack. But, if we don't attack this will do nothing. We must capitalize off of this. That could change everything, both early when he is fresh and late when he is slowing down. We also need to switch your lead leg to the other side and switch your lead hand. You need to become completely different. But you can do it. You are athletic and smart. This is the way, Thad."

Thad began working on the new technique with his college-age wrestling partners. They just kept drilling the same thing, over and over again. But he wasn't sure about it. Rex called in some local boxer types who trained there and their job was to try to hit him. His job was to catch their punch. Even with the headgear on, Thaddeus was getting knocked around. He was very frustrated. Thaddeus Class, for the first time in a long time, was having some doubts. By the end of the workout, he was getting the hang of it. One of the keys was that Billy wasn't going to expect this type of defense. It just wasn't something you do to someone who is a heavy hitter. You always want to take away from someone having a clean shot.

Afterwards, Thad was going to hit some more weights, but he talked to Rex. He said, "I don't know about this. This might be the death of me. Billy punches hard and I can't just expect to catch all these punches, do you think?"

Rex jumped in with, "No, kid, you just need to catch the first ones, which may be the fastest and hardest." They both laughed, because in a sick way they both thought it was funny. "Look the truth is, Thad, we need to have our strategy and be all in on it. You must be completely committed. It is kind of like your faith."

Thad looked up, "What? Paul is having an effect on you, huh?" he said in a tired voice.

"Thad, let's not get carried away. But, seriously, you must be all in on this strategy and I realize we have never done this before. We haven't had to change your fighting style for anyone. But this opponent has studied you for years. He has fought you for years. We both know you are not going to be the stronger or the faster athlete. You must be the smarter, more senior athlete. You are the mentor, and you are about to teach him a lesson that he will not forget. He is ready and in shape. We don't want to go toe-to-toe."

"Ok, Rex, I am in. I am going to finish up in the weight room. I need to finish hard today."

The next day Thaddeus got up and set out to meet Sally at the restaurant. He knew his mother would leave the hospital and go straight to her business. It was a good excuse not to go to church. She hadn't been there for a few weeks anyway, and her world was falling apart. She needed to be back at the restaurant, making sure everything was good. Thaddeus was early and beat his mother there. He wanted to be there when Sally met her for the first time.

When Thaddeus walked into the restaurant and saw Sally, she said, "Wow! Checking on me again?"

"No, I just wanted to be here, I thought my mom might stop by. She is going to get out and come over here, I am sure of it." The restaurant had some business, but when some of the church services let out, that is when it would become busier.

Then in through the door, like she was never even in an accident or in the hospital, she barged in and didn't miss a beat. When Tina and Jana saw her come in, they both went up and said, "There is Mama Class!"

Tina asked, "How are you?"

Debbie, in a way that was typical for her, simply said, "I am good. It is all over now. Everyone is ok. I mostly feel bad for causing the accident. I need to be more careful." She briefly greeted everyone who came to her and they dispelled back to their normal duties.

She looked at Thaddeus and said, "She must be special,

you haven't made it up here this early in years. I guess I figured it out."

"What?" Thaddeus asked.

"As long as I have her here you will come see your mother."

Sally smiled. Debbie was everything she thought she would be. "You must be Sally. I have heard so much about you. Mostly from the people here — I can't depend on Thaddeus to fill me in on what is going on in his life."

"Come on, Mom, it is because you get like this."

Sally reached out her hand and said, "So, you are the great Mama Class. There is so much I need to know from you."

"Really?"

"Yeah, I have been hanging around your son because I am fascinated with how messed up he is."

Debbie laughed, "Ah, yeah, this is going to work just fine." Thaddeus just rolled his eyes.

Debbie said, "Hey, by the way. I can't be around for dinner tonight. I have something I need to take care of tonight. How about you two both come up tomorrow night and I will cook up something for us all?"

Thad was always fascinated at how fast she moved, even after she was just in the hospital and only got out this morning. "You don't have to cook for us, Mom, but what are you talking about, taking care of something later? Do you have a date or something? You don't need to hide something like that from me, I am not a little kid anymore."

"No, you're not, not really. Anyway, I don't want to talk about it."

Sally laughed, "That is a yes."

Debbie jumped in, "Anyway, I can't talk about it, but tonight doesn't work, but tomorrow does. Anyway, Thad, I am going to be making some changes. I am too busy and I need to make some real changes, so I am going to spend the rest of the day with Sally. I promised her she would work through today, anyway. She doesn't know, but I had Jana, Carlos, and Tina spying on her. I am going to make her my manager here, if she wants it."

Sally said, "What?"

Thad said, "Ah, yeah? Ah, what? Mom, you just met her."

"What's wrong, Son, a little afraid you can't dump her now?"

"Wow, Mom, that is awkward."

Sally was shocked. No one had ever given her something so quickly. Debbie looked at her and said, "Listen, I don't know you. All I know is that the people who work for me love you, the customers feel like you belong here, and my son really likes you and you seem to make him happy. You never ran a restaurant but you came in here and ran this place like it was nothing. I need someone I can trust." Sally actually giggled a little, which was strange to Thaddeus because she was so gruff at times. She would smile and laugh but they were much tougher sounds than that giggle. He couldn't believe what she was saying.

Debbie looked at Thad, "Hey, we've got work to do today, Thaddeus Andrew. If you keep standing there you will have to work and you won't make it back to hear Paul preach this morning." Thad smiled at them and kissed them both goodbye.

As Thaddeus walked out the door, Sally looked at Debbie and Debbie said, "That is how it works with him."

Sally laughed a little, "I can't tell you how thankful I am."

"I know, but don't thank me yet, let's get started."

It all happened so fast, Sally couldn't believe it.

At the end of the shift Debbie and Sally walked to the car. Sally's head was spinning. She was so grateful that Debbie included her in the running of her restaurant. She looked up at Debbie and said, "Thank you. I just want you to know that no one has ever given me an opportunity this fast. I have had to work so hard for everything. I just don't know what to say."

Debbie grabbed her by the arm, "Look, Sally, I not only get the best manager in town, I also get to see my son more, too. I get something, too. Don't you worry." She paused and laughed, "Maybe you can get me some grandkids."

Sally said, "Ok, maybe not that thankful yet. I will see you tomorrow Mrs. Class."

"Ah, Sally, just call me Debbie. I've got to go."

Sally laughed and left her with, "Good luck on your date."

"Auh — ok!"

Later that day, Rex pulled up to Debbie's house. He tried to be cleaned up and had a nice button-down shirt on, but he stayed with the jeans. Debbie also tried to stay casual but wore her best, most slimming sweater she could find. They were driving a half-hour to the meeting. Debbie said, "So, why are we driving so far away?"

"This meeting is small, they are unimpressed by celebrities, and they will keep your secrets. That is what you need, right?"

"How do I know that they will be confidential, Rex?"

"Well, this is where I went. This meeting isn't open to just anyone. There are people there who you will recognize. I am not sure who will be there, but they specialize in keeping it quiet if someone's problem might be in the news."

Debbie chimed in again, "So, how can I know again?"

"Because my problems were never published."

"Oh, but I thought it was for celebrities," she smirked.

He laughed, "We are both connected to someone famous and it would leak out and hurt Thad. But, yes, I am a minor celebrity too, you know."

Debbie laughed as she looked over the car. "Rex, why are you helping me?"

"I guess I always thought you had it all together. It is a little intimidating, really. But, here you are, struggling with the same thing I dealt with. I guess I don't want to see anyone go through that, not even you," he laughed. "I am kidding about 'not even you.' I guess, to make a long story short, I care."

Debbie laughed, "Wow! That was painful for all parties involved. How hard is it for big bad Rex Metzger to admit that he cares about someone? The truth is, Rex, you like me."

Rex stopped at a light, smiled at her and said, "Maybe, let's go with that."

Debbie thought to herself, *Maybe I am drunk off the leather seats, or the GITR logo behind my back on the seat, or that he is being nice to me, or that he has helped my kid get to where he is in his career, but maybe Rex isn't that bad.*

Debbie came back to reality. *Ok, Deb, the car is nice, but this isn't high school,* she thought. She then asked, "So, how did you find out about this group?"

"Well, when it comes down to it, the group kind of found me. People like us, Debbie, need to reach out to someone. I got lucky, I guess."

"People like us — you mean minor celebrities?"

"No, Deb, I meant white people," he said jokingly. They both laughed. It was obvious to them that some kind of barrier that always used to be there had been broken.

They pulled up to the office building. The parking lot was

almost empty because it was Sunday. It was the perfect place for this type of meeting. As they were walking in, Debbie stopped and said, "I can't go in."

"Well, you don't have a ride, so… come on, Debbie, you need this. The leader of the group knows you are coming tonight." She huffed, but she went into the building.

They took an elevator up to the fifth floor. Debbie began to go through the normal arguments in the elevator. "How are they going to help me? Who are these people, anyway? What will it do for me to go with them? This is stupid. I need to go home." Rex didn't say anything. They walked to the room. Outside in the hallway, Debbie said, "I will just wait out here. No one knows, Rex, I didn't even tell you, you figured it out. Barbara knows, but that is it."

"Debbie, I am not that smart. I figured it out. Do you think I am the only one who knows, even after the accident? People are kind to you because of Thaddeus, your story, your personality and all the rest, but some people can look and have their doubts."

She went to turn around, and what seemed like from out of nowhere a young woman came walking towards the door. Debbie looked up and said, "Hey, I know you. You are Rachel Santiago."

"Yeah, that is me. Hey Rex. So, you must be Debbie and the mother of the great Thaddeus Class."

"Huh, yeah, that is me."

Rex added, "Rachel is not only a world-famous musician, she also gives back by leading this group."

"You lead it?"

"Yeah, I need to be giving back now."

"But how can you be recovered — you are only what, 27, 28?"

"Hey, Debbie, slow down, how about 25? I started drinking heavily when I was 15. It progressed to other things. I became a functional addict. By 21 I quit. It was really hard to quit and it was really hard to tell anyone. When I became sober, it was my turn to do something for people who can't tell anyone because they are well known." She paused, smiled and then continued, "So, I heard you say you were leaving. Please stay, though. I made a personal promise while I was trying to recover that one day I would provide a safe space for people like you, who just can't talk about it. It is safe here."

Deb smiled at this skinny, relentless young person who was bent on helping her. "I should make you sing it, but ok."

Immediately she broke into tune and sang, "PLLLLEEEE-AASE won't you STAAAAYYY!"

Debbie and Rex smiled and went into the room. She looked at Rex and said, "Wow!"

That night was a small turnout of only eight. Amongst them, country music star Mac Hardy. He was about Debbie's and Rex's age. He said, "Hey, Rex, what is happening?"

Debbie was not a huge country music fan but she recognized Mac. Mac had sung at an event that Thaddeus held benefiting youth literacy in the city. He also sang prior to one of the championship fight cards, which was an odd thing at the time. "Hey, Mac, one of my favorite people to name-drop. I have been using you to get me into everywhere."

"Ah, Rex, I doubt that!"

"So, who is your friend here?"

"This is Debbie Class."

"Ah, the mother of your greatest accomplishment."

Deb smiled, "Yeah, that is me. We met before."

Mac then said, "Yes, I remember, it was at your son's charity event, and I remember you from the fight, too. You looked different than when you were sitting there nervous before your kid's fight. — but I do remember the event."

"Yeah, Thaddeus was so proud of that. You made that event worth it for a lot of people to attend."

"Thank you so much, but your son has the whole world in the palm of his hand."

Debbie asked Rex, "So, did you two meet here?"

Rex jumped in, "Yes, at the end of this group everyone is strongly encouraged to give back in a big way, and since this group is made up of recovering addicts who are also influencers, it isn't that hard. When I hit the point where I was supposed to give back, I was encouraged to help mentor Mac. His sponsor helped him with the sponsor stuff, but I added some coaching. Because of my background with fighters who have a tendency to relapse back into some ugly stuff, I wanted to help with what I knew."

"So, you helped to mentor Mac through this?"

Rex said, "Yes, but you can't ever tell anyone. Thaddeus doesn't even really know how I know Mac."

Deb looked up at him and said, "Wow! I thought you were always in it for the glory!"

He smiled, "I thought that you believed in someone who sees it all anyway and will sort it out later."

"But you said you don't believe that."

Rex nodded, "But you say you do."

Something unexpected happened. Mac Hardy felt uncomfortable because of their chemistry. He jabbed Rex on the shoulder and said, "Great to meet you again, Mama Class."

"It is good to see a familiar face here. Great to see you again." It was funny — Deb still didn't feel that comfortable around some of the people that were in the celebrity realm who knew her family. She looked at Rex and said, "That is cool, what you did for him."

Rex looked at her, "Your secrets are safe here. That is what holds us together."

They sat down and everyone looked at each other. She recognized one guy from a movie she had seen on TV. She had seen another one perform at a comedy club several years before. There were others who were related to someone famous like she was; there was even a struggling pastor there who needed a lot of help. She felt so bad for her. *It is hard enough to be in ministry, but to be a woman in it in New York City!* She really empathized with her. Maybe it was because Debbie always had to look like she had it together since Wayne passed. Or so she thought. *Maybe that was why she was in this mess, maybe it was why the pastor was. Maybe that was the problem.* Her mind raced in circles with these thoughts.

Debra found Rachel's story particularly interesting. Rachel was a young success in the music world, but very much alone — and even drank more responsibly than her mother; her father didn't seem to have much of a role at all. As she talked, Deb thought about how easy it is to judge someone from afar, but people have their own problems. She thought, *I am sure people think my Thaddeus had it easy, but heaven knows he didn't.* She began to tear up. It was her turn to share. She didn't need to. She didn't even need to say who she was. But she stood up and said it. She said, "My name is Debbie Class. My son is the famous one, Thaddeus Class. Rex is his trainer."

Mac cut in, "Come on, Deb, you know Rex is here bragging about him all the time, we know. But we know why he is so tough now! Sorry, Rex."

Debbie laughed a little, and her eyes got a little watery as she looked down. "You all have been so brave. I don't know that I am that brave, but I am so glad to be here." Her voice cracked a little, "I am so glad Rex brought me here. and Rachel and Mac and all of you have been so kind. I don't know that I can do what you have done. But I will try." She sat back down.

Rachel piped up, "We are so glad you are here too, Debbie. And you don't have to speak, but since you did you forgot one thing. You must say it. You don't have to say you're an alcoholic, but you have a problem and you need to address that."

She stood up and said, "You are right! I have never said it. I can't even admit it to myself, I don't think my son even knows or realizes, I have functioned all of these years and it took Rex to corner me. Yes, Rachel," her mouth quivered and moved slowly, "I am an alcoholic!" She sat down and put her head down and some tears came out.

Rachel then added, "You are not weak for coming here and saying it. You are strong for bringing it into the light." She wouldn't have been able to fathom how much better she felt. Everyone was so helpful. At the end of the meeting there was a pledge they recited that Rachel wrote for herself, "I pledge to keep everything here confidential. This place is the safe place for people like me. I promise to be someone who keeps it safe so that our world that we influence can be a better place. Most of all, I am committed to healing and being a healer for people like me."

They stayed and talked for a minute and Rex drove Debra home. On the way home they openly talked about the group. Rex let his guard down and talked about how each of them had played a special part in his life. How they held each other together. This was something that he needed, or he may not have survived, at least that is how Rex told the story. Debra saw a whole new side of Rex now, one that he kept hidden from most of the world. Debbie became more and more enamored with a person who she had never really given a chance to understand her, and she flat-out had chosen to not like or trust. It appeared that maybe she had been wrong about him.

When they got to Debbie's place, Rex walked her to the door. She said, "Thank you, Rex, I can't tell you how much I appreciate this."

"Ah, Debbie, I have been there before, that is all."

"Well, Rex, the truth is I just haven't always been sure that I liked you."

"Oh, come on, Deb, we haven't always been so sure of each other."

"Rex Metzger. The truth is I was sure — and I mean sure — I didn't like you." She said it smiling and shaking her head while looking him in the eye. "Rex, do you want to sit and talk with me a minute?" She looked at him like she would kiss him and he hugged her.

It was kind of awkward, because they had never really touched before and he was avoiding the kiss. He grabbed both her shoulders and bent down a little to look in her eyes, "I have misjudged you, too. I need to go. I am so glad you came, and I look forward to spending next Sunday night with you." He got in the car and pulled away and her heart seemed to go with him, like she was back in high school again.

She got inside the door and realized she was so glad he left. She really did need to relearn how to make better decisions. But the more she thought about him leaving, the more she liked him, and, like she was back in high school, she really liked him. But, more important than all that, she didn't need a drink.

CHAPTER 9

STORMING THE GATES OF HELL

ON MONDAY, BACK in New York City, Billy was destroying his practice opponents. He was training harder and harder because Larry was afraid he would peak too early, so he needed to work out extra hard these next few weeks. It had been a weird time. He reconnected with some old friends. There were times he wanted to talk to Thaddeus, but he couldn't. He knew that bridge was burned and that made him sad, but he took great comfort in how tough he had become. He believed he would knock out the Billy Smith that beat Thaddeus in practice the last time. He was the new and improved Billy, "The Kid!"

There was no question that Billy, Larry, and all the gang believed this was his time. Larry couldn't believe how good he looked. He hadn't seen anyone look this good leading up to a fight, and that included the great Thaddeus Class. With every rep and every minute he was getting stronger, faster, and was in better physical shape than he had ever been before. This was incredible! Larry thought to himself, *I am not going to let it get away this time. Everyone will see that I am the greatest trainer the world has ever seen. I am tired of being in everyone's shadows. This is my time.*

Billy went swimming and lifted during the morning workout. He went to church really fast, but was now back at it again. He chose a different church and it was because he could get in and out fast. Billy's faith was a part of him, but he couldn't go to church long without thinking of Thaddeus and something Thad had taught him. He didn't dare go to Paul's church anymore because of the people there — Paul, and most of all, Thaddeus. He found it too bad that he couldn't share this time with Thaddeus, but he knew this was the path to what he and Larry had always wanted. *Everyone has to lose sometime, and I am the guy who can beat Thaddeus Class. If it is not me, it will be someone else. He is slipping.*

Billy was working out with some temporary practice hands. They were boxers trying to find their way. Billy decided to trade punches with the punchers. Billy had gotten one knockout already. The next guy came in to spar and Billy laid him out in a few minutes. He knocked him out with the headgear on. Then he hit Latimore with a double leg takedown. He dominated him until the buzzer rang. *This is my time,* he thought.

ESPN caught it all. They put the last part of the workout on TV. The interviewer talked to Larry as Billy continued to condition at the end. The reporter looked at Larry and said, "Larry, many people believe Billy "The Kid" Smith is going to be too much for Thaddeus "Pure" Class. Many think that Thaddeus has mentored him and brought him along and now he is a younger and better Thaddeus Class. What do you have to say about that?"

"Well, Thaddeus Class did leave his mark on Billy, but make no mistake about it, Billy has learned how to think and purely at this stage he is the better athlete. He will be in the best shape fight night, while Class is declining. He is still the greatest fighter to step into the Octagon, but he has less than two months left with that title. He should have gotten out. Billy knows him, he wants it more, he is stronger and faster. Thaddeus Class will truly have to have his best night to have a chance but, unfortunately for him, we will have our best fight that night, too."

Across town, Thaddeus Class was feeling the effects of training. It seemed as though he was getting older and needed to care about his diet more. He seemed to not recover from his weightlifting days as fast. He was struggling to focus.

He went takedowns with some of the local wrestlers from NYU. He stayed out there and they kept bringing a fresh body in on him. He didn't seem to have it that day. Rex was very concerned. He didn't train hard over the weekend, and even on a day when Thaddeus was feeling rundown, he should've been able to handle this challenge.

One thing that Rex and Thaddeus had as an advantage was they had been there before, but Rex knew that judgment day could be coming and Thaddeus was starting to know it, too. Thaddeus was starting to doubt if he belonged there anymore. Rex wasn't sure how this was going to play out. He knew that this could be the end. The anger was gone. His mom had some stuff going on. He had a new girlfriend. His faith was a factor in all this. Instead of getting mad, Rex was beginning to see maybe life takes its course and it was ok. But how was he going to get him ready to win this fight? He didn't know. He caught Thaddeus after jumping rope with the rope still in his hand as he looked at him and asked, "Thad, what's wrong? You don't have it today."

"I don't know, Rex. Maybe I don't need this anymore. I don't need revenge on Billy. I miss my friend. I liked things the way they used to be. I was mentoring someone and now he is after me. Larry stabbed us in the back, Billy is coming after me, and it isn't good enough to get me motivated. I used to be able to fall asleep on the couch; now, when I do, I can't get up and I am tired."

Rex seemed to take a different approach this time. He looked at Thad, "You have to find what motivates you. You are the best ever, and this might be your last opportunity to prove it, but if your best isn't put out there we will lose it. Your legacy is everything, but you can't fight not to lose. You have to fight to win! You can't fight scared or nervous or not prepared. You can't back out unless this is going to be your retirement, and even then it will tarnish your legacy. You need to run through this wall and at the end we can look at retiring with both titles!"

He looked into Rex's eyes, "Maybe it is meant to be done right now. I don't know that I want it. I have never felt like this before."

"Ok. I wish I could help. I don't know what to do with this."

Thaddeus looked at him and just shrugged his shoulders and said, "Yeah." At that he left and went off to the shower.

After Thaddeus left the building, he got in the car and called Paul. Paul felt this was serious, so he had him come over to his house. They sat out on the front porch. Paul offered him a glass of wine.

Thad looked at him and said, "Rex is going to kill you. I come over to the pastor's house and he says have a drink while I am in training."

"You're a big guy. You're all keyed up, and you need to slow your mind down." He quoted Paul's letter to Timothy, fitting it to Thaddeus, his young Timothy in the Lord. "Come on, Timothy, just a little wine for your stomach."

"Paul, you and I both know you are way out of context here. Timothy needed the wine for his stomach because the water was bad."

Paul jumped in as he handed him the glass, "But you need something different, you need to breathe a different air. You need to think about what you want, and you need to taste the freedom in your hand for just one glass. You need to feel like you could give it all up for a second, even if it isn't true. Allow yourself to think clearly."

Paul continued, "Look this can't be about you. You are living for God's glory now. You need to score a point for living, right? You need to do this for Jesus if you do it. But you can't fight like you have something to lose. This is the fight of your life. If it is all over, there is no shame in that, but if you want out, it is getting harder as the fight gets closer. The sad reality is Billy proved to not be your friend."

"Paul, I might have done the same thing when I was young. It is different when you still have something to prove."

Paul looked inside the window and could see the TV on. "Have you seen the local news yet? Well, earlier, Larry was interviewed on TV and they are running it again. When it comes on we can listen to it."

"I don't want to! I don't need to hear that guy. What does he have to say?"

Paul asked the tough question because he knew that was why he was there, "Are you satisfied with what you have done? Could you walk away right now, are you done? Do you believe your best days are behind you, or do you desire to be remembered as the best ever?"

"Ok, Paul, you don't understand, what if I am just done? What if I don't desire it anymore?"

Paul jumped back in, "I don't believe you. I have worked out with you. I know what I see in there. I know about your love for it. I know about how it affects your mind and how you think. I know about how you train. I think there is something else."

"Ok, Paul, maybe for the first time I am thinking maybe I can't win. He really lit me up the last time in the practice room the day he left. They know me better than anyone else, almost as if it was planned that one day this would be the path to greatness for them, how they would be a household name. Paul, I can't help but think that this is how I am going down. My first loss to a trainer who cheap-shotted me using the guy I was mentoring. Now there is Sally, and maybe there is more to life than all of this."

Paul said, "Ok, Thad, there is a lot there. First of all, it is great that you are so forgiving of Billy and maybe you need to forgive Larry, too, that could hold you back. But to be fair, Billy cheap-shotted you. Why is it so easy for you to forgive Billy? Forgive, yes, but he did this to you."

"I guess I understand the drive and the pressure and that his next step to fighting me makes sense for him."

Paul came back with, "Are you going to be able to open up and hurt him for real, or are you going to hold back on him?"

"Yeah, I don't know. The closer I get, the less I like this fight. This fight sucks!"

"Ok, since you came to a pastor who competed a little, I have to give you a story. I assume that is why you are here anyway."

Thad, now crouching down with the wine glass in front of him, half gone, put his head down and said, "Ok. If I heard this one from the pulpit already, I am leaving."

"I spent several years trying to let this stuff go. I finally went and talked to a pastor friend of mine at the time. I was helping him with youth ministry stuff, and it was funny what he told me. Now this guy isn't athletic at all, and very leery of anyone talking about the gifts of the Spirit. He trusts God talks to people and stuff, but he doesn't like to go there much. So I kept talking to him about this and I think he got annoyed. He didn't get it, because he was in ministry and knew I wanted to be, but I was still holding on to this wrestling dream in the past. He didn't understand how a college wrestler who was nationally unknown could think of himself as someone who could excel at the next level. I felt with some good coaching and the right environment, and the right people around me, I could still do something. But, what did God want?"

"In a moment of some frustration he said to me, 'You need to give it to God. He will either say thank you, or he will give it back to you.' I don't know that he realized it, but those words changed my life. I went home, I was living alone because Ella and I were engaged. I got quiet and sat on the front closed-in porch and prayed. 'Lord Jesus, thank you for allowing me to compete all these years. I didn't get where I wanted to be. I think that you might have more for me to do on the mat. I may compete more. I may coach, but I am confused right now. My wrestling career has largely been about me. I give it to you. Amen.' Then I did something weird. I listened. This was the only time I have ever heard God speak to me audibly. I have heard Him speak a thousand times, but it was in my mind. He spoke to me in my mind, but this was unlike anything I have ever heard. It was like Elijah looking for the sound, in the wind, the fire and the rain. A wind blew through my little apartment. He said slowly, 'Thank you.'

"I started to cry. I knew it was done. He had something better for me. I had to work so hard at being an athlete and I loved it, but preaching and speaking and leading people came very naturally for me. I wish I could say it was easy and I didn't try to pick it back up once in a while, or figure out how to coach or be around it, but I was always compromising what God was doing in my life. When I fought against it, it made me depressed, but when I finally said yes, I am all in for what you have for me, that is when everything changed, it was when I approached life invading the gates of hell; instead of being on the defense, I became aggressive. Thad, this is what I want you to do. Pray with me. One line and we will sit and listen for a second."

Thad, hanging on every word, set down the empty glass. Paul leaned forward in his chair and continued with a very simple prayer, "Lord Jesus, you know what is best. I thank you for the amazing career I have had. I have gotten to do things no one else has. I think the best still may be ahead of me, I also know you might have something else. As great as it has been, this is yours."

Thaddeus mouthed the words along with him, but continued to say, "This is yours. This is yours. This is yours. Amen."

They both sat back and listened for a second. When the moment was right, Paul looked up and said, "Did you hear that, heaven is moving." Thad slowly looked at him, "No, I don't hear anything."

Paul said, "Me neither, but heaven is moving. Haha!" Thad was slightly annoyed that Paul seemed to make light of such a grand decision. "Grab your glass and come in for a second."

Thaddeus followed him in the door and said, "Thank you, I've got to go to my mom's and meet Sally and my mom for dinner. Thank you so much."

Paul said, "If you meant it, heaven is moving."

"Paul, I just want Him to tell me."

Then Simeon was in the living room, "Dad, look on the TV. Isn't that who Thad is going to fight?"

Paul turned the TV up without saying a word. Then Larry came on while Billy continued to work out in the background. It came in at this moment:

"Larry, many people believe Billy "The Kid" Smith is going to be too much for Thaddeus "Pure" Class. Many think that Thaddeus has mentored him and brought him along and now he is a younger and better Thaddeus Class. What do you have to say about that?"

"Well, Thaddeus Class did leave his mark on Billy, but make no mistake about it, Billy has learned how to think and purely at this stage he is the better athlete. He will be in the best shape fight night, while Class is declining. He is still the greatest fighter to step into the Octagon, but he has less than two months left with that title. He should have gotten out. Billy knows him, he wants it more, he is stronger and faster.

Thaddeus Class will truly have to have his best night to have a chance but, unfortunately for him, we will have our best fight that night, too."

Something happened in the moment. It felt like heaven did move and all of it was inside of Thaddeus Class. There was a holy feeling of joyous irritation. He looked at Billy, working hard and looking better than ever. Thaddeus heard Larry discrediting everything GITR ever built with Billy, and all in the name to take him down. He didn't look at them with anger, though. He looked at them with great purpose. He knew he had something to show Larry and Billy. The next lesson would be painful, but God's good guys do finish first. It is better to live and do it all for the glory of Jesus Christ than anything else.

There was still something else. This fight would be different. He also needed to know if he could put together his best fight ever and win. He knew that God didn't promise that he would win. He ground his teeth together and thought about the ridiculousness of knocking someone out for the glory of God. He thought he needed to read more Old Testament, maybe Samson, to get it. His eyes narrowed and a single tear trickled down his cheek and he breathed and felt relief. It was no longer about his anger, it was something else. It was no longer for his deceased father to see him, it was so his heavenly Father would look on this and say, "Well done, Thaddeus, my good and faithful servant!"

He looked at Paul. Paul looked at him, "I heard it. I don't know what it was, but heaven moved for you, Thaddeus! No matter what happens in that fight, during the training, in your personal life, you must look back on this moment and remember this feeling." Paul put his hand on Thaddeus's head and asked for uncommon joy, protection, and favor for His servant. They both said, "Amen."

Thad hugged Paul, slapped Simeon's hand. "I have to go. Whenever you get there tomorrow, I will already be there. It is go time. You get to prepare me for the best fight I will ever fight. Amen." At that he left.

Simeon looked up at Paul and said, "Dad, were you tough like Thad?"

"Oh, I tried to be. God has me to be there for people like that."

"Good. I need someone to help me be tough like that."

He looked at Simeon, "I don't know what God will do with you, but know that the God inside of you is greater than any person who will stand in front of you, even if it is the giant man you saw working out on TV."

"So, Dad, you want to fight Billy then, too?"

He playfully poked him in the stomach and said, "I just talk about such things these days, but I like getting to work out and help Thaddeus."

"Me too, Dad. You need some new stories." At that Simeon ran and Paul playfully ran him down in the kitchen.

Thaddeus got in the car and his mind was racing. He felt renewed. He didn't realize the burden he had been carrying, but something that Thaddeus saw in that moment on TV was not only the vile motives of Larry, which had always been there, but he saw something else. He saw Billy as a sprinkler. What do I mean by a sprinkler? You see, Thaddeus grew up going to church and around people who were true. Thaddeus always kind of believed, but he wasn't committed to Christ. He "sprinkled" God on the end of his plans, just like Billy did. He would talk about how great he was, or how much he trained, and say something about being blessed at the end. That wasn't God-honoring. It may seem like it to the person, and we may overlook it because we can relate to it ourselves, or it is like us, but God looks upon pride as one of the seven things that He hates. This was now Billy's normal MO.

Thaddeus was thinking more clearly now and he realized that he needed to be honest with himself. He truly had never looked at this fight yet like the other ones. He finally looked at it and realized that deep down he wasn't ready. He was not fast enough, strong enough, his conditioning wasn't where it needed to be yet, and most of all he hadn't put the time into developing the technique. This part would be fun, but he needed to put even more time into this part of it. For the first time, he felt in over his head. Paul always told him, "Faith only seems to make sense when we are in over our heads. We do everything we can, but sometimes we need to wait on God to intervene."

He began to pray and draw close, but not in a sprinkler type of way. He knew God wanted him where he was, and he was more sure than ever before, but he didn't let himself believe for one second that God was guaranteeing he was to be the victor. It isn't right to do that. Sprinklers and prosperity-type people do what Paul called proof-texting, and they make the passage fit, but he knew deep down that God had a part, and He had a part in running through a brick wall, and that wall was named Billy. He wasn't sure as he prayed that this was his last fight, or if he had many more, but he felt alive. He was very excited to have this opportunity. He wasn't afraid of losing what he had anymore. He wasn't going to fight not to lose, he sure wasn't going to train not to lose. He was going to train and fight to win!

He bounced up the steps on the porch of his childhood home and sprung open the door. He walked in and Sally looked at him. "Hey, I thought you were going to be here 30 minutes ago."

He kissed her and kissed his mom and said, "Sorry." They looked at each other in a weird way. "I've got a fight to get ready for and for the first time I am excited about it."

Debbie looked at Thaddeus and smiled, "Rex get in your head again?"

"No, he actually didn't encourage me either way. He feels that if I am not into it, I might want to quit."

Debbie smiled, "Wow! Point for Rex, I guess."

"I think he was wondering, too, if it was time for me to stop. But I really prayed through it with Paul. He told me his story of when he knew it was time for him to be done and we prayed. He promised me heaven would move and I might feel it and I did. I know I am fighting Billy for the right reasons now and it is my fight. Anyway, I can tell you both the whole story later. Let's eat."

They sat down while Debbie prayed for the meal. Debbie prayed before dinner like any single mother would, who successfully raised a man. Debbie did what she had to do, but for years had been going through the motions with her dinner prayers. It wasn't that Thaddeus didn't notice. He figured at least she still prayed. This time when they grabbed hands, Debbie said, "Dear God, I love you. Thank you for my son, thank you for the people in his life, and thank you for sending Sally to keep him in line before I get old." They giggled; she went on a little bit more and ended with, "Allow this food to nourish our bodies. Thank you so much for it and each other. Amen."

Thad also knew something new was going on with his mom. He hadn't heard her sound that thankful since before the day when everything changed, when his dad, Wayne, was gone. So he went in for the kill. "So, Sally and I are trying to figure out if you have a new boyfriend or something. How did this date go?"

Sally reached over and slapped his hand, "Watch out! I've got a knife! Don't bring me into this. You were wondering. I am just getting to know your mom and am not meddling in her business."

"No, I don't have a boyfriend. I just have someone helping me with something."

Thaddeus smiled, "So that is where the more joyful prayer comes from. He can't help you with much without a ring."

Debbie got a little embarrassed. "Yeah, don't worry about that." She laughed.

They continued to eat. It was grilled chicken with green beans. Debbie knew how to cook for a fighter who needed to be lean and not put on any fat, as well as sodium and such. Both Debbie and Thaddeus seemed happy, but for the first time in a long time Sally was also truly happy. She couldn't believe how much she felt like she fit with them. There was so much to be happy about.

At the end of the night Sally rode home with Thad. He drove her straight home because he had to be at the gym early to train in the morning, and she understood. She struggled with needing someone, and that his mom was so nice to her, and how did she get this job so easily. But for tonight she chose to be at peace for now. When they got to her door he hugged her and they kissed a little. He pulled away and said, "I need to go."

She said, "Ok."

He said, "I will call you tomorrow afternoon." He smiled at her and walked back to the car and left.

Sally had left her car in Curlsville, but had a friend who commuted to a job just a block away from the restaurant and would drive her. She just needed to call Kate early and that problem was solved. But none of that even came to mind until Thaddeus drove off. She hadn't felt this out of control in a while. She wasn't sure that she was as disciplined as he was. If he had tried to make a move, she would have definitely let him in. She had great joy when she thought of Thad, but she also was sad because she had always been let down. She was let down by her father and her first husband. She thought, "Now I am falling for a fighter, like some kind of groupie. I guess for tonight I am ok with that." It was all a little confusing for Sally, to say the least.

The next morning Thaddeus opened the door to the gym at five. He had already taken a shower to wake up and feel fresh. He was there to study. He had half a cup of coffee, just enough to get his mind going. He was there and would spend one hour before he and Paul were going to be drilling on the mat. After Paul left, he would grab something to eat and look at tape again. This was going to be a physical season of training, but even more a mental game. He needed to know how to beat an opponent who knew him so well. Billy had perfected much of what Thaddeus had taught him, but also knew how to beat Thad in his current state. It wasn't an easy task.

Thad sat there with a tiny cup of coffee and a whole lot of water. He sat there by himself, waking up to the reality of his opponent. An opponent who had scouted him for years. Billy knew his every move, and he had taught Billy everything he knew. Now Thaddeus was finally studying Billy. On both the practice and fight film he noticed that Billy had even tailored his style to beating him. Had he been doing this for years? It seemed as though he had been doing this for a long time. He stayed away from the tie-ups Thaddeus liked best. He worked ties and forced positions that were not Thad's best. Truly, Larry had done a masterful job. This was an uphill battle.

Thad tried to break down film. He tried to understand his "tells." He also looked for common counters to holds, take-downs, or strikes. He became increasingly frustrated because he didn't have many. This wasn't normal. Everyone has them, but at GITR they had worked incredibly hard to not have any.

About 5:40 a.m. Rex came walking in with a cup of coffee. He walked into his office where Thad was sitting, dressed and intently looking at the screen. Thad's eyes never left the screen when Rex came in. Thaddeus paused the movie; then he put it in slow motion.

Rex took a sip out of his Yeti and looked at Thad and said, "What do you think, Thaddeus?"

Thad looked at him. "I am frustrated. He has no tells, no visible holes in the armor. I think he has tailored his fighting towards challenging me for years. There is a lot that bothers me about that. I am learning nothing about his fighting by watching his fights, yet I need to keep trying. The whole situation is very emotional."

Rex put his palm up, "Thad, what do you think about the fight?"

"That is what I am trying to say. Nothing is harder than this opponent. But, after yesterday, I have never been more focused, I have never felt more committed, I have never known more fully that I am meant to fight this fight. I am fully committed and will not doubt until it is all over. I believe it is going to be the hardest fight I have ever had. He is my toughest opponent, but this is my legacy. More than that, there is a higher purpose."

Rex looked confused while he sipped his coffee, "Yesterday, I was sure you were done. What convinced you?"

"Paul did. We prayed through it, I saw the interview yesterday with Larry and Billy, and God moved in me. I am scared, I feel as though I have a lot to lose. I am not convinced I will win yet; I mean, I am certain, through training, I will get there. I want to win this fight. After this, I might be done, but this is my fight. There is no greater challenge than this." Then he looked at Rex, "What do you think about the fight?"

Rex looked at him, now much more awake. "You are my family. I care about you more than the fight. I also care about you, the fighter. Right now you are considered the best to ever do this sport at your weight class. I only want to go in if we are completely ready. There can't be any fear. There can't be any doubts. We must be smart, but not just smart — we must outsmart them, and you need to become a completely different fighter. We are coming at them with the most sophisticated strategy that you have ever tried to learn. In the end, we win! That is what I think. But, do not think for a minute that this will not be the hardest thing you have ever accomplished." Thad smiled. He stood up and they fist-bumped.

Just then Paul walked in, "What did I miss?"

Rex looked at him, "Hey, you, what business is it of yours to convince my fighter that he is going to fight this monster — and not only that, but that he will win? Huh?" Paul seemed a little stunned. Rex tapped him on the shoulder and laughed it off, "Just @&$&()& with you, Pastor."

Thaddeus looked at Paul and laughed, "Bet you don't hear that every day."

Paul laughed, "That is what I come around here for, the hospitality." He laughed a minute and said, "Well, I will do my part."

Thaddeus looked at him and said, "That is good, we need to figure out how to win."

Rex looked at Thaddeus and said in a serious tone, "Well, I plan on having the greatest fighter I have or GITR has ever trained to have his best fight ever and cement that legacy of greatness right in Larry's and Billy's faces."

Thad looked at him and said, "Look, Rex this can't be about them. I need this to be about what I can do. And where I get my strength from." He looked at Paul and said, "Can you pray for us?"

Paul then looked up at Rex, who was about three inches taller than he was. Rex smiled and said, "Ok, in fact, you can pray for us before any workout you want."

Paul prayed, "Lord, help us to work, live, and act according to your will and for your glory. Help us to be as shrewd as snakes when we make decisions, help our witness to be as gentle as doves, help us to know you. Help us to follow in your ways. Help us not to get injured, and give us uncommon joy, protection and favor. Give us wisdom and protection. Lord, also help Thaddeus Class to win this fight for your glory."

Rex put his ball cap back on and said, "You know, I just don't understand this praying to win thing, but if you guys are ok with it, then I am, too."

Paul put his hand on Rex's shoulder and said, "We have so much to talk about." So, they got to it.

Across town the confidence of Billy "The Kid" Smith was

thriving. He had widened the margin with Latimore and Slippery Pete Durkin to complete dominance, one after another. He had several workout partners, martial artists, boxers, Jiu Jitsu specialists, and some young studs coming out of college wrestling trying to make their mark. He defeated one after another.

(Because the gyms were so close, both gyms had a non-compete clause and were subject to a large legal fine for fraud, and risked never competing in the RTC again.)

After switching partners for the third time, and feeling a little drained after Latimore and then a fresh young body on the attack, a wrestler from Rutgers University who had just graduated and took a job in New York to find a place to train, came in fresh and took Billy down. No one had taken him down in several weeks; he had been dominating in practice like no one had ever seen, not even Latimore, in all the years working out with Thaddeus.

Ron Kroger caught him while he was tired, almost no one can go through three partners in back-to-back seven-minute goes and not get taken down. Ron didn't just catch him because he was tired, he found a weakness. The smart young kid from Rutgers learned how to scout and find a tell. It seemed that after a flurry, especially when he was tired, Billy would take a long, extended reach and stand flat-footed.

Larry immediately jumped on Billy. "Billy, aren't you the best? Attack him!"

When Billy got free he hit Ron with some vicious left hooks, and he went down for a second and didn't know where he was, even though he had the boxing headgear on. Ron got hit again and again and again. When Ron backed out he found his footing as Billy was going in for the kill. This time he reached again and Ron got in deep again on a double leg. He finished the last 30 seconds pounding on Billy. Billy stood up, frustrated, and said, "!@#$!@$ that! #%@#$$ THAT!!!!!" He threw his headgear and stood outside in the hall. Ronnie hit a big move on the champion twice.

This caught Larry's eye. "Ron, your coach told me that you were a diamond in the rough. You just need some pressure. Not many people can say they took Billy "The Kid" down like that.

Ron smiled, "Thanks, Larry, but he was tired."

"Yes, he was, Ron, that is why you will go with him first next time. We will go five-minute go's."

When Billy came back in he overheard some of the same stuff. He walked around and caught his breath. He saw Larry talking to Ron, and he began to stretch a little. It seemed that this first go was very important to him. After all, that was the name of the game, right? Your trainer was always trying to figure out how he would replace you.

Billy needed about ten more minutes to catch his breath and be ready. He started with a slow jog and a warmup. His recovery time was exceptional, because of how much he had learned from Thaddeus, Rex, and Larry about health and recovery.

"So, you are a two-time NCAA All-American. You placed third and then this year you fell to sixth. Why?"

He answered Larry with, "I had some injury."

"What was it?"

"It was my knee."

Larry chimed in with, "All better now?"

He smiled and said, "Seems like it."

Now Billy was mad. He was about to show this guy what fighting with him fresh was really like.

Larry started to pile on Billy a little. "Billy, are you ready to get in here with Ron? Hey, Ron, don't hurt him because you will have to fight instead if he can't take it. Billy, are you gonna let someone come into your gym and destroy you like that? I hope you are rested. Actually, I hope you ate your Wheaties or something."

Both fighters began to bounce and it was time to fight. There was no doubt that this was serious. Billy landed some great punches, but young Ronnie stood in there. There was a flurry of diving in on legs and mat type movement, which ended in Billy landing a nice punch when they hit their feet. Then Ronnie kind of spun out in an awkward way; he came back in and landed an uppercut. Billy went down and then young Ronnie was on top of the champion, and he was unloading on him. He hit him hard a few times. Billy scrambled out of it and came up on top. Billy began to unload on Ron this time. Soon they were back on their feet. The five-minute go ended with Billy on top and the obvious winner. Larry, however, looked and understood they had something there, something for Billy, and something for him. This guy could end up being great. He thought, *Who trained him before? And he can already take it to Billy!*

CHAPTER 10

SPIRITUAL WARFARE

ONE NIGHT, SALLY had another dream. She was at the restaurant and Debbie was being nice to her and the customers loved her and she was truly happy. Thaddeus showed up and they left to go eat dinner. She ate a perfectly-cooked steak with fries and cornbread. She could taste it in her dream. Then she talked about getting dessert, and Thaddeus's face changed into her father's. He looked at her with disgust, "What makes you think you deserve this? Who do you think you are? They don't know who you are, but I do!" At that, he slapped her across the face and when she turned around, she saw Thad, who giggled a little. Then she woke up.

She cried for several minutes. "God, help me, there is something wrong with me. I can't trust him can I, I am not good enough, am I? You don't want me to be happy, do you? What is wrong with me?" At that something happened. She looked at her wall and saw a painting her friend gave her of a child running to Jesus, with the words, "Trust in the Lord with all your heart and lean not on your own understanding."

The word *trust* seemed to move, and the rest of the painting went out of focus. Inside her it was like someone said, "You are my child, trust me!" Not long after that, she fell back asleep.

That same night Thaddeus also had a dream. There were two great armies standing in the valley of Elah where David fought Goliath. And a great champion came out to fight. It was Billy, and he stood even taller and more muscular than right now. Thaddeus wasn't even supposed to be there. He looked and saw the giant. In front of him, he had an armor bearer. That armor bearer was not all that big, but he had an exceptionally large head. The armor bearer shielded all of his weaknesses, while the king instructed Rex to help Thaddeus get ready. The king took his armor off and his shield, and the king's son tried to help Thaddeus with carrying the heavy armor and becoming a different fighter in just a few minutes. When Thaddeus looked out on the battlefield, the armor bearer's shield was getting bigger and the sword of Billy "the giant" was getting larger as he practiced counters to all of Thaddeus's best stuff. Thaddeus looked at Rex and said, "We can't go out there like this. We can't win. He knows me, and I don't have the time to become another fighter. I am me."

As Thaddeus began to grow more and more afraid, he saw his mother and Sally in the distance. They seemed very confident, but they didn't understand the gravity of this opponent like Thaddeus did. Then someone came out of the crowd with a bag and spoke to Thaddeus. It was a familiar voice, but he didn't allow Thaddeus to see his face. He looked in the sack and there were five smooth stones. A voice from the sky rattled the earth, "Take off the armor and take the stones. You will need one of the stones."

Thaddeus looked through the bag and at the very bottom

of the sack was a stone with the face of a man on it. Thaddeus recognized the man. He recognized his face, but he couldn't place him. They worked out together. There was something about this guy that Thaddeus really liked, but he couldn't remember where or when he met him. He thought it was someone younger than he, that he helped at some point, or someone he thought a lot of as a fighter. He wasn't sure who this kid was, so he boldly looked to heaven, "God, who is this face on the stone?"

"You will know him when you meet him. But be yourself. With God all things are possible, without me you can do nothing."

The gravity of it all bothered Thaddeus, but he looked up at the champion and the voice spoke once more from the clouds. "Disciple of David, look at Billy as he blasphemes." Billy spoke about how great he was, and then said something small about God at the end of the sentence. Billy challenged anyone to fight him. Thaddeus looked at Rex, Debbie, and Sally. He looked at the king and his son. He looked at the masses, while all eyes were on him. He walked out on the battlefield with Larry and Billy. The sky got darker and the giant became bigger. Billy and Larry both smiled as they looked at him. They cursed the ground he walked on, and cursed him for being a nice, devoted believer. It got darker and Billy's sword was swung at Thaddeus; he moved out of the way. He took a swing at him with the king's sword and that is when he was knocked to the ground with Larry's shield, and the sword began to come down on Thaddeus and his career was about over. That is when he woke up in a cold sweat like he was working out already. He looked at the clock. It was 4:25 a.m., time to wake up.

He thought about it for a second and he knew that this dream was no normal dream. God had given him dreams before, but this one was very scary; somehow there seemed to be hope. It was dark, yet light at the same time. He took his normal quick shower and he was going to ride his bike over to the gym. It seemed that he would somehow know the way, but he couldn't trust in the wrong thing. And whose face was that on the rock? Weird. Wow! What a dream! He praised God for it as he got ready and rode the mountain bike over to the gym.

When Thaddeus got to the gym, he focused on watching some film, yet he still had this dream that the Lord gave him in the front of his mind. Rex came in and seemed nervous. He began to talk to him about how to stop Billy, but he seemed rushed. He was babbling but not making sense. Thaddeus looked up at him and said, "Rex, slow down, what is the deal?"

"Thad, I am just nervous here, this is a big fight and I think we have a lot to do. You need to become completely different. You need to change your fighting style. We need to confuse him and wear him down with something else. He is going to be ready for your style and better than ever before."

"Rex, I know. That is why I am here at five in the morning watching this film before Paul gets here."

"I know, but I am worried this time."

"Look, Rex, I had a dream about it last night. God has me. He has us."

At that Rex, punched his metal desk. "Come on, Thaddeus! Don't do that!"

Thaddeus looked up at Rex and said, "I will be back. I need to go to the bathroom," and he left the room while on the screen was Thaddeus and Rex in the corner of Billy's winning his championship fight.

Paul walked in and was as smiley as ever. He saw Thaddeus walking to the bathroom from a distance. Thad said in a low voice, "Hey, Paul."

Paul said, "Hello." He walked into the office and he said hi to Rex. Rex tried to say hello, but kind of huffed and walked out of the office in the opposite direction of Thaddeus.

When Paul looked at the television he saw Rex and Thad celebrating with Larry and Billy after Billy's championship fight. *This isn't right,* Paul thought. He also knew that God had him there that morning for more than just another workout. They needed spiritual counsel of some kind. Paul wasn't at his sharpest yet, but he was willing to be there for them, however God wanted him to be.

Not long after, they were all out on the mat and drilling technique. They started with the three moves for Paul and five for Thaddeus. They began to have Paul do technique that was typical for Billy. Thaddeus needed to perfect certain counters to compete with Billy. Thaddeus also was spending the majority of the workout trying to switch to being left-handed in his counters and initial attacks.

Rex started yelling at Thaddeus, "Thad, you are down to 45 days! You need to do this faster. These counters are not fast enough! You must do it faster. You must go harder! Billy is coming for you! Did you like him beating you in your own practice room the last time you saw him?"

Thad's takedowns became crisper. They became stronger with every touch. He was getting faster and smoother. It seemed good to Paul. Thaddeus also seemed to be taking great joy in being in the zone. "This isn't right!" Rex yelled out "You need to go faster. You are putting too much weight on your lead leg." He would pause for a minute and then hit Thaddeus with three more things. "You are reaching too fast. You are reaching with the wrong arm. You're thinking too much. You aren't thinking it through."

Paul wasn't as shaken by it as some pastoral people would be. He knew how these people thought. He also knew this wasn't normal for these two. This was the known greatest fighter and trainer combination in the MMA world. So what had the two of them acting like this?

Finally, after about 40 minutes into the workout, Thaddeus yelled back at Rex, "What is your problem? These are near perfect!"

Rex stopped and looked him in the eye. "Near perfect is usually good enough, but not this time. You need to be perfect!"

He walked towards Rex and smacked his own chest, "I need to be the best version of myself. I am the smarter, more experienced, and better-trained athlete."

"You are smarter, but he is strong, fast, and he knows us. If we are going to make changes we need to be perfect."

"Rex, you are scared. You are coaching me scared, and I refuse to be scared. We win this by being fearless!"

Rex looked at him and yelled, "Whatever!" He then backed off for the rest of the workout. He would chime in once in a while to let him know that he needed to tweak something and that something wasn't right. These technique workouts in the morning were now lasting about an hour and 45 minutes.

Thaddeus hit the showers. He was going to go home and rest for a few hours before going back to lift weights and go live in the afternoon. They were at a stage that the weightlifting was becoming more about the high reps and endurance. There was still a little bit of a power workout mixed in once in a while. They tried to do that on days that he wasn't going live. What is meant by live is some days it was on the mat; some days it was more boxing. But mostly they were putting the headgear on and putting the fight gloves on and getting in the cage, because "it is go time!"

Rex went into his office; this was the time of day that he normally had to himself. There were a few people who were coming in to work out, but he had some time to watch film and relax a little. It was work to watch the old fights, but it was a work he loved.

Paul called the church office as it was almost eight. Bernice was already there and answered the phone. Paul quickly let her know that he would be in later in the morning and to take a message for anyone who needed him. But something came up, so, still sweaty, he walked into Rex's office and sat on a folding chair. Rex didn't like people coming in off the mats or all sweaty and sitting on the couch.

"Hey, Rex, are you doing ok?"

Rex looked up from the screen, "No, I am not, but I don't need a pastor, I told you that before."

Paul said, "Ok. I was just going to ask you if I could drive your car around the block, maybe take it down to Atlantic City today, gamble a little? I might just jump in all sweaty and shower when I get back."

Rex laughed, "Funny, Paul. Look, the reason I don't need a pastor is I don't want someone to tell me I am wrong for how I am treating Thad right now."

"Why would I do that?"

"Because he came in with the end-all today. He isn't scared because he had a dream about it. What am I supposed to do with that?"

As they were talking, Billy's championship fight playing on the TV was at a breakthrough moment that they were all proud of at the time. Rex looked at the TV screen and put his hand up. "Thad needs to be a little scared of that! That other guy was the champion going into that fight!"

Paul said, "Well, let me ask you this, is he normally scared going into championship fights?"

"No, Paul, but he hasn't been the underdog in almost a decade. We have never fought someone that he mentored before. This situation, for me, is unprecedented. Then he comes in here and tells me he is good, because he had a dream."

"Look, Rex, I know what I saw out there in his technique. You and I both know that he picked up some new stuff very quickly and is handling it with precision. It is the first day for much of it. What do you want?"

"Paul, I have trained him before; I know him."

"Yeah, but have you been scared for him before?"

"Yes! The last fight, and he was almost knocked out. I am afraid of his faith."

Paul looked at him strangely. "What?"

"Yeah, Paul, his faith."

Paul was still trying to catch up. Rex continued, "He has lost his edge."

"What do you mean, his edge?"

"He used to be angry. He isn't now. He almost lost against an opponent that isn't half the opponent this one is. We are calling it that he got caught. No, he got saved by the buzzer. But this guy will finish him." He paused for a second, "Paul, I like you, You used to compete, you come in here and drill with the greatest champion the world has ever seen, and you preach on Sundays — and you ride with us out to Curlsville.

You are different. I like you, but I still hate Jesus. I wanted so badly for my little Maggie to be healed, and I saw it happen with someone else's child. I lost Mary, and by the time we could get it back together she died, too. Jesus takes from you, and, quite frankly, He knows I hate Him and He will take this away from me, too."

Paul looked at him and said, "Jesus likes honesty, and He likes that about you."

At that moment Rex stopped looking at Paul as his friend and saw him as Jesus' ambassador. "Paul, I don't give a flying $%$!^@*&% what He likes!"

Paul just looked at him and softly said, "Ok," as he put both his palms up.

Rex continued to talk about how God had failed him and finished with, "God hates me!"

"Look, Rex, God actually provided you with the opportunities you have. He doesn't want to take from you. I told you before. I can't explain why God took your daughter and why your marriage fell apart. I do know that you get to train the best fighter in the world, you run this club, and you have made a new friend in me."

Rex suddenly softened. Paul continued, "Maybe Thad did have a dream and maybe he didn't. But he practiced this morning fearlessly, like the champion he is, and I think that he might be onto something. You and I both know that you need to roll with whatever is going to make him feel good and be confident and be at his best at the end of the day, right? How about you give Jesus a chance for Thaddeus? Maybe this fight will look different. Don't fighters change over their career?"

"Let's be clear. I am going to roll with it for Thaddeus, but this isn't me giving Jesus a chance for me. He had His chance."

Paul smiled and said, "That is fine, but as a friend, I want to ask you something. You seem to not believe in Him until you are mad at Him. I thought you said it was all "just made up.""

"Don't push me, Paul. I will redirect my anger towards you," he smiled.

"Hey now, my best friend is the greatest fighter in the world. Watch out!"

"See you tomorrow, Adkins."

Paul walked into the locker room and Thaddeus was dressed already.

"Hey, Thad, do you want to get some breakfast with me?"

"Yeah, let's do it! I will be in Rex's office, making up with him. Come out when you are ready."

"Don't worry about him. I calmed him down a little."

"Wow! That would be a miracle. I will check on him anyway."

Thaddeus walked into Rex's office. Rex kind of looked at him and just said sheepishly, "Hey, Thad, look. The important thing is you are confident. You are the champ, you have been here before and I believe in you. It is just my job to look out for you and challenge you. I believe in you. I believe if we do things right we win the fight, it is just that it is kind of weird. They have been here, learning us all of this time. It is really, really, what is the word…"

Thad jumped on it, "Annoying! Sounds good, Rex, apology accepted."

"Whatever, yeah, you too, Thad, I guess!" They laughed it off and Thaddeus walked out when he saw Paul walking towards him. It was off to breakfast at the Cornerstone Café.

When Paul and Thaddeus got to Cornerstone, they still

wanted their normal table so they motioned to Tommy and went to their table in the back room, the Thaddeus room. An older waitress who knew them both, Bethany, went to their table. They spoke with her briefly and then ordered their food. She kind of knew what they wanted already, and she went to get them water and coffee. Thaddeus still drank a little coffee while he was training, but mostly water.

When Bethany brought the drinks back, she said to Thad, "Hey, how is Sally doing?"

"Oh, she is good, Bethany. She is working for my mom now."

"Yeah, I heard that. I am sure she is doing great there. Just tell her that we miss her here and to stop by sometime."

"I will. She would love to hear that." At that, Bethany smiled and walked away.

Paul looked up at Thaddeus and asked, "So, Rex said you had a dream, did ya?"

Thaddeus looked at him and laughed, "Man, I shouldn't have told him that, should I? It is just that in my dream it was kind of playing out, and he needed to know that I was ok. He is so worried about this fight, and I actually think it could ruin me, because I don't need that. I usually, actually I always, have his vote of confidence. But he even said it is new territory having someone that we mentored challenging us, and that they were here *spying* on us. It's all very overwhelming."

Paul put his figurative pastor's hat on. "I don't know if you should have told him or not. I used to obsess over things like that, but God wasn't surprised. He gave you the dream. He allowed Rex to be like that, I guess I would have to ask, were you burdened to not tell him the dream? Was it a special instruction to keep it from Rex?"

Thad thought about it. "Well, no."

Paul continued, "So, are you supposed to be a witness to what you have seen and heard?"

"Yes!"

"Look, Thad, pray it through for the future. You might not want to talk about these things with him, but also these conversations have an effect on him. He has changed since I met him, I know that for sure. God is softening his heart and you have been a part of that."

Thad looked at him and said, "Maybe I see it, but he has been through a lot."

Paul jumped back in an apologetic mode, "Let me ask you this. If Rex is reached for the Kingdom and God gets hold of his life, who else would God use but you?"

Thad smiled, "You seem to misunderstand my Kingdom importance. You are the one who has really changed things around there."

"Ah, Thad, you don't get it. I am only in Rex's life because he saw that I could help you by being a practice partner and the spiritual stability that you desire. Also, him being open to that had to do with being desperate, wanting to win, and the softening of the heart, which you were very much a part of."

Thaddeus said, "Yeah, I guess. Well, can you help me with the dream?"

"God can, I know that for sure."

Thaddeus began to tell the dream. "There were two great armies standing in the Valley of Elah, which I didn't realize was the place where the battle of David and Goliath took place. There it was, just like how you preached it. I was standing there, in the Valley of Elah. So much seemed to be at stake. I stood there, as many were concerned: Will we serve them, or will they serve us? But maybe it had to do with them serving God and us representing Him. Well, I am not really sure. It was Billy, and he stood taller and more imposing than ever. I didn't feel like I was even supposed to be there. When I looked closely I saw he had an armor bearer. That armor bearer was not all that big, but he had an exceptionally large head. The armor bearer shielded all of Billy's weaknesses while the king instructed Rex to help me to be ready to go out there and fight. The king took his armor off and his shield, and the king's son tried to help me with carrying the heavy armor and becoming a different fighter in just a few minutes. When I looked out on the battlefield, the armor bearer's shield was getting bigger and the sword of the giant was getting larger as he practiced counters to all of my best techniques. I looked at Rex and said something like, 'We can't win. I am not ready. He knows me, and I don't have the time to become another fighter. I am me.'

"As I began to grow more and more scared, I saw my mom and Sally who were far away. They seemed very confident, but they didn't understand the gravity of this opponent like I did. Then someone with a bag came out of the crowd and spoke to me. It was a familiar voice, but he didn't allow me to see his face. He looked in the sack and there were five smooth stones. A voice from the sky rattled the earth, 'Take off the armor and take the stones. You will need one of the stones.' I searched through the bag and at the bottom of the sack was a weird stone with the face of a man on it. I think it kind of smiled at me with a confident smile. I recognized him from some-where, we worked out together or something. I couldn't quite place him, but I know that I know him from somewhere and that I like him. He was there to help. He might be someone I helped before or something. I don't know. I have mentored some fighters. I wasn't sure who this kid was, so I boldly looked to heaven, 'God, who is this face on the stone?'

"'You will know him when you meet him. Be yourself. With God all things are possible; without me you can do nothing.'"

"The gravity of it all bothered me, but I looked up at the champion and the voice spoke once more from the clouds. 'Disciple of David, look at Billy as he blasphemes.' Billy spoke about how great he was, and then said something small about God at the end of the sentence. Billy challenged anyone to fight him. I looked at Rex, Mom, and Sally. I looked at the king and his son. I looked at the masses while all eyes were on him. I walked out on the battlefield with Larry and Billy. I was terrified and unsure of myself. The sky got darker and the giant became bigger. Billy and Larry both smiled as they looked at me. They cursed the ground I walked on and cursed me for being a nice devoted believer. It got darker and Billy's sword was swung at me, I moved out of the way. He took a swing at me with the king's sword and that was when I was knocked to the ground with Larry's shield, and the sword began to come down on me and the feeling was that my career was about over. That is when I woke up in a cold sweat like I was working out already. I looked at the clock. It was 4:25 a.m., time for me to wake up.

"I woke up being scared and hopeful at the same time, and in a cold sweat like I had already worked out. I know that it was no normal dream. I have been given dreams by God before. This one seemed vivid, and He was trusting me with a lot. I woke up and saw the time and got ready to go work out."

Paul looked at him from across the table and said, "Wow, that is awesome! You are given warning, instruction, hope, etc.

It seems that your fight has some Kingdom importance. I have suspected this all along."

"Glad I can entertain you, Paul. My old friend and former mentor seem to be working for the enemy. They seem to have the power to squash me. The dream ends badly."

"Wait a minute, Thad, you were given a name. You are the Disciple of David. Let's talk about that a minute. That is an awesome title to be given. He was such a great king. Also, we get Jesus through David's lineage. Just like some may look on and believe because of your witness through it all. David was also a man with a problem. What was David's problem? Because if you are a disciple of his, you may take on his problems."

"Ok, Paul, I promise it isn't sexual sin."

"Ah, come on, Thad, I am eating here. I am not talking about that. But you should be aware of that. Be prayerful and accountable, especially leading up to the fight. You need to be planning on understanding where this relationship is headed, because you are susceptible to temptation, just like a person in spiritual leadership. You have sought to be a Christian influence, and it seems that your fight has Christian significance for someone."

"Ah, Paul, I am no saint."

"Yes, Thaddeus, you are one of His saints. When Paul wrote to the saints at Ephesus or Corinth, it was to people like you. When John wrote to the saints of Thyatira, he meant people like you. You are a big influencer now. Do I need to remind you of the press and what they have made of your faith? You must be kidding. You have a following. What is your Face Chat up to these days? We are friends and all, but as your pastor, I have always tried to talk to you about the gravity of such matters. You are a big deal."

"Ok, Paul, but you make this sound like I am like you, or some other preacher, or someone with an even bigger audience than you. You make it sound so grand. It is not."

"Thaddeus, most of what we go through doesn't seem so grand. In fact, it is so ordinary. But being in the center of His will is everything. It means everything, and you can bear so much fruit for the Kingdom. How many talented fighters have you passed up because you work hard, train hard, and study hard? How many people started just like you, but it didn't go anywhere because they couldn't live through the ordinary, day-to-day stuff? I bet there are thousands out there with the talent to be where you are, but you were disciplined and blessed. Discipline is what we are talking about. Face it, Thad, it doesn't get more ordinary than waking up at four and going to work at five and sweating it out. That stuff is so ordinary that very few people can handle it."

"Ok, I get it. I understand. But what about how much hope I feel and then I get destroyed?"

"Look, Thad, let's consider a few things. You are best when you are in over your head. That is what it means to be a disciple of David. That is what I was trying to get to. You are used to being the guy everyone is looking for. You are used to it, but last time you got a little comfortable and almost lost it. You got the knockout, but you were out on your feet."

"Thanks for reminding me, buddy!" Thaddeus snapped back.

"What I am getting at is, remember how there are two types of fighters, the underdog and the front-runner. What if you are actually better as the underdog? The underdog needs to be dependent. He needs to be holy and connected and he is the best witness. The underdog is different. You can get comfortable as the king. King David sinned as he was walking across the top of the castle while the other kings were off fighting wars during the fighting season."

"Wait, Paul, you are saying that part of this is that I am better off as the underdog. That doesn't make any sense. I have always been a front-runner and seem to do better that way."

"Well, what about when you won it and when you first came up through the ranks? What happened then?"

"Look. Paul, it was a long time ago."

"Thad, God is going to help you through this, but there is a lot to this dream. Let's continue, shall we?"

"Please, Paul, that is why I am here, so you can make sense of the roller coaster that is Thaddeus."

Paul came back with, "Yeah, Thaddeus 'Pure Class,' the greatest fighter the Octagon has ever seen, who loves Jesus, is filthy rich, has a great family, a great girlfriend, and the best pastor on earth, ha, ha! I feel so bad for you."

Paul continued, "So, here is the hard part. There is a king, whose name you don't know, but he is in charge of the army of God — or some people, or some army you are on. Or maybe they are a group of people who will be influenced by this. Maybe they are your people. But this army seems to have a king that you don't know or recognize. He is making them nervous, and making Rex put armor on that is his, and trying to make you learn things you don't need. God intervenes with this face of someone you may know or have worked out with. It seems that when you meet the man with the face on the stone you will know it. Take that as a word from God. Also, internalize that you are a disciple of David."

Thaddeus nodded and said, "Ok, I get it."

Paul continued to talk with some urgency. "It seems that this army, Rex, this king, will try to make you a fighter that fits a mold, but you need to take the more unlikely path. This more unlikely path will help you the most. You will understand it better later, because in the dream you will know the face on the stone when you meet him. But if you are not living holy and seeking after God, you might not meet the guy with the face on the stone."

"Ah, Rex could be right, maybe I just had some bad cheese or I fell asleep watching something that had scary commercials. Maybe this fight is on my mind, and David on the battlefield was on my mind, and I made the whole thing up."

"Thaddeus, that is faith."

"What? That is faith?"

"Look, Thad, God shows up in dreams and visions and subtle ways because He wants to give the opportunity to say no. All along we were given the opportunity to have faith. In the Garden of Eden we were there with a choice. 'You can eat from any tree in the garden and you must eat from the tree of life to continue to live forever. But when it comes to the tree of the knowledge of good and evil, when you eat of that you will die.' Unfortunately for you, that tree of judgment, and making judgments, and comparing and reasoning, might just be what puts you down in your dream. You are in a battle, Thad, but it is more spiritual than physical. Obviously, your training is part of it, but your training is not the only thing. Your spirit needs strengthening."

Thad, taking it all in, said, "So, how do I do that?"

Paul smiled and said, "I can help with that. Let's begin to

put a plan together. For now, be my rich friend and pay my bill."

"Funny. I thought you didn't like handouts."

"Yeah, I kind of feel like I work for you these days as your practice dummy. Buying my breakfast is the least you can do." Thad set the money on the table for Bethany and they got up to leave.

As they were walking out the door they continued to talk. Thad said, "Ok, Paul, so here is the million dollar question that I don't get. I am learning all of these new things. I am learning how to fight from the opposite side and I am studying. Is the dream telling me not to do those things?"

"No, Thad, that would be foolish. Part of being yourself is studying and learning and I am watching you pick up these techniques really fast. A normal person can't make changes like you have this fast, and you would adjust and change for any fight."

"So what is it saying then?"

"I think you need to keep your finger on the pulse of what is happening. Don't get overwhelmed or scared. Remember to be yourself. I am no trainer, and am getting out of my professional lane here, but the way I see this fight going is you will need the new stuff to throw him off early. Late in the fight, you will probably look more like yourself. But they didn't teach me fight tactics in seminary." They both laughed and continued to walk down the street to the car.

Sunday night came around again and Rex made plans to drive to Curlsville and pick up Debbie. Along the way, he thought of the irony of his life and hers and his connection to Thaddeus. He thought about Thaddeus, and that he was the only person who could bring them both together. Then he had the thought, "Maybe God does love me." He quickly turned on the radio. He turned it up, and played the music louder. He turned it to the hair band station and blasted some old Queen, but the nudge was still there. It was familiar. He knew the feeling, he knew the voice that was behind it, he knew that it seemed trustworthy, but he had never been able to trust the voice, nor would he ever trust the voice again. He looked up and to the right because he somehow sensed that was where God was and said, "What do you want? I trusted you before and you hurt me."

"I hurt you by giving you a beautiful wife and an amazing child who knew almost nothing but my love. People to help you through it. I blessed you with success — Thad — and now I have blessed you with time with Debbie."

Rex was now in a full-blown conversation with "We Are the Champions" blaring in the background. He said, "I can't trust you again. I can't get past it, but you won't leave me alone. I can't have anything for myself. You even took Thad. It is all a mess. LEAVE ME ALONE!"

"Rex, your desire to win and achieve doesn't even come from you. I am all over you. You are blessed. I love you."

At that, it seemed that Rex was no longer talking to himself, and he felt more alone than he had for a long time. He thought of the irony of the song he was listening to. He thought with intensity. He thought about how blessed his life had been and he began to cry a little. He tried to get control of himself and he cried a little more. He stopped alongside the road for a moment and took a deep breath. Rex wanted desperately to get out of the vehicle, but he was afraid that someone would recognize him.

As he got his composure and began to think about it, he

tried to dismiss everything he was realizing about the blessings he had received. He got back on the road again. He was also noticing that no matter what he did, or if he cursed at God in his heart, there was a warmth and a security in his chest that wouldn't go away. *It seems like it is God and He will not go away,* he thought. He felt comforted, which made him uncomfortable. He got to Debra's house. Truthfully, that was about as deep as he wanted to think right then. He thought, *I will go make myself useful.* But he also couldn't help but think, *Who is prompting me to be more useful? How did this happen?*

He got to Debra's house and walked to the door. He straightened his shirt. Rex had decided to wear a little nicer shirt that he didn't tuck in, but he was having a little harder time not wrinkling it. When Debbie opened the door she swung it open. She was wearing a beautiful blue dress with bright gold earrings. She smiled, and her hair was freshly done that day. She grabbed her purse and said, "Hey, Rex. Let's go."

Rex was stunned a little and said, "Uh, ok." He got the door for her and she was walking fast towards the car.

Rex got in the car and said, "I just want you to know that you look beautiful."

She smiled, "Yeah, well, you know, it is this car. I can't keep riding in this thing and not feel like I need to look good in it."

Rex came back with, "You always look good."

She smiled and the moment seemed to have a little more chemistry than they were both ready for, so he finished with, "It is your mouth that I worry most about." At that they were off to the meeting. They drove and laughed and talked a little.

They seemed to be very comfortable with some light insults. When they pulled into the parking lot, Debbie grabbed his hand, "Seriously, though, Rex, I am so thankful you introduced me to these people. It might have changed my life, or saved it. It did something. And who knows, maybe I will just meet a guy here."

He laughed and thought *So witty and insulting. Somehow I am drawn to this; maybe God does love me.* He looked at her and laughed, "Glad I can help. Just looking out for my fighter, you know." She smiled and they went inside. Rex got the door for her on the way in and they walked to the meeting room.

They walked into the meeting and saw that many of the same faces were there again this week. Mac was there and was happy to see them both, and Rachel walked in and greeted them again. Debbie was even more vulnerable in this meeting, and began to talk some about how her addiction happened and what it had been like to have to keep it a secret all of those years.

It was way out of her comfort zone, but she longed to be driving home with Rex after the meeting. Rex was thinking about how beautiful Debbie was. He was glad to be there with her. He was fascinated with the idea that he actually had a lot in common with her, and she wasn't so bad to be around. He was so proud about how she opened up at the meeting. He felt like he really got to know a different side of her as she spoke about her struggle with alcohol.

After the meeting they spoke with Mac briefly and then they decided to get going. They got to the car and were the first to leave. On their way home they stopped at the BC Café. Rex said, "Hey, let's get some coffee or tea or something. This is part of it, learning how to drink something else. That is, if you have time."

She laughed, "I think I have the time for this."

So, they both got their drinks and sat down on some modern-looking semi-comfortable chairs in the corner. Debbie said, "We have talked a lot about me. How are you?"

"What do you mean, Debbie? I am fine."

"Did I say you weren't fine?"

"Sorry. I don't get asked how I am a lot anymore. Oh, I don't know. I am a little nervous about this fight. This fight solidifies a great career for your son. But, man we have a lot working against us."

Debbie quickly responded, "What do you mean, against you?"

"Well, Thad is at the end of his career. He lost his best friend because he wanted to fight him. He has to fight someone who has scouted him for years to close the skill gap. He is at the top of his game; he will be even better down to this weight class. They stole hundreds of hours of practice film. Thaddeus poured into him things about life, fighting, etc. Also, we are not coming off our best fight. Larry is a great trainer, and I hate to admit it, but maybe better than I." He motioned with his hands, "Do I need to continue?"

"But those obstacles never scared you guys before," she stated. "What is different now?"

"Thad — I don't get him. Sometimes his new-found faith bothers me because that is how I got hurt."

"What do you mean?"

"Well, I was telling him all the things we need to change. He told me everything was going to be good, because he had a dream. I used to know how to motivate him."

"Do you mean control?"

"What is that supposed to mean?" he asked defensively.

"Rex, simply that, as a mother, that is what always got me

about you. You played with Thad's emotions. Maybe he will be even better when his emotions are not rooted in what you think or say. Don't let how you feel destroy the faith he has."

"But, Debbie, what if it hurts him like it did me? I am kind of afraid of God myself."

Debbie came back with, "What are you afraid of? Are you afraid of losing? Are you afraid of looking bad?"

"Deb, you might not believe this, but I care deeply about your son. He is my family. He is all the family I have. But this fight is different. It is great that he feels secure, but the kid that came up through the ranks and is maybe the best ever isn't angry anymore. He isn't as hungry, and this is going to be when he needs it the most."

"Rex, do you know why I don't believe that? I don't believe that because you have trained someone who not only is a great fighter, but now is a good person. You got an old pastor to come in and work out with you guys. It is unbelievable. Look, I understand this disdain you have with the Almighty better than you think. I kind of hate church. God and I are not on real speaking terms, especially since I quit drinking. My faith is weak. I used to hear God talking to me and that sort of thing, but Wayne died and it is almost as if my spirit died that day, too. I have never really said it out loud, but it is true." She paused now, teared up and ready to break.

Rex was shocked, relieved, and sad all at the same time, because he had been through something like that himself. He paused for a second. "Then why do you stick up for his faith? Didn't you believe Wayne would live happily ever after with you? Didn't you believe your life would be different? Didn't you believe Thaddeus wouldn't have it so &*()&)*(& tough?

What makes you hold it together and not say $^@(^$@& Him, I am done?"

She was now more teared up; Rex felt bad and tried to recover, "Deb, I am sorry. We need to go."

As he stood up she stayed seated; she pinned his hand to the table and pulled. "Listen here, Jackass, you are not going to leave here now that we are finally really talking."

He smiled, "Ok," and he sat back down.

Debbie looked at him. "Jesus has never left me, even though I have tried to run from Him. Most of the time I dislike Him. I hurt and am angry, but somehow my kid has become great at something. He has become successful. He has met a girl that might be tougher than he is."

Rex laughed and took a drink, "That is your fault. He was looking for someone tough, like you."

She paused, smiled, and continued, "God sent me someone to help me quit drinking." She got really serious and said, "I suspect you have tried to get away and found you can't, too. Rex, I am terrible at being a Christian and I have felt that for the last several years I am not one. I doubt the existence of God every single day, but you have helped me to see the possibility again." Rex teared up and was kind of speechless.

Debbie continued, "Hey, why is $&@()&$) so serious with you? If you keep this up, I might have to start drinking again. Seriously, Rex, faith is what Thad needs to get through this, and you might not want to be fighting against it much, either."

"Wow! I have never thought of a lot of that. I only think about what God can and has taken from me."

"I thought you didn't believe in God."

"No, maybe that isn't it, Deb. We are just not on speaking terms, either."

She came back with, "Maybe it is just easier to not believe in something than to be mad that someone didn't do something about what you went through."

"Maybe, Deb!"

They lightened up and laughed a little and told stories about Thad. Rex was getting to know Deb and Thad in a different way now, and Debbie saw a new side to Rex — and even her son — through him. They drove home and talked. It felt like they had been on a date together. As Rex walked her to the door he held her hand. When he went to kiss her, they embraced and kissed for a moment. She looked at him and said, "That was great, but there isn't another kiss until you ask me out on a real date. This little alcohol group is not your dating loophole, smooth guy."

He laughed, "I will come up with something."

She said, "Ok, I lied." She gave him another good kiss and went inside.

This time Rex was a little intrigued by her and maybe God as well. *What a strange night,* he thought as he got into the car and drove home. He kind of wondered if Thaddeus would be upset that he was now dating his mom, or if he would be upset if he found out without him being told by one or both of them.

CHAPTER 11

HEROES AND LIARS

REX THEN BEGAN to think about God more intensely during the drive back to the city. He thought about how he fought against the Almighty, only to find out that the people around him all see him as God's vessel, helping them anyway. He really might not be as mad about it today. Could it be possible that God Almighty still did love him and accept him?

As he passed by the BSA Club, he saw a man and a woman pushing each other in the street. The man was pulling the woman's hair. As he got closer, he saw that they both had their hands on her purse. The man took his free hand and smacked her face off the side of the red and white brick building. Her face was now bloody; then he kicked her in the ribs.

Rex quietly parked the car and snuck up behind him. She still had her hand on the purse as the man pulled a knife out of his pocket. Rex said the first thing that came to his mind, which was, "Freeze! Now put your hands up and no one will get hurt. Drop the knife!"

He dropped the knife and turned around to Rex. "Just as

I thought. You are not a cop!" He reached down and picked up the knife. As he ran at him, Rex caught his wrist as he was swinging the knife. It cut Rex under his eye. He was now bleeding good.

The woman reached into her purse which had spilled onto the ground, grabbed her cell phone and dialed 911. "Hello, 911 operator!"

"Yes."

"There is a man here who tried to kill me and take my purse."

"What? Where are you?"

Rex knocked the knife out of the man's hand and threw him to the ground. He tied him up with both legs on top and behind him, arching his back, all while tying up his arms. "Operator, the man now has him down and took the knife away from him. The good man has him down now. Please, hurry! Please get here!"

Rex held the man down for two or three minutes before the police arrived. When they got to the scene they took over. One of the officers looked at Rex, "I know you."

"You do?"

"Everyone knows your face around here. You are the great trainer of Thaddeus Class. He is our hero around here. Tell me your name again, Sir."

"It is Rex."

"Rex Metzger, that is right. Wow! What are you doing up here?"

"Just visiting a friend."

On the ground with some paramedics attending her was the woman. Rex walked over to her. She looked up at him and said, "Sir, you saved my life."

He could see her and tell that she was tough, not small, but not fat. She was even a little muscular. "My name is Rex. Looks like he messed with the wrong girl. Many women would not have put up a fight."

Her lip quivered when she said, "Yeah, it would have gotten me killed if you hadn't been here, Rex! My name is Janet Revis, by the way."

Janet was known for her real estate business locally. She had lived in Curlsville for many years.

"Great to meet you, Janet."

"Great to meet you, you truly saved my life. I am sure of it." She began to cry.

Rex bent down and tapped her on the shoulder. He said to her, "It is ok, you are ok now." He touched her on the shoulder one last time as the paramedics attended to her.

Some people from the local paper were there already and took some pictures. A camera was rolling and this was going to be on the news. A woman medic named Becky said to her, "Mrs. Revis, you will need to come with us. You were hit in the head very hard." Janet agreed and they put her in the ambulance. Another medic quickly put some butterfly stitches on Rex's cut under his eye, to stop the bleeding.

Officer Rodriguez pulled Rex aside, "Hey, sorry about this, but we need to get a statement from you. So, where were you coming from?"

"A friend's house."

"Oh, ok, so you have some friends up here? Whose house were you coming from?"

"Ah, yeah, look, I don't want to get into all that. I just want to say I was driving by. I came from a friend's house and I was going back to the city where I live when I saw this man beating this woman out here. I told him to freeze. When he saw that I didn't really have a gun he tried to attack me with a knife. Once I got the knife away from him, it was easier to get him down and hold him there. Janet then called 911 and everyone was here fast."

Once Officer Rodriguez walked away there was a new face in front of him. The incident at this point was only about 15 or 20 minutes earlier, but someone told the station — or Mercedes Lewis — that it was Rex who saved the day. As soon as the officer walked away the light came on and was shining on him, while Mercedes began to talk. "Mercedes Lewis with Channel 3 News, live at the scene where Rex Metzger saved the day. He witnessed a woman being beaten, mugged, and police believe she was about to be stabbed when Mr. Metzger intervened. Rex, as you know, is the trainer of local fighting legend Thaddeus Class. Rex, tell us how it happened."

"Well, I was in the neighborhood visiting a friend."

"Oh, you have friends out here?"

"Ah, yeah, I know a few people." He continued, "When I drove by here there was a man trying to take a woman's purse and he was hitting her and hurting her. That is when I got out. I then yelled something like 'Freeze,' to make him think it was the police. Then when he saw that I wasn't the police he came at me with the knife and I took him down."

Mercedes jumped back in with, "It helps to have a fighting background, doesn't it? The perpetrator must not have recognized you. There you have it folks, a trainer of a fighting legend was driving through the neighborhood and he just saved someone's life. Maybe this super-hero will be visiting a friend near you when you need it. Mercedes Lewis, Channel 3

News, out!" At that she rolled up the cord and said, "Ok, that is it. Thank you, Rex!" At that she was gone.

When it seemed that the police were done and the story was finished, Rex, not knowing what to do, got in the car to drive home. He was disturbed that a man tried to kill him and Janet. He was disturbed at how shaken up he was. He was worked up and confused. His body hurt. It seemed that he hurt his shoulder a little and his legs felt like they would be sore. He was amazed that he could still move. He didn't feel like he was in shape, and compared to his fighters, he was not. But compared to the guy he had just put away, he was in good enough shape to fight him.

Then it hit him. *Oh, man, this is going to come out that I was visiting Debbie. What am I going to do?*

He called Debbie, trying to figure out how he would tell her. Debbie answered the phone with, "Rex, Rex! Thank God! Thank God, you are OK!"

Rex said calmly, "So, you know then?"

"Well, I know you were being interviewed by Mercedes Lewis. That woman must be everywhere at the right time, waiting for a story to break. But you are ok, right?"

"Yeah, but I have a problem. We really haven't talked to Thaddeus about anything and I don't really have any friends in Curlsville."

"Well, it can't be that bad. What exactly did you tell him?"

"I told him that I don't have any friends in Curlsville."

"Oh, yeah, but you meet people all the time."

"No, not really, I keep to myself."

"Oh, ok. Man, you are boring! That is why I kept away from you all of these years."

"Oh. I just thought you thought I was obnoxious," Rex added.

"Yeah, and maybe a little creepy, since you don't have any friends." She laughed, before continuing in a more serious tone. "Come on, Rex, what do you think he will do?"

"Look, when you are a trainer you have to know your fighter and I know him in a different way than you do, just like you know him in a much different way than I do. The mental part of things is important. The story of how we started to see more of each other, the fact that you haven't dated anyone since his father died. The fact that the two closest people to him are not telling him the truth. Do I need to go on?"

"Let me cut in. I might be the closest to him, but with Sally around you are not in the top two anymore," she laughed. Debra continued, "Ok, I get it! This is bad. I am not sure what we should do."

Then Rex said, "Maybe we don't need to do anything yet, let's see how this works. Debbie, do you think it is unbelievable to have a friend?"

She laughed, "Yes! No one would believe that you have any friends! Haha! How about we talk about it tomorrow, Rex? I am really glad you are ok."

"Thank you, Debbie. I am feeling really shaken up and worried about this. I can't believe this happened, but I will be ok. I am just going to be silent on the way home."

Deb then said, "Sounds good. I will talk to you tomorrow. You are going to be quite a hero around here, now! So proud to be your secret friend out here."

Rex laughed a little and said, "Bye."

As Rex drove on he couldn't believe how weird things had been. He had someone who worried about him. He was kind of a local hero in Thaddeus's hometown. Maybe he was finding purpose and meaning. What was happening to him? He didn't want to get caught up in the emotion of it, but he couldn't help but think that God did somehow watch his back. He also then had the thought, *So, now I am going to start believing something because I feel happy. Wow! I am a hypocrite. My good luck is no different than my bad luck in life. It just happens.* At that he tried to escape it, but he feared deep down in a secret place — mostly secret to himself — that he was fighting against something or someone much greater than he. Best not to fight against God Almighty. No one is harder-nosed than that.

Thaddeus was up early and at the gym studying film before five. He sat there and studied for a long period of time. He rewound and fast-forwarded through several of Billy's flurries. He felt that once Billy started hitting, there was no turning back. He was trying to understand how to slow him down. He knew time was short. Thad knew if he didn't slow him down it could get ugly in the first two rounds. This was an uncomfortable feeling for Thad. He had never been there before, at least not as a professional fighter. Self-doubt had crept in. He knew that he hurt, and that Billy wouldn't be dealing with the same type of soreness. He knew so much was different now. Even his other main practice partners had left him. He had so much going on in his mind over this. Everything was now different.

He was concerned and consumed with the worries of the fight, but also amused about Rex. He had seen on social media already and on the national news that Rex saved a woman's life from Thad's hometown that he actually knew and remembered. Thaddeus had no idea why Rex was there, but he couldn't wait to hear all about it. Rex was always good for a story. He had a gruff way of telling a story that was always memorable in social situations. It was one of his favorite things about the fight world. He really didn't piece anything together about the possibility of Rex going to see his mom, because he didn't see it as likely and he was so consumed with the fight. As he continued to study, he felt stumped by the flurries and he didn't know how to stop this relentless punching attack mixed with Billy's ability to grapple. Now Billy would be leaner, faster, and he would still probably be stronger. Experience would go to Thaddeus, but what was he going to do? He didn't know if the counters he was devising were going to get him through this fight, especially rounds one and two.

As he was still rewinding and watching this winning flurry of Billy's in the championship fight, Rex came walking in. He seemed more agitated than usual, which didn't stop Thaddeus. "Hey, there he is! You are a real hometown hero in my hometown. Is that what you do at night, drive around and keep the neighborhood safe? You are kind of like a superhero where I'm from. A superhero with a cherry red Ferrari." Thaddeus continued to laugh.

Rex came back with, "Yeah, not sure how that happened, but the truth got out. I am one lonely superhero in a sports car. Trying to drive through small towns and hurt evildoers."

"Yeah, Rex, I think they are putting a statue up. Maybe my mom will put one out in front of her restaurant. Oh, wait. She doesn't like you that much. Haha!" Thad laughed and pointed at Rex.

Rex felt uncomfortable with that statement a little, but didn't let on about it. He quickly scratched his nose. "Funny. Wow! You are really enjoying this for six o'clock in the morning."

"No, Rex, I just want you to know in all seriousness that it is a cool thing to do. My hometown is safer and I am proud to know you."

"Thanks, Thad."

Thad tapped him on the shoulder and laughed, "And… if you ever need a sidekick, I am here for you."

"Funny, Thad!"

It was good. Sometimes things got a little too serious between the two of them during fight prep time. They watched some film of Billy and drank some coffee. They mostly concerned themselves with stopping the fighting attack. While they were in the heat of this conversation, Paul came in. "Hey, Rex, I hear you need a sidekick. What do you think? You beat up criminals and I can tell them about Jesus. I've got a mask all picked out already."

Thaddeus was shocked by the coincidence, knowing that neither of them had talked, and he laughed hysterically. "Paul, I can't believe you said that! I just told him I wanted to be his sidekick!"

Paul then said to Rex, "Seriously, though, it was pretty cool. Good thing you were there."

Rex was now uncomfortable, "Yeah, I just did what anyone else would do."

Paul smiled and said, "I don't know. I don't think many would have, and even fewer would have done it without getting themselves killed." He shook his hand and walked off to get dressed.

Thaddeus then asked, since he was starting to feel a little more awake, "Yeah, what were you doing up there?"

"Oh, I had a friend I was visiting up there."

"Who is that, Rex, I know everyone up there."

"Oh, it is someone who just moved there."

"Oh, man, Rex has a girlfriend! Wow! Pigs are flying somewhere."

Rex was uncomfortable and scratched his nose. "Ok, time to go to work," Rex said, feeling really uncomfortable now.

"You know, Rex, I will figure it out. I've got eyes everywhere up there now." Rex gave a fake smile and felt noticeably awkward, due to being uncomfortable with this half-truth, scratched his nose again and moved on.

They went on the mats and were going to start drilling with Paul. Rex then said, "Ok, technique is becoming more and more important. It is time to get serious, guys." Thaddeus and Paul both nodded as they began to warm up.

Across town, Billy was warming up along with several workout partners. Durkin, Latimore, and some college elites, and also among them was the new shining workout partner, Ron Kroger. Ron was simply trying to make a name for himself and get noticed with Larry and Billy. Larry had noticed him and was starting to pay noticeably more attention to him. He noticed that he worked hard and was easy to get along with, but also had a cocky streak. Larry felt like he understood how he thought. Not everyone there shared those same feelings, but why should Larry care? He owns the place, right?

Larry planned on keeping Ron around and using him to train Billy as he climbed the ladder, too. It was a great match-up. As they were all warming up, Billy noticed a conversation Larry was having with Ron. "Ron, you've got to step in on that throw more. You need to commit to the takedown, you can't be worried if you are going to get punched when you break through the defenses like that and have an opportunity to throw."

Ron grabbed one of the college wrestlers there and said,

"Like this coach?" He practiced the setup, stepped in and tossed the guy right to his back. It looked perfect. Larry loved it.

"Perfect!" Larry called out. "This time when you come up, you are not going for the pin like wrestling. You are going to finish him with strikes. Now, we aren't drilling the strikes the same in practice. I want you to stop short of the face once with each hand." So he drilled it again and off they went. He hit him and brought him back down.

Ron stood up and did it again. This time when he hit, he released the workout partner perfectly and was in striking position, ready to put the opponent away. Billy was having a little trouble with this interaction. It was probably because he used to be Ron and now they were fighting Thaddeus. Or maybe it was because he knew Larry, or maybe it was because he knew his own heart and his inability to be loyal. Billy knew, deep in his heart, that he needed to stay away from this kid. This kid would hurt him and may just be someone he'd have to beat one day. They would come after him. Billy thought to himself, *I am the $&*()& champ!* He grabbed Latimore and they began to drill one takedown after another. The moves began to flow and look like art. Latimore had worked out with some greats. Thaddeus, and then both Thaddeus and Billy, and now just Billy. But this had helped him to become a very good fighter as well. Deep down, Latimore didn't like what he saw and the attention that Larry was giving to this Ronnie Kroger, either.

As they were getting ready to go live, Larry said, "Billy, I want you to go with Ron first."

Billy replied, "Ok, Ronnie!"

Ron looked up at the HWT Champion and said, "You can call me Ron, Champ, it is ok."

Billy wasn't sure what to do with his sarcasm. Billy didn't have many in his life that stood up to him, especially not a young buck like this who thought he knew something.

Billy grinned as he got loose. The live goes started, and it was going to be anything goes. Obviously, this was at Larry's discretion. Nothing was to injure the champ, but the striking was still on. Not a lot of clubs do it that way, at least not as much, but Billy would train with Thaddeus the same way. Thaddeus and Billy, along with Rex and Larry, had an understanding — that is, until the day that everything changed.

Billy said a little prayer and walked out to fight Ron. They started out trying to trade punches on their feet. Billy decided to go out aggressive and show this little Ronnie Kroger what was up. Ronnie went after him, or at least appeared to — and backed out.

Ron loved that he was getting to train with Billy. Ron saw this as his big chance. Last time they practiced together Larry noticed him. He wanted to be fighting for the title one day himself. This was going to be something that changed it all for him. He could get the big contract. He could train with the champ until it was his chance to be the champ. He thought that maybe he and Billy could be good training partners. He liked to think that he had something special to offer Billy.

The fight started. Billy ducked down in a flurry and popped back up with his right hook. This was something not many had seen yet out of a flurry from Billy. He learned it at GITR, but he was trying to refine it for the fight against Thaddeus. He didn't really use it on Thad much, because he thought he might need it after the plan was in place. Thad reached on the right side and they believed they could put him out with that punch. They got this idea from what happened with Greg

Wilson in Thaddeus's last fight. Thaddeus, when he was tired, would revert back to some bad habits, and the reach and the open space he gave up would happen again. That was their thought, anyway. This time, though, Billy knew he would hit harder and faster than the Baltimore Bomber. Greg Wilson could hit, but the followup hits would be what would seal the deal. They truly believed they could knock out Thaddeus Class with this exchange. Billy and Larry both had spent considerable time working on setups that worked for this attack.

Ron got hit hard. One thing about Ron was he learned. When Billy hit him he thought he knocked him out. Maybe he would have, but the headgear kept him up. Billy followed up with some punches. He hit him once in the stomach and twice in the face. He screamed at Ron, "What's up today, Ronnie? You thought you could come into my house?" Billy got sloppy and Ron was able to drop into a double leg takedown. He spun around behind, still trying to get his bearings.

Billy rolled out. "What's the matter, Ronnie? Can't stop my hook you little $&*()!#&*($)Q!!!" Another flurry happened. Larry laughed and was clearly amused. This time Ron decided to grab at the wrist with both hands, which was the counter that Thaddeus happened to be working on across town. At that, Billy lifted his arm, creating an opening on Ron's body as he still had hold of his wrist. Billy, having the height advantage, straightened him up and brought his bare foot around with the force of a world cup soccer striker and buckled the knee of the young guy.

"Wow! That is not the counter," Ron thought.

Billy came down with an elbow to the face and struck him with an open hand. "You thought you were ready today, didn't ya, ya little $&*()&#@)*(!&@! Little Ronnie $&*()&#$*#()!"

Ron somehow rolled out and got to his feet a little bloody, but no one was stopping him now.

Ron was a very intelligent fighter and could adapt and think well on his feet. After he rolled out, he hung back a second and thought about the mechanics of what was happening. Ron saw this as a puzzle he needed to solve. This time he decided that he needed to somehow circle into Billy before the punch happened, and when he left himself open he needed to strike him on the same side cheek. The flurry they were in only seemed like a setup. It seemed like something that was only setting up the duck and move. This time Billy was frustrated that Ronnie was still standing, so he darted at him and started into his flurry. Billy ducked a punch from Ron that he made look like he was trying to hit him, but he baited him. When Billy ducked, he hesitated a second, and when Billy was popping back up and beginning the swing with his hook, Ron stepped to the side of the swing and socked Billy on his right cheek. This counter seemed to walk into Billy's power and was quite risky.

The champ was out. Ron put him down. Larry was stunned. First, he was concerned with Billy, his fighter that was getting ready for the biggest fight of his career, but he was also impressed with the gem standing in front him, who could also become an all-time great. At the same time, he knew that he couldn't get too high on someone. *Champions have practice slumps,* he thought. Even though Billy had been a great practice fighter, much of that was due to Thaddeus Class. But it had been a long time since Billy had been knocked out.

The trainers came out and looked at the champion. Billy came to and started to look around, stunned that he had gotten knocked out. "Who hit me?"

Latimore said, "Ron hit you, Champ."

Ron smiled at Billy and said, "He knows me as Little Ronnie. You all right, champ?"

Billy responded with, "Nice shot! It will not happen again!"

Ron smiled at the champ, still lying down, and said, "It happened, and that is all I care about today! And, Champ, I have witnesses!"

At that, Billy looked at the medical trainer they called Trainer Joe, "Joe, get me back up and ready to go!"

Joe looked at him, "Champ, I realize this doesn't happen much to you, but you just got knocked out. You need to go through some protocol. You can come back in and work on technique or lift weights and condition, but you need to make sure you have your bearings before we go live again."

"What the $*#(@)*_$(#)@_!" Billy was now swearing constantly, which was something he seemed to be getting away from while around Thaddeus. He barely even knew he was doing it.

He looked at Larry. Larry looked at him, "Look, Billy, you're the champ. Today isn't your day. We can keep working after they make sure you are ok. It's good for you to have to persevere, but no contact the rest of the night."

"Fine!" Billy then stomped off like a bratty teenager and walked on ahead of the trainers off to the stairs which led up to their room.

Larry turned to talk to Ron. He yelled out, "Everybody get a drink. Let's go one more go and finish strong." He stopped Ron. "You stay here. I don't know how to feel about this. You just knocked out my greatest fighter. Good thing Thaddeus Class and his trainer would consider your counter high risk.

They wouldn't even consider it. But, that was smooth. Is that something you practiced?"

"A little, I guess," Ron responded. "I mean, I have practiced it, but I had to tailor it to what was happening. I have always been good at figuring things out. I went to school to be an engineer. I needed to figure this out. I had to try something. He was killing me."

Larry looked at him and said, "Yeah, let's see if it is a fluke!" Latimore! I need you to go with Ron here!" Larry wanted to see if he could wrangle with a seasoned fighter like Latimore, who wasn't going to make many mistakes but was also an all-out brawler.

Latimore set the timer on the wall by taking the minute hand and putting it on the ten, which was a common amount of time to set. They touched hands at the center of the cage and it was time to go. Everyone else paired up and were set to go as well.

Latimore was a well-rounded competitor. He had fought against and with the best. At different points he had been considered one of the main contenders. He had tried to get back to that status, but injury had set him back and his reason for leaving Rex and Thaddeus was that he blamed Rex for neglecting him after he had Billy to focus on. He felt as though he was getting lost in the shuffle, so when Larry told him that he needed to pack up and go with him, so that he had a chance at being a contender one day again, he jumped at it because he believed he could be.

It was a hard thing, but Thaddeus and Rex both understood, even though it hurt them too. Now a new guy had come into this gym and had hurt the champ and caught the attention of Larry. In Joe's mind, it ain't right. Latimore was now really ticked off!

They set the clock and were going to go for ten minutes. Early on Ron dove in on Latimore's leg, at which he punched Ron hard in the back of the head, just to let him know that he was there. There was no question he meant business. Ron was a little dizzy, and made it back to his feet where Latimore began to go on the attack. Latimore combined his leg attacks with some jabs that hit Ron in the face. Then they scrambled off of one of Latimore's leg attacks. There was a scramble and now a badly shaken up Ron Kroger was on top of Latimore. However, he began to systematically take him apart, he controlled him from the top and continued to elbow him into the back of the head and neck.

His ability to keep Latimore face down was unparalleled by that of Thaddeus Class or Billy "The Kid" Smith. This guy was able to hold him in a way and continued to pound on him. After about one minute straight of this, Larry had to come in and stop the fight. Latimore was mad. When he let him up, he began to yell at Larry. "I was about to take him apart. I just needed to get free. I had him. He was doing good, but I sure wasn't beat yet!"

Larry said, "Look, Joe, maybe you were not going to get hurt, but I can't afford for you to get hurt today too. Your Smokin' %#(@)_*% Joe! Your my %*_%@ guy! You know that, man!" He paused and told Latimore, "Go finish up in the weight area today."

There was still some sparring going on around them. Larry pulled Ron into his office, "Look, kid, I don't know what to think here. You hurt my champ today and another major player here. I would be mad if this wasn't a fighting business."

Ron spoke up, "Sorry, Coach Larry."

"Please sit down on the couch, Ron." He sat down on the couch and Larry sat down on an old office chair he had for his desk.

"Mr. Kroger, why do you do this?"

"What do you mean?"

"Well, it is important to understand someone's why. What is yours?" It began to feel like an interview. Larry began again, "When I met Billy I knew he was something special. You, I don't know. But I suspect you might be."

Ron smiled, "Thanks — I think."

"What I mean is, many people have a good day in practice, but does it translate over? In other words, if you trained against a fighter like Billy, or even Latimore, and had to face them in a public way with millions watching, would you win?"

Without hesitation, Ron looked up from the ground to catch the corner of his eye. "Yes, I think so."

"Wow!" Larry looked at him and said, "I do like you." Latimore saw them in the office together, which infuriated him even more.

"So, let's look at your contract here. We only gave you the same contract as everyone else. We gave you the typical stipend of $800 a week to keep you around and keep you on the non-compete list, so you aren't training with our competitors. But I think I might need to nail you down soon."

"Yes, you should consider that. I would love to be able to focus solely on this as my profession," he replied.

Larry laughed. He liked this kid. He liked him a whole lot. He thought he might have his next champion here, and he knew he had him where he wanted him. He smiled at Kroger and said,

"Let's go hit some weights with the other guys and finish up this workout. We can continue this conversation later."

Ronnie looked at him and smiled, "I look forward to it, Coach!"

They left the office and grabbed the others. They went to the weight area and started working out. Larry put on a different face and went up to the training room to check on Billy. When he got to the training room he saw Billy sitting on the training table, iced up.

"How is the champ doing?"

"Larry, I don't feel like the champ right now. That kid really took me out. I haven't had that happen in a long time."

"Hey, and we saw Thaddeus not have good practices, too, and that didn't hurt him in the competition."

"What? You think this dude is like me, and I am like Thaddeus?"

"No, Billy, you are a bad dude who is going to end Thaddeus's run. This Kroger kid has some potential. I am not going to lie, I just watched him knock out someone who is a great fighter, the best fighter I have ever trained and who is going to prove he is the all-time greatest real soon."

"I heard what you said, Larry. You think this kid is something great. You are putting finding him in the same class as finding me. Well, I am not going to train my replacement."

"Billy, what are you talking about? He isn't replacing you. He is replacing Thaddeus as your workout partner. He is someone who can help take you to that next level. He will help you blow past Thaddeus Class and you will become greater than you could have ever imagined. I believe you will be fine competing against this kid. He is still raw, he isn't you yet. He hasn't even fought anyone."

"Yet? Yeah. Larry, I know how this works, everyone is replaceable. I have seen this before."

"Billy, listen to me. You have trusted me through some hard stuff. We left Rex and Thaddeus together and we are going to take it to them. Trust me on this. This kid can help us."

"No, he is going to help you."

"Where is this coming from? You weren't jealous like this before. You're just a little shaken up. Take the morning off and come in in the afternoon."

"Why, so you can prep little Ronnie? Larry I know you."

"Kid, this is a business. I am sorry that you don't trust me. I have done right by you every time."

"Listen, I will take the morning off only so I can come in in the afternoon and teach little Ronnie a lesson."

"Look, Kid, you're great, you know I believe in you. I hope you realize that! Trust me and we can put this behind us. You need the best workout partners to go where you are going. We may have found one. Trust me, huh? I will see you tomorrow afternoon." At that, Billy looked down and nodded and Larry was off.

"Maybe I shouldn't have left that gym over there," Billy said as he looked at Trainer Joe.

Joe looked up at him from his desk in the corner and said, "You are going somewhere. You are already a champion, but you are trying to beat someone who has never lost and has an amazing legacy. They are going to talk about you beating Thaddeus Class for years. You can't worry about this. They are here for you and training with you. Of course, they will get some licks in. They are studying how to compete against you. You are the main target right now. That is how you will get better! I am sure you saw some practice partners have good days against Thaddeus."

Billy looked up at Joe and said, "Thanks, I needed that."

But deep down he knew that Larry couldn't be trusted. After all, look at what they did to Thaddeus and Rex. He thought, *It is just business,* and he remembered all that he had given up to be here. His mind went there, *There is nothing more important than becoming the greatest, and in a short time from now I will prove I am, in fact, the greatest!*

He got up and left the training room and headed for home. He put some headphones on and pulled up his playlist and thought about how bad of a dude he was. As he walked he thought about beating Thaddeus and beating Ron. He thought to himself, *Man, I hate that kid! … And I don't trust him either!* There was a lot of pressure and raw emotion leading up to a fight like this. He was training hard and was worn down.

If you really break it down, you find this feeling of dislike and distrust towards Ronnie had more to do with how Billy was, and how disloyal he was. We tend to do that, don't we? We project ourselves onto other people. We assume they are like us, when, in fact, they might not be. Thaddeus did it. He didn't think Billy could turn on him. Rex did it, he didn't think Larry would do that to him. That is what we do.

He didn't realize he hated Ronnie because of what he himself did to Thaddeus and the close comparisons that he could make. He did, however, deeply realize that he didn't trust Larry deep down, either. In a typical moment, Billy was way too selfish to self-reflect and realize any of this. Luckily for him, his selfish personality type was that of someone who often seemed to flourish in the fight world.

CHAPTER 12

CHASING OAKS

IN CURLSVILLE, DEBBIE was at home. She realized that she thought about Rex a lot. She liked him, and she couldn't really understand why. She had such mixed feelings about it. How could someone who was faithless and godless be the one who was restoring her faith? It didn't seem right. It didn't seem possible. She thought about after all these years how she just had always wanted her Thaddeus to be whole and healthy, and she couldn't get there with Rex as a barrier. It seemed that he kept him angry. *But, man,* she thought, *he really tried to help me and he is helping me. I am not drinking anymore. He really has been through a lot with his pain, and he lost his whole family. He lost little Maggie and his wife Mary.* It didn't seem right, but she was falling for this roughneck. She didn't understand it, but she might need to make a move soon.

Billy was cleared by the athletic trainers the night before after the Ron Kroger debacle happened. Ronnie came in and worked out a little in the morning. It was just working on technique. He knew the champ wasn't going to put up with how things ended, so he didn't want to lift weights or condition in the morning, but he wanted to sharpen his technique to stand toe-to-toe with the champ in the afternoon. He stayed away from Latimore, who continued to give him dirty looks. It was clear that Ron had shaken up the entire gym.

Larry understood the mental part of this game very well, and he liked the chaos. His mindset was, out of chaos champions are born and some are left behind. However, this type of mindset and talk was what put people on edge, because suddenly Latimore and even Billy Smith started to feel as if they were old news.

Ron worked on counters to strikes, which Larry thought was interesting, and grabbed some workout partners he knew from college. Shots, counters, strikes, timing, he was in the zone. Ron and Michael Costello had worked out in the off-season before and were drilling moves. One would do three and the other would do three. They got a little close to Latimore.

When it was Ron's turn to practice a takedown, Latimore stepped on Ron's shoe and pressed down. "You look pretty good, Ron."

"Thanks. You too!"

"Thanks, Ronnie, but your time isn't yet!"

"Awh, Smokin' Joe, that isn't for you to decide, is it?"

"Maybe it is, maybe it isn't."

Ron smiled at him as he got his foot back and smiled again, "Glad we had this talk." He then looked at him as he began to set up the shot on Michael, "Did you figure out how to stop this yet?" At that, he dove in on his leg. He said, "Hey, I also set it up like this, too." He hit it hard again. "Or, if you react slowly like you might, I also do it this way." He then hit it again and again.

Latimore looked at him with a snarl, "We will see, Ronnie."

"It's Ron, respect the ones that give you a beating." At that, Ron pointed to the other side of the mat and he and Michael found a spot on the other side of the room.

He looked at Michael and laughed it off, "What a douche, huh?" They continued to drill as Larry pondered the events in his mind. Larry looked on and thought, *I really have something here. This kid believes in himself. He came in here out of nowhere and shook these guys up. This kid is going to be amazing.* Larry knew that Ron would be getting himself ready to take it to the champ. He knew that he should offer Michael a contract that would keep him fighting in his club permanently and not just on a month-by-month basis. But for Ron this was going to be a different kind of deal.

By being on the monthly list they couldn't work out with other clubs, but when the month was over they could go wherever they liked. The end of the month was coming up in a week, and Larry planned on taking on a new fighter and a permanent new practice hand. They broke for lunch and would be back in the afternoon.

Meanwhile, Debbie and Sally were getting to know each other better at Mama Class's Kitchen. "Well, Sally, I sure am glad you are here. These customers really do love you here." Debbie said this as she poured them each a fresh cup of coffee, as much of the lunch rush had been cleared out.

"I enjoy this. It isn't much different than being a waitress. I guess I knew I was being prepared for something."

"You know, I hope you don't feel weird about being here or anything. I know I saw an opportunity and I know that you make my son happy. I just don't want you to feel weird if things with Thad change."

Sally felt a little awkward. "Yeah, it is a little bit of pressure, but I am ok with it, and I really like your son."

"I know, Sally, I can tell. You look at him like I used to look at my Wayne."

"Thaddeus doesn't talk a ton about his dad. When he does, it seems that he sees him as a giant."

"Well, Sally, you've got to remember, Thaddeus was just little when the Lord took his dad."

Sally noticed that Debbie gave credit or blame or acknowledgement to God. Debbie's faith didn't usually seem to be front and center as much as it probably was before.

"Oh, Wayne was a giant! I didn't fully appreciate what he was to us until he was gone. Wayne had a deep faith, much deeper than mine. I don't know that he would have struggled with life and Thaddeus and everything to the level I did if it would have been me instead."

Sally was shocked, "What are you talking about? You are a single mother who raised a son who loves Jesus and is a great fighter. He is trained to be an attorney and he would probably be pretty good at that, too. Not to mention, he has recently met a great new love interest." She said this as she put her hands up in the air and bowed at her hips a little with a smirk.

Debbie laughed, "I am sure I don't have to tell you, but my son isn't perfect. There were a lot of hard years there. He needed a father. He got in fights at school and beat kids. He was angry all the time. He excelled in wrestling, boxing, and whatever I could put him in — football, whatever, just so he was hurting someone where it was allowed. It was very hard."

"Is that why you didn't remarry?"

Debbie looked up, a little surprised that she asked such a direct question, but she wasn't threatened because she liked things that way. "I guess, I never found my Wayne again. Maybe I didn't look because it would have been crushing for Thaddeus. Maybe it was a mistake, maybe I should have found someone, I don't know."

"Debbie, stop. Love isn't about filling a job description. It isn't like hiring for a need. You did great!" Sally said this as she looked at Deb and grabbed her wrist.

Things were getting too serious for the two of them, so Debbie said she needed to go to the back and work on something. She left with, "Man, I am glad you are here, and I am so glad you and my Thaddeus are together."

"Me, too!"

Debbie grabbed the pot of coffee and walked towards some customers left in the corner to see if they needed anything like a refill or more food. It was the waitress's responsibility, but she liked to talk with the customers, and it broke the awkwardness these two hard-nosed women felt with each other.

After Sally had taken care of some customers the phone rang. Debra's cell phone had rung a few times, but she had left it by the register. Then the phone at the restaurant rang on the wall. It was behind the bar area, behind the counter. When it was busy, it was always hard to hear the person on the phone. It was a number from the city.

Sally answered, "Hello, Mama Class's."

The voice on the other end hesitated and tried to talk in a higher tone of voice — which was really awkward. "Is this Mama Class? Can I speak to Mama Class?"

"Can I tell her who is calling?"

"Ah, just Roberto."

"OK, I will let her know. Hey Tina, can you tell Debbie that she has a phone call and it is Roberto."

She thought about the number and she knew it was from the city. When she looked at Debbie's cell phone, she saw there were two missed calls on the front screen from someone named Rex. The number was from the city. Was she dating Rex? Her mind was racing. *Wait a minute. She was dating someone and he was up here visiting a friend when he rescued that woman. Oh, man, they haven't told Thaddeus and there is a fight coming up and a big fight, too.*

She grabbed Debbie's phone and started walking back to the back with it. She heard Debbie in her office, giggling like a little girl. "I told you not to call me here."

"Well, yeah, I miss you, too."

"Ok, let's talk tonight. Bye." She giggled as she hung up the phone.

Sally waited a minute and knocked on the door. "Come in, Sally."

"Hey, Debbie, I thought you might want your phone. It was sitting out by the register."

Sally had opened the phone quickly and shut it so that the missed calls were cleared out and not showing up on the lock screen. Debbie didn't realize she knew. She looked at Sally, "Thanks!" Sally felt extremely awkward and wasn't sure if she should be telling Thaddeus about this, or if she should talk to Debbie about it. She didn't know what to do, so she didn't do anything, and quickly handed her the phone and went back to what she was doing before the phone rang.

Afternoon came around and it was time for the excitement that no one was talking about. Billy was going to bring his A-game and square off with Ron again. Billy got there early and began to break a sweat. He was going to need to set a precedent. This was his gym and there was no one who was going to come in here and show him up. Especially some no-name kid that was just here for practice. Billy knew the kid probably had a future, but his future wasn't now.

Ronnie came in not long after Billy. He began to stretch and warm up. He acted cool, and didn't really let on that anything significant was happening that day. But deep down inside he knew that this could be a very interesting day, as he was beginning to prove himself to notable people. He could sense that maybe it was time for a change, and that change would help him to set up a good future for himself.

When it came time to start drilling technique, Latimore and Billy were on one side of the mat while Ronnie grabbed hold of Michael Costello on the other side of the room. There were several groups in between them, all drilling technique. This went on for about 30 minutes. They were told to pick it up, and this went on in a more intense manner for another five minutes. Then they were told to get a drink.

When they all came back in, Larry said, "Billy, you and Ronnie need to pair up, everyone else stay the same. We are going to go for ten minutes. For ten minutes it is live, unless we stop you personally. Let's go!" They smacked hands and the whistle blew.

Billy started out a little conservative, as did Ronnie. They didn't attack very hard at first, for fear of the other's counter-attacks. Billy was trying to watch for the tells that young Ronnie had. He tried to understand if he gave away hints when he would shoot or strike. Finally, after about two minutes, Billy struck Ronnie hard on the cheek. Billy this time didn't overplay his hand like he had the last time they fought. He followed him up, but with cautious jabs instead of something risky, like diving in on a leg.

"What's wrong, Ronnie? Didn't you think I would adjust?" Billy said, as he danced around him. Ron then dove in on his ankle and came up on top behind him for a second. Ron blasted him in the side of the head a few times on each side before Billy rolled out on his feet. At this point they were taking up a lot of mat space because the Octagon would have kept them more contained, but these were the parameters they were given. Billy got a few shots in on Ron and Ron returned fire. The whole time Larry was watching like a hawk. He liked the kid and saw a real future here with him.

As the time went on, Ronnie took a few chances. He took a few shots and ended up taking Billy down again. Billy countered and somehow ended up on Ron, and caught him in the face a few times before it ended. There wasn't much time; there was probably about a minute and a half left on the timer and neither fighter had really outdone the other yet. There was some urgency as they both continued to fight. Billy came in swinging and leaving the right side open again. Ron saw the opening but decided to roll out the other way this time. There was something about it that he didn't want to do it again. He couldn't believe it and he thought to himself, *He didn't learn the first time! Is he showing me how to knock him out, or what?* With about 45 seconds left, Billy then connected with some heavy blows followed by a double leg takedown. He somehow finished the go on top of Ronnie, who was on his back with Billy's thumb in his throat, cutting off his airway.

He screamed, "You think you can beat me, kid? This is my house!"

The buzzer on the wall rang and everyone stopped but Billy kept going. Latimore walked over and laughed, "Hey, that is why you are the champ."

Larry yelled out, "Billy! Let him go!" At that Billy let him go. He let him out and Ron gasped for air.

Billy yelled out, "Larry, I hope you are not going to keep this guy around here very long!"

Larry yelled back, "What is wrong Billy, feel threatened?"

"No, just reminding you to take the trash out once in a while!"

Ronnie went to get a drink. He sat by himself in the hall. The next set of goes would be less striking, but they would rotate fighters, and thus fighting styles, on the champion. Whenever one person got tired, another would go in and fight. Larry would also let them know if it was Jiu-Jitsu, boxing, kickboxing, wrestling, etc.

When Ronnie came back in he needed to start with Billy. Larry always wanted the fighter that was standing out to wear the champion down first. The clock was set for another seven minutes. Billy looked at him and nodded, "Back for more?" Ronnie winked at him and nodded back. This made Billy angry. Truthfully, it is because it would have been normal for him to do such a thing. Billy would have looked up at an older fighter and let him know that he still had something left for him.

Larry announced, "All right, first fighters; boxing, GO!" The clock started and Ron was only supposed to go until he was tired. He stepped in and caught the champ on the jaw. He seemed to have caught Billy off balance and they sparred into the wall. Billy rolled out off the wall, and planted him with a vicious jab. He hit Ron again and again for another 30 seconds straight. Billy planted him with some more shots and then he went for the hook again. Ronnie saw it coming from a mile away and quickly got to the other side after moving out of the way. Billy exposed himself and Ron cracked him on the jaw, knocking Billy down.

Billy went down before anyone even rotated in. Billy wasn't even sure what happened. Billy got back up and circled in on Ronnie. This time he hit him with a jab and caught him with that hook that Ronnie didn't see coming the first time. Ron went down and had some trouble getting back up.

Red Jackson walked over to Larry and tapped him on the shoulder. "You'd better sign that one. He has heart." Durkin and Latimore heard him and they didn't like it very much. Red is kind of a puppet master type of coach. He didn't mind stirring the pot in this crazy man's game. That was something Larry loved about him. He preyed on emotions to get the most out of people. What made it so effective was Red didn't talk a lot. So when he said something, people unconsciously assumed it was important. Larry was aware of this, but the fighters didn't reflect on it enough to understand why it worked.

Larry looked at Latimore and said, "Get in there! Jiu-Jitsu!" Ronnie walked to the other side of the room and got a drink of water out of the fountain. He sat there for a minute and watched the champ. He thought to himself. "I can beat him! I know how to now!"

About at minute six it looked like Durkin, who was right before Ron, was going to get to stay in there. Slippery Pete, an experienced grappler who was fresh, was taking it to Billy at the end of the go, as expected. Billy went through several tough partners, but he needed to dig deep right now. They were wrestling and going takedowns. Billy got the final take-down and rode him out until the end of the time. Billy got a drink. The others began to drill moves over and over again. After about six or seven minutes, Billy came back into the room and drilled with Latimore. The last ten minutes were drilling moves and it was intense. At the end they were done. Ronnie would have liked to go with Billy again, but what a joy to know that he had a formula for the champion. After he thought about it, he thought maybe it was good that he didn't go back against him again today anyway.

Larry grabbed Ronnie's sweaty arm and said, "We need to talk about your contract. I won't need you here in the afternoon tomorrow. Let's talk about it at lunch tomorrow." Ronnie smiled and agreed. His confidence now soared. Billy and Latimore looked on with an irritated spirit.

The next day Billy was doing his normal training in the morning, and was going to have more live goes with Ronnie, Latimore, Durkin and the others. It was a brutal 45 minutes. First they drilled for about 15 minutes. The last 25 minutes was two ten-minute goes with a five-minute break. The champ was then going to hit some weights.

Ronnie and Billy did one live go for ten minutes. It was a lot of mat work. Situations were given and they would have to fight their way out of them. It was one situation after another. Striking was minimal and light. Billy won this battle hands down and looked like the champion today. Ron Kroger looked good, but he was a step behind Billy most of the morning. This was good, because the focus was on Billy and it had to be about Billy right now.

Ronnie went and got showered up and waited for Larry. Larry took a little longer while he stayed and motivated Billy with the weights and his conditioning. Billy was going to come back in the afternoon and just drill and work on technique. It wasn't going to have the same type of intensity this workout had.

Ronnie sat in Larry's office and waited for Larry. Once Larry got changed and walked down the hall, he came to his office and saw Ronnie texting on his phone. Larry called out, "Hey, Ronnie, you ready?" "Yeah, Coach, I am ready!"

Ron grabbed his gym bag and started walking. Larry looked at him, "Just call me Larry." As they walked out the door, Latimore saw them leaving together and knew that he was taking him out to eat. He knew they were going to Moedoe's and Larry would be offering him something to make him a permanent fighter. He knew the drill very well, actually.

Latimore thought to himself, "Ah, $*(#)_* no!" This was something he knew all too much about with Larry and with Rex. He thought to himself *this can't happen.* Currently, Ron wasn't being compensated to the level he deserved because he was a no-name. In fact, he was a great secret now. This could be the find that really separated Larry from Rex and everyone else. No one was even going to realize where he came from. Latimore looked on and thought, *This ain't going to happen.*

Larry had reservations at Moedoe's and they went in. He joked around with the hostess because they knew each other, and he took a private booth in the back. Ronnie sat across from Larry, a little nervous; he knew he was facing a giant and they were in his domain right now. He sat there and looked at him and thought, *I am in his ring now. This is his Octagon. No matter how excited you get, Ron, don't sign anything tonight.*

Larry began, "So, I have been really impressed with you, Ron. You show a lot of promise. You are raw. You are not there yet, but I see a beautiful canvas to work with. You are a thinker and a competitor. I think you could be great for our club and for Billy. Maybe one day you will be a champ yourself."

Ron looked at him and smiled, "Thanks, Larry, I appreciate that."

Larry went on, "That is why I want to make you an offer to be an exclusive fighter at our club."

"Really?"

"Well, yeah, Ron, what did you think you were doing here?"

Ron smiled. He thought, *I will buy a new car, a new house, everything will be new. I have finally made it. I can just pull my current car right into the junk. Finally!*

Larry reached into a professional-looking folder he had with him. "Now, here is the deal. We need you to be committed to being a workout partner for Billy. You may also be asked to train others like Latimore. This also gives us the exclusive rights to you as a fighter, and we will get the standard percentage off of your fight purse."

Ron looked at it. Something didn't feel quite right, but the offer was huge. It was bigger than he thought it could be! He knew he wouldn't be rich, but for a young guy coming out of school, he could pay off some bills and buy a new house and get a car. It was great, and he would get to do what he loved. He would get to chase his dreams! They would also be investing in him and would want him to win.

Sunday morning came around again and the fight was getting closer and closer. The people who gathered at Trinity Bible Church seemed to keep to themselves around Thaddeus when he had a fight coming up soon. Many of the people who went to church there kind of knew to not ask him for autographs on Sunday because he liked to just go and be a part of the congregation. Also, people knew him and some of the luster had worn off. Most important, Sally was sitting there with Thaddeus and couldn't be prouder. People would not say much to her, because she was a guest and with Thaddeus, but they were so glad she was there.

When Paul got up to preach he had a fresh black eye and said, "So excited to talk to you today about what it means to be true to yourself. Thaddeus, you can vouch for it — I am much too old to be fighting, and I am a terrible fighter!" The church roared, starting with Paul's own kids in the front row.

He continued with talking about being true to what God calls you to do, speaking words from the Apostle Paul in Second Corinthians, and talking about how we are all molded for something different. Thaddeus took in a lot of the message and thought about how God was using him, going to use him, etc.

As he got to a place in the sermon about secrets and not being true, and how our sin always finds us out, Paul said, "Brothers and sisters, it isn't good when they find out you are lying and not being true. It isn't good even to lie to protect someone." Suddenly, Sally felt this overwhelming weight of knowing that Rex and Deb were probably seeing each other, but they were within a month away from the fight, and Thad needed to have no distractions. He was so focused on this fight and nothing else. Sally truly didn't know what to do.

Forty-five minutes away in Curlsville, Deb was in church and thinking about the mess she was in. She thought about how it could be a distraction for Thad, and that she was already a distraction for Rex. She thought about how confusing it all was, but she felt giddy inside. She hadn't felt this happy in years, and she surely hadn't felt this happy in church, that was for sure.

Barbara spoke with her after church, "So, Deb, what is

going on with you? You seem so happy. What is his name?" Deb was kind of taken aback by the question, but Barbara was very insightful. They were alone, off by themselves. She looked at Deb, "It is your kid's trainer, isn't it?"

"What? How did you know that?"

"Well, you are not usually this happy in church! I also saw this newscast and he claimed he had friends around here. He doesn't have any friends! Haha!"

Debra was blushing a little and said, "Listen, Barbara, I would like to talk about this later, but I can't right now. Please do not say anything about this!" Barbara made the motion with her hand like she was turning a key and locking her lips. She then pretended to throw away the key. Deb said hi to a few people and needed to head out, and so she did. Deb turned to leave and Barbara saw someone she needed to talk to and moved on.

Deb left, and knew she needed to leave so she could meet up with Thaddeus and Sally. She drove home to finish preparing lunch for them all. There was some meat cooking and Thaddeus was at the stage of the fight preparation where he needed to regulate what he ate for the best performance, not so much for weight. It was understood that there wouldn't be a lot of starches or carbs there. The meat would be somewhat lean; she had all of the details like this down. She knew the drill.

Back in the city, Thad and Sally were leaving church. They were trying to slip out the back when little Johnny Zarka came up to him and said, "Hey, Thad, I hear you are going to knock out your friend who used to come to church with you." Johnny was only six years old — and quite bold. He had become quite comfortable around Thad.

Thaddeus always stopped and talked to him, even though he had his coat on and was giving every social clue that he was trying to leave the parking lot right then and move on to the next thing. He looked at Johnny and said, "Yeah, I hope so."

Johnny had trouble understanding and looked at Thaddeus and said, "But, Thad, I thought you guys were friends and were trying to help each other, that is what you told me before."

Thad teared up a little and looked at little Johnny. He couldn't help but think, *man it is hard when kids understand better than adults do.* He said, "Yeah, Johnny. Sometimes people aren't who you think they are. But, that is ok, God is good, right?"

He looked at Thad eye-to-eye now, because Thad knelt down to talk to him. "Are you who you say you are?"

Wow! Sally looked with awe at the boy's mother, Mary, who was standing nearby. She nudged Sally and said, "Thaddeus and Johnny really connect. Thaddeus has always made time for him. He even has come to some of his school functions before. I think they connect because we lost Johnny's dad two years ago. Thad can relate to what the kid is going through. He actually told me he doesn't want the kid to go through the anger he went through. The kid needs someone to tell him it will be alright once in a while."

Sally teared up and smiled. She looked at Mary and said, "I am so sorry about your loss."

Mary looked at her and said, "Thank you! But, listen, I have learned by watching your guy there that God is good. You know, he gave his testimony here not long ago. God is good! My son has needed him and some others around here to show him that. Thad told me that maybe he wouldn't be a fighter today and would have a different life, if he hadn't had to go through the pain and anger he went through without a father." Sally was blown away.

They got to the car. Thad could feel Sally smiling. Thad looked at her and said, "What?"

She finally burst, and she punched him in the shoulder, "I can't believe you never told me any of this. You spoke at your church and gave a testimony about your life. You are in this young kid's life who doesn't have a father. Why wouldn't you tell me any of this?"

"Sally, it never came up."

"Look, when you are trying to impress a girl, let it come up. Because you really help that kid."

"Look, Sally, I try not to be seen doing things like this. That isn't what it is about. I actually know what it is like to be that kid without a father and trying to make sense of life. It is horrible. No one should have to go through it."

Sally jumped in, "But, Thad, it worked out for you." She grabbed his hand and smiled.

He grinned a little as he put the car in drive and began to pull out of the parking space. "Yeah, it did. It did work out, and maybe it was part of God's plan and all of that, but I wrestled for a long time with it being His plan, even after I became successful as a fighter. It is so hard looking that kid in the face who met Billy and knows that Billy and I helped each other, and now I need to get in there and try to hurt him."

Sally looked at him, "Are you having second thoughts?"

"Sometimes, Sally. I really tried to help Billy, just like I did little Johnny Zarka. Now it is all just confusing."

She leaned in to speak to Thad and said, "Look at me Thad."

Thad replied with, "For a second, but I am driving here."

She looked at him and said, "He ain't like you! He took advantage of you and is willing to throw you away in an instant. He ain't playin'. You need to teach him a lesson. That seems to be a God-honoring thing. Little Johnny can't have the end of the story being that nice guys finish last. You need to win, for God's glory, for the nice fighters out there."

Thad laughed, "Sounds like a pretty small club, The Nice Fighter Club, that is."

"It is, and they are counting on you."

After that the conversation lightened, and Sally couldn't figure out how she was in Thaddeus's car, going to dinner at his mom's house — who was now letting her run her restaurant. It scared her some to realize that she was out of control and now somewhat dependent on a man. She didn't like it, but she did like Thaddeus a lot — and his mom, and the job. She felt in awe of him, because he was a better person than she thought he could be, but deep inside she was concerned. Experience had told her that men are not what they seem. Especially an internationally-known person like Thaddeus Class can't be all that he was cracked up to be at home — but maybe she was wrong. She hoped, but didn't really think she was.

They laughed and joked. It was truly perfect. When they got to the house, Thad said something kind of funny that struck Sally weird and she suddenly remembered she may know something that Thad didn't know that he would want to know. Thad looked at the house he grew up in and said something like, "I wonder if my mom does have a boyfriend, and who it is, you know, what is he like? It is kind of a weird thing, you know. I mean no one can replace your dad, right?"

Sally knew the topic was heavy even though she couldn't

relate at all. She would have replaced her dad most days growing up, yet still loved him somehow. She thought for a moment, but knew that she wasn't completely sure. So, she just awkwardly said, "I don't know. She is a good judge of character. I am sure he is a great guy."

Thad said, "Yeah, I guess! I am hungry. Let's go eat."

They walked up the three wooden steps in front of the house that led to the porch and walked across the porch to where the front door was. They walked in and were greeted by a little white poodle. "What?" Sally said, followed by Thad's, "Mom, what is this?"

She looked at him and said, "It is a dog. What do you think it is? This is Sammie, my ferocious guard dog." As she said that, he was wagging his tail and licking Sally's face.

"Really, Mom? You are going to take care of a dog now."

"Maybe!"

Sally chimed in with, "Hey, whatever! He doesn't shed!"

At that Thaddeus said, "Whoa! This must be contagious." Then Sammie came up to him and licked his hand gently. Thad kind of stomped his feet and the dog started jumping, bobbing and weaving. This dog was ready to play.

Deb looked at him and said, "Oh, yeah, he is a fighter!" Thad got down and grabbed a paw and started to wrestle with this tiny little dog. They were ready to eat and they sat down.

When they were all seated, they started to pray. Deb grabbed both their hands and said, "Dear Lord, thank you for bringing us all together, and we pray this food will nourish us. Help us to serve you and do your will today as we walk in your joy. In Jesus' name, Amen."

Thad looked up and said, "Ok, Mom, I've got to ask. Your prayers are better. You got a dog. You seem happy. You don't appear to be drinking or anything, what is going on? Your new boyfriend isn't spending the night here or anything, is he?"

Deb smiled and her mind went back to when Thad was a boy and thought his mom was going to go on a date and he went to the guy and told him he would beat him up if he tried to get fresh with his Mama! It was embarrassing for Deb, but funny.

"Ah, Thad, you have always been so protective of your Mama! But don't forget I gave birth to and raised a fighter. I can take care of myself."

Sally laughed, but the topic was making her a little uncomfortable. Deb continued, "Look, Thad, nothing like that is going on here. It is all by the book!" She added, "But I can keep you updated, if you like."

"Got It, Mom! Got It! Too far!" They all laughed.

Deb wanted to get away from the current topic so she began to look to something else. "So, Thad, did Sally tell you how well she is taking care of things at the restaurant?"

"Well, she hasn't said much, but I can tell that she loves it and I know she is doing well there!"

Deb added, "I knew she could do it!" She and Deb smiled at each other.

Sally replied, "Thank you, Deb! It has been a great experience! I enjoy it! And being around you helps me to understand why your son is so messed up!"

They all laughed.

The conversation continued. They didn't talk much about the up-and-coming fight initially. They talked about the food and all hung out for a little cup of coffee with some whipped cream on top. This helped Thaddeus feel like he was treating himself. It was a weird little thing he started while training a few years back, especially when the diet restrictions really started in his training.

Before too long it was time to go. Sally needed to get back and run some errands and Thaddeus was going back to get a light run in that night. They needed to start heading back to the city, while Rex would be making his way towards Deb to go out later. Rex and Deb already felt weird about it, and Sally did, too, because she had a strong assumption and she didn't know what to do about it.

CHAPTER 13

ANSWERED PRAYER

BACK IN THE city Billy was hitting it hard. He tried to listen to a podcast earlier with some preacher on it, but the phone rang. He got off track talking to some girl he met recently. He went to the gym and was studying film. He set his mind to work out hard, knowing that Thaddeus would not workout as hard on Sunday. In preparing for a fight with Thaddeus, this was one of those mental edge types of things. Where Thaddeus was using Sunday as somewhat of a rest day, Billy was going to lift hard and run hard and really push himself. He knew that he was going to hurt when it was all over and he would go into tomorrow's workout a little tired. Larry would be there with him to help push him. In Billy's mind, he was working hard when Thaddeus was not. It was a confidence boast, just another one of those subtle games a fighter plays with himself.

Larry let Billy kind of decide what workout he wanted to do that day. Larry wanted Billy to be motivated and gain a mental edge with this type of workout more than anything. It didn't matter so much what he did that day, or even for how long. It was about how hard he trained.

When Billy got to the gym he decided to do some circuit lifting which would be followed by some hills. They had a private type of alley that not many people used. The people that did go on it knew Billy and Larry, so it wasn't a big deal.

There was a lot of screaming in the weight room that day. At this point it is high reps and low weight, but they had adopted a match strength type of approach, like Thaddeus did. Technique with the weights at this point wasn't as important, because they needed match strength. Billy needed to be strong at the end of the fight as well as at the beginning. Afterwards, it was to the hill. It was cold, and Billy was already sweaty, so he had the hat and the gloves and the sweats on.

Larry told Billy on the way out to the hill, "Today is when you make the big gains. You know he isn't training hard today. You know that he isn't doing what you are doing!" As he said it, there was drool coming out the side of his mouth and you could see his cold breath in the wind. "It is time, Billy!" Every one of these hills is a round! Get to the top! Beat him on this hill, Billy! This is where you beat him before you even get in the Octagon!"

Billy stretched a little and it was a go. "If you are going to win, Billy, you need to fight all the way to the top! You are the champ! You are going to take him down! This is going to be unforgettable! It starts right here!" By this point, Larry was yelling and it was time. He blew the whistle and kept time for the first one.

Larry didn't really know how fast Billy should ascend up this hill. He did, however, know that this was going to be the fight of his life and if he did it fast the first time, he was going to push him not to lose much speed the second time up. The key for Larry was to really push him with a hard time to beat on the first time up.

Billy was a much faster runner than Thaddeus, and in his mind he not only thought about the fight, but he thought about beating Thad up the hill. He thought about punching Thad so hard that he couldn't get back up. He thought about all the people who doubted him, and all the pain he had in his life. He thought about having no father and he pushed it harder up that hill. He went for it.

Billy reached the fire hydrant that marked the spot for the finish line. In his mind he beat Thaddeus walking into the ring. He won the staredown. He beat him in the Octagon. He fought him hard. Some words came to him about how to win a staredown and what it means to be ready and mentally prepared. Then he realized most of what he said in his head was similar to things Thad said. Then he was mad at God. He thought, *So, the only way for me to accomplish my dreams is through my mentor. That seems so wrong. Thanks a lot!*

He had such intense feelings as he was coming back down the mountain and letting his body take him down the hill, that when he hit and touched his hand to the sidewalk he exploded, and in his mind it was round two. This time they were grappling and he threw Thaddeus over his head like he did the last day they'd seen each other. He got on top and pummeled him as the crowd was in awe and the announcers were baffled. It was historic.

Billy pushed it so hard up the hill that he beat his original time, and when he reached the hydrant he let out a deep grunt. He turned right around and began his rest down the hill, but still pumping his arms as he went back down.

When he got to the bottom, Larry knew that Billy really let it all out on that one, but the problem was there were three more rounds in the fight, and Larry wanted him to go through the wall today. When Billy hit the bottom his hand touched the ground and Larry yelled out, "Win this fight in the third round!" and Billy took off again. He recovered. He was in the best shape of his life. He was stronger, had more muscular endurance, had more lung capacity. He had more confidence and knew more about fighting and competing than he had at any other point. He was going to dethrone the great Thaddeus Class. He knew it deep within his soul. He would beat him. He was better the last time they fought, maybe the last several times, and on that day he would be better than Thaddeus, too. He was reaching for greatness as he sprinted up the hill.

He got to the top and didn't want to slow down much. He turned around and went back down the hill, letting the hill take him down. When he hit the bottom Larry yelled again, "The fourth round. This needs to be the greatest round of your life!" He continued to yell and push him while Billy thought about what it would be like to see Thaddeus Class beginning to falter and get tired. In his mind, he kicked and punched. He countered any shot Thaddeus had. He scrambled, and was now on top of him, beating him down from behind. Thaddeus rolled over on his face and Billy caught him with his head up against the mat. He hit him and Thaddeus was out. Just then Billy reached the top of the hill, and as he touched the fire hydrant he lifted his hands in the air in victory. Then he ran back down.

This time at the bottom of the hill Larry was screaming at him. "It isn't over! You need to put him away now." This time Billy was punching and clawing in his mind's eye. Thaddeus

Class was squirming and Billy caught him in a choke and he began to squeeze. He squeezed as he continued to knee him in the back and he was going out. At that he continued to punch Thad and give shots to the ribs. He put him away as he hit the top of the hill and yelled! "$&@#)(YEAH!!! I AM THE $&@#*()&$@)* Champ!"

He jogged back down and went back inside to jump some rope. Billy had never felt better and Larry had never seen someone who was more ready. Larry thought, *It will be a historic night! Larry you're a genius!* Billy was making great gains every single day and would hit a nice peak on fight night if everything continued to progress the same. At that he went back inside while Billy finished the last 15 minutes jumping rope before calling it a day.

Later on that night, Deb was focused on making herself feel beautiful. She wanted to put some makeup on and look good, but not let on that she put any time or effort into it. She couldn't wear sweatpants or something like that, but she was going to wear jeans and make them look good. She noticed that when Rex would come and pick her up he was starting to dress nicer, too. It was a weird stage because they were dating and going to these meetings and not telling Thad, and now there had been some press with Rex in Curlsville. Thaddeus — and Sally, for that matter — could put a timeline together of when this all started. It made them nervous, and people would recognize him and the car, and it really wouldn't be long until the very awkward conversation came out. It wouldn't be a big deal, but all parties involved were not into distractions during the training leading up to the big fight, and especially not a fight this big.

Rex pulled up in his Ferrari and clicked the lock as he

walked to the door. Deb, looking more radiant than ever, opened the door as he was beginning to knock. "Deb, I almost hit you."

She looked at him, smiled and said, "You wouldn't dare." She then kissed him on the nose as she walked by him. They got in the car and they were off. It was beginning to feel like they were old friends. They both were able to talk about their addiction problems. They were able to talk about life and loss and anger and pain. They even talked about God. Both of them were disappointed when they got to the parking lot because it was time to enter the meeting. They both knew it was to be an interesting night, the email from Rachel said the topic was, "Secrets." They both wondered if they completely knew the other, and if they truly knew what made the other tick. Deb looked at the car and giggled inside. *He must really like me, because this is way too elaborate of a plan just to try to get into someone's pants.* Rex opened her door and they went inside.

The next day Ron came in to New Horizons. He came in at the normal time in the morning. He stood looking in at his locker and was starting to get some clothes out of it. Latimore walked up behind him and said, "So, what do you think you are doing kid?"

"Well, Smokin' Joe, I was about to get changed, but since you are creeping me out behind me, I might not take my pants off just yet."

Latimore walked around in front of him at his open locker. "So, you think you are one of us now?" Some others were close by, looking on. "I remember being you, being asked to go to the local restaurant. I remember being asked to be around to train Thaddeus and all the good treatment. Then they put that contract in front of my face, and I thought I made it. Well, it seems they have forgotten about me, kid!"

Ronnie looked at him, a little taken aback. Latimore was now only about six inches from his face. "Look man I am sorry to hear about that. We are all just trying to get there."

"Yeah, just know Ron, it ain't happening for you through here. I won't let it, and the champ don't like you either."

"Whatever. Leave me alone so I can get dressed now, please."

Ronnie got dressed and walked by Larry's office. He was talking with an old retired fighter in his office. He yelled out, "Hey, Ronnie! You got some paperwork for me today?"

"I have some legal eyes on it!"

"Wow, Ronnie, you came to play, but lawyers?"

"Ok, Larry, it is me. I am looking at it! I am pretty excited about the opportunity. Give me until Thursday!"

"Sounds good, Ronnie." At that Larry felt satisfied and went back to what he was doing before.

Ronnie went out on the mat. He jogged for a few minutes and stretched. As he was stretching out his quads, Billy came walking behind him and stepped on his hand. "Oooh! Sorry about that Ronnie!"

"All good, champ!" He acted like it didn't even phase him. It was strange, because he wanted to be there. He was doing well, but was even the HWT Champion of the world threatened by him there? *How can that guy be insecure? I guess it isn't about what you have done or what you have.* This was truly a very odd situation.

But Ronnie was a thinker. He was not interested in playing games. This was the opportunity that he had and he needed to run with it now. Ron and Mike Costello partnered up and they practiced together. Costello was someone that was easy-going and Ron could relate to. Ron thought, *He might be my only friend here.* Their friendship went back to competing against each other on the college wrestling mat.

As Ron and Mike worked on takedowns they also worked on the setups to strikes. They worked on some footwork together. After about 45 minutes, it was time to do some live goes. Larry took Costello and put him with the champ. Ron went with Latimore. They were not supposed to strike, kick, or do any locks or submissions that could injure someone. They set the clock for seven minutes. Costello got taken down early by the champ. Costello was on his face early and trying to get to where he could face the champ. Billy was really taking it to him.

Latimore came to play today. He and Ron were really scrapping. About four or five minutes into what looked like a wrestling match, Latimore kicked Ron in the thigh and caught him in the forehead with a right hook. Ronnie was sent across the room reeling as Latimore ran at him. When Latimore went to tackle him, Ron snapped him down and tried to go behind, back to their feet. Latimore punched him in the leg and then in the face.

Ron was down. Larry yelled at Latimore, "Joe, what the *()$__#(@*_(are you doing?" "What is wrong Larry? I didn't hurt your precious prospect!"

Larry looked at Latimore and said, "Get out of here! Go! Come back tomorrow! You know the rules and I told you what we were doing! You can't be striking people who don't expect it!" Latimore stomped off to the locker room.

The whistle blew and everyone went to take a water break. Larry walked up to Ron, "How are you doing?"

"Coach, I can go."

Larry was happy because Billy needed someone else to jump in. "Hey, Ronnie, I will tell you what, go stretch out that leg, get on the bike for this next go, and you can go with the champ the last one. Sound good?"

So when everyone came back in Ronnie got on an Airdyne bike close to where Costello and Billy were going live. Larry cut the music in the corner and said, "Hey! Listen up! We are going this way for a reason. Fight with no strikes, no submission holds that will choke someone out or injure them. Yes, it is mat work mostly, but we don't need to strike all the time. We are getting closer to the big day; we don't want to be getting hurt. The clock is set for seven minutes again. Same partners! Go!"

As they started to circle, Ronnie was watching the champ and Costello. Costello was a good wrestler, but adjusting to fighting as a new sport. He was working as an assistant coach at NYU but was really trying to make it as a fighter. Costello was circling and trying to feel out the champ.

Ron noticed another hole in the champ's armor. He thought to himself, "Not only does Billy leave that one side open where he can be knocked out while countering his best punch, while he circles, ever so slightly, he crosses his feet." Ron reasoned out that at heavyweight no one was probably quite athletic enough to expose it.

It was a lazy habit. It might be one that he was just picking up right now, but as attentive to detail as those guys were around there, he couldn't believe it was happening. Suddenly, as Ron pedaled the bike, he felt better. He didn't feel good, but the pain made him push and realize that there was something worth fighting for. He got to try to stand down the champion again. He pedaled and looked on as Costello was dominated by Billy yet again.

There was another break in the action and they all got a drink except for Ronnie Kroger. Larry said, "Ok, last go today, make it good!" He looked in the direction of Ronnie and Billy and said, "Full on fight, punch, kick, choke — anything that is legal. If someone taps out, you are done." It was another seven-minute go. As Ronnie and Billy bumped hands, they both knew it was go time. They may have had head gear on, but there was no reason to believe someone might not get knocked out.

They exchanged some hands. Billy came in with some punches he connected on. He masterfully set up that hook. Ron ducked and decided for some reason not to put him away, but to spin around behind him and take him down. Ronnie got mad and they exchanged more blows. They fought each other hard. Both connected on some punches; with about 30 seconds left they started circling and taking shots and throwing punches. Ron pushed and pulled until finally he got Billy to cross his feet. The moment Billy crossed his feet Ron dove in on his feet and took him right down. He finished the last 20 seconds on top of Billy, punching him while Billy was sitting on the mat trying to defend himself and pulling Ron's leg close and burying his head in his stomach.

Larry called time and announced that it was done. As Ron was walking out, Larry shouted at him, "Bring me that paperwork."

Ron said, "I will, Thursday!" Larry was excited and so was Ron, but Billy and Latimore didn't appear to share that same sentiment.

It was funny how when Billy was with Rex's gym he acted

with more integrity, and when Thaddeus was his influence and not his opponent, he was a better, more faithful person. Latimore was not a very well-rounded person anymore. It seemed that from the top down everyone around there ran on anger. For Ron, this was going to be his big break though, and he was looking forward to having the signing over so he would know what would happen next.

Costello grabbed Ron and said, "Hey, let's grab something to eat."

"Where do you want to go?"

Costello replied with, "The dyna across the street is fine!"

"Sounds good." They showered up and were out the door in a few minutes. They walked across the street to the local place. It was nothing special. They were going to get a good meal and be off for a day. They were both looking forward to recharging.

When they sat down, Costello looked at Ronnie, who had a fresh black eye, and said, "Hey, man, congrats on the contract!"

"Oh, you heard about that? I didn't even sign it yet."

"What? Why?"

"Well, I don't know if I will survive these guys and there is something about the atmosphere that tells me what Latimore told me already. He told me that I will never be one of them."

"Look, Ron, I am signing mine, which is just going to make me a workout partner for them. I am just a practice dummy and I am able to be here and grow, but it is nothing compared to yours. I can't even really quit my coaching job, but both incomes together make it real nice, though. This is your big break, Ron! Don't look the gift horse in the mouf! These guys will have to ease up on you! It is just odd that you came in here and can get some licks in on the champ and beat up on Latimore already! You have star powa! It rocked their security, man!"

"You see, Mike, that is the problem. The problem is I can already rock their security! Maybe I don't need to be around insecure people, even if they are the best at what they do."

"Look, Ronnie, I told you before. This is a dirty business and it attracts dirty people. But you are something special! You made the first big step. I am jealous. It is normal to think there is some catch. But there isn't — you finally made it! I plan to be where you are by next year!"

"Yeah, I think you will, Mike! Congratulations to you too, man! This is big for you too! It will be great for your coaching career, income and all of that, and you are in the room! You are going to be fighting for them before too long!"

"Thanks, man, but listen to me, Ronnie! Do not turn this down! Bring that form in and sign your life over on Thursday! You will not regret it in the long term! Yeah, you will have to deal with them, but make no mistake about it. They respect you. I don't know if you will ever be one of them, but you scare them."

"I guess you are right!"

"Ronnie, you know I am right!" They laughed and joked about old times and new beginnings and parted ways that afternoon.

Costello walked back to the gym and grabbed his stuff. He walked by Larry's office, but Larry didn't see him standing there. He was on the phone with someone. He said, "Yeah, I am hiring on a new fighter, a guy that has some potential as a practice hand. Yeah, this young gun I got, he has real potential, so does the practice hand, I think, but he is a little older and needs some work. One of them you will definitely see contending out there. I just need to get his paperwork! It was the right move getting away from those guys, and now we are going to take over!"

Costello walked on, a little agitated that he was called the "practice hand" and referred to as having "some potential," or maybe it sounded like. It may have just confirmed everything he thought they thought, but it hurt. He knew he could be better. Deep down he was strongly convicted that he would show them.

The tension of the fighting environment was hot. There was something about it that day that seemed a little off. Costello walked in early, and walked into Larry's office with his paperwork. He looked Larry straight in the eye and said, "You won't regret it! I will exceed your expectations of me, Coach!"

Larry laughed, "I hope so! I think this could really go somewhere! Wherever it goes! Glad to have you aboard! Maybe you can get some more of your college wrestlers training in here!"

They shook hands, and Michael said, "Hope so, Sir!"

When Costello left the office he looked out in the hall and was walking with great relief. Larry yelled out, "When your buddy giant killer gets here, send him in!" Michael, a little irritated with the situation, smiled and said, "Sure thing, boss!"

When Ronnie got to the gym he pulled in in his rusty little thirteen-year-old car. He looked at the mess of wrappers on the floor while smelling the old car smell. His feet felt a little numb from the cold that somehow blew in from under the gas pedals. At that, a new BMZ pulled out of the parking lot and it was off. It was black, and the wheels were shiny and the young girl driving gave him a smile. He looked at the car and pulled the document out that would change it all. He signed it and folded it in two.

As Ron got out of the car, he was walking in believing it was all good and everything would be changed. He looked up and saw an electronic billboard across the street. He saw Thaddeus Class on the board. He saw him driving the same type of BMZ that had just pulled out. He put some sunglasses on and drove down the road. The commercial then said, "Integrity, Grit, and Pure Class."

He stood there for a second and thought, *this is odd. Why do I feel the need to sabotage myself? It is just a coincidence. It is a weak one, at that. There is no reason to believe this has anything to do with that.* Deep down he knew it did. Something in the innermost parts of his soul gave him a check that associating with the wrong people would not be the best decision. His mother always told him not to do business with people who were desperate or unethical. These people had everything, but they were greedy for the glory more than anything else, and their anger made them unethical.

He closed his eyes and thought for a second. He knew he couldn't turn down his big break. *God must give me a sign if He wants me to do something different. I have gone after it all of these years.* Then he walked inside. On the way in he saw Mike. Mike smiled and said, "Hey, it is the big day, little Ronnie has made it today! After you get rid of that roller skate out there and get yourself a real car, you are buying me lunch."

"Mike, you're crazy! I wouldn't waste my money on you."

"Hey, the big boss wants to see you. He is waiting on your paperwork!"

He walked into Larry's office and Larry saw Ronnie. "Hey, Killa! Look man, I gotta go! You got the paperwork? I have a little thing going on! I have a little family type of emergency! I will be back about halfway through the workout! Leave the paperwork on my desk! It is a big day!" He took the paperwork and set it on his desk. "Kid, you might be a star." He shook Ronnie's hand and left. Ronnie left the paperwork on the desk.

Latimore was in charge of the workout. Ronnie and Michael walked in and saw this. Latimore began drilling with the champ. He yelled out, "We are going to drill anything you want for 45 minutes and at the end we will get a drink and go live!"

Costello and Ronnie worked out practicing new moves and holds. They worked out well together. Costello was a seasoned wrestling coach and drilling partner. Working out with Costello kept Ron feeling more at home at New Horizons. He started to think. *This is my place now! They are investing in me now. I have finally made it!*

Everyone stayed with their usual partners and at the end Latimore yelled out, "Costello! You go with the champ!" Latimore said, "No strikes or kicks with Michael and the Champ. Everyone else, it is ten minutes all you got. If someone taps out you are done!" Latimore looked at Ronnie and said, "You're with me, punk."

"Whatever! No one uses that word anymore, old man!" At that he turned his back on Latimore and Latimore punched him in the ribs.

Ronnie went down, and he kneed him in the face. Ronnie thought he might have broken a rib. He crawled off the mat. Latimore looked at him and said, "I don't care what they pay you, you will not be one of us." Latimore laughed and grabbed a different partner. Everything seemed to go on. Costello cared about him, but he had his hands full getting beat by Billy.

Ronnie walked out, finally understanding that he wouldn't be one of them. That was the truth. He didn't want to be. Talk about a sign, *be careful what you pray for, I guess.* He walked into Larry's office. The door was open and the paperwork was still on his desk, untouched. He grabbed it off the desk and stumbled out the door.

He got back into his cold car and he could barely breathe. He was gasping, and he could see his breath in the car. The car was cold. He turned the key and it wouldn't quite turn over. He yelled out, &@*#(*()#@ ME! $#()_$*@#* ME!" He looked at the paper on the seat and started to get out of the car. When he got to his feet, he looked up and saw the same electronic billboard again. He saw Thaddeus again. It said it again, "Integrity, Grit, and Pure Class!"

He knew deep in the places of himself that no one knew of but him that he didn't belong in this place. He wasn't going to be there. Latimore was right! He wasn't going to be there forever! He was never going to be one of them! He was different from them.

But, what would he do now?

Tensions were running high at GITR. Thaddeus looked like an animal. He was covered in sweat, scaling the rope in the middle of the gym floor. He got to the top and rang the bell in the ceiling and began his descent. When he got to the mat he was greeted by a fresh body who immediately dove in on his legs and buried his head. Even though he had a very protective headgear on, when the champ caught him in the front or the back of the head, it would shake his brain inside his skull. Thaddeus was hitting the wall. He trained hard this week, but the young practice hand known as Hoss, now was in deep and was trying to get behind him. It looked like Thad may give up a takedown and expose himself to some shots.

Rex immediately called out, "Get out of there! I ain't letting you out! You think you will feel your best the whole fight? You must get out, now!"

Thaddeus found some energy somewhere. He created some space between him and his opponent and found himself upside down with Hoss's leg. He came out the back. Took him down clean, and pounded his head three times from behind. Hoss got to his feet and leaned on the champ when Thaddeus planted him flat on his back. He tossed him beautifully. Thaddeus was now looking like he would be in fight shape. After one shot to the face Rex blew the whistle.

Thaddeus then went into some squats, push-ups, and a set of pull-ups. This man was a beast. But he knew he needed to be a beast, because he trained the wild beast he would fight, and this was what it all came down to. God was with him, everyone could see it — even Rex, if he could be honest with himself, which he rarely was.

Thaddeus began to jump rope for about five minutes. Rex looked at him and said, "Get a drink. I don't want your workout partners to get cold." Thaddeus saluted him and went to get a drink. Even though Thaddeus Class had become a model Christian, Rex still looked for Thad's edge to come out in his personality. When a fighter is highly trained and feeling confident and healthy, they get a little rude and edgy. They begin to fight with a chip on their shoulder. Thaddeus was going to need a big chip on his shoulder, but that humility might just serve him well, too.

When Thad saluted or rolled his eyes or talked back to Rex, Rex considered it a good sign. Thaddeus hit this point at about this stage of his training every single time. Rex couldn't help but think, *maybe the Son of God doesn't hate me.* Then he reflected on what a weird thought that was for the gym. He then hoped he wasn't losing his personal edge. Competitively speaking, he had come to be more comfortable when he felt disdain for the Almighty.

Thaddeus went to get a drink and was at the stage where he would get by himself a lot in the hallway during the rest times. It was still cold outside, but not much wind or air got in so it didn't affect him in any way. None of his workout partners dared to talk to Thaddeus unless he was already speaking to them.

Something clicked with him that week. Only a few weeks leading up to this moment, he couldn't see himself fighting Billy. He couldn't see a title fight going down this way. Now he not only saw it, but welcomed it, and thought of it as maybe the best thing or last thing that he ever would do for Billy. This was going to be the fight of his life.

When Thaddeus trained and when he was by himself, he saw the cocky smirk on Billy's face. He remembered in his mind's eye being planted into the cage, where some of the blood from his forehead and nose could still be seen on the cage. Rex made sure it was left there for Thaddeus to see while he trained (very smart). It seemed like yesterday. He could still feel the sting in his heart and the loss of a friendship. He was getting past it and was getting ready to kick Billy's head in, all for the glory of God, which made perfect sense in his brain.

He was healthy, strong, and focused. It was going to be a great fight. Thaddeus knew he was in for the fight of his life, but was he ready? He knew that confidence came with more training and knowing how his body recovered. He was very focused, and when it came to the peaking process he knew everything he needed to know. But this fight was so weird. He knew this could be his last fight, and if it was, he needed to win. He needed to do it for himself, Rex, GITR, Sally, his mom, the fans, etc. But even more, this was his last opportunity to disciple Billy. He had taught him how to fight, but he had also taught him about righteousness. It was God Almighty that would have to help him. It was God who would be there and see him through it all. Most of all, it needed to be for God's glory. *Knock 'em out for the glory of God,* he thought to himself again and again. "Wow!" He reflected on the strange world that he lived in.

Across town Billy was between workout partners. He took a breather as he looked at the new poster that Larry put up in the corner of the matted room. He stared at it for a minute as Larry came into the room. "Hey, Billy, what do you think of the picture? It was taken after your last fight!"

Billy turned and said, "I remember it very well! I remember that moment getting my hand raised, but where are you?"

"Oh, I am in the corner. This was your poster. It looks like you are standing all by yourself on top of the world."

Billy remembered the moment, and how Thad was the first person to call him "champ" and welcome him to the club. He was the first one to express happiness over it. He bragged about him and built into him. He teared up a little. He missed his friend. He knew that he did wrong. To say that he did wrong was an understatement.

Larry looked at him and said, "Everything has a cost. We already got you a title, now let's go make you a legend."

Billy thought, *Yeah, everything has a cost. Let's do it!* Billy went back into the room and it wasn't fun. He destroyed his partners. Everyone was there except for Ron Kroger, who called in sick and wanted to rest up a little.

When he left, he felt empty and sad. He may have even felt ashamed, but he really wasn't very honest with how he felt with himself anyway. He should have loved his workout, but he didn't. He hurt! He began to think, "I need to do something about this."

Whenever he thought about Thaddeus, he just went harder and convinced himself that the best compliment to a mentor or a teacher is to leave them in the dust. He finished with his last partner, Michael Costello. He looked superior to them all and looked ready. It was hard to see to the untrained eye, but it was there. It was a hairline crack in the otherwise flawless mental armor. Billy was beginning to hurt. Red didn't notice it, because he didn't have the relationship with Billy that Larry did. But Larry and Billy both knew it was there, even though they never spoke of it. Every fighter is always overcoming something new every fight. I don't think either of them thought much about it, or wanted to. For one, it was just another obstacle, and for two, they didn't really like what they did. They only considered it something that needed to be done. It was a transaction. It had a heavy cost, but it was a good investment. It sounded good on paper anyway.

Later that night, Billy fell asleep a little early and was sound asleep when his phone buzzed. He opened his eyes and thought, *I bet it is her.* He read her text and told her how to get to see him. He met this cute little girl grabbing some groceries. She recognized him. He thought she was cool, so he let her up into his skyline penthouse.

Her name was Katarina. Kat was very beautiful. She was very in shape and confident. She was short and strong. Even though she was never a gymnast, she was built that way. Katarina knocked on the door at about nine p.m.

The fact is Billy never stood a chance. Kat recently gave "the girls" some extra size, shape, and lift. She got up in the middle of the night and left. When Billy woke up in the morning, he told God he was sorry, but in a weird way. It was one of those apologies a child gives, but they will turn right back around and do it again. Billy was somewhat pride-filled and self-deceived. He didn't see it as being caught with his hand in the cookie jar. He kind of thought somewhere deep in his soul that how he lived didn't really matter, because God had saved him. This may be true about his final destination, but tragically wrong about how to represent Him peacefully along the way.

When Billy was working out with Thaddeus he wouldn't have acted this way. He seemed to really understand how to live and what God wanted from Him. He also took a lot of spiritual cues from Thaddeus. No, Billy didn't need Thaddeus to be motivated to work out. But he did need Thaddeus to be motivated to be a good person. Temptation at the top is great. Since leaving Thaddeus behind, it appeared that obedience to God was left behind, too! This was very confusing. When he woke up, images from the night before filled his mind and he couldn't help but think of it all the time, but now it was time for him to work out and he had to go.

In Billy's mind, the world owed him. He worked hard to get to where he was. He worked hard to be the champ, and now he was going to take more. He was going to take everything he could get. It is funny how we compare ourselves and our sins to others. To most ,Billy was ok because we put ourselves in his shoes. Of course, he was going to go out and see how much the girls loved him now as the champ. Of course, that was normal. *He was only a guy. He couldn't help it, right? People don't understand how hard it is to be me, either.* Those were the thoughts that fed his justification, and who in his life was going to tell him otherwise?

This is how our sin compounds. All of our decisions do. It is no secret. It isn't rocket science. It is just how it is. He turned on his mentor. He turned on Thaddeus and Rex and GITR. He acted wrong, but really it wasn't ever about serving God. It was about getting what he could. When push comes to shove, we all typically serve with false motives. This provides success with a funny loophole for ruining people.

I am not saying that Billy can't win the fight or his career will take a dive. It was very reasonable to believe that Billy would win the title and be a double champion. The odds still had Billy by a lot. He was younger, stronger, and faster. Thaddeus had taught him everything he knew, so this was going to make him the opponent that Thaddeus didn't want to face. However, we are talking about the legend of Thaddeus Class. In the long run, don't you want to live with peace? Who would you rather be? On fight night the target was on Thaddeus's back, so maybe on that night, I would rather be Billy. But as for the rest of my life... there is peace in living a life of Pure Class.

CHAPTER 14

FAITH

EARLY ONE MORNING Thaddeus Class was up and working out with Paul. They watched some film and were on the mat experimenting with technique. A stranger walked in. They couldn't see his face. Thaddeus saw him and suddenly it jolted the memory of his dream. Rex was a little agitated and looked at the stranger with the hood up and said, "Gym is closed!"

Ronnie responded, "Hey, man, I just wanted to stop by and see the champion train a little." He removed his hood. Thaddeus remembered his face from the face on the stone in his dream.

Rex recognized him and turned red. "$(#*)_** No! NO! NO! NO!" Ronnie was a little taken aback. Rex continued, "You think I am an idiot? I know you, you are working out with Billy! Get out of here, before I have the champ kick your head in."

"I decided I didn't want to fight for them. Check the exemptions list. I am not on it. My contract ran out and they offered me another one and I didn't take it."

Rex smiled and said, "Yeah, those workout contracts aren't that good." Ronnie laughed it off.

Rex looked at him and continued, "Hey, man, look, it is a bad look! I will get accused of stealing you away from them. There is bad blood. Not to mention it could put both titles in jeopardy if your contract is somehow still good there. Having you here changes everything."

"Rex, maybe I can help you win!"

Rex laughed it off, "Maybe Thaddeus has done a little of that before you walked through here."

Ronnie turned around with his hand up and gym bag up and defensively said, "Ok." He walked back towards the door that he had just walked through.

Thaddeus and Paul stood still for a minute. Thad had told Paul about the dream, but it wasn't at the front of Paul's mind. When Ronnie put his hood up and began to walk away with his gym bag in hand, Thaddeus said, "Wait!"

Rex looked and said, "What?"

He pulled Rex aside and told Paul, "Paul, get to know our guest a little."

Thaddeus didn't want to tell Rex he had some kind of weird dream about the guy, but he did have some weird sense that this meeting might just be important. "Rex, I believe this guy can help! I worked out with him before. I have seen him before and maybe he can help us. It isn't illegal. They didn't keep him happy. What is the worst that can happen? Is he going to go and tell Billy how I fight?"

"Thad, we can't have it! If he comes in here and goes back over there, he has everything to gain and nothing to lose."

"Maybe we need to have faith once in a while. Maybe we need to acknowledge that we are being blessed sometimes."

"Thad, stop! I can't! If it is faith, it will come around again. I am not sure!"

Thad thought it was a weird response, and maybe even one he would have heard his mother say to him. Thad thought that was really odd, but quickly forgot when Rex walked back out into the open room to the mats. "What did you say your name was?"

Ronnie looked at him and said, "Rex, my friends call me Ronnie. Now that I know Paul, I know all of you."

"Listen, I can't let you train here. Check back after the fight."

"Ok, I understand!"

Rex looked at him and said, "Good luck to you!"

Ronnie turned and started to walk again. Rex wanted to forget the whole thing. He had Paul and Thad start where they left off. Paul was mimicking the movements of Billy and they were simulating what it would look like in slow motion.

They were all unaware that Ronnie was still standing there. "One last thing! You're making a big mistake!"

Rex was furious, because he now was certain that he was a spy. He decided to take the bait before he bit his head off. "What mistake is that?"

Ronnie dropped his bag and pointed. He walked towards him, "Right there you are asking him to circle out there. But Billy has been getting lazy and crossing his feet in this scenario. You can take him down by getting both legs if you time it just right!"

Rex then asked him, "How do you know this?"

"I did it!"

Rex then looked at him and said, "Ok, prodigy, what else?"

Rex was now strangely interested, because early on he and

Thaddeus worked and worked and worked on getting Billy to break that habit. For some reason, Larry felt that Billy was athletic enough that it didn't really matter. Thaddeus was trying to train him to be able to beat anyone, even someone like him. That was who Thaddeus was; he was very unselfish.

He had Paul mimic the movement of Billy and he dove in on the leg and got into striking position. Ron continued, "Here is another scenario: when he moves in on this right hook, he takes a breather even if he misses. But no one wants to circle into his power, for fear that he will do something different and they might just get knocked out. If you duck this just right, and move into his power, you end up here, in a knockout type of position, and he will do it over and over again!"

"Ok, Ronnie, why are you here? Would they not offer you a contract?"

"They offered me one and here it is." He handed it to him.

"Ronnie, this is signed. You need to leave!"

"No, check the list. I took it off his desk yesterday. Larry had a family emergency."

For Rex the story checked out, because his old pal Larry did have an aunt who had passed away the day before, and he found out through a common friend they shared.

Ronnie looked at him, "Look give me a shot! I wanted to come here because I think you are probably different than they are. When I got the offer, a guy named Latimore was pretty hard on me, and Billy doesn't want me there. I think maybe I threatened them when I had a few good goes with Billy. I think because I was committed not to make the same mistake twice with him it threw him off. I was a little smarter than he was. Anyway! I want a shot!"

Thaddeus pulled Paul aside and said, "What do you think?"

"I don't know, man! It seems a little risky."

Rex was now a little more interested in what Paul had to say but cut in and said, "Yeah, we can't do this."

Thaddeus began to lobby. "Rex, I believe this is an opportunity that is placed before us and we need it. After all, can't you look at the list and check with Charlie Pigeon to make sure the list is up to date and all of that, and get some assurance?"

"I guess — and we would be trusting that snake Charlie not to talk to Larry!"

"I think we need to go for it! It is an act of faith, Rex, and you should take my side on this, but it is your gym."

"Ok, Thad! I will trust you because you have built this place too! But know this could be a disaster!"

Rex shook Ronnie's hand, not knowing what just happened and said, "I am set to talk with Charlie Pigeon this morning at about ten on the phone. Barring that everything is clear and legal, welcome aboard."

Ronnie looked at him and said, "You won't regret it, sir."

"I already do! We will talk about your contract tomorrow!"

Ronnie shook Paul's hand and Thaddeus's as well. "I look forward to learning from you, champ!" They shook hands and Ronnie grabbed his bag and left, ecstatic.

The next morning it was understood that Ronnie would be working out in the live goes in the afternoon. Rex was a little concerned and wanted Thad to understand. "Just so you understand, this guy could help us, he could hurt us. I am not very sure about him."

"Well, Rex, I will take that as a unanimous yes, coming from you."

Paul just laughed as they were starting to stretch and get ready for some drilling. "What are you laughing at, Pastor, I might just kick you out, too!"

"Come on, Rex, I am the most stable thing you've got going around here."

"Oh, yeah, a mega-church pastor who hasn't gotten over his wrestling career, still trying to relive that."

Paul nodded at Thaddeus and smiled, "The bar isn't real high, that cat right there is a lawyer and he chooses to fight instead. Come on, Rex you don't keep real classy company!"

Rex went back to it. "Look, Thad, you need to be a little cautious with this guy. They offered him a big contract over there. I don't know why he wouldn't take it. He made it. I am not going to offer him much yet. It doesn't add up."

Thaddeus came back with, "So, you are saying he could be shady because he was offered a big contract by our competitor and wants to come over here for nothing. I say he could be the best thing that has happened to us in a very long time, because he might just have standards above what he saw over there and he had the guts to walk in here. I am going to choose faith on this one."

Rex looked at Paul, "Ok, Pastor, we need you now, I might need to give you a raise. What do you think? Is the champ here on the side of faith on this?"

Paul looked at Thad and said, "It is too early to tell. If I am being objective, I think you both make good points."

Thad looked at Paul, "Come on, man! What are you talking about? This is faith!"

"Think, Thaddeus. Faith isn't worth anything if it is in the wrong thing. It doesn't have to be blind. It just has to know the one who you are putting the faith in. Did God send him?

How am I supposed to know that? Faith can't be a cop-out, it is then too hard to argue with."

"That is it! I have decided! You are going to start buying your own lunches."

Paul said, "No, I am not!" They laughed it off and began to drill.

At this stage Rex was beginning to get a little more technically involved. He was starting to yell at Thaddeus a little to go faster and to go harder, but what had always been important for Thaddeus was he could do the movements when he was tired. At the end of this workout he was beginning to wear himself down a little. He would have some fresh live goes in the afternoon, followed by some intense weight training that focused on muscular endurance.

He looked smooth drilling technique, but Rex was concerned. He thought something was missing. It might be that he had been through a lot, and it might have been the personal nature of it, but he didn't seem as focused as he had been getting ready for past fights. There was a fire that hadn't been lit yet. There was something about when the animal meets the scholar. First, his body needed to be getting worn down, and second, the animal comes out. Finally, when he was rested and rebuilt, the animal drive was there and the mind and the body were rested when it all came together. That was the finished product that you wanted to see on fight night. That was what made that night worth millions for both fighters.

Many people don't realize the intense chess match that goes into these fights. The wrestler, the boxer, the martial artist, all need to come out as it gets closer to fight time. Let's face it, this wasn't just any other fight. This was Billy "The Kid" Smith, trained by Larry Rossi, and he knew Thad; he knew them both better than they knew themselves. The animal and the scholar needed to show up and be on time.

After lunch they came back for that second workout. It was going to be a brief warmup and live goes. Only this time there would be a fresh set of eyes in there. The first live go was going to be with the new guy. Ronnie was going to get a ten-minute shot at the champ.

They sat around stretching after some jogging and there was some laughing and joking around. Ronnie was just getting to know the guys. With Rex standing there he said, "Hey, I heard we get trained here by Curlsville's own Superhero."

"Yeah, we do."

Rex rubbed his nose a few times. Thaddeus then said, "Good thing he is up there protecting the city. My mom still lives there."

At that, Rex rubbed his eyes and his nose several times. Everyone was laughing. The whole exchange made Ronnie stop and think about what he just saw.

They got started with about ten guys in the room. Most of them were going to get a few minutes fresh fighting the champ, while he had to keep fighting everyone. At least, that was the plan. Rex looked at Thaddeus and smiled, and then he looked at Ronnie and said, "Well, the list and Charlie said you are all clear. Let's see what you've got."

They stepped inside the cage and Ronnie waited for the champ to get in. The timer was set. They would have two five-minute periods and anything would go.

Rex was being a little liberal with how he wanted to conduct his gym, but he knew that Thaddeus needed the live goes and he would reserve the right to stop it at any time. Thaddeus was fresh, he was tired from the morning workout, but he felt good and ready. He circled Ronnie. They both tried to throw some punches at each other. Thaddeus saw his opening and went for it. They scrambled for a few seconds, but within the first minute he had Ronnie on his back while Thaddeus hit him in the face a few times. Ron was able to counter and get back to his feet.

When Thaddeus went back to the same move again, this time Ronnie hit him with an uppercut. This time he swept his legs and knocked Thaddeus back. Rex was impressed, and the other workout partners looked on. Ronnie was taking it to him. There was no question that this guy was for real. They scrambled again and Thaddeus came out on top, pushing Ronnie's head against the cage. The bell rang.

Rex was impressed that Ronnie could stay with Thaddeus. Was this guy this good or was Thaddeus slipping? Was it somewhere in the middle? They went back to their corners. Thaddeus tapped him and said, "Good go, Ronnie!"

Ronnie took his mouthpiece out and looked at him and said, "One question for you, Thad. How long have you been letting your trainer hang out with your mom on the weekends?"

Thad looked at him and said, "What did you say?"

Ronnie laughed, "How can you be an attorney; you haven't thought of this possibility? I guess that is why you became a fighter! It was on the news, Thaddeus. Our hero Rex was in Curlsville visiting a friend. I have only been around him a few days and I know that the man doesn't have any friends. Come on, man!"

Suddenly, Thaddeus turned to look at Rex. Rex had a little smirk. "He is crazy!" In that moment Thaddeus was back on the playground again when someone said something about his mom. It was shortly after his dad had died and he simply beat the older boy on the playground down. It might have been the moment that told him he could be a fighter, and it was a bit of a renewal of those vows. He hit a double leg to three or four punches to the face like Rex hadn't seen him do in years. Ronnie got to his feet and Thaddeus tried it again, but Ronnie had thought of a new counter already. He thought, *I need to slow him down.* Somehow, Thaddeus was taken down to his back. Thaddeus got out and ran at him again. Thaddeus swept his feet with precision and began to go to work on him.

Rex said, "Keep going, the clock starts now!" The young fighter had some counters and really showed he could fight at that level, but Thaddeus showed why he was the best in the world at that moment. Thaddeus threw him into the cage and hit him in the ribs a couple of times. Ronnie found himself just trying to slow him down for the last 30 seconds, and finally the timer on the wall rang.

Rex sat and wondered how this little lie was going to hurt him, but he couldn't help but wonder what he was seeing. Was he seeing a new fighter that could really be something? With Thaddeus he also saw the animal come out. The attention that it was putting on him was embarrassing, but at least the beast showed up.

Thad huffed and left the cage to get a drink. He took his mouthpiece out and looked at Rex. Thaddeus said something out of character. "Ok, now I hate him! Get him out of here!"

"Oh no, Thad. I am going to keep him."

He looked at Rex and said while being short of breath, "Look, man, I have been wondering ever since the news, why you didn't tell me you were dating my mom. What is the big secret?"

"Look, Thad, I know I should have told you, but it is kind of weird. How did you know?"

"I didn't until just now. Wow, Rex! Get rid of Ronnie! I was wrong!"

"Son, I am sorry that I didn't tell you that I went out with your mom. It was wrong not to talk to you. But I am not getting rid of this guy!"

He motioned to Ronnie. "Stay warm — you will go again in a minute." Thad was going to go another ten minutes, only every two minutes someone new would come into the mix. The first opponent was a college kid named Nate Armstrong. He had some boxing and wrestling experience. He came in and Thaddeus circled him once before ducking his left and laying him out. He knocked him out.

"Send me someone else." Another guy came in, this time a local college wrestler. This time the champ stutter-stepped and kicked him on the side of the knee, buckling him to the floor. Finally, the third guy came in. It was Ronnie. Ronnie circled and decided to dive in on Thad's legs. Thaddeus made him pay dearly with a few knees to the face. Ronnie backed out and hit him with a few jabs, and his athleticism kept him from trouble. Thaddeus controlled his emotions for a moment and circled, like a predator waiting to pounce. He had that sensation in his mouth where it begins to water with the realization that he loved what he was doing. He attacked, and it was like he could feel the hair on his back stand up — but somehow Ronnie kept moving.

Thaddeus landed an uppercut and dived in on an ankle, which led to him being on top. The buzzer rang and the next hand was to come in. Thaddeus didn't slow down. He was now training at a level that he hadn't in years. He was starting to feel younger. It was like he had been born all over again.

At the end of the ten minutes Ronnie was the only one to stand in there with him for two minutes. Everyone else pulled out early. As they went to get a drink, Thaddeus climbed to the top of the cage and when his hand hit the top he back-flipped off. He began shadow drilling when his bare feet hit the canvas. He started to do some squats and push ups. He was pushing it until the end.

He was panting, frustrated, yet fully alive. The animal was coming out. Rex looked at him when he began to slow down and it looked like he was done. Come on two minutes and he continued to shadow drill and do push ups. Rex called time after two minutes when Thaddeus climbed the cage again, did a back-flip, and finished in his stance. He wanted to put his hands on the top of his head, but he didn't because it was time to be tough.

Rex softly spoke to him and told him, "Get a drink!" They came back for one more go after that. Ronnie stayed out of the live goes at Rex's request and Thaddeus had never looked better. When the workout was over Rex went to his office and told Thad to go shower. Rex told him, "Tomorrow will be your last weight-lifting day before the fight."

Thad said, "Why not tonight?"

"I made reservations at Carmine's."

"Rex, you are a real piece of work, you know that?"

"Not for me. For you and Ronnie! You need to eat with him and get to know him. This will be that last big steak dinner for you before the fight."

"Rex! You need to get rid of this guy! This is toxic! He is dangerous! He irritates me!"

"I know, Thad, and that is what I like about him! Maybe you are the one who needs to have faith! Haha!"

Rex was really proud of that zinger. Ronnie came out of the locker room slowly. He looked at them both and smiled. "Have fun, ladies."

Ronnie laughed a little even though it hurt, while Thaddeus didn't break a smile. He turned around and looked at Rex and said, "This new conversation ain't over!" Rex knew he was talking about the new discovery that Rex had been dating Debra but they chose not to tell him. With that, it was off to Carmine's.

They sat down at the table, both of them looking bruised and beaten. Thaddeus was not even looking in his direction. Ronnie looked at him, "Come on man, let's try to get along here."

All Thad had for him was, "Why?"

Quickly, Ronnie came back with, "How about why not? I said some things I shouldn't. I pointed out something you didn't know! It was mean and to get you going. Sorry!"

"Nah! Don't be." Thad softened. "I told Rex I wanted you in the room. I got what I asked for. Now you will probably be there a lot more. I can't believe I didn't see that Rex was dating my mom! What is wrong with me?"

Ron answered, "There is nothing wrong with seeing the good in people. Don't hold it against them, they have probably had to spend a lot of time together following you around."

Thad smiled and said, "Remember what happened last time you started talking about my mom." Ron smiled. Thaddeus continued, "How did you pick that up that fast anyway?"

"Thad, I just notice things. I can read people. From what

I know and have observed of you, so can you. But maybe you get blinded by the people closest to you."

"Maybe. But, really, how did you know?"

"I knew something was wrong because Rex scratched his nose every time your mom was mentioned. He has a tell."

"What?"

"Thad, people are people, whether they are fighting or in everyday life."

"What does that mean?"

"Thad, it means he has a tell. Before the workout, he kept scratching his nose when he was talking to you and you mentioned your mom. Every time your mom came up, he scratched his nose. He did it like three or four times. I then thought that was odd and I processed what I knew about him, which is what everyone knows about him. Number one, he is your trainer and number two, he helped stop a crime in your hometown. So, I suspected it. I mostly thought I could get a good yo-mama joke in; boy, that backfired! I took an old-fashioned beatin' after that."

Thaddeus laughed out loud. He knew he liked this kid. The people Thaddeus seemed to get close to were people who were honest and bold. They were sincere, and really didn't care what you thought. I am not talking about someone who walks around and commonly says, "And I don't care what you think, I will do what I want." They actually do care what you think. Oddly enough, it is their main focus. Thad knew that.

They laughed as the conversation continued. Thaddeus was glad that it seemed like something new was happening. Thad looked at Ron and said, "Thanks!"

Ronnie said, "For what?"

"For helping me find something that I haven't had for a while."

Ronnie laughed and said, "Hopefully, you can help me to find it too! It was tough being on the other end of that!"

"Yeah, I didn't realize it, but maybe I lost a step when Billy changed — or before that. I am not sure."

They ordered some food and laughed and joked around a little, getting to know each other. Over dinner it got serious. "Thad, can I ask you something?"

Thaddeus looked at Ronnie and said, "Where am I going to go? My food is here."

He laughed a little and said, "Look, Thaddeus, I was over there with those guys and they are great fighters! But they don't function like you guys at all!"

Thad became very curious, "How do you mean?"

Ron continued, "You're a Bible guy. I stick to Mark! Jesus seems to be to the point in that one. It basically says the same thing as Matthew, but in half the pages, ya' know? Billy is like the seed that fell on the rock type of guy."

Thad looked at him blankly; he was amazed at what had unfolded from the dream, to the truth coming out about his mom, to having a new workout partner who turned down Billy and Larry, to even this moment. Not knowing what to say, Thaddeus just replied with, "What do you mean?"

Ron returned with, "Ya' know, it is about Mark three or four Jesus tells the story where the guy throws the seeds. It lands in a few different spots."

Thaddeus nodded his head and said, "Yeah, the Parable of the Sower."

"Some land on the rock and it is only temporary. It doesn't take root. It seems to me that when he became champ or took the opportunity to want to fight you, something better came along and his faith didn't have any root. He still has a verse hanging in his locker. He might go to church or something, but it isn't probably what it was for him."

Thad's face got a little disfigured. Reflecting on Billy's spiritual immaturity caused him great pain. "Ah, Billy will be ok. He is just a little confused right now. He has faith."

Ronnie looked at Thad and said, "Wow! You still want to protect him. How can you want to rip someone's head off and care about him at the same time?"

Thad laughed and looked at him. "I am sitting here with you right now, aren't I?"

"Just know with me, Thad, 'Ronnie Kroger don't change for nobody.'"

Thad actually enjoyed the conversation. They ate. Thad paid the bill and they went their separate ways.

Sally was going to be getting off from work. Thaddeus decided he was going to go and surprise her and hang out with her for a few hours. It was understood that they would meet up at Mama Class's Kitchen. The Kitchen was closed and Thad texted her to let him in. He walked in and said, "Sally, hey babe!" She jumped up from the papers she was looking at on the table. Thad knew his mom wasn't around because she didn't like doing any paperwork out in the restaurant. But he asked anyway, after giving her a hug and a kiss, "Hey, is my mom here?"

"No, she is running some errands, what's up?"

"No, I just didn't want to talk to her right now."

"Why?" She had to ask because it didn't seem that Thad was ever sick of talking to his mother.

"I found out something today. My mom has been dating Rex."

Sally's face went pale. He continued, "He has been coming up here and visiting her sometimes. It has been at least since when he helped that girl and was on the news up here. It probably wasn't when she was in the hospital. I don't know." He sighed, and already had his lawyer hat on. He sat down on the stool at the bar area.

"Wait, Sally, why are you not saying anything? You knew this already, didn't you?"

She paused and blurted out. "I ah, I… I .. I wasn't sure. There were some weird calls and I heard her talking and I didn't know."

Thad looked at her and said, "How could you not tell me? Why is everyone keeping secrets from me?"

Sally looked at him, "Thad, I wasn't sure! You need to calm down."

"Calm down? My trainer is dating my mom and everyone who is close to me knows but will not tell me, even though I have a fight coming up! What do you mean, calm down?"

She put both hands on his shoulders and looked him straight in the eyes. "You told me you don't want distractions."

"Well, this worked out great! And no, I don't need any distractions right now, so maybe we should stay away from each other until after the fight." He intended those to be his last words before stomping out.

She said, "Thad, wait. Come on! I am sorry!"

He said, "Sally, I need to be alone! Sorry," and he walked out.

Sally then felt horrible and wondered how this would

affect their relationship. She wondered what was going on. She thought, *Did I just get dumped? Am I going to ruin his training?*

Deb came walking in the door. "Hey, did I just see my son leaving? What was he doing here?"

"Oh, he is mad at me."

Deb took the bait. "Why? What do you mean?"

"He is mad that you are dating Rex and I didn't tell him or wasn't sure and didn't mention it. I don't know."

Deb was baffled. She put her hand on her own forehead. "Sally, I am so sorry."

Sally said, "Look, I am all done. I am going home. Don't worry about it." She walked out and said, "I will see you tomorrow!"

Deb wasn't sure she would. She sat down, sad and angry with herself. She sat down, afraid that she had hurt her son before the biggest fight of his life, and messed up everything between Sally and him. She avoided dating all of those years because of how he would respond, and now this had messed everything up. She went back to the fridge and cracked open the bottle and poured herself a tall glass of Merlot. She drank a few glasses and then she called Barbara to take her home.

Barbara walked in and saw Deb. She knew something was wrong. "What happened?"

"Barb, I am justh a tarrible person!"

"No, you are not, Deb. You might be a little intoxicated, but not a bad person."

"Look, I meshed my son's relationship up. I meshed his fight up. All 'cause I am dating Rex — and now my kid knows."

"Deb, I told you you needed to tell him."

Deb looked at her and said, "Stop judging me, Barrbaara!"

Barb smiled, "I am not judging you. What can I do to help?"

Deb looked at Barbara and said, "Barb, you are my only friend."

She looked at her and said, "Deb, you know that isn't true." She helped her to her car and told her she would take her home. "Deb, do you have to come in early tomorrow?"

"No, I can go home and sleep."

Deb looked at her phone and she had 14 missed calls, mostly from Rex. She said, "I need to call him."

"No!" Barb said. "Bad idea."

She took her phone and texted for her, "I am not feeling well. Going to sleep!"

Rex texted back, "Ok, but call me in the morning."

Barb texted him and said, "OK."

Deb got in the passenger side of the car and fell asleep before she put her seatbelt on. Barb had to put her belt on for her.

They went to Deb's home. Barb called her husband, Ted, and decided to stay there with Deb. Ted brought Barbara over a sandwich and kissed her goodnight at the door. Barb stayed there until Deb woke up in the morning.

CHAPTER 15

RESTORATION

THE NEXT DAY Thaddeus got to the gym and walked inside. Rex was already there, watching some film on Billy. At this point Thad was furious with Rex. He walked in and grabbed the remote and shut the TV off. Rex looked up; Thad started as Rex sipped his coffee. "Were you going to tell me that you are dating my mom? How did this happen? Why won't anyone tell me? I am fighting with Sally now."

Rex chimed in, "I told you she would be a distraction."

Thad got instantly mad and he fired back with, "WHAT? We are fighting because of you! She thought you were dating but didn't want me to be distracted. She didn't tell me, either! Rex, you were on the news up there! Why would you lie to me? Why is my mom lying to me? What is going on?"

"Your mom and I can do whatever we want. I don't have to check with you!"

"What do you mean 'have to'? Why do you choose to lie to me? I thought you were better than that! I am going to get changed. Keep it professional today, Mr. Metzger."

At that he stomped off as Paul was walking in. Paul looked at Rex and said, "What is this all about?"

"Me, him, I don't know, just pray for us. We need you here, pastor."

Paul chuckled and looked at him and said, "Huh?" He walked off to get dressed, too.

Rex laughed to himself and thought, "Well, maybe lying is always wrong." Deep down, this was one of those things he held onto as problems with the Bible. He thought that even Christians believe that there are problems with telling the truth all the time. *If we all lied a little selectively the world would be a better place.* This was an ideal he liked to replay in his head. *Well, Rex you tried that one. Cross that one off the problems list, and put it in the other column.*

Deep inside he heard a voice that was not his own and it simply and calmly said, "Seems like maybe we are working towards a single column after all, huh?"

Meanwhile, across town in the early morning workout, Latimore was taking the beating of his life. Billy nor Thaddeus had ever done anything to Latimore like Billy was doing to him that day. Everything he tried Billy had an answer for. No one in the room had ever seen anyone fight the way Billy was fighting. He was breaking his body down one more time before the final days of the fight where he would bring his body to peak condition. These next few days were critical for a fighter. Tension was mounting, but no one at New Horizons had any doubt about what Billy could do. Larry was ecstatic, to say the least!

The only lingering uncertainty was that Billy was fighting Thaddeus Class. Yes, he was doing things no one had seen before. Yes, he was young and in his prime. Yes, they knew

Thaddeus — and the last time they were in the Octagon together, Billy showed him it was now his time. But you can't ever forget Thaddeus Class had been nothing short of brilliant when the spotlight came on. Everyone knew he would be ready. Thad would be smart and he would be well prepared, everyone knew that. His mind would be even more brilliant. His body may begin to decline, but his mat intelligence would continue to improve.

When that go was over it was Costello's turn. After a break, he came in fresh and was able to hang with Billy for a few minutes. Then Billy began to go to work on him. About six or seven minutes in he hit him with a left hook that put Michael out cold. Billy laughed and said, "Oh, and ask him when he wakes up where little Ronnie has been. I wasn't done with him." He smiled at Red and Larry as he said it. Larry was beginning to wonder the same thing.

A college guy had to get in the Octagon with Billy for the last three minutes. He made Larry reset the clock for five minutes. He punished that kid for two extra minutes. Then he went into some squats and ran in a circle for an extra two more minutes before getting a drink.

Those early morning goes were important for Billy's psyche because he knew that Thaddeus did his drilling in the morning. He also had another mind game that he was planning for Thaddeus.

It looked like it might be a normal drilling day for Thaddeus and his group until Thad got mad at Rex for something unimportant and there was yelling and all kinds of broken communication. When it was all over Rex said, "I am going to my office."

Thad said, "Good!"

About that same time Ron Kroger came walking in. He started to watch them as Paul was mimicking the movements of Billy. Paul had gotten used to doing this for drilling technique.

Ronnie said, "Thad, stop! Listen, if you are going to win, you must duck all of his punches to the inside. Stop practicing catching the punch. I tried it and he almost broke my leg with one of those kicks. He lifted my arm and hit me with it. You need to duck into those hooks and uppercuts."

"Ronnie, I can't do it every time or he will knock me out!"

"Look, Thad, you're right, it can't be every time, but he will get sloppy. Keep practicing the counter when he crosses his legs. I am telling you, catching it will get you hurt."

Thad internalized this information and kept practicing the same thing over and over again. Thad began to change up his stance a little. He began to mess with his footing. He started to get back into this strategy of going left handed at the beginning of the fight, and the different ways he needed to fight. Billy would take a round to get used to each new stance. It would need to be a masterpiece, but he needed to work those counters — especially this duck from several different stances and positions. This would not be easy.

Ronnie's presence gave Thaddeus and Paul peace. A measure of peace in this atmosphere was important for them to have a chance at winning. Rex looked on and felt very out of control. He felt very awkward about the whole thing. It was the most awkward he ever felt in his own gym. He was losing control. He thought, *Who has the reins? Is it God? Weird, huh?* His personal life was now screwing up the relationship between him and his fighter. It was all happening at the wrong time, but this guy was piecing it all back together and it was as if Thad really did know something about this guy, or something about something. He couldn't quite figure it out. He sat there and wondered if this was God's great comeback for him. Put him in a relationship that would screw everything up. The bad guys would win. The relationship would not work out. His fighter that had made him and he had become like family to would hate him? Was this how it would go for him? *Well, God I was starting to like you but it looks like you are screwing me over again. What the heck? I don't get it.* He heard that voice again and something that said, "Calm down, Rex! You will be just fine!" He wanted to be mad at God, but it appeared that the anger was gone and he couldn't. It was as if someone did something to it, or took it away. *Huh?* he thought to himself, and stood in utter disbelief. He had been angry so long he didn't quite know what to do or how to act. He actually noticed that he could think more clearly.

After the workout, he called Deb. Deb answered.

"Hey, Rex." She didn't seem very excited to talk to him. He halfway expected that.

"How are you today, Deb?"

"Oh, I have been better. My son's girlfriend is here; she isn't saying much. She is kind of mad at me. My son is mad at me, although we haven't talked, and I assume he is really mad at you." Deb was thinking this was not the time, but she needed to end this thing with Rex. She needed to set herself aside one more time for her Thaddeus.

She didn't go looking for love all of those years after Wayne because her love was lost in that accident and she needed to raise a man. She knew that she could bring a man into it and mess everything up. "You know, Rex, maybe we need to talk about this. I am not sure this is good, what we are doing here. Maybe we are wrong."

Rex said, "What? You are breaking up with me? Are you serious? Deb, we shouldn't have lied, but other than that, this isn't wrong. The hard part about it is over. Now that he knows, we can talk about it."

"Rex, I've got to go. We can talk later. I've got the lunch rush coming in right now. Focus on getting my son's head back on straight before the big fight. Sorry."

Rex started to hurt again. He let himself really be drawn in by someone again and the thought of having to end it like this really hurt him. He did something weird. He hung up the phone and looked up. He laughed, because he always felt like God was up and to the right and he would meekly look up there to try to make eye contact with God Almighty. He said, "Lord, I trust you. Forgive me. Help me to get her back and restore things with Thaddeus. Amen." This was simple. He had been right beside him all of these years. He wasn't just up and to the right, He was beside him and above him and everywhere. A weird sensation pierced through his body. He knew that he would never be the same. It appeared to be falling apart around him, but he finally knew. God is good!

On the other end, Deb was able to hide behind the smile but she was a wreck, too. She thought about how disgusting it was that she couldn't stay away from the alcohol, but developed a taste for it again and fully intended to be tasting some more today.

Sally kept talking with customers and Deb couldn't help but notice just how beautiful she was. She thought, *My son has done well. Man, I hope I didn't screw up his life too badly.* She began to pray, "God, work it all out and help me to see my part."

Sally kept thinking in her mind that she messed everything up. She was praying something similar. "Lord, help me, guide me. Amen." You see, Sally was a doer. She wasn't going to just pray it, she wanted to accompany it with action.

Later on, back at the gym, the one not praying was Thaddeus. He was getting tired and irritable. Rex was especially nervous because they were in that window where those were the last really physical goes before the fight night. Thaddeus warmed up and practiced some key counters and now it was go time. Thaddeus entered the cage with Ronnie.

As they start to go, you could tell that Thaddeus didn't have the same look about him that he had yesterday. Ronnie began to work on taking him down. Ronnie dove in on an ankle. He seemed to be working the ties and taking his time with the champ. Thaddeus took a few shots, a few kicks, a few punches, and didn't really connect. At the halfway point not much had really happened.

Thaddeus went to the corner and put his head down. This wasn't typical behavior for Thaddeus. After a minute, someone rang the bell and he got to his feet slowly again. Now they would go five more minutes and this would be the only go with only one partner. Thaddeus took a bad shot and let his guard down enough for Ron to get some good licks in. Thaddeus fell down and struggled to get back up.

Afterwards, Ron pulled Thaddeus aside. "Hey, man I don't know what is going on with you today, but looks like you need to work on those counters. Look, let me mimic his stance for you." Ronnie mimicked Billy 's movements and let Thaddeus slowly work through the counters. Thaddeus went and got a drink. Something happened in the hallway and he was able to regain his focus.

Rex's experience had taught him that if you are focused on

one fighter and that one fighter is distracted that day, yeah, they need to work through it, but it is ok to make some changes. Rex then said, "Here you go, fellas. All five of you are going to rotate in on Thaddeus. Each one of you will come in fresh every two minutes or when you get tired. Alright! Ready, go!"

Thaddeus had the toughest fight first with Ronnie, but knew that he would probably see him again at the end of the go. Thaddeus, knowing the end was in sight for this workout day, and knowing how important these next few days would be, was going to push through it. He went after Ron right away. He knew he had to hit him first and hard. He hit him in the head, then kicked him in the thigh. Ron dove in on Thaddeus's ankle. Thad was able to wiggle free. Thad then shot in on a single leg takedown that resulted in him coming up behind Ronnie. He tied him up and tried to lock up a solid choke hold from behind. It looked like Ron was going to be going under.

Ron kept fighting and wedged his hand inside Thad's arm around his throat. Rex called time at the end of the two minutes. Thaddeus jumped off of Ron and another partner came to the center. This partner was a college student who was an experienced boxer and had some MMA experience. He tried to punch first. Thaddeus saw it coming and ducked into it, like he had been practicing for Billy. He ducked and let out a roar, as he hit him in the mouth after dodging an amazing punch. After much scrambling, partner number three came in and he wasn't very good but he had a lot of energy and really tied Thaddeus up. Eventually, Thaddeus got the takedown and he got on top of his opponent and started to inflict pain, pain as if it was personal.

Thaddeus was wearing down. This was the time when

Ronnie should be able to come in at the end and beat him. Thaddeus worked his way through two more practice hands who went longer than the allotted time and Rex announced, "Ok, Ronnie, get in there and beat the champ for three minutes." But there was something about it. He remembered Billy being told that. He knew that he saw some of the same star quality in Ronnie, but maybe he was a more solid person who was interested in his own success right away. There was hope and vision and thankfulness and competitiveness and frustration towards Billy that all rolled into a moment. With everything Thaddeus had left he set up a shot, faked it, and backed into a boxing type of stance. He kicked Ronnie twice in the thigh. He shot in on a leg and took him down and continued to unload on him. Ronnie got free only to be taken down again. The champ was digging deep. He was depleted. Ronnie caught him with a forearm and slowed him down a little. Ron got in on his leg. Thaddeus wiggled away and the round ended with Thad on top of Ronnie. It was a good ending.

"Ronnie, help Thaddeus with some of those counters he missed on you for two minutes while he is tired, and then, Thad, you go home."

Thad sarcastically said to Rex, "Don't think you are my dad now." It would have been funny, but you could tell he didn't mean it to be and it sounded worse through a man gasping to catch his breath. Thaddeus thanked Ron and gave Rex the stinkeye. He had already gone to the locker room in his mind, and he was going to go home, eat, and spend some time by himself.

By the time Thaddeus made it home he had 15 missed calls. More than half were from Sally, one from Paul, who left a message, and several were from his mom. She left one message, as did Sally. It seemed that everything was kind of taking a weird turn right before the fight. Thad had never liked when things like this happened. He liked to have everything as under control as he possibly could before a fight. That way, if he got sick or injured or something traumatic happened, there was some margin. He had been around a long time, and it was hard for everything to come together on that one glorious evening every time.

He texted everyone back and let them know he was ok. He told them all he would talk to them the next day. He wanted to stay on track and fulfill what he always did the Wednesday before fight week. Every single time on Wednesday a week and a half before the fight, he would run the hill. The hill was a hill he picked out many years before. He got in this routine and before he could start easing his foot off the gas he wanted to give his legs one more go. He wanted to push his lungs and all of his muscles climbing the hill.

As he sprinted to the top of this quarter-mile incline, he thought about his opponent and what the fight would look like. At the very top he thought about being victorious in that round — or whatever it was. He had to start running by 4:30 a.m. It didn't matter what the weather was, he would be on that hill. It took him about 20 minutes to drive there. Part of the psychology of the run was that while Billy was sleeping, he was up and going.

Thaddeus went to bed and couldn't stop thinking about what he would do next. The man was a machine, and that was something that gave him a superhuman-type of edge in this contest. He went to bed thinking about it and it helped him to not feel the pressure of the fight and experience the loneliness, depression, anxiety or hurt that was going on in his life right then. He had a great night's sleep. He woke up at 4. He got there at 4:20.

It was a bit foggy that morning. *God loves you,* he thought. He jogged around for a minute and began to stretch. When he looked up on the hill there was someone standing there. He stood at the top and looked down at him. He waved, and got in his car. It was Billy. He yelled down in a condescending tone, "Hey, big brother, I figured you wanted the hill at 4:30; that is why I ran it before you got here. I wanted to be done with it before you needed it!"

Billy got into his sky blue Maserati and drove off. He revved the engine good, and pealed out when he left. *The man is a snake,* Thaddeus thought. Somehow Billy knew that if he beat Thaddeus there, that was a mental game that would give him more confidence and make Thaddeus feel less confident.

The frigid air struck him on the cheek. His lips were dry, his body hurt, and he stood in front of the hill. He thought about the audacity of the mind games, but also how much Billy wanted it. Then he thought *Well, of course he wants it. He cashed in our friendship. He risked a lot to be able to take me on, and Billy wouldn't take me on if he didn't think he would win.* In that moment it felt as if he had no one. He felt sad because he used to think they were close. Not a soul really cared.

Just then someone came walking up the road. It was an elderly man. He looked at him and said, "Hey, I know you. You are that fighter."

Thaddeus looked at the man and said, "How do you know that?"

"You visited my grandson in the hospital. His name was Greg."

"Yeah, I am sorry, Sir. I remember."

"Yeah, we lost him probably within a year after that. You came to the hospital. You held his hand and when it was time to go he said that Jesus had him. I ain't no fightin' fan, but I decided that day that I was a Thaddeus Class fan."

Thaddeus remembered them and was speechless. He looked at the man and said, "Yeah, I had a hard time with that one. I knew that I needed to get away after that. It is good to see you again. How are you doing?" They spoke for about a minute. They didn't shake because it was cold.

"The world needs more of you. Let's knock him out! You better get to it. I don't want to interrupt your workout." At that, the man looked at him and said, "Thank you. When you beat that guy, I will be watching. My money is on you." The man got in the car as Thaddeus nodded.

Thaddeus exploded up that hill, stronger than ever before. He thought about the first round. He thought about winning. He thought about the good guys winning, and he thought about what it would look like to win it all for Jesus and do it with Pure Class!

When Thad got to the gym it was time to drill with Paul and Ronnie for an extended period of time. He got in some good conditioning, but it is important the movements are natural when you are already tired. They were getting to the last big workout days before they needed to get easier leading up to the fight. Everything had been done right, except Thad's mind was a mess. He was mad at everyone close to him. He couldn't take it. He pushed through the workout, but he knew that Billy beat him to the hill in the morning and that was symbolic of how things were going. *I guess I have had my time,* and he continued in his mind being tempted to dwell on some ridiculous thoughts. Then he thought, *That man was there to thank me. I ran that hill way better than Billy. I am training harder than he is right now. This is my time! It is still my time!*

He left without saying much to Rex. Things were tense, but before a fight they usually are. Rex was kind of mad at him because he and his mom weren't dating anymore. Thad got showered up and wanted to go home before he came back and went live in the afternoon.

When he got to his car he saw someone from a distance standing nearby. He thought, *Great, a groupie, and I can't even get to my car and go home and eat without someone being there.* Not knowing who it was, he yelled out, "Hey, do you mind getting off my car? I am going to be leaving here." At that she turned around and lowered her hood. It was Debra.

"Ah, Thaddeus, I came to see you." Thad was happy to see his mom. He was irritated with her, but he didn't let that stand in his way. "Hey, I know that you are on a schedule. I can ride with you and come back with you when you come back to workout here in a few hours, if that works."

Thad said, "Sounds good. I need to be back here about 2:30." They got in the car and started to drive over to his apartment where Thad had some food prepared.

"Look, son, I have really made some mistakes lately and I am sorry. Rex and I have been dating. I have started drinking heavily again. I am a mess, and I feel like I am messing things up with you and Sally."

All of a sudden Thad was furious. "Rex got you drinking again!" He could feel the tiny hairs on his back stand up as he said it. "What?" He was noticeably mad. "Wait until I talk to him." He reached for his phone while he drove.

"Thaddeus, wait! No, you've got it wrong! He got me to stop drinking! We went to a secret recovery meeting led by Rachel Santiago. There were people there you know, and wouldn't believe, but I am not allowed to say. He recognized that I was probably drinking when I wrecked and he took me where he got help. When I broke it off with him, I started drinking again!"

"Wait! Mom, you broke up with him?"

"Yeah, we can't have this relationship together. It ain't going to work! Then, I guess Sally knew or might know. I should have been honest with you."

"So, you broke up with Rex because you think it will affect me?"

"Yes."

"Mom, that is crazy! I didn't realize how big of a problem this was for you, but you were driving drunk. I didn't know this was a problem. But he did and found a place for you to get better. I can't hardly argue with that! Sounds like you should stick with him!"

"I don't know if it will work out, son."

"Well, you better figure it out!"

"Thaddeus, you don't have to dabble in my dating life."

"Mom, I can't believe after everything with Dad that you would drink and drive."

"Thaddeus, look, I am sorry. I made a mistake. Thanks to Rex I am getting help — or was, anyway." Thad just shook his head. Debra knew it was a lot to take in.

They pulled up to the apartment and went inside. Sally was cooking some chicken, they knew the exact amount Thad would have cooked himself and with the exact amount of spices with a little bit of a green vegetable on the side. He looked up at Sally who smiled at him. "Sally, what are you doing here?"

"I told your mom that I knew what you would eat. I offered to cook while she went to meet you. She let me in."

He looked at Deb and said, "What did you just tell me about dabbling in your life?"

"I don't know! But, you are welcome!" Thaddeus sat down as the food was ready and they also grabbed some plates and ate a little. Deb prayed and they ate.

Thad took a bite of the chicken. Sally looked at him. "How is it?"

"Chicken's great! You, you are a little tough!"

Deb laughed and said, "Glad everything is all good again." They ate and seemed to act like nothing had happened.

When Thad got back to the gym, Paul was standing there in the parking lot waiting for Thad. He looked at him and said, "Paul what are you doing here? You are usually not here in the afternoon. You gonna try and go live with me today?"

"No, champ, I ain't stupid! I am just here to let you know that I appreciate how you have brought me in here. It has been a big deal for me. It has helped me to go back and wake up something that was dead, and I feel so alive since I have been able to help. I am just here to help if I see something, or to be here any way I can." They bumped hands and walked inside.

When they walked inside he saw Rex. Rex looked at him and said, "Thad, you are late!"

He smiled at him, "Ah, come on, Rex, let's get to work. And, by the way, you and I need to talk after this. You want to go to the coffee shop with me?"

Rex didn't know what to make of it. He looked at him and said, "Sure, but don't be breaking your diet over it."

Thad looked at him and said, "Don't worry!"

Thad warmed up with Ronnie for a while, working on the

counters that they had developed for Billy when he would miss a punch or get out of position, or crossed his feet in his stance. Ronnie was improving every day, and was giving Thaddeus a good fight when they went live, especially a tired Thaddeus who had already worked out twice that day.

This was the day Thaddeus had to leave it all here. He had to leave it here and feel good about the product. Yeah, he was tired, he was edgy and a little weak. If he was not careful he could get sick really easily right now. But this was the day he needed to hit his peak. He was on schedule and believed he would give the best performance of his life on fight night.

Ronnie and Thaddeus shook hands and it began. They were going to fight for ten minutes. Ronnie tried something different. He was moving fast. He was fresh. He struck him hard. Now, at this stage, Thaddeus had on not only a headgear, but other protections like rib pads, which is exactly where he got hit.

Thad felt that shot through the pads and went down for a second. Ronnie followed up and kept fighting. He didn't lay off. When Thad got to his feet and stumbled a little, he dove in on a leg and was back. He got Ronnie down and was able to go to work on him for the rest of the go. Thaddeus let him know what it was going to be like to fight Thaddeus Class.

Next, the fighters got a drink and Thaddeus went with Ronnie again. They fought another ten minutes before getting a drink, and it seemed that Thaddeus was getting better as the afternoon went on. He was a beast. Ronnie had never seen anything like it. He was not just another fighter, he was legendary, and he might just put together the best fight anyone had ever seen. Thaddeus dominated again.

In the final fight, Thaddeus would fight for ten minutes

straight against alternating opponents. There would be three college-age guys rotating in. One a martial artist, one a boxer, and one a wrestler. First, the wrestler. Thaddeus went upper body, tying him up before kicking him in the thigh and sweeping his leg. He beat him until he was called off. Next, the boxer came in. Thaddeus boxed with him for a second before seeing the opening for the double leg takedown.

They were called back to their feet because Rex yelled, "You can't hit that on Billy! He will see it coming!"

They went back to their feet when Thaddeus yelled at the young college-age practice hand, "Danny, I am going to do it again!" He smacked him in the head and hit him with it again, finishing with a flurry of punches on top of him. He looked at Rex and said, "I don't care who sees it! He can't stop it!" Rex was happy, his edge was back. But would it be enough?

Thaddeus continued to pummel all three of them. At the end of the go he ran sprints and jumped rope and pushed until there was nothing left. Tomorrow he would be off. He was starting to look ready. Now the recovery game.

Across town at New Horizons, Billy was beating everyone they put in front of him. This was the best he had ever looked. It was the best anyone had ever seen him. It was the best that Larry had ever seen him. No one in the room doubted that it was his time. Costello was glad to be there. Latimore felt like things were shifting. Most of all, Billy didn't believe that Thaddeus Class would touch him. In his mind, Thad had made the mistake of telling him everything he knew already, and Thaddeus Class was no spring chicken.

So back at GITR, practice ended and Thaddeus went to Cornerstone with Rex. They went in and Thaddeus ordered some kind of low-fat caramel latte-something and Rex looked at him and said, "What are you doing? Your diet is important these last few days!" He looked at Rex and smiled and got his drink and sat down. Rex then sat down, too.

Rex looked at him and said, "What do you want to talk about?"

"Ah, Rex, we don't need to talk about anything! I am not staying!"

"He looked at him and said, "What is wrong with you? Are you losing your mind before the fight?"

"Yes, and you'd better work it out!"

At that moment, Debbie walked in and said, "Thad you didn't tell me Rex would be here!"

Thad stood up and pulled out his chair. "I got your drink for you already. You and Rex need to talk this out, but the two of you can't be fighting through this week. It was easier when you were lying to me."

Deb looked at him, "Is this revenge for bringing Sally to your house?"

"Yes! I will see you guys later!"

At that he left. He stomped out the door and didn't look back. They looked at each other and laughed. "Deb, I am sorry for starting this with you. I wish I would have thought this through. The fact is, you make me want to be better. You help me to believe and think differently. You give me hope."

"No, Rex, you make me better. I got drunk as soon as we broke up!"

"What? Why?"

"I don't know. I know it was stupid and it was just once. And I shouldn't need you to get me through it, but I guess I do, or might, or choose to? Look, I haven't let myself feel this way in a long time. Can we try this again?" She said it as she grabbed his hand, and they both knew it was right. Rex could see in Deb's eyes that everything was right with the world.

When Thaddeus left he called Sally. She picked up. "Hello?"

"Look, Sally, I am sorry. I know we ate together the other day and we talked a little, but my mom was there and everything. I have been doing a lot of thinking. I have learned this time around that it isn't everyone's job to make me happy."

"Wow! Look at you, the champ might not be so selfish."

"Haha, I had that coming. What I mean is, my strength has to come from within or from God, who is within or outside of me or whatever. I can't let this stuff rattle me. My life is complicated and I can't expect people to have to do everything perfectly. So, I am sorry."

"Thad, it is fine. And for me, I am sorry, too. No more secrets."

Thad laughed and said, "Deal." They talked for another ten minutes and everything seemed right once again. Thad was starting to get some peace back. He was feeling a little restful for the stage he was in. The truth was, God was on his side and no matter if he won or not, he was going into the Octagon fearless.

That night Billy was home thinking about the fight. Billy knew he had never fought better than he was in practice right then. He never felt healthier. He knew that he and Larry should have left Rex and Thad long ago. It was his time now, and he mulled it over for hours and hours, about his game plan and how the fight was to go. About eight o'clock there was a knock on the door. It was her again. He opened the door and said, "Hey, Kat." She walked into the apartment and dropped her coat, wearing nothing underneath. She grabbed him and threw him down. Once again, he never stood a chance.

About 4 a.m., Billy had a dream. He was training with Thaddeus again. They worked out and were sitting on the mat laughing. There was a mutual respect. Thaddeus looked at Billy and spoke some verses to him that they had spoken about before. It was Proverbs 5:3-6, "For the lips of an adulteress drip honey, and her speech is smoother than oil; but in the end she is bitter as gall, sharp as a double-edged sword. Her feet go down to death; her steps lead straight to the grave. She gives no thought to the way of life; her paths are crooked, but she knows it not."

"Which is it, Billy, are you more like her or like me?" Thaddeus pointed to the corner of the room and Kat stood in the long coat she had on that covered her. Billy turned to reason with Thaddeus and he was gone. Instead, Larry was there and he smiled at him. He woke up and looked beside him. Kat had already left, and the sudden realization of his loneliness filled the room.

Billy gasped and sat up in bed. His confidence was shaken and he was suddenly irritated with God. He looked up and yelled, "So, was I supposed to be in his shadow forever?" He shook his fist at the sky and shouted, "You, you tricked me!" Deep down he knew that Thaddeus loved seeing him succeed and he would have helped him. But it was over now. Billy did 20 push-ups and went back to sleep. Even though deep down, because the verse was quoted more specifically than he would have remembered it, he knew God was speaking to him.

Sunday morning, now within fight week. Thaddeus was going to do just a light little workout later that would help to burn some calories, but for the most part he was just going to go to church. He got his mom to meet him and Sally there, and they would come back to his place for a light little lunch.

Amazingly enough, Rex would be there too. Rex would pick up Debra and bring her to the city and they would all go to church. Rex hadn't been to church in years, and he halfway expected Paul to have split personalities. He couldn't be that nice and real up front. *I know how this goes, but Paul has earned my ear so I will give it to him.* He also had found something new. He experienced peace and joy like he hadn't in a long time. He also had someone that he enjoyed being around, and they had pain and struggle and her son in common.

Rex was nervous, like God might strike him down for coming through the door. He was sad that it took him this long to make it back to church. It was irritating that he had to admit to himself that he had been throwing his little temper tantrum with God all of this time.

He pulled up to the house and was nervous to see Deb. She opened the door with a simple type of beauty. Her hair was pulled back, she had a little bit of make-up on. She smiled as he said, "You look great, as always."

"You, too." She handed him a Bible. "Carry this, so you can fit in."

"Yeah, I forgot I am going to need to try to fit in."

"Now, Rex, is that what I said?"

The Bible had a trendy-looking cover from about 20 years ago. He said, "Did you give me a children's Bible?"

"No, it is a teen edition. Read the inside."

He opened it to the back of the front cover and it said, "To Thaddeus. I love you and so do both of your fathers in heaven." Rex smiled. "Rex, I tried back then. It didn't all stick, I guess."

"I don't know, Deb, raise a child up in the way they should go and they will return to it when they are old. I always tell him, he is getting old." She smiled at him as they walked to the car arm in arm.

When they pulled into the church parking lot, Thaddeus and Sally were standing in the narthex area of the church. Thad was talking to little Johnny Zarka again, and a few other kids were around. He was talking to them about fighting. One of them said, "My mom told me that Christians shouldn't fight." Sally looked at him, smiled and thought, *How is he going to handle this one?*

He looked at the little boy and said, "Yeah, fighting isn't a good way to handle your problems. The fights I do are organized. They are like a game of football, or basketball. We have some rules. What makes fighting and being a Christian hard is I only want to do things where I can talk about Jesus and what He has done in my life. Fighting isn't always the nicest thing out there, but Jesus, He was a fighter."

Some mothers standing close cringed a little. The kids looked confused. "Look, Jesus would have never thrown a punch at someone, but he told the people if the Romans make you carry their big heavy armor for them for a mile, carry it for two miles. When they put Jesus on a cross, He hung there and willingly died for us. And when it was finished and He did what He needed to do for us, He said, "It is finished."

"Man, what Jesus went through for us and without sinning, I will never be as tough as Jesus."

Little Johnny piped up and said, "Thad, do you think Billy is as tough as Jesus?"

Thad laughed and said, "Man, I hope not. No, Johnny,

no one is as tough as Jesus." The boys were captivated and just then Rex and Debra came walking through the door.

Rex looked dressed up and more than a little uncomfortable. He looked at Thaddeus and smiled and said, "Well, kid, I didn't get struck by lightning yet."

Thad and Sally laughed, "Haha!"

Deb looked and said, "I will hold his hand so God can get us both with one shot." They laughed it off and decided to take their seats. Thad found his usual seat toward the back and the service started. Deb and Sally sat by each other, and Rex and Thaddeus sat on either side of them.

The worship music was great and there was much time to reflect. A passage of Scripture was read out of the Gospel of John. It was John 2, where Jesus turned the water into wine. Paul spoke of His time in Israel and seeing the location of the wedding at Cana in Galilee. He spoke of some historical parts of it, but he didn't want his audience to miss the point.

He brought it back home with, "Look what Mary said, 'Do whatever He tells you.' The mother of Jesus knew something. Whatever Jesus says, listen. She may have learned this the hard way when He stayed back in Jerusalem when the family made their pilgrimage to the temple, and He stayed there to talk with the religious leaders. When they asked Jesus why, He responded, 'Didn't you know I needed to be about my Father's business?' But, when it comes down to it, do what He tells you. This is the principle."

He paused and went on in a much softer tone, "Several months ago, a very large man who made me a little uncomfortable came into my office and we talked and he wanted me to work out with Thaddeus Class. Sorry, Rex, it is a good story, I promise. I know you are just a guest, but you like attention, it is cool right?" Rex nodded back at him. "So, I started to work out, drilling or practicing moves. Look, I am not going to fight anyone, don't worry, and I am not leaving to start anything new, but what you don't know is, I was starting to think my time here was done. It had gotten stale here. And please, don't be offended, you are not stale. You are very much alive," he said with both palms out. "But, maybe I have been. Yes, the church is growing and ministries are happening, but I needed my soul to be fed with some type of challenge. Helping Thaddeus Class prepare for maybe the greatest organized fight of all time helped me to realize that I am not done and there is so much more to fight for here. I was reminded of a time that has long past, and what it was to bleed and sweat and compete. I watched how greatness prepares for the challenge. So, when I said, 'God, how can I follow after Mary's advice and do whatever you tell me to do,' He is telling me to keep fighting for this church and the souls of this community. Thank you, Rex and Thaddeus! Thank you Jesus!"

Ella was sitting in the front row, beaming with pride, sighing in relief. A single tear fell down her cheek and Simeon and Elizabeth both smiled as their dad spoke. He continued with much more about the text and taught it well, like he always did, but a passion was revived and a sense of divine purpose for him. He felt young again! As Pastor Adkins continued to preach and connect all the dots, he talked about opportunities in the church and serving the community and the homeless need; Thaddeus and Rex both felt they got to be a part of something that was worth so much more than fighting. Not even Thaddeus thought Paul was thinking about leaving the church. Thaddeus thought to himself, *Maybe this fight really is bigger than just what happens in the Octagon.*

CHAPTER 16

SHOWTIME

FINALLY, IT WAS time for the weigh-in. That rat Charlie Pigeon was there, creating a circus mess. He had already gotten under the skin of Rex, but Thaddeus stayed classy. He actually planned for the annoyance of Charlie Pigeon. He tried to anticipate difficult interactions that happen before fights. Thad was unusually nervous for the weigh-in. His weight was fine, but the gravity of it all was really hitting him.

Something deep inside of him was telling him that he wasn't quite prepared. He called on the Lord. He mouthed the words, "Please, Jesus, help!" They came and got him. It was time. On one side of the stage behind a curtain he stood — Billy, in just a pair of shorts. He was down to weight and leaner than Thaddeus had ever seen him. He knew that by tomorrow night Billy would be about twelve pounds heavier, just by eating and drinking some fluids. Thaddeus was sure that Billy was in the very best shape of his life. Billy's eyes locked onto Thad. The problem Thad was going to have at that moment was he had taught Billy all of his mind games and his normal routine wasn't going to work. The only way into Billy's head was authenticity. Billy's own betrayal would have to be his own worst enemy.

Rex saw Larry standing beside Billy and Red Jackson and he said to Thad, "I can't wait until you destroy them. They don't have a chance!" First, Billy was called out of respect to Thaddeus. Both were champions, but he was coming down to Thaddeus's weight class and Thad was the legend.

So they called Billy to the scale. He weighed in at exactly at 213. What a specimen he was. The sports announcers covering the weigh-in were oohing and awwing. One of them stated, "Thaddeus Class has never faced a physical specimen like this before, and I can't wait to see how fast Billy "The Kid" Smith will move at his new weight."

Thaddeus weighed in about two-tenths of a pound less than Billy. He obviously didn't have as far to go. Thaddeus was impressive and everyone was used to him having the most impressive body in the Octagon, but Billy got his weight down well and looked like the athlete of the future. What if Thaddeus couldn't keep up with the HWT champion? This was a real question in the minds of the observers.

They announced Thaddeus's weight and then they brought the two fighters together. Billy was ready. He would not break eye contact. Thaddeus looked very confidently into his eyes. But the feeling that Thaddeus felt was not like anything he had ever experienced before. Oddly enough, he had been preparing for it, but it still caught him by surprise. He was angry, frustrated, aggressive, and genuinely cared for Billy, all at the same time. Billy looked as though he was a wild animal and could rip Thaddeus's head off at any moment. Their noses were almost touching. Thaddeus, in a calm voice, simply said with a smile, "Missed you, Buddy." Then he slightly winked his right eye.

It broke Billy's concentration. Thaddeus then reached out his hand without breaking eye contact, and shook Billy's hand. Billy said, "Whatever! It has always been about you, hasn't it? Good luck!" Billy stepped to the side and forward towards the front of the stage and flexed for the crowd. The media got some good shots. Thaddeus did the same thing. After this spectacle was over, the next time they would see each other would be in the Octagon.

Paul looked on as the spotlight was on both Thaddeus and Billy. He had seen the weigh-ins before, but he wasn't standing there feeling the tension. He thought, *Rex even told me he would have trained me. I could be standing here, maybe for my title fight. Why didn't I pursue this? I rolled off the couch and was able to work out with Thaddeus. Maybe I wouldn't have been a champion. Probably not, but it would have been nice to see what I could have done. Maybe I will never know; well, I won't know. How will I know? It is over now. Why did I not pursue this again?* Then he thought. *Oh, Yeah, God asked me to do something else. I just preached that I need to do whatever Jesus tells me to do."* The answer was right, but not good enough for the moment. He ached and hurt, even though he knew that to do God's will you had to give up certain things. Parts of you have to die, so they can be raised to life again. He struggled with why he had disciplined himself as a young athlete. What was the purpose of it all? Then he thought, *I guess to have the opportunity of faith you have to have the opportunity of doubt.* The truth was, something within him hurt, and it hurt really badly, it never truly went away. *Huh? Weird!* he thought. *I have been successful in ministry, life, and family, and I am still looking back, wanting to see if I can win fights. What is this feeling? I just told the church that this all convinced me to be all in, and now I am feeling this thing again.*

As they were leaving through a hallway, away from Billy, Thaddeus told Paul, "I need for you to come to my room, I need to talk some things through with you again."

Paul said, "Not a problem, I will be right up."

Paul knocked on the door and Thaddeus was in the room by himself. "Come in."

Paul looked at him and said, "What's up?"

"I don't know, Paul. I feel ready and I am jittery and I know the challenge will be great, but I wasn't ready for the feelings I have. I mentored him. I care about his success. I also kind of hate him for what he did to me. And Larry — I can't stand how they betrayed me, and it is quite an out-of-control type of thing. I don't even understand what I feel." As Thaddeus talked, he was beginning to shake a little and he gritted his teeth and tears were beginning to come out as he spoke. He was visibly upset, grieving, nervous, all of these things were coming together, right then.

"Look, Thad, I don't know what you're going through. I have mentored people who later turned on me. I never had to fight them, but man, I would have liked to have knocked them out! It would be great if pastors got to get in the Octagon with ex-treasurers and board members. What do you think?"

"Paul, shut up man! I need my pastor! I am having a crisis!"

"Right. Look, Thad, this is going to be your biggest challenge. If he beats you, you've missed your last chance to help him. You will have missed your last chance to show him that righteousness wins. You'll miss your last chance to make him think. This is the most important lesson you will give him.

You live clean! You work hard! You still have it, and God will bless you!"

"Paul, you and I both know that there is no Biblical promise that I am going to win this! God doesn't need me to win!"

"Thaddeus, you want this to be bigger than about fighting, right?"

"Yes!"

"Well, it is! Your trainer is coming to church. Your mom has found something in him. You and Sally have something special. I am reconnecting with what it means to fight for my ministry. I almost gave up on the church. I almost packed up and left too early, but you helped to remind me to fight."

"Look, Paul, what if I can't beat him? I never fought someone who has me in age, size, strength, and I taught him everything I know!"

"You may have taught him, but he didn't learn it all. He turned on you for this. He doesn't value you like you do him. He still has a lot to learn and you are going to teach it to him. But even if you don't, this whole thing has been worth it for so many people involved." At that, Paul hit him on the shoulder. "You might want to get some rest."

"Nah, hang out with me for a minute."

"Sure thing, Champ," and Paul stayed there for a little while, talking about life and anything but fighting.

Thaddeus got up to use the bathroom and Paul was left sitting there by himself. He heard the voice of God from within him. "Do you get it now? You have a unique past and a unique gift and I have positioned you uniquely. Just like I had many people in Corinth that didn't know me yet, there are many people in this fight world that will know me, too."

Wow! That word Paul had was etched on his heart at that

moment and he knew what to do. He knew that God Almighty had put Thad in his life. Thaddeus needed Paul there at the most challenging moment of his career. Paul correctly understood his job was to help Thaddeus see God clearly during this time.

Thaddeus came back from the bathroom. Paul looked at Thad with a renewed sense of strength. He stood up and looked at Thaddeus face-to-face. He said to him with both hands on his shoulders, "Thaddeus, never doubt who you are. You are a child of God. You bring light to the world. You taught this kid how to fight, but he is not you. You have another lesson to teach him and God is going to teach you one, too. You are the best at this, but most importantly, you are God's child!" He paused and looked deeply into his eyes, "Do you know that?"

He looked at him and a peace fell over his face. "I do, and I have a purpose and I am going to win for the glory of God and the good of Billy!" Joy returned to the face of Thaddeus, he got it!

In another room Billy sat with Larry. Billy was happy to be eating and drinking some water. He was eating some lean meat, trying to recharge after making weight. Larry looked at him, "Ah, Billy, did you see him? He won't look much different tomorrow. He is probably weaker than when you fought him last time. You have all the advantages. You trained hard. You will be the one to dethrone the great Thaddeus Class. You are going to be so stacked by tomorrow night! You will be recharged. I can't wait to see it all happen. Everything we have worked for is coming together right now. You truly are the best fighter I have ever trained. Proud of you! As long as you stick to the plan you will be fine. But remember, you are fighting a great fighter — but this is your time."

Larry and Billy were relaxed for what they were about to do. It was probably because they felt good in their process and they did it their way. In their mind, "We got this!" They believed it was their time. Billy believed he couldn't be beat! He was a champion and he was about to be a double champ, a champion of two weight classes.

Sally knocked on Thaddeus's door. Thad answered. She looked pale. She said, "Hey, I know I shouldn't stay long and I want to stay out of the way. I just want to talk with you for a minute."

Thad looked at her, holding the door, "Sure!"

At that, Paul got up and walked to the door. "Praying for you, Champ. I can't wait until tomorrow. It is going to be great." And he left.

Paul nodded at Sally and smiled. She nervously smiled and said, "See you tomorrow, Pastor." She turned to Thad and was a little stiff and hesitated, "Hey, I am a little new to all of this, but I am really glad to be here with you. I am rooting for you. I just wanted to see how you are doing. It was kind of weird, but I got this feeling when you were face-to-face with him, it was like I was experiencing what you were in that moment. I had no idea how close you were to him. You really did a lot for him to get here, didn't you?"

Thad teared up and smiled a little, "Yeah, I don't know how to talk about it. I was talking with Paul about it a little, but it is hard. It might be hard to fight him."

"Look, what you need to know is, I don't know anything about fighting. In fact, watching this in person is gonna be a different type of experience for me. But you taught me that I can love again. You taught me that this isn't over, that things are worth fighting for. You put up with me turning you down for dates and you kept coming around. Billy doesn't have that type of commitment, but don't win it to teach Billy, or any of that. You need to win this because that is what you do. No matter what happens, I am going to be here for you, but I feel like I should tell you, this will be emotional, but this is nothing you can't handle. Make sure the best man wins!!!" She kissed him on the cheek, and looked him in the eye. "I love you."

"You, too."

She smiled and said, "Get some rest. You're the champ."

There was something different about him. He smiled and said, "About to be a double champ, huh?"

"That is right!" And she left.

Thad was alone and he needed to relax. He opened his Bible to the story of David and Goliath and thought about his dream. He reflected on something in the story. Most people think that David and Goliath is, in fact, about David and Goliath. But really, it is about David and Saul. Paul taught him that. David was burdened by the Philistine cursing the God of Israel. Saul was the most trained, had the best weapons, probably had the armor bearer to go out and stand in front of him with the shield. He was head and shoulders above the rest, and he should have been out there fighting.

But it was David that felt the burden and only saw Goliath as an obstacle. As Thaddeus read this story, a peace came over him as he realized he couldn't be thinking about winning for Rex — or Billy — or Sally — or even himself. What he stood for is what is right, and what is right is doing things right for God's glory. The little Johnny Zarkas of the world — and Simeon Adkins — needed to see it. More than that, at the end of the day, it must be for God. He knew he needed to please the audience of one. God was with him and he must experience that. As he read, he became tired and would put it down for a little while. When he got nervous about the fight, he would read again. Eventually, it was time for bed and he felt at peace. The stage wasn't too big, because it was God's stage and he was only along for the ride.

"It is ringside with Mark and Rich. This is going to be a clash for the ages. The hometown Vegas odds has the legendary champion as a three-to-one underdog. The reasoning is simple. Billy 'The Kid' has a similar fight style. But he is younger, faster, and stronger. We haven't seen him fight at this weight class yet, so this will be fascinating. It is a case of teacher versus student and the teacher has taught him everything he knows. I think tonight will be the night that we finally see Thaddeus Class defeated. What do you think, Mark?"

"Look, I understand the odds, but if you needed to win one more fight to probably go down in history as the greatest fighter to ever fight, wouldn't you find the stuff for one more showdown? Yes, he taught him, mentored him, and trained him, but don't you think he thought this moment might come? One day the guy who he helped would be trying to fight him. He knew how good he was, he probably assumed he could get down to weight. Emotions are running high. But I am going to go with Thaddeus Class."

Rich spoke back up, "My money is literally on the safe bet, Billy 'The Kid' Smith."

Rich transitions, "Let's go down to the Octagon: Here comes one of the fighters right now. Billy 'The Kid' is making his way to the Octagon. What is he wearing? He has the hood up and he appears to be gliding to the ring. He has his entourage with him and he looks to be on a mission. He has his fans and the ladies love this guy. Billy has the best chance of beating Thaddeus Class of anyone we have ever seen so far. This is going to be some fight."

As he hit the Octagon, Billy's robe came off. "Ah, Mark, you gonna change your bet yet? This man is massive. He is here to inflict pain." The crowd cheered as he bounced around and took a good leap up in the air. Rich again, "Look at that vertical. This guy truly is the total package and is fighting a legend at exactly the right time."

"Rich, don't speak too fast because here comes the teacher. He is coming to ringside with his people. He is led by Rex Metzger, the owner of GITR and legendary trainer of Thaddeus Class. There is a Gorilla already in the ring. Believe me, Rex has no love loss for Larry Rossi or for Billy Smith. He helped to train them only for this thing to turn on him. They will be ready."

"Ah, Mark, it is just business. It was time to do something else. The fact is, one of these two men leaves a champion of two weight classes tonight, and the other with no title at all."

"Rich, look for Thaddeus Class to show you pure class tonight."

As the announcers continued to broadcast, Thaddeus smelled the ammonia mixed with the arena food mixed with sweat, and he had that feeling that sunk in his stomach. This time it was worse than before. This time it seemed to paralyze him a little. He had a moment of doubt. Right on cue, Rex reached back and said, "You are the greatest fighter of all time. You will prove it tonight. Just be you. Look who is with you. Me, Paul, Ronnie, and look over there at Sally and your mom." They smiled at him on the way. Both of them looked like they could throw up. There was no doubt this fight had a different feel. Just as he got that surge of confidence back, and the inner feeling of a security that comes from knowing a Savior, he could see the top of Billy's head. It was time to turn it on! When he went to make eye contact with Billy, Billy and Larry saw Ronnie. Ronnie blew them a kiss from behind Thad's back.

It stunned them. Larry shook his head while Billy looked surprised. He said to Larry, "Isn't this illegal?"

"Billy, we never signed him. He was free to go. We will have to talk about it later." As he got closer to the Octagon it became apparent that Thaddeus Class was beginning to believe he owned this piece of real estate, and Billy looked up, breaking eye contact first to go into moving around, throwing some punches and taking some shots. It was time to go, and Thad was beginning to win the mental game.

The fighters were announced. They went to the center to shake hands. Billy was a little rattled by Ronnie. He looked at Thad and said, "New coach?"

Thad smiled and said softly, "New Billy." Billy was stung by it like you would expect a spoiled brat to be. It made him ache a little.

He got back to the corner and told Larry. "I am going to kill him!!!!" The bell rang and Billy came out really aggressive. Billy knew he could start fast with Thaddeus and Thaddeus would not be able to keep up with him. Billy was certain he was at superior conditioning and strength. Billy felt unstoppable and Larry felt it, too.

Billy got to the center, snuck in the first punch to the face and a swift kick to the thigh. An average person's leg would have broken. Thaddeus was slowed down right from the beginning. He switched legs and went left-handed right away. Luckily for Thad, the moment lent to Billy forgetting the game plan at the beginning. In other words, it wasn't controlled aggression, which was what Thaddeus was known for.

Billy was then stunned because it appeared that Thaddeus was able to now fight quite adequately left-handed. Billy thought, "It is just because I kicked him in the leg; this can't be real." So he tested him and over-committed on punches. Thaddeus quickly took him down and began to go to work on top. He got several closed fists on Billy's ribs. He held Billy down from behind as Billy tried to get away. He kneed him in the ribs several times, and took Billy's head and smacked it off the mat. This first round, to everyone's surprise, had been all Thaddeus. He controlled the rest of the period and when they got to their feet, Billy was bloodied and battered and beginning to believe he made a big mistake.

When Billy got back to the corner, Larry grabbed hold of him. "What are you doing? Listen, he just caught you. You need to go out and strike hard. He can't keep up with you. This left-handed stuff, it can't last. Even he will have to go back to what he knows. Just like we planned." As Larry was talking, Billy began to nod and believe again. The trainer put some clotting solution over his eyebrow to make some bleeding stop. They wiped the blood and the ref cleared them to return.

Thaddeus was very encouraged in his corner and Rex said, "Stick to it! We went left early, but stick to it!" When they returned to the center of the Octagon, Billy got the first punch in again and shot deep on the left side. He was extra aggressive because he knew Thaddeus didn't normally lead with that leg. This time Billy took him down clean as he began to pound on him from on top. He got some vicious rib shots in and smacked his head against the cage. Everyone thought Thaddeus was knocked out. But, Thaddeus somehow managed to scramble back to his feet as he still led with his left foot. Red yelled out at Billy about some adjustments he needed to make. The brains in Billy's corner were adjusting and figuring it out as well. So Rex and Thaddeus would keep having to adjust, too. Thad was more comfortable with the intellectual side of this fight than the athletic side, even though Billy had two of the best minds this sport had ever seen in his corner. Thad knew how to adjust, and Ronnie and Rex would help him throughout the fight with that.

He noticed ever so slightly that Billy was beginning to give up that left side and over-commit when he came in on the hook. He was beginning to cross his feet. The rest of the round kind of worked out to some scrambling that amounted to nothing, but the round went to Billy.

Going into the third round of five, they had an even fight, and one for the ages so far. In Thaddeus's corner they were beginning to be concerned. Rex said, "Why didn't you take advantage of what he is giving you. We practiced it!"

"I am hurt, but I want to wait because I might only have one real chance. It will get worse as the fight goes on." Ronnie nodded.

Paul said, "Look, Rex, Billy is going to get more confident and will over-commit as he slows down."

Rex looked at Thad and said, "Ok!"

Thad looked at Rex and said, "I am going to stick to the left side, he is slower when I do that. He isn't ready for it."

"But, Thad, so are you!"

"Rex, we came in here with a plan and it is an even fight so far! I still believe it! Let's see it through!"

It was time to get back to their feet and fight. Thaddeus

got to the center a little before Billy and he stuck with the new stance. After a flurry, three minutes into the round Billy came in with that vicious right hook. Thaddeus tried to catch the punch like they originally practiced, even though he was thoroughly warned by Ronnie not to try that. Just like Billy did to Ron in practice, Billy lifted up his arm and hit Thaddeus with another kick, this time it was in the ribs. Then he caught him with a good fist in the face. Thad seemed to get away for a second and another kick came in, catching him in the thigh, which brought him down. When Billy came down to punch downward, Thaddeus was able to scramble and change styles. He tied him up with some Jiu Jitsu and some wrestling holds to slow the big guy down, but it looked like this might finally be the end of an era. The bell rang and after three Thaddeus was clearly down by a round. He was having trouble breathing, and he was going to need to fight through it. Billy strutted back to his corner while Thaddeus stumbled.

He looked up and saw Debbie teared up and Sally latched onto her. Thaddeus was in pain. He looked over at Billy and Larry laughing and Latimore smiling on. Thaddeus thought, "This can't be how this ends!" They tried massaging his chest and kept him warm. They were afraid that he had broken a rib. Rex was considering throwing in the towel.

Thad looked at Rex, "All I have is ten minutes to finish this thing! I've got two five-minute rounds. You can't stop this! I know you are thinking about it! But we have trained for this! We are on the side of what is right in this thing! This is bigger than fighting, Rex! You said so!"

"Look, Thad, you need to show me that you can still win this! I believe in you, but you've got to do something. Go back to your normal stance."

Ron looked at Rex and said, "Let me talk to him!" Rex nodded. He jumped up on the outside of the cage. And was at ear level with Thaddeus. "Thad, you know he is going for that hook. The way to put him away is to duck and look into that hook like we practiced. I know, because I knocked him out that way. He will give it to you. Wait for it! It will be historic!" At that, Thad returned to the center of the Octagon.

The fourth round was starting and Thaddeus met Billy in the center of the Octagon. He got one good street punch in and Billy fell to the ground. Billy was shocked, as Thaddeus unloaded several shots to the face. Thad tied him up and worked on him for a minute. Billy was able to counter and get back to his feet. Thaddeus was back in the left-handed stance and was taken down by Billy again.

Thaddeus was now having more trouble breathing. He thought that if he got hit in the ribs again, he might die. He somehow countered out and he caught Billy reaching. He slapped him open-handed and tackled him to the ground. They ended up back on their feet while Thaddeus had both of his legs. He lifted Billy in the air, slammed him on his back, and began to punch down on his face. This lasted for a few minutes. Billy scrambled out. He was battered and moving more slowly, but Billy was forced to dance around and avoid contact for the rest of the round. Round four went to Thaddeus Class, and this decision between two champions was going to be a fight to the finish.

Thaddeus was in so much pain he couldn't sit down. He hurt and agonized over what was happening. He kind of leaned on the cage; had to straighten up his back. Rex looked at him, "You have been like a son to me and you have taught me so much through this. You have to finish him. You have to find what you've got. What makes you Thaddeus Class and what makes him Billy is you have that special something! You will get out of this! You are five minutes away from being considered the greatest ever! You are the best! Let loose the last round! You have to forget the pain! You have been through it before!"

He looked up and head-butted Rex and he saw the look in his eye and the animal drool in the corner of his mouth. He looked at his mom and Sally, knowing their stomachs were tied in knots. He looked at the speechless preacher and at Ronnie. Ronnie smiled, "You will have an opportunity to put him away with that counter this round. You know it is the way!" Thaddeus made an attempt at smiling. This was it. It was time to dig deep. Then he looked at Billy, already standing, and Larry, beginning to congratulate him early. It would be a wild one, but here we go.

Thaddeus went back left-handed again. They scrambled and he switched back to his normal stance. Billy became over confident and began to swing at him. Here came the hook. He finally threw it slowly enough again that Thaddeus could risk trying to catch his arm. He caught his arm and spun behind him. Billy turned into him as Thaddeus kneed him in the chest twice. They went back to punching. The hook came again, and Thad caught it again, but Billy was able to muscle out of it and hit Thaddeus with some brutal jabs with his left arm. Ronnie and Rex were scared because he seemed to be focusing on catching the hook.

But Thad knew Billy and he knew Larry. Thad had caught that hook twice. They were going to think he would continue to do just that the rest of the fight. Thad over-committed on trying to catch some jabs. He wanted Billy to think this was a new strategy. Thaddeus got hit hard a few times and had to circle out. At that, Billy started running at him. Thad circled again and even looked a little dazed. Billy was running at him. The act worked!!!

Billy set it up with a jab, and here came the hook. It was like it was in slow motion and Thaddeus ducked into it just like Ronnie had shown him. He came up and uppercut Billy and punched him in the ribs several times. Billy somehow flurried out and came back dazed. As he tried to dance and get fancy he crossed his feet. Thaddeus got in deep on a double leg but this time instead of taking him down he stood him up belly-to-belly and arched his back, driving Billy face-first into the cage and dragging his nose down it, just like Billy did to him so many months ago. It was bloody and painful, and when Billy got up, Thaddeus finished him with an uppercut and kicked him in the ribs.

Billy went down and couldn't get up. It would be remembered as the greatest knockout in history. What a fight, but Thaddeus Class was the hero. He was the one who couldn't be beat! It was over! Thaddeus Class stood over top of Billy and he felt triumph. He felt sad. He felt a lot of things, but he looked back in the corner and he saw Ronnie smiling. He saw Paul and Rex were side-hugging and jumping up and down. He looked back and saw Deb and Sally hug each other. He couldn't believe that he saw all of these people come together. He couldn't believe that he saw something so special happen as a result of so much betrayal and hurt.

He looked up and saw Larry. Larry, who now trained a fighter under Rex and GITR to win the title and held it only a short while before Billy's reign was over. Larry was dumbfounded, and knew that Billy may have been good enough to beat every other fighter that day ever, except for the one in front of him. Larry realized that greed may have cost him the title he always longed for. Billy climbed the ladder and won only to lose it right away.

Thaddeus began to walk to Larry. He looked up and their eyes met. Larry, knowing the pain and the hurt that he caused Thaddeus, was a little afraid to look at him. Thad looked at him and said, "Larry, you trained him well. I consider this the greatest victory of my career. I want you to know. I don't hold it against you or him. I get it." He stuck his hand out and said, "Good luck to you."

Larry shook his hand. "You know, Thad, I don't think like you at all, but what you did here tonight, I didn't expect. I don't doubt that we deserved it. You proved you could still do it tonight. It was a mistake to go after you so fast." They shook hands.

Larry walked to the center of the Octagon to help with Billy, who was now awake. The trainers got him up. Larry grabbed him and unexpectedly told him, "Look, Billy you gave it your best. It wasn't your night tonight." At that Billy began to cry, but he held it in as he needed to walk to the center.

Thaddeus slapped hands with everyone in the corner. He hugged Rex and pointed out at his mom and Sally. It was emotional. As he turned to walk back, he was met by a very rattled Billy Smith. Very weakly out of one swollen eye he looked at him and said softly, "Ya know, Thad, I wish it wouldn't have worked out the way it did. It really wasn't gooood that, things kinda… Ya know it,… ah."

"Billy, I forgive you, buddy! It hurt, but we gotta move on. You're still the best fighter I ever fought with or against. Good luck to you!"

They hugged and shook hands. The ref came and stood

between them and it was announced by knockout, "The winner and now uncontested, undisputed double champion, The original Gorilla in the Ring of GITR, Thaddeus Pure Class!"

Debbie smiled at Rex, and then it happened. The next interaction was what she was worried about. Rex caught Larry in the corner of his eye and walked towards him and Billy as they were walking away. Larry looked up and said, "Here to gloat, Rex?"

Larry was standing and Billy stayed seated with Latimore standing ringside with Pete Durkin, Red Jackson, and some others. "I just want you to know. I don't hold it against you for leaving. I never gave you the credit you deserved. I understand you and Billy wanting more of the spotlight. I understand Latimore and Durkin, how you guys could think I didn't give you enough attention. I understand the pressure you feel to succeed now. Larry, I get it. To all of you, I am sorry for my part and do not hold anything against any of you. Billy, I am proud to have been part of your story tonight." He shook hands with everyone in the corner and he walked away.

Some kind of weird weight was lifted off his shoulders. He felt free. He felt alive. As for the fight and the death Rex died to himself, "It is finished!" As for the life and his new future, he had hope and he felt brand new like a baby, yet seasoned like an old saint. He no longer fought against God. He was thankful, he had defeated his toughest foe yet, himself. But through Christ, he must die to himself daily. His friends Thad, Paul, and Deb would help him with that. Something new was about to happen.

The End… or is it just the beginning?